Praise for *Emb...*

"A fun, fast farce . . . Deft [and] sly."
—L.A. Taggart, *San Francisco Chronicle*

"[A] terrific comic novel . . . Colorful and affectionate."
—Connie Ogle, *Star Tribune* (Minneapolis)

"Don't take this book too seriously, and it will entertain you, seriously."
—Ellen Akins, *The Washington Post*

"Part comedy, part insightful social and cultural critique, part sheer delight . . . [with a] whip-smart sense of humor . . . Crouch brings memorable characters to life one brilliant detail, one deft bite of dialogue at a time."
—Stephanie Hunt, *The Post and Courier* (Charleston, S.C.)

"Delightful, humorous and shocking . . . A page-turner filled with astute commentary."
—Emily Burack, *Alma*

"Entertaining and insightful . . . , reaching notes of genuine triumph without sacrificing the wry comedy, while the red dust and heat of Namibia radiate off the page. This is a blast."
—*Publishers Weekly*

"With wit and tenderness, [*Embassy Wife*] explores the complicated nature of race, power, marriage, colonization, diplomacy, and community. A sharp, funny, page-turning romp."
—*Kirkus Reviews*

"Smart, funny [and written] with heart . . . while propelling the novel through mysteries and deception."
—*The National Book Review*

"The story's setting is vivid, [Crouch's] wit dark and bone-dry . . . [Her] satire is cutting . . . As armchair tourism goes, it's quite a ride."
—Margot Harrison, *Seven Days*

"*Embassy Wife* showcases Katie Crouch's mastery of the three skills I most value as a reader and writer: keen and sensitive observation of human behavior, a wry sense of humor, and authenticity of character. Namibia comes off the page with its dusty heat, its slow pace of life, its nascent and unfolding place in history, and the sheer pressure of the drama that unfolds."

—Rémy Ngamije, author of *The Eternal Audience of One*

Liniers

KATIE CROUCH

Embassy Wife

Katie Crouch is the *New York Times* bestselling author of *Girls in Trucks*, *Men and Dogs*, and *Abroad*. She has also written essays for *The New York Times*, *Glamour*, *The Guardian*, *Slate*, *Salon*, and *Tin House*. A former resident of Namibia and San Francisco, Crouch now lives in Vermont with her family and teaches creative writing at Dartmouth College.

ALSO BY KATIE CROUCH

Abroad

Men and Dogs

Girls in Trucks

Embassy Wife

Picador / Farrar, Straus and Giroux / New York

Embassy Wife

Katie Crouch

Picador
120 Broadway, New York 10271

Copyright © 2021 by Katie Crouch

All rights reserved

Printed in the United States of America

Originally published in 2021 by Farrar, Straus and Giroux
First paperback edition, 2022

The Library of Congress has cataloged the Farrar, Straus and Giroux
hardcover edition as follows:

Names: Crouch, Katie, author.
Title: Embassy wife / Katie Crouch.
Description: First edition. | New York : Farrar, Straus and Giroux, 2021.
Identifiers: LCCN 2021005690 | ISBN 9780374280345 (hardcover)
Subjects: GSAFD: Satire.
Classification: LCC PS3603.R683 E46 2021 | DDC 813/.6—dc23
LC record available at https://lccn.loc.gov/2021005690

Paperback ISBN: 978-1-250-84932-8

Our books may be purchased in bulk for promotional, educational, or business
use. Please contact your local bookseller or the Macmillan Corporate and
Premium Sales Department at 1-800-221-7945, extension 5442, or by email
at MacmillanSpecialMarkets@macmillan.com.

Picador® is a U.S. registered trademark and is used by Macmillan Publishing Group,
LLC, under license from Pan Books Limited.

For book club information, please visit facebook.com/picadorbookclub or
email marketing@picadorusa.com.

picadorusa.com • instagram.com/picador
twitter.com/picador usa • facebook.com/picadorusa

1 3 5 7 9 10 8 6 4 2

To Paulina Nepembe, with love and admiration

Summer

'N Man kan sy verlede nie ongedaan maak nie. Kan 'n sebra sy strepe uitvee?
A man cannot undo his past. Can a zebra undo his stripes?
—Afrikaans proverb

Namibia, the country planted firmly above the west side of South Africa, is mostly desert. If you live in Windhoek, the capital as well as the only settlement that might qualify as a "city," you are surrounded by brown, dry hills. Drive straight west, and the hills turn to scrub and then desert, all the way to the sea. Drive south, and you have scrub and sand again, until you meet the towering red dunes of Sossusvlei. Drive east, and you'll hit the Kalahari Desert before facing the crocodiles of the Okavango Delta. Eventually, if you drive north, you'll find some greenery, though it takes nine hours, and first you must go through the giant salt pan of Etosha National Park, where, if you get out of your car to take a photo or pee, there is a distinct chance that you will be eaten by a lion.

This was a summary thus far of the observations of one Amanda Evans, a very recent forty-one-year-old transplant from California. Amanda was an American living in Africa with nothing to do. She knew her situation wasn't particularly unique, but she wanted to make herself useful. She'd booked an interview to manage an orphanage, but in the meantime she took notes about the place that she supposed might be a travelogue/journal/memory book for her daughter. Amanda tried to keep her notes as objective as possible, though she had to admit some of her unhappiness might be seeping out onto the page:

We swim every afternoon, after skimming off the crust of dead wasps on the pool.

I sneeze red dust. I pee red dust. If we leave the windows open, when we come back the white floor and walls are covered in red, red, red.

It's like everything has been turned up on the contrast filter: The colors are brighter. The sun is hotter. The animals are bigger. The sky is farther away. The bugs are the size of birds, the birds the size of pterodactyls. The poor people are poorer. The rich people are richer. And everybody has a gun.

At the moment it was 6:45 on Tuesday morning, and Amanda, notebook in hand, was trying to figure out the Namibian expat scene. As she sat in the long line of cars waiting outside the gate of the Windhoek International School, she noted that there was a distinct order to things, at least in the school queue. The children of Chinese businessmen, it seemed, led the charge, their chauffeurs having been idling outside since 6:15. The Americans were next (other than Amanda), driven by their mothers, who talked to each other on their cell phones from various makes of white and silver SUVs emblazoned with red diplomatic plates. Next, the Europeans, cool and elegant in diesel Mercedes sedans and legitimately beaten-up Land Rovers. The Afrikaans families were few and far between, having so many school options in Windhoek where their own language was spoken. Yet a few did opt for an international curriculum, just in case their kids wanted to roam farther than a water-starved country inhabited by just 2.4 million people, and those forward-thinking parents rumbled up in loaded bakkies right before the bell. The wealthy African internationals—the Botswanans, the diamond-rich Angolans—didn't line up at all. Instead, they preferred to arrive well after the bell rang, when they could convene among themselves in the parking lot beside their black shiny BMWs and late-model Range Rovers.

None of these patterns were scientific, and—as Amanda was always careful to say whenever she made any observations about her new continent out loud—she was no expert. But as the mother of a third-grader at the Windhoek International School, this was what Amanda Evans had observed during her nine weeks and three days so far in the country of Namibia. She wasn't counting, necessarily, but her daughter, Meg, had been marking the days off in crayon on her *Dog of the Month* calendar. Every morning, a new big purple X marked twenty-four more hours gone.

Today was February first. Amanda had gotten a later start than usual, so was far enough back in the line to watch the other Americans from a distance. Persephone Wilder, in her gleaming 4Runner, had the window down. Amanda was vaguely surprised at this, as lowered windows were strictly against U.S. Embassy security rules, and Persephone, with her glossy red hair, creamy skin, and daily uniform of some iteration of white, didn't seem at first glance like a rule-breaker. But that was definitely her arm sticking out of the window, and even from back here Amanda could make out Persephone's ponytail bobbing back and forth as she talked.

Kayla Grant waited behind Persephone in a silver Prado. Her windows were tinted jet-black, so Amanda couldn't see her, but she could hear Beyoncé vibrating from the car. Shoshana Levin was behind Kayla, her Highlander still covered in white dust from a family trip to Sossusvlei. The Levins, Amanda noticed, had added a pop-up tent to their roof, an impressive investment given the fact that Shoshana's husband supposedly had only a year left on his post.

Amanda's car had red plates also, because of her husband's consultant position as "special academic advisor" to the embassy. Her car, however, was a relatively modest Subaru Outback. The Evans family had been in Namibia just two days when they'd purchased it, but Mark declared it the "perfect" car, not wanting to be like those "Boer dickwad rednecks" who sprang for enormous gas-guzzlers. Twenty-one years prior, Mark had spent a year in Namibia with the Peace Corps, so he was confident, he told Amanda, that he knew how to get around the country. But then, the very next weekend on a trip to the Kalahari, the family had gotten stuck in sand two hundred kilometers from the nearest farm, with no cell reception. Which, Amanda had thought as they waited for seven hours in the desert until a bakkie stopped to help them, made Mark, in some ways, the biggest dickwad of all.

What *was* a dickwad, anyway?

"Google says it's 'a blockage in the urethra.' Of, like, a man, I think."

Amanda blinked. Since coming to Namibia, something was happening where the private things inside her head were trickling out of her mouth in word form without her knowing it.

"Meg, give me back my phone."

"Okay. What's a urethra?"

"I don't know, exactly," Amanda said. She frowned. How could that be one more thing she didn't know?

"Okay. The line's moving, Mom. You can go."

Amanda looked in the rearview at her daughter. Meg's green eyes, shaded by bangs, met her own, then slid back down to her notebook, leaving only a view of the top of her hat. Given the intensity of the Namibian sun, all students at the Windhoek International School were required to wear wide-brimmed sun hats anytime they stepped outside, even if they were heading to the restroom in a rainstorm. Meg's navy-blue hat was a comparatively sober choice, as many of the students wore brightly colored hats adorned with patches, sew-on jewels, and even cloth flowers. From afar, the school looked like a drunken garden party, populated by gnomes.

Amanda inched forward. Her WIS badge was properly registered and displayed correctly on the dash, just as the emails from Petra, the school receptionist, had instructed. *No entrance without a badge, ever, ever, EVER!!!!* Amanda did not know Petra, but she was already keenly aware of her fondness for exclamation points. Not that Amanda had ever seen anyone so much as glance at her badge. Today, the guard, a stunning Damara woman dressed like a New York cop, kept her eyes glued to her phone as she waved the cars through with a slight flick of her hand.

By the time Amanda entered the lot, the spots nearest the classrooms were already taken. A Swiss mother hurled her car into the Zebra-striped crosswalk, disregarding the waving arms of Headmaster Pierre, the French-Canadian head of the school, who stood in the parking lot each morning trying to instill some sense of order. (Another observation Amanda had jotted in her book: *Europeans are not very good at waiting.*) As she put the car in park, the furious scribbling from the backseat got a little more intense.

"I packed you one of those Afrikaner donuts," Amanda said, breaking the heavy silence.

"They're called koeksisters, Mom. Anyway, Miss Ruby doesn't allow sweets."

"Maybe you can eat it in the bathroom?"

There was a pause. Amanda could only hope it was because her daughter was appreciating her mother's love, as opposed to embarking upon a lifelong eating disorder.

"Okay. Thanks."

Around them, the staccato bursts of car doors opening and slamming again. Her daughter, however, remained steadfast, hunching down farther in the backseat. Amanda waited two more minutes, until it was really time to put an end to this stalling.

"Lolo?" she finally said, resorting to the nickname she'd been using for Meg since she was a baby. "You know what Miss Ruby said about pre-classroom prep."

"Didn't have that at my old school. Where we studied, you know, normal things. And we didn't have to wear these stupid hats."

Amanda sighed in agreement. Namibia wasn't *my* idea, sister. Only this time she concentrated on keeping her mouth shut. She might be a bit tired today, but the last thing Mark needed coming his way, she supposed, was more passive aggression about the move—or direct aggression, for that matter.

Across the parking lot, Persephone Wilder, wearing a white moto leather jacket over a white sundress, was herding her twins and older daughter toward their respective classrooms. She seemed to carry her own halo of light, like a dove that had accidentally swallowed a uranium pellet.

"How about ice cream after school?" Amanda asked the hunkered little form behind her.

Meg shrugged. In California, sugar had been so savagely parsed out that a dollop of honey counted as a special treat. In Namibia, not even marshmallow-covered donuts were enough to excite Meg anymore.

"Or . . . trampoline-shopping?"

Amanda held her breath. The trampoline was the big gun, the special surprise Mark wanted to save for a birthday or an excellent report card. And here Amanda was, bringing it out in month three.

"Okay."

From the rearview mirror, Amanda detected a tiny smile. She did an inner fist pump.

"See you at one-thirty, then. Have a *great* day!" She winced at her own false enthusiasm. When had she become the sort of woman who bribed and pandered? Meg slid out of the car as if she hadn't heard her.

Trampolines. Lies. False promises. How many other betrayals to her family would Africa require?

Oh, Namibia, Amanda thought idly as she stared at her daughter's small figure as she trudged across the lot toward the school, built, according to the WIS brochure, to resemble a traditional African rural village. Will you be the end of me? She shook her head, checking her attitude. It's only two years, she lectured herself. Again. These were the words Mark had used when he'd come home from the library that day seven months ago, his eyes brighter than she'd seen them in years. She still distinctly remembered where she'd been—her Los Gatos kitchen, making salmon in the sous vide. Meg had been doing homework upstairs. Amanda was listening to Ella Fitzgerald on her father's old record player, answering work emails in a carefully calibrated, decisive, but non-bitchy manner while the salmon burbled away. Everyone was safe. Life was beautiful. They were ripe for a good screwing over.

"It's just two years, and they've picked *me*, Mandi. Me. The first time I applied!"

"Applied for what, now?" Amanda's chest had done that thing where it constricted and expanded at the same time. "Sorry—what did you apply for?"

"A Fulbright. A goddamned Fulbright."

"Oh—so, it's money?"

"Well, actually—"

Oh no, she thought. It was a well, actually. Which always meant the shit was about to hit the fan.

"Mark."

"I've actually been applying for lots of things . . . fellowships. I didn't want to bother you with it because, you know, there are so many things I don't get. But I got Jaime to help a little . . . Did I even tell you Jaime was here for that seminar?"

Jaime was a college rowing buddy of Mark's. He was the friend who'd managed to accomplish everything Mark hadn't. Jaime had made the Olympic rowing team after college. Achieved academic success. Now he had transitioned into a successful nonfiction writer who penned bestsellers about newly "discovered" historical facts. Tall, blond, and toned, Jaime couldn't stay with a woman for more than five seconds. Before he'd discovered Burning Man, Jaime had been James.

"Anyway, his rec must have helped my application somehow. They emailed today, and then *called* me. A Fulbright's usually one year, see, but they're interested in my topic and want me to advise, as well. So they'll pay for two years of scholarly research, *and* for school for Meg . . ."

"Wow." Amanda closed her laptop. "So . . . let's slow down. I mean, I'm sure I could find work in Paris. The visa part won't be easy, but—"

"Oh. Well, actually . . . it's not Paris."

Amanda regarded her husband, his tousled brown hair, shot through with gray, his big chocolate-drop eyes. The first time she had seen Mark, all those years ago, she'd wanted to put those eyes—no, his whole being—into her mouth, pelican-style, and keep him there forever. His gangly body still besotted her, which was why, when she first heard this plan to uproot the family to God knew where, she promised herself not to lose it.

"I thought you were writing about how community discord indi-rectly caused parts of the Holocaust. In France. Paris. Haven't you even narrowed down the causal percentages by, like, arrondissement? Isn't that what you write about all day? France?"

"Well, actually . . ."

Amanda leaned on the counter, trying to catch his eye. "Mark?"

"I shifted last year from *that* holocaust to holocausts in general—"

"Does your dean know this?"

"—and, as Jaime agreed, there was a holocaust in Namibia that's practically unresearched. When the Germans tried to eradicate the Nama people in the early 1900s. Did you know that? No, right? See, it's *wide* open—"

"A wide-open holocaust?"

Mark paused and made eye contact at last, only to take a deep breath and look away again to focus on the succulents on the back porch. "Wide open. Yes. So I changed my focus from France to Namibia, and Jaime was right. It worked."

"Amazing," Amanda tried weakly.

"Plus, since I've already been there, I speak a bit of Oshiwambo, which is very similar to Nama, I think. They liked that, too. Like I said, they've even made me a special advisor on the Nama thing, which means we get diplomatic status . . ."

Amanda opened the fridge, looking for a way to get her out of this. But there was only Trader Joe's seltzer. And probiotic kefir. And an ancient salad growing its own mini-universe of mold, encased in a plastic salad container that would take two thousand years to disintegrate.

"Special advisor?" she asked, slamming the fridge door harder than necessary. "How can you advise the government on the Nama when I've never even heard the word *Nama* out of your mouth until now?"

"The point is, it's two years. Africa, Mandi! I've been there before. I know the ropes. Think of the adventure it'll be for you, though. And think of the learning opportunities for Meg."

"Look," Amanda said. "Look. I'm all for adventure. And I'm so proud of you. I am." She stopped herself. Was she really? Yes. Yes. He was her *husband*. "But what about my job?" She noted, with alarm, that her voice had risen an octave. "They just gave me this huge promotion. I can't just leave *now*."

"Mandi." Mark said her name as if it were a statement. As if proclaiming, after giving it some thought, that this was what she was, a noun.

"Yes."

He walked over and took her hands. She felt her body go stiff. They touched each other so seldom now, other than during prescribed sessions in bed. She still loved the feel of his fingers, and after all these years she continued to crave his body at night if he was away. But here in the kitchen, when she was supposed to be doing work and getting dinner ready, she had to admit his physical affection annoyed her.

"How long have I been an assistant professor at that lame school?" he asked now.

She squeezed his fingers apologetically and moved back to the cutting board.

"Santa Clara's not lame. Just because it's not Stanford . . ."

"Well?"

"Um . . ." She concentrated on the carrots. "Seven years?"

"Nine, Mandi. I'm a laughingstock. This, on the other hand. This is major. Now I can be the breadwinner, for once. Do you know how emasculating it was, having you rocket up from receptionist to head of a whole fucking department? You didn't even like that job at first. *I was the one who was supposed to become this star professor——*"

"Emasculation isn't a thing anymore. Also, I was an assistant, not a receptionist."

"Just give me two years," Mark said. "Please? I mean, I stayed home with Meg all that time, didn't I? It's my turn, Amanda."

The words. Amanda recognized them. And for years, she had known they were coming. But here they were now, floating in the air, suspended. Amanda could almost see them there, bumping lightly off her skull.

"Your turn."

"Yes." Mark was staring at her now with expectation. Amanda

looked around. How she loved that kitchen. She loved the marble she'd had reclaimed from a condemned house in Saratoga. She loved the Viking range she'd saved up for, the gallery of Meg's stick people and rainbows she'd had framed and arranged on the wall.

"Okay," she said after a while. He grabbed her and hugged her tight, letting her go only when she gave a little squeal indicating she couldn't breathe.

"And actually," Mark said after planting one huge kiss on her cheek, "everything will be just the same when you come back."

Amanda shook her head now, steeped in the memory of the rest of that conversation. How she had said okay, because even after all these years, she still felt like he might find someone better. And he was right—it was his turn. How her boss had told her she'd age out of Silicon Valley within a year, much less two. How they'd ended up selling the house because the realtor told them managing a rental from Africa was going to be a nightmare, and, well, with the market at an all-time high . . . How their daughter had burst into tears over having to leave third grade in the middle of the year, then proceeded not to talk to Amanda for a week.

That, certainly, was the worst part. Worse than giving up the job she'd grown to love, worse than selling the house. Amanda's daughter had never cut her off before. From the moment that tiny wonder had exploded from her body, Meg and Amanda existed in comfortable symbiosis. Moods were communicated without the bother of words. When either was plagued by some sort of anxiety, one pitched, the other caught.

Mainly, Amanda thought, it had to do with Meg's supernatural sense of intuition. "You look tired, Mom," her daughter had said once when she was just three years old. "Maybe you need a nap." Her precociousness progressed from there. "I like your hair, but you could use more layers in the front." "Mom, after you hang out with Tara's mom, you get a little mean, I've noticed. I think she's too competitive."

"Siamese twins," Mark would grumble when he felt particularly left out. "Besties." Which would be true, except Amanda and Meg weren' friends. Not really. Amanda made certain to avoid the creepy, overly familiar manner of the Silicon Valley mothers and daughters who wore matching outfits and sat in chairs, hand in hand, while having false eyelashes applied. She didn't want that. And more importantly, she and Meg didn't need it.

Amanda and Meg's bond was maddening to her husband. So Amanda worked hard as well to make him feel included. Love in a family is supposed to be even, but everyone knows it's not. Meg loved Amanda more than she loved Mark, and as his wife, Amanda was constantly trying to make up for that fact. If he wanted to go to Namibia, they'd fucking go.

But there was a cost. Because now, for the first time in her life, Meg was shutting her out. The loss was physical to Amanda. She could feel the sadness spreading, black and oily, through her veins. And worse, it made her furious at her husband, with whom she had once been so in love she'd nearly tattooed his name on her lower back.

(Thank God for her fear of needles. Thank f-ing God.)

The thought of her growing isolation brought tears to Amanda's eyes, which pissed her off only further, which was why she was banging her forehead lightly against the steering wheel when someone tapped sharply on her window.

"All-i-son."

Amanda raised her head and turned, slowly. It was Persephone Wilder, even more resplendent up close, and she was determinedly calling Amanda by the wrong name.

Amanda rolled down her window. The hot air blew in as if from a vent.

"Hi. I don't know if we've met. I'm Persephone Wilder."

"We have," Amanda said. Three times, she didn't say. Because why drive home the point that Amanda's appearance was so nondescript that even the volunteer community liaison—whose unofficial job it was to meet and greet new Americans—couldn't remember her?

"Oh dear. *I'm* sorry."

"It's okay. Also, it's Amanda."

"Where?"

"No. I'm Amanda. Not Allison. My name. Amanda Evans."

"Sorry?"

"Oh. Shame."

"Shame. Shame! As in, 'sorry.' Or, 'pity.' Or, 'too bad.' It's an Afrikaans phrase."

"Are you from South Africa?"

Persephone straightened up, resting her hands on her narrow hips. "No! Well. We're all from Southern Africa now, aren't we? But no. I'm from Virginia. Still, whenever I'm at a post, I try to become as local as possible, you know?"

Because locals always dress like the love child of Lilly Pulitzer and Moses, Amanda thought. And then: Please let me not have said that one out loud.

"Wrong foot, wrong shoe! Okay. Well. Amanda, I assume you have children."

"If I don't, call the cops, because this would be a weird place for me to park."

Persephone smacked her head. "Shame! Amanda, as you can see, I can sometimes be, pardon my Oshiwambo, a real dum-dum."

Despite her foul mood, Amanda felt her insides begin to thaw.

"Well, what I was trying to say, before I dug myself into even more of a hole, is that I'm unofficially the greeter around here, and there's nothing I'd love more than to arrange a little meet-'n'-greet coffee hour with the other spouses. Or maybe, if we get ambitious, even a little afternoon braai. Which means barbecue. Which I'm sure you know. Do you think you would like to—"

And then something amazing happened. There, in the school parking lot, two men wearing blue workmen's clothes marched toward Persephone carrying a large dead oryx. As Amanda gaped, they unceremoniously tossed the carcass at her feet. She closed her eyes and opened them again, just to make sure it wasn't the residual effect of the Ambien she'd been relying on to get her through her sleepless nights. But no, when she looked, the oryx carcass was still there, its tongue lolling dangerously close to Persephone's polished toenails.

"Oh my God." Amanda grabbed an old airplane blanket from the backseat to cover the body, and got out of the car. Out of the corner of her eye, she saw someone coming toward her.

It was a woman. An African woman. Though was she really just a woman? Amanda wondered. Because a creature that beautiful, she surely could not be cut of the same cloth as herself. This goddess was half a foot taller than either her or Persephone; every limb seemed to stream from her body, graceful as water. Her skin was dark, polished, and pore-less; her face, a masterpiece of planes and curves, centered by long-lashed eyes the color of maple syrup. Her figure, which was magnificent, was shown off in a sheath dress so well tailored, it was obviously conceived just for her. To top it all off, she wore exactly the sort of high heels with red soles Melania Trump favored when visiting prisons for toddlers.

"Wow," Amanda breathed, soliciting a snort of annoyance from the other woman beside her.

"Persephone," the woman said. Not a greeting—a command. "The meat you ordered for International Day."

Amanda was surprised to see that Persephone Wilder responded with a huge smile.

"Why, thank you, Mila. So wonderful of you. It's a bit early, as the event isn't for months, but—"

"You need to be prepared, Per-she-fo-NEE." Mila enunciated each syllable with what seemed to be disdain. "The day does sneak up on you. And tell Adam to call me about our meeting tomorrow." She paused and looked at Amanda. "Please."

"Oh, I'm sorry. This is—"

But the woman named Mila had already turned and floated away. Persephone put her hand on her forehead, tapping her hairline with her index finger.

"Wow," Amanda said again. Persephone shot her a murderous look.

"Oh. Sorry."

"She's a government wife," Persephone said. "I *have* to be nice to her. But she is such a . . . a . . . *monitor lizard.*"

"A stunning one," said Amanda.

"Shame," Persephone said. "*Damned* shame." She looked at the brown playing field, where some tiny hatted figures limply kicked a soccer ball back and forth in the scorching sun. "Actually, monitor lizards are amazing animals. They can live for months on an ounce of water, and their tails are strong enough to beat off lions."

"Huh," Amanda said, still staring at the dead oryx.

"Though my favorite animal, of course, is the rhino." Amanda cocked her head. Persephone Wilder seemed to be talking to her own personal God. "So extraordinary. So elegant."

"Yup, they're nice," Amanda answered, bewildered. She held up the airplane blanket. Persephone took it, smiled, and threw it over the corpse.

"Good sirs," she called to the two men in blue, though they were standing right beside her. "There's a ten in it for each of you. Just place this neatly in the trunk. Thank you." She turned back to Amanda. "Well Amanda Evans. It looks like I'm off to the butcher. But tell you what. Follow me, and afterward we'll go to my house."

"Well, I—"

"Oh, come. You're an unemployed expat in Namibia. What *else* do you have to do? I'd say I'll make you coffee, but the truth is—despite the fact that it's forty minutes shy of eight a.m.—I'm already in need of a real drink."

2

Persephone Wilder really did try to be generous toward everyone. It was her duty, after all, as a representative of the State Department. But Mila Shilongo . . . now, there was a piece of work.

It wasn't Persephone's fault that the PTA had voted her in as president over Mila. Everyone had seen the level of nepotism and, frankly, corruption that had gone on at last year's International Day fundraiser during Mila's term as head of the organization. It was supposed to be the PTA's biggest event, for Lord's sake, and in Mila's hands the whole thing was just a messy, drunken, hot party that probably lost as much money as it made.

Though perhaps, she thought as she wove through the clogged streets of Windhoek, Persephone did have *one* other problem with Mila. Persephone's husband, Adam, was obsessed with the woman. The two had been working together on a publicity project having to do with road safety in Namibia. Mila's husband, Josephat, was the minister of transportation, which for some reason gave Mila the right to handle his media relations. Adam, meanwhile, was representing the U.S. Embassy, which was funding the project. The arrangement made no sense to Persephone, but she'd learned long ago not to look too long and hard at State Department enterprises. Still, whatever this was, it had turned into a work duty Adam was entirely too enthusiastic about.

"That woman! She's like Beyoncé and David Bowie's wife melded into perfection!" he'd crowed the other day after a meeting.

"You're being a little race-specific, dear."

"Fine. Throw in Scarlett Johansson. My God! That ass!"

Maybe that had nudged Persephone to campaign with glittery signs, phone calls, and teensy favors just to ensure her PTA presidential win. Persephone knew how much the PTA meant to Mila, yet the victory brought her surprisingly little satisfaction. Especially when, the other day after a government reception, Adam had muttered: "Damn. That Josephat Shilongo must have an amazing time in bed."

Persephone wrinkled her nose. Sometimes Adam could be so crude.

Yet as a State Department wife whose husband was obviously being groomed for an ambassadorship within a post or two, she could not let her dislike of the wife of the minister of transportation show. Particularly to the other wives. Oh, she might let a tiny diamond of discontent slip at an opportune moment, in the name of camaraderie at, say, an International Women's Association of Namibia coffee. But as volunteer community liaison officer, it was her unofficial job to show a good attitude at all times, in order to steer the others toward the correct psychological state.

After all, it took grit to be a State Department spouse. Patience. The ability to pretend you were not living in a house that looked like a jail. The ability to find a way to throw a brilliant pool party during a drought. The ability to suffer through afternoons of craft-making and Nia dance. The ability not to hate your husband (or wife!) for roping you into this life.

Persephone's Namibia was different than Amanda's, in that it was something to be conquered rather than feared. She had three years to visit the highlights of this mammoth tract of red dirt and diamond mines; three years to ferry her children to all the best campgrounds and oasis resorts and game parks, to experience Namibia's *Best of*, to photograph her children at progressively remote settings (#worldasclassroom #statedepartmentlife #livingthedream). Persephone was impossible to discourage, but she had to admit, sub-Saharan Africa was challenging. So far they had camped in Etosha, where one of the twins got bitten while trying to feed a zebra; Swakopmund, where Adam had almost drowned trying to impress their (former) babysitter; and four different lodges in the Namib Desert, all of which served only "game," a dish that, to Americans, was basically a food-poisoning Russian roulette.

Because she was squinting into a white shield of high noon sun that rendered her Ray-Bans useless, Persephone's SUV stopped just short of a red light at the intersection of Hosea and Mandume Avenues. This was Windhoek's ground zero; everything in town radiated from here. Men in state-issued blue jumpsuits hawked Namibian papers from the median. Farther down, children in torn, donated clothes, their feet bare, white, and cracked from pavement burns, defended their territory, knocking on the car windows for coins and bits of food. Taxis—tiny, brightly colored, driven by Blacks—wove dangerously in and out of the SUVs and massive safari-outfitted pickup trucks driven by whites. All the while, the sun beat down, slamming against the roof, pressing incessantly against the car windows.

Your entire life, Persephone observed, could be defined by which way was home from this huge intersection. A turn to the right would take you to Pioneerspark, a bland, flat, Afrikaans middle-class neighborhood. Years ago, this was the Old Location, a tract of land the German government set aside for the Blacks to live in. The Old Location wasn't elegant, but it was comfortable, centered around a pretty stone church and dotted with small kitchen gardens. After the South African government took over, it was decided that this land, which was comparatively fertile and convenient to town, should be given to the whites. One by one, the Black families were forcibly removed, culminating finally in the 1968 uprising, which resulted in eleven deaths. The houses, their gardens, and the school were razed to make way for ranch houses and bungalows and garages for bakkies that still remained there today.

People of color still came to Pioneerspark, of course, but only to bring in deliveries and to slip in and out of service doors. To get to their homes now, they had to turn left instead of right at the Hosea-Mandume intersection and travel the three miles to Katutura, the new Location, where the soil was even crueler, where the shops were protected by metal bars on the doors and dogs chained outside, where riverbeds dried up for eleven months of the year, then flooded during the rainy season, carrying away the most vulnerable shacks and drowning children.

Katutura, in one of Namibia's many tribal languages, translates literally as *The Place Where We Don't Want to Live*. Persephone was proud to say she had even been there once, on an embassy cultural field trip. There was a tour guide hired by the State Department who shielded Persephone and the other wives from speaking to anyone and herded them on and off the air-conditioned bus. From the bus, the women peered at houses, which ranged from stone bungalows to corrugated tin shacks. The orange clay streets snaked up and down a rugged hill; the market smelled of cow blood and sour milk.

The light turned green, finally. Persephone pressed her foot on the gas, for she was going neither to Pioneerspark nor to Katutura. She, along with the wealthiest Namibians of any color and the other expatriates with money, was headed to the green hills that rose in a comforting, motherly fashion above this dustbin of a city. Her air-conditioned car would now glide up Nelson Mandela Avenue, where she would soon turn off onto a lovely street and retreat to her large, cool house, which, like all the others in her neighborhood, had a veranda, a garden, a pool, and a huge electric security gate to keep out Afrikaners and Blacks alike.

Persephone didn't take these things for granted, mind you. She spoke daily with her maid, Frida, about the crime in Katutura, and someday would take her own children, also, on that ghastly tour, so they could have a concept of how lucky they were. She was an empathetic person, and she did her part with the local charities and thought often about the unfortunates of the world. And now she was almost home, and *what*, she wondered, did she have in the fridge to serve Amanda Evans for breakfast?

Persephone checked her rearview mirror to make sure the Incoming was still in her wake. She seemed pleasant enough. No initial signs of crippling homesickness, culture shock, nervous breakdown, or eating disorders, all of which Persephone had dealt with in her time. She seemed sporty, kind of, but not like Shoshana, with her hundred-mile desert mountain bike races and Kilimanjaro marathons. She seemed funny, but not bitter. Smart, but not obnoxious. No flags as of yet— like, say, Kayla's constant exclamations about the glorious affordability of the help, or Carol Li's gluttonous application of hand sanitizer before and after every trip outside of her own gate. Shoshana was bearable, sometimes. Kayla and Carol were a drag. In short, Persephone was fostering high hopes for Amanda.

She was in the relative safety and calm of the affluent Eros neighborhood now. One last raring of the motor to get her up the almost vertical hill, and they were in front of the gate. Persephone leaned out to punch in the code and waved at Amanda, who waved back. The gate slid open with a thundering groan, and the cars slipped side by side into the huge circular driveway.

Amanda stepped out, pausing momentarily to take a good look at the house. Persephone smiled broadly, crinkling her eyes at the corners to hide the fact that she was actually checking Amanda out. Silver Birks, black Athleta travel skirt, gauzy tank, crafty-looking infinity scarf. The outfit, for a beginner, was a solid B.

"Quite a place," Amanda said.

Persephone tilted her head, testing the air for snideness. She'd given up being self-conscious about assigned residences long ago. It wasn't her fault that the allotted housing for State Department employees in Namibia allowed for a thousand feet per family member, a pool, a recreation area, and a garden. A State Department family living in a mansion while assigned to Africa was normal. Slightly less normal was the herd of life-sized bronze rhinos scattered throughout the garden. (A Chardonnay-fueled, questionable purchase made during the auction portion of the Marine Ball.)

Amanda was inspecting one now.

"You really do love rhinos," she said.

"I'm crazy about them. They're so . . . sexy." Persephone flushed. "Or something. And people keep killing them here. It's maddening. I'd love to just sit out there in the bush with them and pick off any poachers who came along."

"You run that by the ambassador yet?"

"Not as such. But let me tell you, rhinoceros bodyguard? It's my dream job. Here . . . let me show you around," Persephone said, leading Amanda away from the sculptures and up a flight of stairs. "This is the terrace. Breezy, isn't it? My colleague Margo holds yoga classes here sometimes. I'll get you on the WhatsApp list. Come in. Here's the kitchen, the living room, the other living room, the kids' wing . . ."

She gestured grandly at the white-tiled floors, the cavernous rooms, the State Department furniture. Did she enjoy pretending she was Zsa Zsa Gabor at such moments? Maybe, she would later admit to her Afrikaans therapist, who would nod sagely and murmur, *Shame.*

"Mimosa?"

"Sure," Amanda said. Persephone handed Amanda a bottle of cold prosecco and grabbed a box of Ceres and two glasses. She'd intended to sit by the pool, but Elifas, the gardener, had already sealed it up after the weekend, and basking next to a blue plastic tarp didn't have quite the same effect. Instead they settled under the lapa, where Persephone prepared to deliver her standard Incomings speech. (Homesickness is normal, there's a nurse who prescribes at the Klein Windhoek Pharmacy, go to the back of Woolworth's for almost-American tastes and decent wine.) Yet Amanda dug in first.

"So who was the gorgeous woman who gifted you that carcass?"

"It was an oryx." Persephone paused and took a sip, the bubbles pleasantly tickling her nose. "And that was Mila Shilongo. Classic government wife. They're from up north. Completely corrupt husband."

"What makes you say that?"

Persephone rolled her eyes. "Because they're rich as King David. I mean, really, I heard they jet off to the U.S. and stay at Canyon Ranch once a year. What are they doing that could earn them a fancy house in Klein Windhoek *and* a game ranch?" She fiddled with the strap on her shoe, making a mental note to rein herself in. Gossip was strictly against her rules. "I'm just saying, if there's any government money that's not going towards the roads, it's just criminal. More people die in car accidents here than any other way."

"I believe it. Mark was in an accident, too. Back when he was here in the nineties."

"Oh, that's right. We knew that."

"We?"

"The point is," Persephone went on hurriedly, "Minister Shilongo is in charge of all roads, and the international trucks who use those roads. There are all sorts of fees they have to pay, and *someone's* getting them." She adjusted her ponytail. "Also, she's been in charge of this fiasco called International Day for years. *I* want to run International Day. I just know I could show them how to do it and actually make money. Oh, and I forgot to mention that Mila has a real thing for my husband." Hmmm, she thought. Perhaps she was getting close to gossip territory now. "But she can be very nice, too."

"Sounds like you adore her."

"Well." Persephone turned to fluff the outdoor pillows on her chair, concentrating on acting as if all the information Amanda would tell her about herself was news. For one of the things Persephone definitely could *not* tell Amanda was that a file about each new embassy family was circulated among a disclosed few, which, naturally, included Persephone. She knew that Amanda was forty-one—old for an Incoming. She knew that little Meg had been attending private school. She knew that Mark had been in the Peace Corps but had to go home because he was in some sort of bus accident. She knew that now Mark was working on a PhD and researching the turn of the century concentration camps on Shark Island. And she knew that Amanda had worked for a large tech company, that she was very good at it, and now she wasn't working at all.

She added a tad more champagne to her own glass.

"And how are you settling into Windhoek?"

Amanda shrugged. "I'm fine. You know. It's a disruption, but we're up for it. Or I'm up for it. My daughter, not so much."

"Meg?"

"Oh!" Amanda raised her eyebrows. "I hadn't realized I'd mentioned her to you."

"You must have," Persephone said hurriedly. "Back at school."

"Yeah, well. I had to promise to buy her a trampoline just to get her out of the car this morning."

Persephone grunted, looking at the spoils of her own children: trampoline, badminton court, pool volleyball net, and the Jonestown colony of dolls splayed grotesquely across the Astroturf.

"And what are you going to do? While you're here, I mean. Will you work?"

Amanda looked a bit hopeless, suddenly. "Looked into it, but the visa process won't work."

"Well. There's a lot here for Trailers, anyway. I can get you involved in anything. International Women's Association . . . Society of Diplomatic Spouses . . ."

"Wait. Trailers?"

Persephone looked at Amanda, perplexed. "Trailing Spouses." Hadn't this woman been briefed on anything? "That's what they call us. Officially. Spouses who follow State Department workers to different posts."

"That's so belittling," Amanda said, screwing up her face as if she'd eaten a bad pepper.

"I guess I've gotten used to it. It makes me feel . . ." Persephone paused, weighing her words. Adam would chew her out if any negativity got back to him. "Less lonely, I guess. In my situation. I mean, I could have a job at the embassy, if I wanted to. Angie, the security officer's wife, is a receptionist. And Aaron, whose wife is another doctor at the CDC, he works as a driver. But I'd rather . . ." She stopped again. Do nothing? Supervise Elifas, who was more competent than herself at everything? "Be with the kids."

"Why don't they just call us Sandbags?" Amanda mused. "Or Deadweight?"

"That's not really . . ." Persephone changed tack. "I think of it as being part of the most overqualified stay-at-home moms' and dads' club in the world. I mean, Kayla's an architect. Shoshana's a psychologist. Margo's a midwife. You're a manager."

"COO."

"Right. Back home, if I were a housewife, I'd be surrounded by other ladies who obsess over making school lunches and going to barre class. Here, I guess we do that, too, but everyone's really smart. Even if we are really smart at doing nothing."

"Well," Amanda said, sitting up slightly. "I won't be doing nothing. I've already made connections with an organization over in Katutura. For orphans, foster kids, that kind of thing. They want me to help them manage the place part-time."

"They said that?" Persephone asked, trying not to laugh. "That they want you to . . . manage?"

"Yes."

"And what is it called?"

"Um . . ." Amanda reached for her phone. "Our Hope Children's Hostel. Actually, what time is it? I'm supposed to be over there at ten. Hey, I better go."

Persephone gathered herself and rose to escort her guest out. "Well . . . great! Let me just get the gate for you, darling. And let me know about that meet 'n' greet!"

"Thanks," Amanda said. "And thanks for the mimosa. It's nice to have a friend in a strange land."

Persephone patted her arm, practically glowing. Community liaison duty for the day, aced!

"Byyyyyye!" she called as she watched Amanda's Subaru slide into the street. She did feel badly about sending her new friend into a den of wolves as hungry as the Our Hope Children's Hostel. Poor Amanda Evans was *not* in for a good morning.

Ah, well. If she was excited about it, who was Persephone to bring her down? It was not the job of the Embassy Wife to dampen anyone's enthusiasm. Diplomacy was tricky, after all. You had to break the new ones in slow.

3

Mark Evans had always been a star. He walked with the easy gait of those used to being looked at; he spoke with the humble self-assuredness of a boy who knows his future will be better than most. Preordained, his mother said sometimes, to the annoyance of his only-slightly-above-average brother and sister. Standing six-foot-three and filling out at two hundred and ten pounds, Mark had been both the varsity basketball and lacrosse MVP of his high school. He'd then been recruited by Brown to play lacrosse, only to be poached by the crew team, because they had a shorter season and better parties.

Mark's four years at Brown had been effortless and legendary, marked with aced premed classes despite leading his boats to victory at countless weekend regattas. His entrance into med school was assumed. Instead, to his parents' annoyance and worry, Mark chose to join the Peace Corps. He was such a well-known senior in the Class of '95 that the news caused a ripple through campus, which both alienated him from the other athletes and, to Mark's delight, opened a whole new range of bedroom doors of socially conscious eco-hotties.

That summer Mark was dispatched to Namibia, a place no one had ever heard of. His luck seemed to turn as soon as he set foot in the country. In Mark's family's mind, it was as if he were disappearing into blank space. He sent them long, boring letters of his progress at the health clinic where he had made the important decision, he told them, not to become a doctor. And then he had gotten into a bus accident. ("He was riding buses!" his mother shrieked. "In Africa!") But this, after all, had turned out to be a good thing, because—to the family's great relief—he'd been sent home early.

Mark's mother never fully understood what had occurred in that horrid country, but when her son returned from Namibia in 1997 to take up residence in his high school bedroom, he seemed, she whispered to her closest friends, "a bit broken." He was, of course, though he wouldn't be able to admit it until many years later. The accident had shattered his leg, and everything else.

As the dull, housebound weeks dragged on in Highland Park, he wondered at all that had happened at home while he was gone. It was like he returned to the movie of his life and everyone else had pushed fast-forward. Both of his college girlfriends were engaged. His former Brown roommates were VPs at various Wall Street firms; Mark didn't know what that meant other than they seemed ridiculously rich and confident. His parents were older, his siblings more self-involved. He skulked in his mother's house for two months, suffering the shame inflicted by his mother's friends when they asked what he was *doing* with himself these days. His classmates still living in HP couldn't believe it. Mark Evans, that cocky prick, had fucking boomeranged? Finally he couldn't stand it anymore. He went to Boston to stay with James.

While Mark was away, James had finished his master's degree in history at Harvard in one year, and now was moving on to his PhD, focusing on homosexuality in Nordic Viking culture. Mark still felt too numb to care much, but he was impressed by James's lifestyle. His friend had his own handsome cubby in the Widener Library and a cozy room in a house in Somerville where other good-looking graduate students came and went, drinking wine and talking about politics and cooking communal stir-fries. James had been his one friend that he knew, someday, would really make it. He was able to turn everyday happenings—band performances, pot-laced study groups—into sought-after events. Mark couldn't imagine how James would spin a PhD in history into something grand, but he was impressed with the fact that his friend had a purpose. Over beers at Grendel's, he confessed his envy.

"You can do it, too, man," James said. "You should. You were always better at school than I was. I had all Bs in history."

"So how did Harvard happen?"

"Prof Chapman at Brown? He loved me. Like, inappropriately. And Harvard liked my angle. Who else writes about gay Vikings? No one. That's what it's about. The angle."

"But you're not gay," Mark pointed out.

"Who cares? I could be. It's my angle." James looked at him thoughtfully. "Yours should be something Jewish."

"What? What does that mean?"

"You're, like, the best-looking Jewish guy ever. You could be, like, the Jewish Sebastian Junger."

Mark drew a circle in the beads of moisture on the outside of his beer. "How do you know Sebastian Junger's not Jewish himself?"

"Isn't there something in ancient Israel that interests you? You could search for some ancient scrolls or something."

"I don't know. I've been twice—"

"Teen Tour?" James grinned.

"Maccabiah Games, fuck you very much. The Israelis are kind of rude. The country didn't speak to me." He paused, looking at a pair of girls playing with the jukebox. While he was away, the waistline of the jeans women wore had plummeted to the lower hip. One of the girls was wearing a yellow thong; it snaked up above her belt loops. At one time, this would have propelled him either to make an opening remark or, if that seemed too difficult, to head to a bathroom stall to whack off. Now it just made him want to cry.

"I liked Namibia," he finally said.

"No one knows or cares about fucking Namibia, Mark. You're not going to sell a Namibian history course to Yale. Don't you speak Spanish or something?"

"French. And Ovambo."

"Do France. Jewishness and France. The Holocaust is big. It's like, *Schindler's List* legitimized the fucking thing."

"My grandmother was an Auschwitz survivor, you ass. It's always been legitimate."

"Yeah, but now it's popular. That's what's important. Don't look at me like that. It's 1997, and colleges are trying to sex up. A good-looking TA working on a thesis about the Jewish French Resistance, or whatever? You can sell that."

Mark spent the next month sneaking into the Harvard libraries with James's card and researching Jews in France. He put together an article entitled "Neighborly Death Sentence" and submitted it to a history magazine, which, to his delight, ran it. He sent it around with his application to schools. Dartmouth admitted him into their PhD program, and, because of his All-American crew status, said he could make extra money as the assistant coach.

Dartmouth. It was a place someone like Mark Evans was made for. Brown had felt like a female school to him, with her soft lawns, cozy brick buildings, and lax, loose curriculum. Dartmouth was a male place, tough and square, and it threw its fatherly arms open for him, then pushed him gently forward, encouraging him to heal. At first Mark hurled himself into his studies. He had a ridiculous amount of time, which reminded him of the Peace Corps. He was supposed to spend it working in the library, which he did, in his own private study office. Then Father Dartmouth gave him grants to go twice to France, where he did some interviews and poked in archives and learned about Burgundy wine.

Everyone knew it was officially against Dartmouth policy to date students. Everyone also knew, if you were a man, this rule was meant to be broken. Besides, the decree made the sex with undergraduates even more exciting. The last woman Mark had loved—the one who'd pushed him into this chasm—was measured, wise, and shy. The trajectory away from her was to grasp for anything but; hence the subjects of Mark's attention at Dartmouth were uniformly tall, blond, willowy, arty, and completely unreasonable. They hated that he had to leave their bed at 4:00 a.m. to coach; they couldn't stand that every weekend was spent on rivers and lakes at other campuses.

During his second spring in Hanover, Mark fell in with a senior, a sailing team champion named Whitney. She was blond, of course, but she varied from the others in that she understood an athlete's schedule and had a wry sense of humor. She'd also grown up in a mansion in Darien that had once belonged to Charles Lindbergh, had a trust fund that she dipped into regularly for trips with Mark to New York and Montreal, and was truly filthy in bed.

Mark was pretty sure, in his entire life from now on, that he would never find a better partner in the world than Whitney Chase. That spring, she graduated, and, instead of following her friends to New York, moved to Vermont with Mark. She was gone half of the time at international regattas, which Mark appreciated. Then Whitney returned one frigid April day, radiant from a J-24 victory in Malta, with news. She was leaving him for an Olympic dinghy sailor named Hans.

"Dinghies?" Mark said. "Even the sport sounds stupid."

"He's a silver medalist," she said impatiently. "Anyway. Mark. You're great. But you're really unfocused. Frankly, my loser alarm has been going off for a while now. And you're obsessed with 'what you went through' in Namibia. Which is boring."

"I went through a lot in Namibia," he said. "I can't talk about it. But Whitney, people died."

"Boring," she said.

It took her leaving for him to realize it. Mark was no longer a god. He was a human person and, yes, Whitney was right. A loser, in the literal sense. He had lost something he would never get back, and the ghost of that happening was creeping through the rest of his life. Whitney leaving was proof. Mark had never been left by a woman before. He couldn't believe the hollow feeling in the pit of his stomach, or how the empty drawers where Whitney's clothes had been made him cry. He still made it to practice, barking orders through the megaphone from the motorboat. Other than that, he'd lain on the sofa, drinking whiskey. He was becoming really fond of whiskey.

After a month, Mark had lost fifteen pounds. His jeans only fit when he punched new holes into his belt. Then, on an achingly beautiful day in May, Mark went into Dan and Whit's for beer and something to eat. As he stood absently looking into a fogged-up cooler of sandwiches, he felt a hand on his arm. It was a coxswain whose name he couldn't remember. Yes, he could. Amanda. Her brown hair was shiny and clean. She smelled like fabric softener.

"Those look gross," she said. "Come to my house. I'll make spaghetti."

Without a word, Mark had taken hold of her hand. He held it all the way from Norwich to Hanover, and continued to hold it, even while she made the pasta. Her housemates stared and exchanged glances. Coach is holding Amanda Pruitt's hand! Mark didn't give a shit what they thought. He knew, from his past, that he needed carrying. He was sure she was the woman to do it.

How right he'd been, he often thought. Amanda was a rock. She set up their home, she made their friends, she had their child, she mothered that child. She did so many things that he didn't even think about them anymore. He loved her, he appreciated her, he bragged about her. But he didn't have to look for anything, ever, because it was already there. Dinner was made, finances were sorted, his clothes were where they were supposed to be. Was that boring? He didn't let himself think about it. He'd had the opposite of boring, and he'd nearly died.

Then, five years ago—a decade into their marriage—Amanda Pruitt had started to let his hand go. Maybe it had started when she'd gotten that big Silicon Valley job. Or maybe it was when she and their daughter started to get so annoyingly, unnaturally close. At first he'd thought it was a normal mother-child bond; after all, Amanda was an orphan, so it made sense that she'd be more attached than other mothers. But once Meg started talking, it became clear that Amanda would much rather have a conversation with her daughter than with her husband. She would take Meg on day-long, mysterious "dates" to the beach or into the city; the two would return from their adventures without him, flushed and giddy. Which was fine, he guessed. Except for a long time now his wife was going on twice as many dates with their kid than with him.

Perhaps that's why he had brought them all back to Namibia? To get her attention? He knew it wasn't true, but he did want to show her the place. Because if there was one person living in Windhoek who truly had a crush on Namibia, it was Mark. Amanda's husband had lived in Ovamboland when he was twenty-two, just when a young person is ripe to declare allegiance to a wild and spectacular land. He'd fallen, hard. In particular, he lusted for her bleakest bits, the tracts of wind-scoured bush partitioned off every fifty miles or so with nothing but old barbed wire; the treeless mountains scarred by quarries; the treacherous northern coast littered with rusting shipwrecks where angry waves crashed onto brown beaches, making swimming impossible. Mark loved the scrubby, bristly plants that could survive on nothing more than the mist of the sea, blown in from three hundred miles away; the hornbills and oryx and impalas that dotted the expanse of sand. Most of all he loved the nights. Darkness in Namibia was so much thicker than at home. It had a smell, of woodsmoke and cooling earth. The sky was enormous and inky. And the sleeping veld—with her singing insects, searching birds, bellowing elephants, and all sorts of other unsaid creatures—it was the loudest place he'd ever heard in his life.

She'll love it, he'd thought. She'll love it because I did. But now that he had engineered their return, nothing was going right. Amanda was even more indifferent to him now than she had been at home. In fact, now the lack of warmth had gone up a notch to irritation. Which was dangerous, and not only for their marriage. Because Mark wasn't just in Namibia to reclaim his past. He had a ghost to put to bed, one his wife could never meet.

As Mark toweled off after a midafternoon swim in the pool of their rented house, he heard Amanda's car outside. They'd let the house (Namibians didn't say "rent") from an English South African family who'd given up on the safari business and moved back to one of the shires, but had left their furniture and knickknacks in case they wanted to return. As hunters, the landlords had shot everything in their path from muskrats to lions, and all kills, it seemed, deserved to be mounted. Meg and Amanda had been so freaked out by the heads that Mark spent much of the first week hauling the trophies to the unused bedroom, where they covered the floor and scared the shit out of any guest who wandered in there to find themselves stared down by twenty-five pairs of glassy, lifeless eyes.

But the pool was clean(ish), and the place had a nice view. And another useful feature was that every time someone went in or out of the compound, the alarm gave off a pleasant, hushed *beep*. It was a sound Mark found jarring yet helpful. If a beep went off, it meant Amanda had to park, sort through her things, drag herself and her grocery bag/workout clothes/curio shopping plunder across the blazing driveway and into the house. This gave Mark about three minutes, which was just enough time to clear away his files, close and log out of his emails, and hide his burner phone.

Because here was the truth of it: Mark had never applied for the Fulbright in France. He hadn't actually applied for his Fulbright at all. James had written the entire thing, just so Mark could come back to Namibia, find the girls, and put the whole thing to rest.

It started a year ago, while he was sitting in his windowless basement office in Santa Clara. His wife's career was rocketing ahead, while his own, it seemed, had stalled. Yet Mark knew he wasn't fated to be this unsuccessful. He was not meant to be wasting away in a basement office while his best friend James made the bestseller lists—while *all* the other rowers from his boat at Brown bought third homes from their hedge fund jobs. He was blocked. Depressed. And he knew exactly why.

Only James knew the full truth. Mark, unable to take the guilt of it, unloaded on him the same night at Grendel's when his friend had talked him into academia. And James, his shameless best friend who had slept with his wife's sister during their wedding weekend . . . James, who later still sued that very same wife for alimony . . . even no-morals James had been flummoxed.

"You just *left* them?" he'd whispered, horrified.

Mark nodded.

"You can't tell anyone, man. No one. You could go to jail for that. Not to mention hell."

Once he saw James's reaction, Mark knew that anyone else who heard the truth would never be able to love him. Because when you do something like that, you stop being a whole person. Now it was more than two decades later—twenty years of carrying around this horrible secret—and Mark wanted to be a whole person. He wanted it for himself, and he wanted it for his family. It had taken him that long to face it, but now it was decided. He would find those girls. He would make up for what he had done to them. No matter how much money it took. Even if it meant he had to go to jail for a while.

So he had called James. Or Jaime. Whatever he called himself now. National Book Award nominee. Best friend. Former crew asshole girl-friend stealer.

"I'll get you in there," James had said over the phone when he'd asked him to do it. "But solve the problem, man, all right? I can't listen to this bullshit anymore. You've got a hot wife who makes a ton—"

"Back off my wife."

"An adorable kid. So when you're done, promise me you'll find a new job, okay? You can't be an assistant prof at fifty."

"You're the whole reason I went into history. You said I was good at it."

"I was wrong. Hey, I gotta go, my editor's calling. Look, I'll do the Fulbright thing for you. Send me your Social Security number."

So, thanks to Jaime, they were in Africa, where Meg was despondent and his wife was bored out of her mind. Which was why Mark was exceedingly glad she was taking on this new orphanage job. Once Amanda actually had something to do, she would be less in his business, and he could stop lying so much about what he was doing, where he was going. And with any luck she would be happier, period. After all, what smart person likes sitting around with nothing to do? None of them, that's who. Which was why the Hopeful Orphans Children's Hotel, or whatever it was, was going to be a godsend.

"Hey!" he called when he saw her emerge from the car. Meg was trailing after her, which was a little weird, as she was supposed to be in her after-school activity. The Windhoek International School day started at 7:15 because of the heat and petered out at 1:30, but any parent who could afford it threw their kids into paid extracurriculars meant to stretch the school day until three. These were not clubs meant to pad a résumé for Yale; the offerings ranged from yoga under a thatched roof to playing with plastic action figures. Still, it was worth a hundred bucks a month for the hours of freedom, so the Evanses happily doled out the cash. So why wasn't Meg doing one of them? he wondered.

"How was your meeting?" Mark asked. "And why's Meg home?"

"Meg is home because she got in a boxing match with a student," Amanda said.

"Wait, what?" Mark planted his fists into his sides, then shook them loose again, out of fear of looking too much like an old man.

"I got a call from the scary Afrikaans receptionist while I was at the orphanage. She punched someone."

"I didn't mean to!" Meg cried.

"We know, sweetheart," Amanda said, putting her arm around her.

"Here, sit down on the porch with us." She led Meg to the comfy over-stuffed outdoor chairs. "Just relax." They sat across from each other, stretching their tan legs over the bamboo-and-glass coffee table that was sticky with rings from cold drinks during happier times.

"Wait," Mark said. "Wait. No relaxing. Meg, what the hell is going on?"

"You owe me a dollar!" Meg cried. Mark clenched his jaw, rubbing his back molars back and forth, wincing as they made a sort of horrible clicking. It was a bad habit he had, one that his dentist had warned him about and that his wife hated. Though she wasn't noticing now, because she didn't seem to care about anything he did since the relocation.

"Hey," Amanda said, sinking farther back into the purple cheetah print. "The swear jar was your idea." It was true. Mark had instituted it just last week. He'd caught Meg happily eavesdropping on her mother as Amanda video-chatted with her best friend back in Los Gatos. After hearing "fucking Namibia" four times in two minutes, he'd lost patience and started charging.

"Meg," Mark said now. "Just tell us what happened."

"You won't get in trouble," Amanda added soothingly. Their daughter crossed her twig-like arms over her chest. "Did someone call you something?"

"No."

"We won't be disappointed in you," Amanda said. "We just want to make certain that—"

"It's fine, okay?" Meg burst out. "I'll fix it. I'll *apologize*. I just don't want to talk about it anymore."

"Don't speak to your mother that way," Mark said, still towering over them. He liked being tall, other than when he was standing and everyone else was sitting, as his lanky, wilting form inevitably made him feel like a Truffula tree from *The Lorax*. "It's not acceptable. You're already in enough trouble."

"You just said I *wasn't* in trouble," Meg protested.

"Well, you might be," Mark said. "First I have to hear what happened."

"Wait. No. Lolo, you're definitely not," Amanda said. "But we do need to sort this out."

"Mandi, follow my lead here."

"But—"

"Okay, Meg. Start."

"I don't *want* to *talk* about it."

"Well, you have to," Mark said. "You can't just—"

"Actually, let's let her have a pass," Amanda said.

Mark put his hands on the back of his head and looked at the sky, willing himself not to explode. Amanda spoiled the shit out of their daughter. It was her one main blind spot. First it was because of their "bond." Then it was because she felt guilty about spending so much time at work. Now it was that she felt bad about dragging their daughter to Namibia. All he knew was that if they didn't get a handle on the situation, Meg was going to end up being a grade-A asshole.

"Meg, why don't you go for a swim?" he said.

"No." His daughter glared at him before slipping away into the tiled cave of the house. Leaving Amanda to stew in her righteousness, he went to the kitchen, fetched two glasses and a bottle of wine, and poured a large, crisp portion for his wife.

"Here you go," he said, coming back out.

She shook her head and pushed it back toward him. "Mark, it's the middle of the day. All people in Namibia seem to be able to do is offer me alcohol. I mean, booze doesn't solve problems."

"It does take the edge off, though," Mark said. "And if we smoke pot in Nam we'll go to jail."

Amanda sat down and pushed her chair back into the precious shade. "The school called my phone at eleven, while I was at the orphanage," she said, drawing her legs up under her. "The receptionist said Meg had gotten into a fistfight with another girl, which seemed totally implausible to me. But she won't talk about it. So there's no way for me to defend her against these International School psychopath moms."

Mark sighed. He knew Amanda was making great sacrifices, but he wished she wouldn't remind him of it every other minute. After all, the yard, shaded by banana trees and carpeted with artificial, droughtproof grass, was inarguably lovely, particularly when the nighttime breeze rustled through the hanging leaves. And having a pool and a swing set and two spare bedrooms, Mark thought, was pretty fucking awesome. Which was why he wished that the women in his life would spend a little less time complaining and developing unhealthy new habits such as boxing other girls out of the ring, and a little more time just enjoying themselves.

He poured himself some wine. "As usual, she worships you, ignores me."

"Because you're mean to her."

"I'm a disciplinarian, Mandi. I want better health for her. It's not right that you let her get away with everything and that she eats only Kraft mac and cheese."

"It's Annie's Organic."

"It's disgusting. It's poisoning her brain, and what's more, it's clearly making her violent."

"She's nine, Mark. And too skinny. She needs calories. If I can make Namibia bearable because of mac and cheese—"

"Namibia is perfectly bearable. Come on. It's a fascinating, beautiful country."

"It's a parking lot for four-by-fours."

"Moving on," he said, just to show she hadn't won. In response, she grabbed a bottle of almond oil sitting on the ground and started smoothing it into her legs. The air was so dry that everyone in the family had rough patches all over—knees, cheeks, noses. Ever the problem-solver, Amanda had stocked almost every room in the house with some type of moisturizer to prevent chapping. Though Mark was pretty sure, watching Amanda slather oil into her skin, this was just another way for her to torture him. Because if their sexual encounters had been an endangered species back in the States, here in Namibia they'd become all but extinct.

"Why don't you tell me about your meeting at the orphanage?"

"Well . . ." She took a sip of wine.

"Yes?"

"I gave them five thousand Namibian."

"Wow. That's generous."

"They said that it was their volunteer fee."

"Wait. I thought they had a job for you."

"Yeah. Me, too."

"Uh-oh."

"I gave them the money, and then I was sent to help someone scrub an old refrigerator."

"Sounds like a promising start," he said encouragingly as Meg padded by on her way to the kitchen. Mark watched her pour a huge glass of juice. "That's, like, a cup of sugar you're about to put into your body," he yelled.

Amanda rolled her eyes. "They said I could come back, if I wanted, but they clearly hoped I wouldn't. I'll just give it a pass."

"Are you talking about the orphanage, Mom?" Meg said, drawing closer, glass in hand.

"I am, sweetheart. It's not working out the way I wanted it to."

"Why?" Meg asked. She gulped down the rest of her juice, set the glass on the table, and sat on her mother's lap. It was ridiculous, as far as Mark was concerned. Their daughter, who was almost as tall as Amanda, teetered on her mother's knee, slipping off and then wedging herself up again. But his wife didn't seem to mind.

"I wanted to help the kids," Amanda said, smoothing Meg's hair, "but they wouldn't even let me near the bucket to clean an old kitchen."

"So there were kids there? Like me?"

"Not like you. No. They don't have parents."

"Like *you* didn't."

Mark could see his wife's legs stiffen, could feel the impact those words had on her gut at being reminded that she was an orphan. He rubbed his forehead in frustration at Meg's blunder. But then again, he hadn't considered Amanda's real reasons for wanting to get involved with the orphanage, other than boredom. Another fail for him, another point for Meg. Not that he was competing with his nine-year-old daughter.

"They're sort of like me," Amanda replied after a moment. "But I had Grandpa, didn't I?"

"But he's not your real dad."

"He's dad enough," Amanda said crisply. "Anyway, they wouldn't let me meet any of them."

"And it makes you sad."

"Well . . ." Amanda said. Mark tried to catch her eye, but she avoided him. "It would make me really happy to help."

"I'm sorry, Mom," Meg said, giving her a hug.

"It's okay, sweetheart," Amanda said. "Nothing for you to worry about."

"I'm sorry, too," Mark tried. "And, Meg, you need to—"

But his daughter had already gotten up and disappeared. Amanda stared in the direction of her exit, wearing a small frown, then turned her attention reluctantly back to him. "Did you know they call us Trailing Spouses? Like, we just trail around after our husbands because we're too lame to get our own jobs?"

"It works the other way, too, you know. Spouses who follow their wives around. That's what I've basically been doing for a decade."

"You weren't following. You were working, in one place."

"Anyway, you should be happy. How often in life does one get to be a government-sponsored concubine?" He looked at her legs again.

"The Fulbright is paying a stipend for you, too, you know. It's not very big, but it's something. So maybe you should be putting a bit more time into pleasuring this spouse you're trailing."

Amanda picked up a wooden spoon and threw it at him, narrowly missing Mark's head. "I'm going to take a bath," she said. "I'll be out in an hour."

She grabbed her goblet of wine and left, leaving Mark alone with a family of yellow weaver birds. He watched as they flew back and forth from their teardrop nests made of reeds. The male weavers were a brilliant, shocking yellow, streaked with jet-black. They looked like flying buttercups. From skimming the *Peterson's*, Mark knew the males collected the grass and wove the outside of the nests, while the females lined their little houses with feathers and leaves. It was an episode of *Planet Earth*, right here in their backyard. Even David Attenborough would be impressed. Couldn't his wife and daughter stop leaving him and appreciate what he had done for them?

"Fuck it," Mark said to the birds.

"*Dollar,*" Meg called from down the hall. Her voice was so soft, Mark could barely make out the sound.

A mile away from the Evanses' bungalow, on a hill in Ludwigsdorf nestled in the midst of a few other houses so large they might well have been hotels, Mila Shilongo was overseeing supper.

Mila hadn't touched a stove herself in five years, but she kept a close eye on Libertina, who had a tendency to over-boil rice and ruin good cuts of meat with too much braai spice. Though Mila had bought Libertina two blue uniform sets, the housekeeper insisted on wearing her traditional Herero dresses, complete with double-horned cap. Libertina was perfectly sweet to the Shilongos; Mila had never caught her even rolling an eye. Still, she couldn't help thinking—given the centuries of bloody wars between her own tribe and Libertina's—that the long, printed dresses were something of a small fok jou to her Oshiwambo employers. At first it had annoyed Mila, but it no longer did. She knew what it was to work for someone else, and how one had to seize every opportunity for personal dignity.

Libertina's traditionally clad, stooped form was glaringly out of place in the Shilongos' gargantuan home, constructed solely of white brick, white tile, and glass. The furniture was all either black or white, the rugs were almost all trophy skins. Mila loved her house. It was clean, neat, huge, and appropriately opulent.

"Don't boil that rice too long, Libertina," she said now, pouring herself a tiny bit of wine. The old woman glanced at the glass, her face as unreadable as blank paper. Ignoring what she guessed was a judgment, Mila stepped out to the patio to relax and look out over her own version of Namibia.

It surprised Mila daily that she still lived in this country. When she was a girl, she and her sisters would make their way to school early to beat the sun. While the others scrabbled and ran in the flat red play yard, Mila would slip into the empty classroom and pull out the worn atlas, donated some fifteen years before by a German family. She didn't read German and didn't want to, but she would run her finger over the images of countries across the sea, places that must be cool and kind, dotted with trees and mountains. She imagined that the place called Frankreich must be entirely pink, the way it was shown on the map. Pink grass, pink trees and buildings, a cotton-candy sky. Kanada offered aquamarine mountains and royal blue cities; Australien would be entirely canary yellow, ocean to sea. She knew this to be true because in the book Namibia was exactly the color it was in real life: an ugly burnt orange, same as the clay in the plot outside her hut where nothing would grow, same as the dust that blew all the way up from the desert and coated the inside of her mouth.

Mila's Namibia was a different place than the country Persephone and her friend were visiting. Those women, Mila thought, with their hand sanitizer and their white clothes, would never actually live here. They would say they did once they went back to the United States. *When I lived in Africa . . .* they would tell people at parties. But they hadn't really, even if they stayed for three years, or ten. Those women could go home when they wanted to, when their friend got malaria, or if they got tired of the snakes in the garden. The Americans saw elephants as novelties to be photographed; Mila knew them as nuisances that trampled villages and shat gallons of dung in the yard. The Americans saw the vast red dunes in the Namib Desert as a natural wonder; Mila knew they were a waste of space, deadly to any living being but the ant or the oryx. The Americans spent thousands chasing lions around with cameras; Mila's uncle had been killed by a pack while herding goats outside of Ovji. From their air-conditioned trucks, the Americans didn't feel the eye-scorching heat. They didn't know what it was like to have to lie down half of the day just to survive, your sweat pooling under your back, trickling out of every crevice. They didn't know that families battled, sometimes violently, over a single shade-bearing tree. They didn't know what it was to live with twelve people in a small mud house, fighting over the grainy TV, bickering over the radio, batting the flies that boomeranged in through the window as soon as the morning light hit the ground. And though Mila did not live that way now and never would again, she was tired of Namibia, and she was tired of the visitors. But there was no leaving this place for her. There'd been a single flash of hope, years ago, but that, like so many other flames, had flickered and died.

Out of the corner of her eye, a flash of purple. It was Taimi, fluttering next to the pool. She could have been a lilac-breasted roller, fluttering in from Katima. Watching her brought Mila's mind back to the unpleasant business of the trouble that morning. She sighed heavily. From the start, Mila had been against her daughter going to the International School. There were other private institutions—St. George's, for one, and St. Paul's—that followed the proper African calendar. Why would she want Taimi to be in school when the rest of Namibia was on summer break? It made no sense. And, if they really wanted Taimi to be clever, Mila had pointed out to Josephat, even better boarding schools awaited in South Africa. Certainly they had the money for it.

But Josephat had been adamant about their daughter staying in Windhoek. As a boy, his mother had left him with his grandmother in Oshakati while she went to Walvis Bay to work in a hotel. She only visited him every six weeks, which meant Josephat suffered a long, lonely childhood in his grandmother's hut, unprotected from her nightly demands that he scrub her heels with a mixture of paste made of sand and salt. Even today, Josephat still harbored a revulsion toward feet, which meant Mila could only wear shoes with closed toes in his presence. No small sacrifice, she often thought, in a charred land such as this.

Josephat's experience also brought on the decree that no child of his would grow up outside of his house, now that he was a rich man. Their older daughter, Anna, could do whatever she wanted . . . and she did.

Josephat's success had arrived too late to give her the benefit of a proper education. But Taimi! *She* would have the best Windhoek could offer, which was an international certificate. So, the International School it was, along with its den of international mothers, those lazy women who lounged about the coffee hut all morning and couldn't drive properly on the left side of the road.

And who were these children, Mila wondered, Taimi's classmates? How stupid could the Americans be? How could they not know that Taimi's father was in the government, that striking his child could almost be construed as an offense against the state itself? And, what was more, how could they not know who *Mila* was?

She looked at her phone, checking to see if Josephat had called yet. Only texts from Adam Wilder, wanting to meet again about their project. Damn Josephat, getting this idiot involved in their affairs. She supposed it was important to have relationships with diplomats to distract from rumors of corruption, but this one! First of all, it had stirred up the wrath of the Gecko, though Mila had certainly put her in her place today. More irritatingly, the man could not have a conversation with her without staring at her breasts.

Mila sat in a chaise lounge to wait. She had never liked Persephone Wilder, with her constant criticisms and her ideas of "how things could be better in Namibia," if only the Namibians would listen. She sat there, lording over those PTA meetings with her soy matcha chai. Bringing a takeaway cup to a coffee hour in someone's home! Disgusting! Now the Gecko (Mila's favorite name for her) had nominated herself as the new PTA president, and—*boom!*—won the election. She would, she said, take charge of the first project at hand, International Day, and give it "new life," unmistakably suggesting that Mila's party hadn't been sufficient. Now, as if all of that weren't enough, Persephone was apparently enlisting another woman to attack her through her own child. The thought made her toes curl.

"Taimi!" Mila shouted. "Come here."

Her daughter sashayed around the pool, taking her time to come to her mother. Oh, this child. Mila shook her head as Taimi swung her hips from side to side and jangled the bracelets she had taken to wearing on her ankles.

"What are you doing, walking like that? Do you want people to think you're a little prostitute? Your father will be home at any minute, and he will not be pleased to see you wearing almost nothing."

"My father loves me no matter what I wear."

Mila nodded in reluctant agreement. Taimi was Josephat's true joy—which was precisely why she was so very spoiled.

"I am still trying to interpret what happened between you and the new American girl today." Mila folded her arms over her chest and looked at her daughter through narrowed eyes. "She had no reason to attack you? None?"

Taimi did a leap and a pirouette, landing inches from the edge of the pool.

"Answer me when I am talking to you."

"Well. Perhaps a *little* reason."

"Yes?"

"We were playing a game."

"What game?"

"A pretend game."

"Of what?"

Taimi stood still, studying the sky.

"Taimi?"

"Ministers."

"What?"

"We were pretending to be ministers."

Mila adjusted her position in her seat.

"Government ministers?"

"Exactly." Taimi beamed. "Like Papa."

"And you were minister of what?"

"I was president."

"Aha." Mila tried to conceal her approval.

"The new girl was the minister of trampolines. Phalana was minister of swings."

"I see. So how did the minister of trampolines get so out of control?"

"I asked her where she was keeping her *other* wife."

Mila's smile faded. "Taimi Shilongo. What are you talking about?"

"I said, Where does the minister of trampolines keep her other wife? And she asked me what I meant. And I said, '*You* know what I mean. The minister has a *secret*.' And she hit me. With her fist."

"Well." Mila paused, a bit confounded by her daughter's precociousness. "What *did* you mean? What secret?"

"Mila! Taimi!"

Josephat was home. Taimi did another pirouette, stopped dead, then gave her mother a dazzling smile before dashing away toward her father's voice.

"Papa!"

Josephat emerged onto the balcony, looking tired yet still perfectly pressed. Mila loved that about him; he was a big man, yet no matter what the weather, he seemed never to perspire. He picked up his daughter and twirled her around. Mila sighed. Obviously, she wasn't going to get to the bottom of this tonight, which meant she probably wouldn't at all, ever.

"Taimi, go tell Libertina to put dinner on."

Her daughter skipped away. Josephat sat in the chair next to her, looking out over the city. Mila smiled. They did not have a traditional relationship, God knew that. Yet she couldn't help being overwhelmed every time she saw him.

"So?" Mila leaned over and kissed his cheek. "Where were you just now?"

"Meetings."

Mila rolled her eyes. The ministers loved having meetings. They loved planning the meetings, they loved meeting to plan. Actually getting things done, that was a different story. "I have news," she said.

"Yes?"

"A foreign girl struck Taimi today."

"What?" Josephat turned, his face rigid with anger. He and his sisters had been beaten every day of their childhood by his grandmother, usually with a broom handle. Mila knew this would set him off. "Is she going back to her country?"

"No, but she was sent home for the day. I believe Taimi may have said something unkind."

"I don't care. This is not acceptable, Mila. We didn't work this hard to have Taimi have the same childhood we did."

Mila glanced at the Jacuzzi burbling at Josephat's feet. "I do not think she's in danger of facing our hardships, Jo."

"Who is this girl?"

"An embassy child."

Her husband groaned. "American?"

"Naturally." She rubbed his arm. He had such lovely forearms . . . ropy, the color of gleaming teak.

"Shame. They think they can come here and do whatever they want." His lack of physical response chilled her; Mila took her hand back.

"Well, the American Mr. Wilder certainly thinks he can do what he wants with *me*."

"Adam Wilder makes us look good, my dear. He is necessary. But the others? What are the Americans even doing in Namibia?"

"You mean *Nam*-bia?"

Josephat smiled. The American president's mash-up of "Namibia" and "Zambia" in a speech in front of the world mangling their country's name had happened some months before.

"Exactly. They don't even know where they are! And they think we're . . . a 'shithole.' Did you hear that one?"

"I did."

"Awful people," Josephat said. "I was talking to one businessman today, here to sell me cement or some what-what-what."

"Was he bidding for a road-building job?"

"Not properly," Josephat said. Mila nodded. This meant he was a contractor who didn't understand that there was no way Josephat would purchase his materials unless he was guaranteed a secret kickback.

"He was ignorant, then," Mila suggested.

Josephat shrugged and got up out of his chair to get a closer look at the view. "Not knowledgeable of Africa, my dear. Anyway, he said he didn't have the same views as the White House. 'He's not *my* president,' this man said."

Mila and Josephat burst into laughter together. Americans actually thought they could excuse themselves individually from their leader! As if the world didn't think *Mugabe* when they met a man from Zimbabwe. Or as if a girl whose mother was a whore would ever be anything other than a whore's daughter.

Josephat put his arm around Mila's shoulders as they looked at the city. She wished he would encircle her waist. For the last few years, he had been withholding affection, seemingly curling into himself more and more. She couldn't remember when it started, and she didn't know what she had done. But he was the floor of her ocean; without him, her carefully constructed world would crack open and fall away. The new lack of security caused her physical pain.

"Who are these new embassy people anyway?" he asked finally. "I'll have them followed."

"They're no one. I'll deal with it tomorrow when I go into the school."

Josephat patted her shoulder. "And did you deliver the oryx to Adam Wilder's wife?"

"I did."

"Was she grateful?"

"Persephone Wilder can butcher it with her teeth, that much I know."

Josephat laughed. "You are a queen." He released her and went to the kitchen to pour himself some water. "Still, I don't want Taimi affected. What's to be done about the conflict?"

"I'm going tomorrow to meet with the girl's mother. If you don't mind, I'll take the motorcade. Just to prove the point."

"That's fine," Josephat said. They had agreed long ago to take everything they could from his position. For what was the point of government perks if you weren't going to use them? "But, Mila, I want you to befriend this new American woman. Mrs. Wilder is one thing, But I don't want Taimi isolated from every single American family."

"Taimi could never be isolated. Not in a million years."

"Yes, but we want her to have American friends. It's the whole point of this school. Perhaps she will do an exchange when she is older. This woman, she is not Mrs. Wilder. Be kind to her."

Mila tossed her head, pouting a bit.

"Mila?"

"I will listen to her side of things."

"I'll arrange for her dossier to be sent over. What's her name?"

"I didn't get it."

"I'll get Reggie to find out."

"Reggie works with you again?" Mila felt an unpleasant twist in her stomach. "I thought you two had a falling-out."

"Focus, Mila. The Americans. Let's get her on our side, hmmm? You never know. You might like her."

"Stop it."

"Please do it, Mila. For Taimi. And me." Josephat finished his water and put the glass down. Then he took both her hands in his and kissed her cheek. Mila looked at his face, blushing. He smelled of vanilla. She could almost feel his precious skin against hers. The moment instilled a beat of hope. "I'm going to take a shower," he said, still holding her hands.

"Shall I join you?" she dared.

Josephat gave a half laugh and kissed her cheek again. "You're so funny, darling. I'll be down in half an hour."

She could feel the rejection physically, cold as a sharp wind. She watched her husband climb the stairs, then went into the kitchen to keep Libertina from daydreaming and letting the pap turn into cement.

Like Josephat, Mila grew up in the north. She was the second eldest of four sisters. The family lived in Onesi, a village seventy long kilometers west of Oshakati.

The girls' mother was Olivia, a notoriously skilled seamstress with equally notoriously questionable judgment. The sisters had three different fathers between them, the cause of constant rivalry. Yet the eldest, Selma, and the second youngest, Sophia, had the same father—Tega. No one would call Tega a good man, as he drank, and had two other houses of children. Still, he was there in the flesh, not dead of TB or HIV, and not just some dim memory from a night at a drunken braai. His very existence made Selma and Sophia feel vastly superior to Mila and Saara, who had fathers somewhere, though their names and faces were lost in the beer-soaked stories of nights at the local shebeen.

Onesi. It was a small town, a typical Ovambo village consisting of a carefully planned group of round huts with walled-off yards. Gardens of mud, perhaps a tree to provide a shady corner. Communal, poor, gossipy, Onesi was—like many towns of this nature—also loud. Goat bleats, rooster crows, shrieking children, women gossiping, men laughing, radios blaring church hymns and tinny rock, whining dogs, angry chickens, hungry goats, wind, rain. If you wanted quiet in Onesi, Olivia liked to say, you had to die for it. Years later, when Josephat was designing the glass castle in Ludwigsdorf for Mila, she insisted on walls so insulated she could hear nothing from the streets or neighbors.

Mila had the bad luck of being an uncommonly beautiful girl growing up in a spectacularly poor place. The contrast turned up her prettiness so much it brought on harsh feedback, same as the volume dial on their ancient radio. None of the village women liked her. She was a favorite as a toddler, but at six or seven, it became apparent what she would become, and all affection dropped away. As an adult woman in a world of comfort and laws, Mila found beauty is a pleasant thing; in an impoverished place run by men with too little to do, it was a black mark. Older boys were forever trying to corner her in the back of the schoolhouse; they grabbed her thighs in passing and tugged harshly on the hem of her dresses. When they could catch her ear, they whispered the things they could do if they could get her alone. By fourteen, all the men were wild to get Mila by herself. If she was alone on the way home from school or to the shops, she took to running. Often her sandals were too flimsy to be of use, so she'd put them in her knapsack. Her bare heels grew thick from wear on the pavement. Her body became more lithe as she learned how to pump her legs and lungs faster for speed.

But being fast didn't always help. Sometimes the boys would reach out a stick and trip her. One night Dominic, an old neighbor who was always drunk but still strong, was able to grab her by the arm and pull her toward his house. Her sister Saara saw it happening from a few feet back, where she was playing with her friends. Running to the fire, she grabbed an unspooled hanger her sisters used for cooking meat, then scuttled over and whipped Dominic until, yelping, he slunk away in retreat. Mila and Saara hadn't been particularly close before, as one was shy, the other the opposite. But now an alliance was formed, and the sisters protected each other, warding off the jackals so their fine bodies could be used later, for proper things.

Saara was the youngest and the one everyone liked. She wasn't stunning like Mila, but she was fine-looking, and she was quick with jokes and had a voice the village gossips said would get her on that idol show in Johannesburg, the one on the TV. Her father was rumored to be from Rehoboth—how else to explain her light skin and almond-shaped eyes the color of jade? Tega loved her best even though she wasn't his daughter; one day he passed Saara some candy, and Selma, in a fit of jealousy, took a coal from underneath the potjie and set fire to Saara's dress. When Olivia came back from the well to see her youngest screaming with legs burned and blistering, and her two eldest trying to gouge each other's eyes out with sticks, she dropped her bucket, spilling the hard-earned water onto the dry, cracked mud. Then she went inside, filled a plastic Pick n Pay bag with clothes, and left. Olivia never visited the hut again, but simply sent for Sophia—the most reasonable of the four—to collect a small amount of money every week for their needs.

At fourteen (Selma), thirteen (Mila), twelve (Sophia), and eleven (Saara), the girls were completely alone. As they grew, their house became nicknamed the Beautiful House. Tega bought padlocks for the doors and tied a large dog to the shepherd's tree outside. Within weeks, more than one man had a scar on his ankle after walking by and checking to see if a window, perhaps, might be cracked for a little view.

It was filthy, the Beautiful House. Plastic bags batted against wire fences. Mole rats darted in and out. When the girls did their laundry, ants would crawl up the line onto the shirts and dresses, so that every piece of clothing had to be beaten with a stick before it could be worn.

By the time they could walk, the girls paired off against each other in their race to become something else. They competed for the teachers' affections. They fought over every odd job that was batted their way. Selma and Sophia had an advantage, in that Tega sometimes passed his real daughters some money after he'd been drinking. By sixteen and eighteen, they had enough to travel to Katuura, where they found a cousin and commandeered a corner in her house.

As soon as they left, Saara and Mila scoured the place for clothing. Before, Mila would never have given her sister the satisfaction of wearing her used rags, but now she riffled through the old dresses, rescuing a sleeve here and a skirt there. Neither girl could sew, so they went to their mother's new hut, fifteen kilometers away.

It was an ugly place, much worse than the Beautiful House. The walls were dark green, and coated with something that glistened gruesomely, as if someone had smeared them with lard. The only decently kept item in the hut was Olivia's sewing machine, which stood in a cleanish corner under a bare bulb, surrounded by finished pillowcases the color of jewels. The girls were shocked to find their mother barely recognizable. Her curves, which once had poured into precariously tight shirts and dresses, had now shriveled into nothing. She had sores on her face, and her daughters could see her bones through her skin.

Mila and Saara stood rooted to their spot by the front door. "Sophia didn't tell us you were hungry," Mila finally said.

"I'm not hungry," Olivia answered, using a chair next to her bed to pull herself up. "I have the AIDS." Her head was bald in patches. "Why are you here? For money?"

"We are hoping you can make us some clothes," Mila said. "So we can get good jobs at a hotel."

Olivia shook at the loveliness of her daughter's voice and swiveled her head at her. Mila was seventeen now. Olivia put her clawlike hand on her arm and led her out into the lane. In the sunlight, the chasm between illness and vitality opened between them even further.

Five dresses: three for Mila, two for Saara. It was the last work Olivia completed in her life, and the result was conservative but exquisite. Mila was given a black suit embroidered with cobalt thread, a knee-length sheath of purple and black, and a looser sundress that was burgundy in front, blue in the back. (Creativity was required, as materials were limited.) Saara was presented with a green suit and a pink Ovambo sundress—Olivia had raided her own material for that. Mila donned her suit, Saara her Ovambo dress. They crept out of their mother's house without saying goodbye.

The year was 1994. The girls hitched a ride with a farmer to Oshakati. Wearing their hand-sewn finery, they marched into the Oshakati Country Hotel. Saara went to the reception desk as Mila hung back.

"Please tell the manager," Saara said in a clear voice, "that we are educated ladies, and we would like to give you the *opportunity* to let us work at this fine hotel."

The receptionist, a man, laughed quietly in order to scorn her while not disturbing the guests. Then he caught sight of Mila. As he hesitated, Saara turned around and gave her sister a sly smile. It happened this way often. People would believe one thing, and then, looking at Mila, change their mind.

"I'll be back in a moment," the receptionist said begrudgingly, obviously disgusted with his own susceptibility to beauty. As luck would have it, the manager who appeared was a rather rough-looking white woman who introduced herself as Mrs. Ferreira. She took the girls out back by the trash bins, and grilled them, hard.

"You must not steal," she said. "You must get tested for TB and HIV. The tests will come out of your wages. You must not speak socially to guests. You must not steal. Did I say that already? I'll say it again. Do it and I will call the police. You can have one job between you as a maid, and one bed in the staff house. There are no men in the women's side ever, no women in the men's side. There is no liquor, ever. And, for God's sake, do not get yourselves pregnant. If you get pregnant, you will be fired and tossed out."

"Yes, miss," Mila and Saara murmured. Mila dug her nails into the back of Saara's hand.

Now it was more than two decades later, and Mila Shilongo, once a girl who had so little her dying mother had to sew her a dress out of discarded clothes, sat in a white enamel chair grand enough to serve as a throne. She looked out at the baked hills of Windhoek, washed pink in the waning sun. Already the lights of the houses along Nelson Mandela Avenue were beginning to glitter below. And to the north, beyond Eros, she could see the glow of Katutura, where Selma still lived, and where Mila, too, might have been fated to be, had she and Josephat had not been quite so clever. In certain weather, you could hear the distant sounds of the Location, pulsating with grief and joy and car engines and yelling and real life. It called to her, clearly as fine music. When it did, Mila pulled her soundproof windows shut.

5

Persephone Wilder was thirty-eight years old. She was not worried about her age, nor did she hide it. For one thing, it helped her keep her dates straight. She knew, for example, that it had been twelve years since she'd taken on State Department life. Never one to do things halfway, she'd jumped in as enthusiastically and gracefully (she hoped) as Esther Williams jackknifing into William Hearst's Neptune Pool.

Persephone was twenty-six then, and by that point she had already supported Adam during his slog through law school. After his graduation, Adam had gotten a job as an associate at a middling firm, and it turned out he didn't like law at all. More alarmingly, he wasn't very good at it. And though Persephone had been making a very fine living for them both ever since college as the personal assistant to celebrity chef and homemaker Doni Oppenheimer, the bloom was off the rose. She was tired of Doni, and, as hard as Persephone worked to stay in a cloud of cheerful denial, it was becoming increasingly clear that Doni was tired of *her*.

Not that she hadn't learned invaluable lessons from the woman. No condiments on the table outside of serving bowls, ever! Decisions—whether it be the color of one's socks or one's choice of marriage partner—should take no longer than forty-five seconds and should never be regretted! Pick a designer for life and if you can, meet them! Always order the third most expensive wine on the menu! Goose down, no substitutes, no questions! A hangover can be solved by a fur collar and large sunglasses in the winter, an iced whiskey and a nap in the summer!

Oh, she was brilliant, Doni was, but she was a notorious Svengali, and even a girl of Persephone's fine constitution could only take so much gaslighting for sport. ("Persephone, I won't need you until eleven tomorrow! Have a nice morning, *darling!*" to be followed with, "Persephone, you are over two hours late! I am *beyond* disappointed!")

After all those years of service, Doni had started attacking Persephone in her classic, underhanded way—pointedly commenting on the brilliance of certain designers two to three years Persephone's junior . . . dropping story after story about her little niece's acceptance to business school . . . ("She's only twenty-three and she really knows what she *wants*. As every woman *should*, Persephone!")

So if Adam was going to fail at law, then he had damn well better pick up something else, she told him, in soft, wifely terms. Because she was ready to retire. This was when, over a plate of gnocchi Doni Oppenheimer would have thrown against the wall for its gummy texture, Adam had brought up the Foreign Service exam.

"You mean, work for the government?" Persephone had responded.

"As a . . . bureaucrat?" The words fell out of her mouth like stale raisins.

Living in Washington, she'd sometimes fantasized about Adam's potential career in politics. He wasn't especially political, though, and when he did show an interest, he tended to lean distressingly to the right. (Persephone had grown up in a benevolently Republican house, only to drift over to the other side at UVA.) Being elected to serve was noble and even glamorous. But being employed *by* the government, that just made Persephone think of ill-fitting Docker pants and very bad shoes.

"No, no. I'd be a *diplomat*," Adam said, even as he studied another woman at the bar, one of his less appealing habits. Very good-looking people like Adam, Persephone had observed, got away with things like that. It had shown an uncharacteristic lapse of foresight, her marrying such a handsome man. Junior year he had dropped a note on her book while she was studying, asking her to his Psi Phi formal, and her study partner, Betsy, had literally screamed with shock and envy. She knew it was one of her faults, but Persephone thrived on other people's envy.

"A diplomat," Persephone said, pouring herself more wine to wash away her pointless negative thinking. "Tell me more about that."

So he did. He would take the Foreign Service exam. It would require some studying, but nothing like the bar, so he was sure he could hack it. There were some current events questions. Some public speaking tests. A personal statement that, of course, she would prep him for.

"And so, if you do end up getting the job?"

"Then we go. Somewhere. All our expenses paid. They come pick up our things—a whole houseful!—and take it to, you know, wherever we're going. And they give you a house over there *and* travel expenses. My fraternity brother Treef . . . remember Treef? Yeah, he wasn't the most . . . anyway, Treef lives in Harare now, which is sort of dodgy, but he has this huge mansion with a pool and his wife hangs out at the country club all day and all he does is manage the office."

Persephone wrinkled her nose. "Well, you wouldn't be doing *that.*"

"No. I'd be higher up. A lawyer. Embassy counsel. And maybe, if I did well, which I'm sure I will—I mean, how hard can it *be?* Well . . ." He leaned in to whisper, "Ambassador. Which would make you . . ."

"*Mrs.* Ambassador." She'd sat back, pleased already with this happy inevitability.

That was the thing about Adam. He was so smooth, you thought you were going out for gnocchi, and the next thing you knew, you were signing up to leave your home country for the rest of your life. And he managed to make it feel like it was *your* dream.

The night before the exam she'd fed her husband a large helping of bland tuna pasta (Doni always had this meal before award shows and galas) and gave him some Benadryl for a good sleep. For confidence, a blow job in the morning, followed by eggs. And, with that, she sent him off. As expected, Adam had aced the public speaking portion. On the rest he did just fine. A few weeks later, he received a job offer: legal counsel in Kuwait, starting in four months.

At the time, Kuwait sounded fine to Persephone. She didn't know exactly where it was, but she was twenty-six, so that was forgivable. As promised, some very nice movers with a clipboard had come and emptied out their town house, while she and Adam attended some rather alarming trainings on world health and disaster preparedness and international security. Adam was even sent to some secret location, where he learned how to try to survive an explosion, drive in reverse at sixty miles an hour, and shoot a machine gun (a boot camp experience that made Persephone green with jealousy). Then a government car had come to take them to the airport. They showed their special diplomatic passports, which let them cut all the lines, then got onto the plane and flew away.

That was three posts ago. After Kuwait came Laos (wonderful food, shitty health care), Romania (grim, but pleasantly close to Paris, or at least Vienna), and now Namibia. Back in Kuwait, she'd invested in a world map backed by corkboard, placing little color-coded pins, red for places they'd actually lived, green for places they'd just visited. It was the first thing she hung in every kitchen, with the world by now satisfyingly covered in protruding dots.

There is much to be waded through when your spouse is in the service. And at the beginning, she wasn't always good at it. But because of an inner ear imbalance, Persephone fell a lot (once into a pool while wearing a sari given to her by a Trailer from Mumbai). She liked wine a bit too much (not the reason for the fall, she still swore to Adam) and was sometimes prone to laughing uncontrollably at inappropriate moments. Like funerals, for instance. Or commemorative ceremonies for World War I battles.

But, damn it, after twelve years and three children, she was better than most. Which was why last year she had decided she'd officially graduated. Persephone was no longer a Trailing Spouse. She didn't just follow Adam around, languishing in his shadow. No. Persephone Wilder was a person who uplifted the State Department by providing excellent support for her husband, her family, *and* her peers. She was something else entirely: an Embassy Wife.

Persephone knew perfectly well how antiquated this sounded. In fact, she had only once let out her true thoughts about her role. This was with her siblings, over cocktails on the porch at the farm a couple of years ago. They, too, were spending their trust funds in serving their country—her sister as an immigration lawyer; her brother, a high school teacher. So she'd assumed they'd understand. But instead, they had both just stared at her, openmouthed, before suddenly roaring with laughter into their Goslings Dark 'n' Stormies (her family's signature drink).

"Embassy . . . *Wife?*" her sister had gasped out between squawks. "You don't think that's a little sick? I mean, you were a Jefferson Scholar, Perse! You could have done anything."

The point, really, was that during a time when her president—whom she, as a State Department representative, could not directly disparage—was doing his best to paint Americans as a country of rude, orange Oompa Loompas who shoved others out of the way for photo ops and paid off porn stars, Persephone was working as hard as she could to be a vision of grace, empathy, and kindness. She was *listening* to people. Paying attention to what they needed. And she was talking to them, whether they wanted to or not.

Today's Embassy Wife task: a quick coffee with her new (best?) friend Amanda in order to hear about the orphanage fail. No surprise there. The minute Amanda had told her about her appointment, Persephone knew quite well that Our Hope Children's Hostel most certainly did not want Amanda to "help manage," or make them "more efficient," or help them save money, or anything of the sort. Neither did the Katutura Women's Collective, the Namibian Christian Orphanage, or any of the essential organizations that aided the less fortunate citizens of this country. The administrations of these organizations had been contacted by every well-meaning American coming to Namibia for an extended period of time—every Trailing Spouse, every junior-year-abroad student, every tourist looking to "make a difference." Arriving with fantasies of wearing flattering safari clothing (already an impossibility), they would go around looking to help "manage" or "teach" or "counsel wayward children." Whatever. It was a nonstarter. Shoshana had tried to save sick baboons, only to be marooned in a pen at N/aàn ku sê, forgotten by the paying college-age volunteer, and then mauled by a baby cheetah; Margo had hung out at the women's clinic offering free ultrasounds until she was asked to leave when she wondered aloud why all the donated baby formula was being loaded into the back of the head nurse's bakkie.

Ah! Here Amanda was now, already sitting at a courtyard table. Persephone hurried into the courtyard of Stellenbosch, a veritable fantasyland in the middle of the desert. Built by a homesick South African marooned in Windhoek due to marriage, the restaurant replicated one of the lovely villas built a thousand miles south in the actual town of Stellenbosch, a green jewel of Cape Town's wine country. Here in Stellenbosch Namibia, green vines grew, birds chirped, and a fountain trickled with a seemingly endless supply of water, impervious to the barren scrub and dust blowing by outside.

"Amanda! My, you look lovely." And she did: black linen skirt, a crisp white shirt. Was that Prada? Lord.

"Oh, this is the dressiest I've got. I have to go to the school to meet with the headmaster, and I want to look, you know, as intimidating as I can. They say Meg hit another student." She shook her head. "But I *know* her. I just can't believe she would do something like that."

"I'm sure it was nothing," Persephone said. Though, having witnessed a decade of the antics of diplomatic children, she was pretty sure little Meg was capable of far more mischief than her mother imagined she was. "Why don't you eat something?"

"I already ordered a milk tart."

Pie before noon! Now Persephone really liked her.

"Well, Headmaster Pierre is a lovely man, anyway. Very Canadian and understanding. Likes scotch. African enough to accept a bribe, in case it's necessary."

"Well, it's not just him. I'm also meeting the mother of the girl she hit. It was your friend—Mila Shilongo."

"No!" Persephone flagged the waiter down for coffee. "Amazing. She probably deserved it."

"Persephone."

"Fine, fine. I'll stay out of it. It's just . . . well. You already know Mila and I have some friction."

"I do."

"It'll be fine, my dear. Don't worry. So what happened at the or-phanage, darling?"

Amanda told her. The fee, the blow-off. No surprise there.

"Don't worry about it. There will be lots of opportunities to help. I told you about the International Women's Association of Namibia, didn't I? We do a fashion show that raises money for schools, and then there's this Nearly New sale. Also once a year we go to the Katutura Nursing Home and take a bunch of elderly ladies to lunch out at a game ranch. We need to be clearer, actually. Last year they had no idea what was going on, and some thought they were being kidnapped. One lady was so frightened she had to go to the hospital once we got back. But it's all very well intentioned."

The milk tart came, a lush, creamy disk of deliciousness. Still, Amanda looked glum. "Those are all good ideas," she said. "Pretty much. I just want to do something, you know?" She attacked the tart. "I feel like I have something to offer. But maybe I don't."

"You *do*," Persephone reassured her.

"And now I have to go to this damned school appointment."

"Shall I come with you?" Persephone asked. "To the school?"

"Thanks," Amanda said, standing. "But I've got this."

"All right." Just then, through the white stone archway, something caught Persephone's eye. Amanda's handsome but rumpled husband, clutching his laptop and an armful of files. "Amanda, is that Mark?"

"Oh," Amanda said. "So it is." Only it seemed to Persephone that Amanda was hiding from her husband, as she had gotten up from the table and was ducking behind an Italianate pillar.

"Shouldn't you say hello?"

"You know, I actually have to leave now to get to the meeting," Amanda said nervously. When Persephone gave her a quizzical frown, Amanda relented. "Well, we're friends, right Persephone? So I'll just tell you . . . I really don't want him to come to the school with me."

"You don't?" Persephone tried not to look too curious.

"It's a long story. Let's just say he's a bit controlling where Meg is concerned? And that might not be that helpful at the meeting . . . and also, he doesn't even *know* about the meeting. So I'm just going to slip out before he sees me."

"Well. That was a quick coffee date," Persephone said, feeling a tad put out. "But ten-four, doll. Good luck."

"Thank you."

Persephone watched Amanda ridiculously over-tip the car guard—rookie!—and waited until she drove away before she herself innocently approached Mark Evans, who had made himself comfy at a café table on the other side of the fountain.

"Why, hello!" Persephone said. Mark Evans jumped, covering his papers. Despite his quickness, Persephone caught what they were: old obituaries from *The Namibian.* Intriguing.

"It's Persephone, from the State Department?" she said. Mark blanched and nodded rigorously. "How are you settling in, Mark?"

"Good, good."

"Mind if I sit?"

"Sure." He shoved his papers away and gave her an easy, professory grin.

Too late, she thought. I've seen them.

"You know, I'm the official community liaison. So if you have any questions . . ."

"Oh. Great, great."

"I'm just adoring your wife, getting to know her and all," Persephone said. "Is that all for the book you're working on? I'm very interested in the Nama genocide issue, actually."

"That?" He scratched the back of his head furiously. "Ah, well, it's part of it. Hard to talk about until I'm finished."

"Oh, I'm sure."

"You know, I just remembered, I have an appointment at the archive." He jumped up, shaking the delicate café table. "Would you excuse me, Persephone?"

"Of course!" She beamed up at him. "Press on. I'm *for* financial retributions, by the way. For the Herero, specifically. They'd have to give about a fifth to the Nama, too. What *was* the Nama-to-Herero ratio again?"

"I'd, um, have to look at my notes."

"It'll be tough to parse out. And *most* horrendous, of course, was the concentration camp in Walvis. A national travesty."

"Yes. Um, I'll see you," Mark mumbled, practically running out the door. Persephone sat alone in the courtyard, listening to the water in the fountain burble.

Well, Persephone thought.

It was clear to her now Mark Evans was most definitely *not* here to study the Nama holocaust. Persephone Wilder always did her history homework before moving to any country. And she happened to know that, while the incident most certainly was a national travesty, the horrors of 1905 did not occur in Walvis Bay, but in Lüderitz. Had the professor been seriously interested in the subject, he would have been unable to resist mansplaining her mistake. No, her new friend's husband was covering for something. Because not only did Mark Evans not know anything about the supposed topic of his research, he didn't seem particularly interested in Namibian history at all.

This was nothing Persephone would tell anyone. Not yet, anyway. For this was what Embassy Wives did—gather information. Their findings, of course, would not be parsed out until there was a very good reason. But the reason, in Persephone's experience, always came in the end.

So, Professor Evans, Persephone thought. What, exactly, are you hiding?

6

Forty-one years before Amanda moved to Namibia on her husband's whim, her mother dressed her in a pink flannel dress. She changed Amanda's diaper—though she was surely not called Amanda then, but instead another name no one would ever know—and wrapped her in a receiving blanket. Then she drove her to the fire station in Charleston, South Carolina, and left the infant on the front step.

The Meeting Street fire station was an official safe haven for foundlings, so no inquiry was made as to where the baby might have come from. The deputy chief made the discovery. He hadn't come out because of her cries; even as a newborn, her new mother, Merritt, said, Amanda acted as if she was in the world to cause as little trouble as possible. What the deputy chief noticed, as he sat up drinking Sanka and watching *M*A*S*H*, was the screech of tires around the block. Thinking it was a group of drunk teenagers he had to report, he went outside to see if they would come back around again. The car was gone, but at his feet, in a milk crate, was a tiny face looking up at him, its expression mirroring his own in wonder and surprise.

Abandoned babies in milk crates weren't common in downtown Charleston; word traveled fast. And that next Sunday, the fate of Baby X, as *The Post and Courier* called her, was the mainstay of a sermon at St. Michael's Church. Merritt Pruitt, who usually stayed to make certain the coffee urns were full, was so moved she went straight home to speak about it with her husband, Albert.

Merritt and Albert were old Charlestonians with plenty of

money, but no designs on grandeur. They came from a long line of merchants, having owned Pruitt's Furniture on King for three generations. Theirs was a somber, dark mansion at the end of Society Street, rife with antiques and inherited silver, short on lamps and natural light.

There was no question that the adoption of baby Amanda, as she came to be known throughout town that week, was the most surprising and generous thing they had ever done. Indeed, soon the event became the main source of the family's local identity.

So, though Amanda never really knew who she was, she also never really wondered. She was Amanda Pruitt, the little miracle who had saved her mother and father. Her adoption was never a secret. The Pruitts' theory was that letting Amanda know the truth was much kinder than a jolting, TV-drama revelation later in life. She was far from spoiled, but she enjoyed the same privileges as the other downtown Charleston girls: private education at the Day School, cotillion lessons, riding lessons, ballet.

Merritt, who was forty-eight when she brought Amanda home, unleashed the physical affection she'd been saving up for the baby she never had. She slept with Amanda until the child was two, and even after insisted on adjoining rooms. She hugged and cuddled her daughter so much it drove Albert to worry, with the fuss over strained baby food, and then later the obsession with healthy school lunches and purified water. Bridge and travel were things of the past; obviously, her friends said, the woman had just been passing her time, waiting for motherhood to happen. And it was a good thing she had never been silly enough to get a job, as now she channeled any potential professional energy into ensuring Amanda's well-being.

Albert fathered mostly from afar, giving the fatherly lectures on cleanliness and manners his own father had given to him in the same house. Once a week he gave Amanda five dollars, instructing her to bike over to First Federal on Broad and put it into her savings account. They had started the practice when Amanda was seven, and Albert reasoned—correctly—that if she did the same until she left for college, she would have a respectable nest egg. On Sundays, he took her through the newspaper, explaining current events, both national and international, no matter how alarming and ghastly. *The Post and Courier* was too sanitized, so he made special arrangements with Burbage's to carry *The New York Times*. He inspected Amanda's room, Navy-style, at seven on Saturday mornings. Other than that, he left things to Merritt.

When Amanda was twelve, Merritt went to the grocery store for mayonnaise (the main ingredient of Amanda's favorite chicken salad). Merritt was a healthy woman who walked the Battery every day and loved swimming, so who could blame her for never having a doctor scan her brain? She collapsed at the Harris Teeter, dying instantly of an aneurysm, her fashionably tanned arm stretched out among the broken shards of a Duke's jar.

Amanda had been at swimming class. It was one of those warm Charleston days in which the very air, heavy with jasmine and the pungent tinge of the marsh, swelled with unnamed possibility; perhaps a kiss from the boy who looked at her sometimes in math class, or a sleepover invitation from a new best friend. Returning home, she wore her wet bathing suit under her school clothes, her hair still damp and smelling of bleach. She parked her bike in the basement and climbed the back stairs to find her father sitting in the dark in his study.

"Merritt is dead," he said. His daughter didn't say anything, so he cleared his throat and began again. "Your mother. She died in the grocery store." Albert got up and hesitantly put a hand on her shoulder, then took it away. "I expect you'll need a bit of a serious cry. And that's okay, so you do that. I'm going to lie down myself for an hour with this glass of bourbon. Then we'll go to the mortuary to arrange things and say our private goodbye."

Amanda waited until she heard his feet on the stairs, then collapsed onto the floor, wailing. She must have screamed and cried for the entire hour, because the next thing she knew her father tapped her shoulder to tell her to wash her face, because it was time to go.

Was Amanda Pruitt fated to take care of men? By thirteen, she was running the house on Society Street, doing all the cooking and household management. Merritt's intention had been for Amanda to be a downtown Charleston girl like her older nieces—traveling in pastel herds on ribboned Schwinns, soaking in good manners by gossiping in ladies' kitchens, and spending idle afternoons in each other's bedrooms studying while sucking on candy from Lakeside-Schwettmann's. It seemed to Albert that Amanda was cut from a different cloth.

Amanda was serious. She had to be—there was no alternative. She fitted her bicycle with baskets so she could pick up various sundries without a car. She learned to plan meals for the week and order groceries from Burbage's, which delivered for a small fee. Albert didn't mind the cooking repertoire of a preteen, as long as there was food on the table when he got home. Amanda's initial menu offered hot dogs, cheese sandwiches, and peanut butter, though she eventually graduated to Hamburger Helper, chicken cooked in Campbell's mushroom soup, egg noodles with butter, and pasta with mayonnaise and tuna. Meals were usually enjoyed in front of the television. During commercials, Albert would press the mute button and ask her, gingerly, if everything was fine. Sometimes they would play bridge after dinner, a game Amanda, like Merritt, was freakishly good at.

Something happened to Amanda the day her mother died that she was too young to explain properly. Later she would guess that it was one of her aortas turning to ash, causing her to feel less than other women. And the way it happened, the suddenness and the indignity of it, both made her seethe with anger. But the truth was, Amanda liked her life. She liked the responsibility, and the freedom it provided. She managed the household accounts, so if she wanted, say, a shirt from the Gap, she didn't have to beg anyone for it. At sixteen, she took over her dead mother's car. As long as the bills were paid and the house was run well, curfews were not an issue.

"If you need to know about sex . . ." Albert started saying, during a break between *Miami Vice* and *Law & Order.*

"Uh-huh?"

"There are books I can purchase. Would you like a book?"

"Sure." She had already been penetrated by Alec Freeman at a beach party, but there certainly seemed to be more to know than the rough, sandy pumping he had introduced her to. The next day, *The Joy of Sex* and *Our Bodies, Ourselves* appeared on her bed, wrapped in brown paper.

As is often the case with children allowed to make their own choices, Amanda Pruit ended up not only managing, but acing school and her social life. Amanda knew, because Albert had told her, that she was only of average intelligence. Yet it seemed that she was born to work. And in some situations, her teachers gave her a little extra leniency. After all—as more than one instructor murmured in the teachers' lounge, the words winding their way through the blue smoke—the girl had been left on the street as a *baby*, for God's sake. And then her adopted mother had to go and die beside a jar of *mayonnaise.*

Though, if Amanda knew she was gaining advantage because people felt sorry for her, she didn't mind it. Wins were wins. She had friends, but she wasn't reliant on a clique to coddle her. Senior year she had a boyfriend, Jack, whom she liked enough, and he served his purpose, which was for her to learn properly about sex before college. And when time for college came, there wasn't much to think about there, either. Albert had gone to Dartmouth.

Amanda had garnered no expectations about college. It was Albert's opinion that his good experience there was information enough for his daughter, so he did not see the point of spending the money on a college visit. Amanda arrived having never seen it. To her surprise, she loved the place on contact. The thrill of knowing that, for the next four years, it would be hers. She liked to walk around during the empty hours, categorizing her favorite pieces of it. The cold brick pressed against her knuckles. The dusty scars in the grass where the boys cut across the green to the dorm. The far-off echoes of shouted commands from the playing fields. The sight of soiled formal gowns in the morning. The way her ears burned in the New Hampshire wind.

The work was harder than at her school in Charleston, but Amanda managed. Many students had trouble, she noticed, because of drinking. Alcohol held no novelty for Amanda; she'd been enjoying beer and wine with Albert since she was thirteen. As she had at home, she went to parties when she felt like it. She also slept with boys when she felt like it, then politely avoided them when they saw her on campus. Amanda was open to a college boyfriend, but she was the type of person who called things what they were, and the sex she was having seemed healthy but underwhelming. She was disappointed in these drunk fraternity brothers, with their grim dorm-bed techniques and fleeting attention spans.

It quickly became apparent that she would need to get involved in a sport. Dartmouth was a sports school; Amanda had run track in Charleston, just to kill time, but here, not playing a sport was, if not a crime, an obvious missed opportunity. A boy who lived on her hall—another one-night, disappointing tryst, but at least he had a sense of humor—told her his crew boat was looking for a coxswain. He also knew, from his night with her, that Amanda was small, strong, and decisive, all crucial qualities for a woman in charge of directing eight rowers in a boat. He took her down to the boathouse and introduced her to Mark, the coach.

Decades later, Amanda would muse that there were two or three moments in her life, tiny and crystalline as the tanzanite Mark would buy her in a jewelry shop, that caused her entire fate to pivot. One was her abandonment as an infant. The other was the death of her adopted mother. When Amanda Pruitt saw Mark Evans standing in front of the Dartmouth Boathouse by the Connecticut River, she knew right away that fate was turning monumentally once again.

Mark Evans stood tall and alone on that wooden tongue of a floating dock, arms folded, his open flannel shirt fluttering behind. Crew boats streamed past, and the fall sun reflected silver off the usually mottled green river. Every once in a while he would raise an old megaphone to his red lips and call out directions; the words scudded out tinny and muddied over the water.

"Pull. No . . . PULL," he called. "And lean on the hammer!"

How intoxicating it was, to see this beautiful boy-man controlling all those willing hands. He had an inherent possession of easy, Kennedy-like confidence. This sort of handsomeness was not rare at Dartmouth, but something else drew her, something deeper she could intuit from years of filling gaps and solving problems in her father's house. Mark Evans would need her. Not yet, but soon.

Amanda was born pragmatic. Waiting did not mean uselessness. It did not mean mooning over her coach or remaining idle until he gave a sign. That would be pathetic, and a waste of time. So she watched with detached interest while he wasted himself on blond Susannahs, Mary Beths, Whitneys. It didn't bother her, and she made use of the time herself with a Bobby, a Shaheed, and a Graham—nice boys with crew bodies and bright futures. These boys liked Amanda, and their mothers loved her. Then, three years later, there Mark was, standing in front of a sandwich cooler in the town across the river, tears running down his face, fogging up a pair of glasses she had never seen before. Amanda loved those glasses instantly; they chipped away at the intimidating nature of his perfect looks. It was those glasses, in fact, that gave her the courage to offer dinner.

"Sure," he'd said. "Let's go." When he looked at her, she felt a stirring. The cinders in her chest were crackling into something dangerous. Life is starting, she'd thought as Mark Evans wrapped his big hand around hers. It's time.

And life had started, hadn't it? Amanda thought now as she navigated toward the school. Life with Mark, at least for the first decade, had been exactly what she'd always wanted. There was travel, and sex,

and shacking up in a Bernal Heights apartment. There was a wedding
Albert was uncharacteristically generous over. It was hard to remember now all of the right things, because they had come so easily. Good-
looking, athletic friends, progressive dinner parties, trips to Lake
Tahoe. A move to the South Bay, the birth of Meg, Amanda's new job,
Mark's teaching. More money had followed, just the way it was supposed to, right? She didn't want to be flippant about it, but it was all
part of the expected trajectory. As was success. As was happiness. The
aging process was inevitable, but it would be softened by just enough
Botox and the right schedule of relentless workouts. What wouldn't
change was her love for Mark. She had waited for him. She was his
person.

And yet. Something had been happening to her. It wasn't just that
she was pissed off because he'd made her give up her job and move to
a sun-beaten African desert. Sometime in the last two or three years,
she had begun fantasizing about his death. Not a murder, of course. Nor
anything as painful and slow as cancer. A quick biking accident, perhaps, where he felt nothing. A freak sailing snafu.

She didn't know when it had started, exactly. Was it when he
completely stopped giving a shit about his job? Or when it suddenly
occurred to her that perhaps he'd never truly cared about history at
all? No books around the house, no trips to France to track down the
World War II families he was supposedly writing about . . . And then
there was one evening when he'd missed dinner, and she hadn't cared.
Then it happened again, and she found she was actually relieved. No,
glad.

In fact, if they missed each other because he was out for a row or
she had a late meeting, she found that she was grateful. His stories
about the history department were narcissistic and mind-numbing, she
started noticing. And everything he said to Meg was pretty much just
wrong. No longer endearing to her was the way he was always late, or
how he forgot his wallet when he was taking her to dinner, or his fits
about finding his keys, only to discover sheepishly that they were in his

pocket. In fact, these incidents were causing a curious reaction on her skin. Hives. She was becoming allergic to her husband.

She knew she would never go as far as leaving. Amanda Evans, who had come very close to having no family, knew full well how invaluable it was to have managed to build one. But a painless, convenient death, leaving her and Meg free to live a cozy life of reading in bed and girl trips to Mexico and Europe? Not to mention freedom from Mark's family and whatever was supposed to happen once he actually got his PhD and was able to find a job only in somewhere like Bumblefuck, Idaho? It intruded on her thoughts often enough to erode the very shame of it.

Amanda, nothing if not a problem-solver, knew there was surely a way to get back to the old place again. There was a time when she'd lie in her room at Dartmouth, pressing her legs together as she thought about peeling Mark Evans down to the skin. It wasn't a different person who did that. It was just a version of herself who needed some layers chipped away.

So this wasn't a burning problem, she'd told herself. She could get back to where she'd been. She could. It was part of the reason she'd said yes to Namibia in the first place. Only now everything was going wrong here, too, and here she was, sitting in the reception area of the International School, having pointedly left her husband behind because his competitive nature would inevitably fuck everything up.

Amanda shifted nervously on the reception-area couch, which was not as cheap as one would have expected. She looked at her watch—10:29. Albert had taught her that successful people were always early. Not on time, not late, but early, and well prepared. "This gives you the advantage of intolerance," he'd told her once. Albert's tips were the most useful of her life, more relevant than pretty much anything she'd learned in her online business school classes. Be early, and always call people back.

At 10:30 on the dot, Headmaster Pierre popped his head out. That was another surprising aspect of Namibia: Unlike the adages she'd heard about "Africa time," appointments in Windhoek were highly punctual. Perhaps it was a residual from the German colonial era, she thought. That, good beer, and weird-looking sausages.

"Hello, there, Mrs. Evans," he said. "Looks like Mrs. Shilongo isn't here yet. Ha ha . . . we—*ahem*—can't exactly start without her . . . so . . . do you mind waiting?"

His face was flushed and round and lovable, like a Disney hound dog. She could hear her father telling her to feign intolerance, but scolding this man would have been like beating a kitten.

"I suppose we'll have to wait," Amanda said, trying to sound stern. "If we're going to get to the bottom of this."

The headmaster nodded and backed into his office. From the reception desk, Petra shot Amanda a reproachful look. Amanda was confused for a moment, before remembering one of Persephone's nuggets of "non-gossip."

("I'm not saying I know anything," her new friend had said. "But the headmaster and Petra are most definitely having an affair.")

Suddenly Amanda heard a blast of sirens. Not one, but at least three of them. She shot up from the sofa and went to the door. As the wailing got louder and louder, Amanda gripped the counter and turned to Petra, who wasn't even looking up from her desktop.

"What's happening?" she gasped. "Is there an emergency?" The receptionist didn't answer, but simply shook her head, bored. Amanda watched, transfixed, as two screeching police cars, followed by a black Land Rover, tore into the parking lot, synchronized as fighter jets. When they screeched to a halt, still in formation, she could see children's faces popping into the classroom windows.

Headmaster Pierre appeared beside Amanda's shoulder. "That'll be Mrs. Shilongo," he said brightly.

The driver of a Land Rover jumped out—a Secret Service type with a not-so-secret pistol in his belt—then circled the vehicle and opened the passenger door. Amanda herself had dressed up for the occasion, wearing her very best Silicon Valley Prada armor. But when Mila Shilongo stepped out of her vehicle, the woman looked as though she were headed to St. George's Chapel at Windsor as Meghan Markle's personal wedding guest. Mrs. Shilongo had graduated from the short shift modeled the other day to an ankle-length dress of the most beautiful African material Amanda had ever seen—a kaleidoscope of blues and violets, shot through with what looked like real silver thread. Like the other dress Amanda had seen her wearing, this had clearly been tailored just for Mila, and—who knew?—had perhaps been sewn on her body that very morning. Though it didn't matter what this woman wore. In dirty jeans and a flannel shirt, she'd still be the most astonishingly lovely thing Amanda would see that day. Or year, for that matter.

Amanda wasn't intimidated by beauty, as Persephone seemed to be. Instead, she was interested by it. Prettiness was an advantage Amanda would never have. She'd done well without it; indeed, at places like Dartmouth and Silicon Valley, it might have even gotten in her way. She'd always appreciated being average, if not forgettable. So it was fascinating to her how people seemed to physically melt as this woman came closer. The security guards seemed impervious behind their dark glasses, but she could feel the headmaster beginning to quiver, could sense the receptionist's irate aura grow even heavier. As for Amanda, she continued to appreciate the works of natural art that were Mila's perfectly symmetrical cheekbones, shoulders, and eyes.

Mila didn't bother to close the car door, as there were four men waiting to do it for her. As she strode up the cracked cement path, they stood aside, holding their weapons loosely. Six feet from the entrance, Mila paused and put her hand out. One of the guards stepped forward and she leaned down, her obsidian curls spilling over as she adjusted a delicate strap on her golden shoe.

Jesus, Amanda thought. Or actually, once again, she must have thought it out loud, because Headmaster Pierre murmured in agreement.

Both of them backed up as Mrs. Shilongo entered a few moments later, pressing neatly against the wall to allow her progress. She smelled of jasmine and sugar and everything in the world that was delicious.

"Ladies!" the headmaster said, recovering. "Welcome! Please . . . step into my office."

Amanda could feel Petra's withering gaze. Trying to gain some ground, she stepped forward and entered first, claiming the armchair closest to the headmaster's desk—zebra hide. Mrs. Shilongo entered behind her, standing in the middle of the room. She didn't sit immediately, choosing instead to tower over Amanda until the headmaster had himself settled.

"I am Mila Shilongo," she announced, offering her hand. The diamonds were massive. From Amanda's awkward angle, the gesture might have suggested that Amanda should kiss her fingers, royalty-style. Instead she jumped up and gave her best American handshake.

"We've met, actually. I'm Amanda. How are you?" Mila didn't answer, but pressed her fingers in a series of complicated ways—the Oshiwambo hand greeting. Only then did she adjust her skirt to lower herself into the free chair.

"Well," Headmaster Pierre said. "Ladies! Obviously, this is not the most positive of pretexts for a meeting. But I am quite happy—*quite* happy—that you have both agreed to be here. To discuss . . . the incident."

"Yes," Amanda said, sitting up as straight as she could. "I just wanted to clear up——"

"Mrs. Evans," Mila Shilongo interrupted. "I am here to say that I am very sorry."

Headmaster Pierre and Amanda looked at each other in surprise.

"Amanda. May I call you that? Good. Yes. Amanda. Our children were playing. And you cannot help sometimes that your girl is overcome by sin. It happens to all children."

"Sin?"

"Well," the headmaster said. "Let's——"

"I am not saying only your daughter. Taimi is possessed by him, too. It's sin. Satan in the play yard. He took our girls, and he played his tricks. The only way to defeat him is to catch him out."

Amanda tried to focus on the Big Five diorama on Pierre's desk.

"You know, Headmaster," Mila continued, "it is silly to have a meeting without the girls here. We were not there, so how can we know what it was the devil made them do? I think they should come. Yes. Good, then. Bring them here." Mila rose and pulled the door open. "You there! We need Taimi Shilongo! Go and get her. And bring the Evans girl, too!"

Amanda sank down, listening to the slow, angry creak of Petra's chair.

"Excuse me?" the receptionist said incredulously. Petra was old-school Afrikaans, the type who grew up during apartheid and was perfectly happy going to the beach with only people of her skin color, thank you very much. Amanda guessed she had never received an order by a Black African in her life.

"Taimi Shilongo and . . ." And with that, Mila turned and looked at Amanda, eyebrows raised.

"Meg?" Amanda offered in a small voice.

"Meg. *Evans*. Grade three. Now, not now-now. Thank you." Mila spun around again and sank back into her throne, failing to notice as Headmaster Pierre sprinted out into the hallway to try to repair the damage. The door slammed behind him, and the two women sat quietly for several awkward moments. Then Mila turned her body toward Amanda, unleashing a mind-blowing smile.

"You are from the United States?"

"Yes." Amanda nodded vigorously. "California."

"Very nice," Mila confirmed. "We have been, of course. Two times. You live near Disneyland."

"Well, that's Southern California. We're——"

"Do you like Namibia?"

Amanda paused to consider the question in light of the day she was having so far. "Not very much," she said.

Mila stared at her, and Amanda braced herself, waiting for the oncoming wrath. But then Taimi's mother threw back her head and laughed. The sound was full-throated and generous. It felt like warm afternoon sunlight.

"Yes. What's to like? There are no trees. It is much too hot, then much too cold. There is nothing to do. There is no water."

"Well. I like the animals."

"Is it?" Mila said, raising her eyebrows. "Then you must come to our farm. It's up north. We keep all of them there. Giraffes, lions. It is very famous. You'll come."

I will? Amanda wondered.

"Ah. But I hear the girls coming. Let's not make too much of this, now. Let's just clear this up and move on, yeah?"

"Easier said than done," grumbled Headmaster Pierre as he returned, his face still flushed from running to fetch the students. Taimi bounced in now, followed by Meg, who shuffled behind her, looking down at the floor. Amanda felt her heart twist in her chest as she took in Meg's wilted hat, her downturned mouth, her sunburned arms.

Fuck Mark, she thought, her breath growing short with fury. Fuck him for bringing us to this miserable place.

Out of the corner of her eye, she saw Petra stalk to the door and slam it shut on them all. There was nowhere for the girls to sit, so instead they stood in front of the headmaster, vulnerable as subjects on trial.

"Well, girls," Headmaster Pierre began, "I just wanted to get a sense of what might have happened yesterday."

"I said something that made her very angry," Taimi said.

"I thought you were playing Ministers," Mila said. "What would make her angry about that?"

"We were," Taimi said. "But then I asked about other families."

"Other . . . families?" Amanda repeated.

"Men with mistresses."

The headmaster chortled, while Mila let out what could only be described as a yawp. "Taimi! *Mistresses!* Where did you get such an idea?"

Taimi opened her mouth to answer.

"No," Mila said quickly. "Do not speak. I do not want to hear it. God gives us one wife. One husband."

Amanda looked at Meg, who glowered back at her under the lip of her hat.

"Meg, honey? Why did you hit Taimi?"

Meg's lip started to quiver.

"I don't want to tell."

"You have to," Amanda said, trying, for once, to sound stern.

"Well, technically you don't *have to*," Headmaster Pierre said, folding his hands over his stomach. "Let's stick to the rule books here! I don't want any"—he glanced at Mila—"talk later about this not being completely official. Though, dear, you might as well tell your mother what happened. I don't see what it could possibly hurt."

Meg looked at the headmaster, then back at her mother. "Okay."

"Well?" he asked, looking not a little fearful at what he might hear.

"Um . . . Taimi . . . was talking about how parents have secrets."

"Secrets," Amanda repeated.

"Well, you and Daddy have secrets. And I don't know what a mattress is exactly——"

"*Mistress*," Taimi corrected, smiling at Headmaster Pierre.

"——but maybe you and Daddy have one. I thought. Maybe. And that's why you're always fighting. And it made me mad."

Amanda bit the inside of her cheek. It was something she used to do at particularly caustic GiaTech meetings to keep from crying.

"Meg," she said, channeling all her energy into keeping her voice level and positive. "We're not *always* fighting."

There was a heavy silence, as her daughter's lack of reply challenged the validity of that statement.

"Well. There's no mistress, anyway."

"That's settled!" Headmaster Pierre crowed, dabbing his forehead with a handkerchief. "Now—"

"Then why do you whisper?" Meg pressed.

"Daddy's just distracted. He worries about work. His book and everything. That's all."

"That's why you fight?"

"We don't fight. We talk."

"Really?"

Amanda swallowed.

"Yes."

"Really really?"

Amanda nodded. *You fucking liar.*

"Well." Headmaster Pierre clapped his hands together and stood. "That's sorted. Nice work, girls! No more slapping each other around, eh? All friends here."

Meg pushed her hat up until the brim stuck up vertically from her head, like a navy-blue halo. She took a step toward her mother and put her hands on her hips.

"Taimi," Mila commanded. "Embrace your friend."

Taimi jumped forward and folded Meg into her arms. "Come on!" she said, hooking her arm around Meg. The girls opened the door and trotted out, not bothering to look back. The headmaster followed. Mila regarded the activity in the hallway, then rose to close the office door.

"Instant besties," Amanda said, trying to lighten the mood. She could almost hear the effort splatter onto the floor.

"Amanda Evans," Mila said sternly. "What is happening in your family?"

Amanda thought of all the cheerful ways to brush off Mila Shilongo's curiosity. Then she got very, very tired.

"My husband is having a nervous breakdown, I think."

"He is breaking down?"

"In the States we call it a midlife crisis . . ."

"No, no. We call it the same," Mila said impatiently. "Well. Not Ovambos. Not Germans. Afrikaners, sometimes. Herero men, they break down often." She shook her head. "You must tell him to be stronger. Life is not long."

"No. Well. In the U.S. it is. Life expectancy, I mean. My father's almost eighty, and I'm thinking of finding him a home—"

"You must protect your daughter from this. The breaking down. Her father cannot break down in front of her."

"No, he doesn't. It's subtler than that, you know? But . . . anyway. We're fine."

"It does not seem fine."

"I overshared. I'm sorry. I never do that."

Mila didn't answer.

"Maybe marriage is more complicated where we come from. I'm probably overthinking it . . . Anyway, I never tell Mark any of this. Which is super-dishonest, I guess."

"Please," Mila said. "Remember where you are. There are many different levels of truth here in Namibia."

Amanda squinted—a bad habit she'd developed since turning forty. It happened every time she took a swallow of wine, and when she didn't understand something right away. "What does that mean?"

"Sometimes we tell people things that may not be completely true, because that version helps more people. Or we arrange things in a fashion—I'm talking about management, you see—that might not look completely legitimate but will benefit more people. We speak eleven different languages here. Did you know that? We have nine different tribes, all with their own cultures and ways of doing things. How could we not have different versions of what's true?"

"I don't know," Amanda said doubtfully. "I've kind of always thought whatever happens, happens."

"No. A crocodile eats your goat by the river. Someone else saw the same thing, and said it was a leopard. The third person said it was a poacher. The goat is still gone. Do you see?"

"Sure," Amanda said. "Well. Not really. No, I don't get it."

"You will be fine," Mila said, standing and, to Amanda's surprise, grabbing both of her wrists to pull her up. It was dizzying, being that close to her. "And we will be friends, Mrs. Evans."

"We will," Amanda said. And to her surprise, she meant it.

7

Everyone knew there was at least one spy posted in each U.S. Embassy around the world. A CIA ace, posing as a humble diplomat.

It was a common pastime of the Trailers to guess who it might be. In fact, just last week the Namibian contingent had played the *who-is-it–here?* game at Crafts and Cocktails. Kayla and Shoshana were convinced it was Trevor, a young operations assistant who always seemed to be MIA at functions. Persephone never said anything, because such conversations, obviously, were immensely unpatriotic. But she knew it was definitely *not* Trevor. First of all, he would have been awfully obvious. Plus he was phenomenally good at his actual position, a difficult task of scoping out and renting properties secure and enormous enough to house the American diplomats. No, it was becoming increasingly clear that the CIA plant in question in the Namibian Embassy was her very own husband—Adam.

The first hint was privacy screens on all his devices. Then there were the hushed conversations in the olive grove, and the constant trips made upon the flimsiest of excuses. The nail in the coffin was that, ever since hitting sub-Saharan Africa, Adam had become absolutely dreadful at his embassy job. Persephone had to admit he'd never exactly blown the top off his roles in Kuwait or eastern Europe, but in Namibia it had gotten especially bad. Which was exactly how she knew he *must* be spending his time doing something else.

For example:

"These Americans in jail for supposedly trafficking marijuana," she said on the morning of Amanda's meet-'n-'greet breakfast as she and Adam sat together, perusing *The Namibian* over their morning coffee. "They've been waiting for a trial for quite a while now. Isn't that your area?"

"Sort of."

"Sort of? If you're not advising these men, who is?"

"You know the ambo has me ass-over-elbow, babe. Which is why I'm headed out today."

"But, darling. Have you been to see them in jail lately? They must be so uncomfortable."

"Giving them cookies is consular work. Anyway, why are you being such a little bitch? Stressed over your breakfast party?"

Persephone arched her back in annoyance. She abhorred the *b*-word, unless one was speaking of whelping full-bred puppies. Though perhaps she was grumpy, as she had risen at 5:00 a.m. to prepare for the party, and by 7:00 she'd already hit some roadblocks. First: Shoshana's text reminder that she didn't eat gluten. Persephone had already been down to the bakery at the Puma station, elbowing old German ladies out of the way for the famous baguettes and chocolate croissants; now she had to send Sally, the second-newest Trailing Spouse and therefore the most gullible, on an emergency trip to Woolworth's. Minutes later, Kayla called, saying she would be late, if she made it at all. Then Margo called on the landline. *Were kids okay? She figured no, but little Noah was doing his "elimination training" and had to be monitored at all times with the potty bowl, so* . . . Yes, Margo. Of course! Ugh. Then there was a sewage backup in the mini-olive grove—something that happened often enough, but did it *have* to take place on the day of her party? And now, on top of it all, Adam had coolly told her on his way out that he'd be away on government business for the next three days. Starting now.

"And I'll actually be away next week, too."

"Oh, darling. *Next* week? We've volunteered to host the embassy 'braai. I'm running the entire thing. You're supposed to man the grill." Adam paused, espresso cup in hand, and shot her his Mr. Politics smile. Persephone's husband was the sort of man one might brush off as blandly handsome, until the moment that smile of his transformed him totally. She had seen more doors than she cared to remember open just by a flash of those perfect teeth, those sexy wrinkles at the corners of his green eyes. Her husband's smile promised, wrongly, that he was worthy of your secrets.

"My sweet. I know the braai is crucial," he said. "Well, I don't, really. Not half as crucial as opening the new PEPFAR center in Rundu, anyway. The Namibian president is coming to cut the ribbon with the ambo, and what the fuck does she know about Rundu? And if that thing isn't done, it's my ass on the line. So I'm just going to have to fucking set up camp up there, you know?"

Ugh. It seemed a bit early in the day for all this swearing.

"Again, I'm not certain what Rundu has to do with being legal counsel . . ."

"You know I can't answer every one of your questions, honey. It's the State Department."

"Well, I just don't know why you didn't tell me this before," she said.

"I don't know how to grill. Namibians don't even let you use gas. Or charcoal! They use wood. Dry branches they go out and gather from the veld. How am I supposed to do that?"

"Why don't you get your hot friend Mila to help you?"

"Oh, I *hate* you."

Adam came behind her, circling his arms around her waist. He bit her ear, then growled something completely unmentionable. Her face safely out of his line of sight, Persephone rolled her eyes. How Adam did adore dirty talk.

"You taking the kids to school today?" he whispered.

"They're going on the diplomatic shuttle," she said, still pouting.

"Frida!" Adam called down the hall. "Get the tykes on the bus, okay?"

"Yes, meneer."

And then Adam pulled Persephone into the laundry room and,

muttering at her as if she were a sex worker in Bangkok, very efficiently did the thing he'd promised, in just the amount of time he had before heading to the airport.

It was somewhat exciting, having a husband who was a spy, even if he couldn't exactly tell her that fact. It made the sex a bit more titillating, she supposed, though maybe not just now, because she did *not* enjoy that angle. Persephone didn't care what the other Trailing Spouses said about sex. No woman did. Honestly. Right now all that mattered was that she had to come up with something different to wear than this freshly pressed dress with the awkward stain it had just acquired. Shame.

Adam and Persephone had much more sex than she let on, especially to the other Trailers. Though from powder room conversations at State Department functions—not the fundraisers, but the parties where free wine was served—she knew Foreign Service marrieds tended to have much more sex than normal U.S. couples, anyway. For one thing, everyone was well rested. All the mothers had hired help, so there was no excuse of the kids tiring you out. The job offered constant vacations to exotic locales. You had to attend at least one evening function a week, where the only way to get through it was at least a tiny bit of alcohol. Some embassies had gone through a full course of in-house swinging; apparently there had been quite a to-do in the Haitian consulate over the last few years. But Windhoek, with its camel thorn trees and brown crabby grass, wasn't exactly the sort of place that inspired orgies.

Suffice to say that the members of the U.S. Embassy community in Namibia—whether breadwinner or spouse—had a lot of sex with their own partners. And after a fishbowl of bad wine from the Erongo, the girls had a tendency to get a *little* competitive about how far they'd go. Kayla dressed up in outfits. Shoshana and Barry had tried a threesome. Margo liked it from behind. No, *behind* behind. Oh, it went on, and on. This husband loved dildos up his rear, that person made home porn movies. It was a bit tiresome, to know so many details about the people you saw every single day.

That sort of bragging wasn't for Persephone. She didn't need to, because she knew perfectly well that she and Adam had more sex than any of them. Nor did she think it vain to acknowledge that as a fit thirty-eight-year-old who still looked pretty terrific in white skinny jeans, she inspired a lot of sex. It was part of her job. No matter how modern attitudes got, or how empowered mothers became, as an Embassy Wife (or Husband!), lots of sex was something you signed up for. After all, if your working spouse wanted it, what could you say? I'm too busy right now, because I have to run to the Puma station for croissants?

She stood in front of the mirror, attacking the rat's nest Adam had made of the back of her head and trying to decide which iteration of white to put on . . Fashion, Persephone had learned the hard way, varied from post to post. Go on wearing your Lululemon or your Rag & Bone in Namibia, and you'd look not just elitist, but disrespectful. Backtrack to cargo pants and T-shirts, on the other hand, and you'd look like Safari Sam, fresh off the overland bus.

Persephone had been around long enough to know that most Incomings, upon arrival, panicked and spent thousands of dollars on Amazon. These men and women would clog the State Department pouch with various articles of light travel clothing, which they would undoubtedly wear once and then give to their housekeepers. Not Persephone. Not anymore. Her uniform was white, other than workout clothes, for which she opted for pure black. She didn't look like other international women, and she never looked like she was trying to look like a local. She had her own style. She was an—no, *the*—Embassy Wife.

Wait. Someone was hovering outside the door. Frida.

"Miss Persephone?"

"Yes, Miss Frida. Come in."

Persephone had asked Frida a million times to stop calling her *Miss*. She loved having help, but she didn't like the platitudes that came with the classic African household. She wasn't Scarlett O'Hara, for heaven's sake. Well. Maybe she was Karen Blixen, but the baroness started a school for her help, and fretted no end about the plight of her staff.

Anyway. The point was, even though she had been born in a university hospital in Charlottesville, and Frida had likely been born somewhere unimaginable, Persephone was an American, which meant they were both women and humans, and no one should be calling anyone *Miss.* But Frida wouldn't stop, even though Persephone had commanded and begged. So now Persephone mirrored the effort, to keep things on the up-and-up. Which was too bad, because saying "Miss Frida" every time Persephone needed the housekeeper to do something was a real mouthful.

"Lucy went to the van without her shoes, Miss," Frida said now. "I thought they were in her rucksack, but I just found them."

"Lucy! What is *wrong* with her? Oh, I hate bus mornings. She'll just have to go to class looking like a street child from Katutura. I mean—sorry," Frida lived in Katutura, along with almost every other domestic worker in Windhoek. "I mean, I know *you* wear shoes! And that every-one in Katutura, in fact, favors footwear. Except some people. Though Afrikaners really hate shoes, don't they? I always see those children in the grocery store shoeless. Even at the doctor's office, no shoes! And cer-tainly they can afford—never mind. I don't know what I'm talking about. And how are you doing today, Miss Frida?"

"I am fine, Miss Persephone," Frida said, smiling inscrutably. At her? With her? She was fairly certain Frida thought she was a complete idiot, though she hoped not, because she really liked Frida, who was wise, and had three children of her own she never mentioned or complained about, and could solve the most difficult household problem with a min-imum of discussion or fretting. And here Persephone had gone, dis-paraging the Location. She was no better than that lady in the gym she'd randomly talked to who longed for apartheid because the traffic had been better controlled by the white government. Which might have been true, technically, but it was an appalling thing to say, all the same.

"Miss Frida? I've been meaning to give you something." She strode over to her closet. The doors opened with a bang, and clothes—disgustingly wasteful, barely worn clothes—came spilling out. Persephone looked at the heap, then grabbed two of her least favorite dresses and a sweater. "*Won't* you take these? It would be such a help. And these shoes." She nabbed a pair of gold sandals she'd only worn once because the soles were too slippery. "They are perfect for your feet."

"Okay, miss." Frida took the pile of clothes, her face completely neutral, neither grateful nor offended. "Thank you, miss."

"Oh, Frida, can't we just try and call me Persephone?"

"Yes, Miss . . . Persephone."

"Oh, Miss yourself! All right. Forget it. Let's get ready for this breakfast, shall we? The ladies are coming now-now. I'll make the coffee, you warm the croissants?"

The two moved around the house together, putting out food from the hidden bakery, Woolworth's, and SPAR, and arranging flowers and napkins. The breakfast was to start at 10:00, but in the nines, Persephone was still in the middle of making eggs-in-a-hole (a last-minute decision) when the bell rang and Shoshana's car appeared in her video viewer.

"Oh, Miss Frida," Persephone said. "Shoshana is ten minutes early. So awful. No one should ever be *early* to a party."

"No," Frida agreed.

"Let's let her wait a minute," Persephone said, flipping an egg. Twenty seconds later, Shoshana buzzed again. Persephone glanced at the screen, enjoying the view of her friend tapping her nails against the wheel. "All right," she said, when they heard the buzzer the third time. "Buzz her in. But, Frida! Miss Frida. Do not call Shoshana *Miss*."

Frida gave Persephone a perplexed glance and went to usher in their first guest. Moments later Shosh entered, looking—to Persephone's eye—absolutely horrid in damp, stained workout gear.

"Perse!" Shoshana crowed. "*So* sorry. Didn't have time to change. I'm training for the Desert Dash, you know, so I had to fit in an 80K ride after CrossFit. In this heat! Brutal."

"Well, you're early," Persephone said pointedly. "Would you like to use my shower?"

"Nah. We're all friends here. Hey, can I have a coffee? Iced? No? I always keep old coffee in the fridge, you know, and presto! Oh well. Anyway, this new person isn't, like, a new ambassador's wife or anything. She's not even embassy, is she? Her husband's like a teacher or something?"

"He has a *Fulbright*. Very prestigious. He's advising on the Nama situation."

"Don't know much about that one. Speaking of which, did I tell you we've pretty much nailed our next post? Almost definitely Belgium, baby. Barry's gonna be the next chargé."

"You did tell me," Persephone said, pouring (hot) coffee for Shoshana. She found Shoshana's athleticism inspiring, and her sense of humor charming. Her constant awareness of the State Department pecking order, on the other hand, was less endearing. Particularly when Shosh's husband would soon be the second-in-command, outranking Adam.

"Sally will be here soon. She ran out and got you gluten-free croissants."

"Oh my God. I shouldn't have bugged you about it. That is so nice, but those things have some sort of xanthan gum in them or something. You shouldn't eat gluten-free baked goods, it's like pouring glue in your gut, *literally*. No, my Amazon box came today. I'm cool with black coffee and my protein shake."

"And your Charmin?"

"Shhhhh." Shoshana giggled. It was no secret that the Levins used the diplomatic pouch—an age-old privilege dating back to the very beginning of the Foreign Service, meant for only the most precious of items—to receive American toilet paper. As if they didn't have perfectly good toilet paper here. A tiny bit scratchy, but who cared? Yet the truth was everyone, from the ambassador down to the college girl from Iowa who worked as a receptionist, abused the pouch. The back halls of the embassy, unseen by visitors, were stacked floor-to-ceiling with boxes shipped from Amazon Prime. At first Persephone had tried to rein her own ordering in, out of principle, not to mention Adam's lectures.

"It's not like it's free for the government to send Tide Pods from Des Moines to Kuwait," he told her, back when she first discovered the pouch. "The taxpayers shoulder that bill."

And so she had done her best to go local. She really had. But it was so much easier to press *Buy Now* than to live with your children's rashes from Namibian laundry detergent, or comb SPAR for organic black beans, or convince your daughter that South African OTEES were the same thing as Life cereal. And so, compliments of the U.S. government, shipping containers toting all of their Amazon items arrived every week.

Keeping her orders squarely in the middle realm of abuse, Persephone made a point of going to pick up the boxes herself, unpacking them and hiding the Amazon packaging before Adam got home. So far, she had been lucky. Whenever she'd come to the embassy to collect her loot, he hadn't been there. Kayla was the biggest abuser, anyway. Last year, she had pouched a live fourteen-foot Christmas tree from Vermont.

At ten o'clock exactly, the other guests started to arrive. Even in slow-paced continents like Africa, State Department people tended to be prompt, particularly when food was involved. (If free alcohol was on the menu, they were early.) Within half an hour, Persephone's assigned Foreign Service furniture was filled with Shoshana, Kayla, and Margo, along with half a dozen other Trailers who shook Amanda's hand before pairing off to talk among themselves. Persephone tried not to glare too hard at the knots of women forming in her kitchen, but she found them so . . . base. If you were eating someone's meet-'n'-greet croissants, for Lord's sake, you were meant to *meet* and *greet* the person. And make them feel welcome. Honestly. Had these spouses been raised in a barn?

No, no, she thought. She mustn't go down that rabbit hole. This was a party! And she was actually feeling warmer than usual toward Margo, who had parked herself on the sofa next to Amanda almost immediately. It was also fortunate that Persephone's new close friend

Amanda seemed not to mind at all when Margo removed little Noah's diaper and pointed to the silver bowl she'd placed at her feet.

"It's a way of potty training," Margo explained. "You make the right choice available to your child. And, well, hope for the best! Anyway, as I was saying, there are all *sorts* of ways to dress up these chairs."

Persephone busied herself with passing out croissants and coffee. All State Department houses, other than the ambassadors', of course, were furnished with exactly the same government-issued furniture, designed by an American who could only be a depressed, color-blind man in some cinder-block basement. Every piece, from the dining chairs to the sofas to the tables, was unbreakable and at just the wrong height for everyone. And you could bounce a quarter off the rubber-filled sofa cushions. Even now, the sitting guests looked strained, their legs bracing against the floor to keep themselves from slipping down or to the side. Those with the most State Department experience passed these events standing.

"I custom-made my own slipcovers from local fabric," Margo said. "And the other thing you can do is have big pillows made by a local for, like, a dollar. Even a lampshade cover to help the light . . ."

"I wouldn't fuck with the lampshade," said Kayla. Her husband was the facilities manager, meaning he was in charge of all the housing and furniture. Kayla, therefore, saw this as her jurisdiction as well. "Though slipcovers are a good idea. Because one weird stain, and you have to pay your deposit."

"Happened to us at our last post," chimed in Shoshana, who was balanced precariously on the arm of a love seat, her muddy running shoe pressed against the coffee table. "Four hundred bucks for a coffee stain. It was my most expensive purchase in Madagascar."

Persephone smiled graciously, noting that Shosh was now enthusiastically scarfing down a regular, gluttonous chocolate croissant.

"I'll be careful," Amanda said. "Thanks." Persephone tried to catch her eye, but Amanda had turned back to Margo, and was nodding with great respect and concentration at Margo's instructions on how to make a papier-mâché bird feeder.

She has good manners, she thought, feeling her approval of her new friend grow. And that was it, wasn't it? Persephone mused as she went to refill the carafes of coffee and soy matcha tea. It wasn't a class issue. No, *manners* were the key characteristic that separated the wheat from the chaff—or the Trailing Spouses from the true Embassy Wives.

"Then we went to the Gondwana in the Erongo," Kayla was saying. "You know about the embassy discount, right, Amanda? And oh my God. It was so *cheap*. Yes, there were frogs in the pool, but I was like, who cares? All four of us get this awesome room and all this food for ninety American bucks? You should go up there. Seriously."

"We will. Thanks," Amanda said.

"And do you have a housekeeper yet?" Shoshana asked. "Or a nanny?"

"I don't use a nanny," Margo said as she plucked a turd off the floor and threw it back into the elimination bowl. "Noah and I are bonding. No nannies."

"If you don't get a nanny here, you're fucking crazy," Kayla said. "Also as you need to, so you can help out the economy."

"My daughter is in school all day . . ." Amanda said. "She's beyond a nanny, I think."

"It's eighty bucks a week for a full-time person," Kayla said. "U.S. dollars. And that's, like, if you're super-generous. Why not just have someone there to make soup and fold laundry?"

"Kayla has two nannies," Shoshana said.

"Look. I'm here to live the life I want to live," said Kayla, lifting her chin. "I don't think there's any shame in that."

"You're in Namibia because your husband is serving the U.S. State Department," Persephone said, a tad tersely, putting more gluten in front of Shoshana. "So I trust you're here out of *service*."

"And thank God for that," said Kayla. "Amanda, in terms of posts, you scored. Namibia is Africa *light*. Good malls, good roads, good coffee shops. No danger of getting into a tight spot with a warlord."

"Totally." Everyone was paying attention now. "Africa light" was a favorite Trailer topic.

"Our last post in Dar es Salaam? Holy shit. I mean, our house was huge. And the help was even cheaper. But traffic was so bad it took two hours to get two miles."

Amanda nodded. Persephone was impressed at how placid she was, how she looked as if she was really listening and cared.

"Hey, Amanda, I found you on LinkedIn before I came over," said Jeffrey, the finance manager's husband. The gossip among the Trailers was that he was a secret drinker. Though perhaps *secret* wasn't the word, because only a moment ago he had fairly blatantly added whiskey to his coffee cup from a flask. "COO. Pretty impressive. What will you do while you're here?"

"I've been trying to find a volunteer opportunity I like. One where they actually need me."

"Well. We all do IWAN," Shoshana said. "International Women's something. It's sort of half coffee and wine and chatting, but the other half is outreach, raising money for scholarships, that kind of whatever. Or you can volunteer over at Penduka. Where they teach women to empower themselves by making pot holders and things."

"I guess I was hoping to do something a little more . . . direct," said Amanda.

"Only you can't," Kayla said. "The Namibians don't want meddling. People here just want to do things *their way*."

"They'll be happy to take your money, though," Jeffrey said.

"Yas, queen."

"I don't think that's true at all," Persephone said. "I think you're being awfully negative, especially to a newcomer."

"Exactly." Margo nodded. "How much did the women from Katutura nursing home love it when we took them to brunch?"

"You only think they loved it. The woman I was hosting thought she was being kidnapped," Kayla said. "She cried all the way there."

"Come on. You're giving the wrong impression," Persephone said.

"You *can* get directly involved. And I'm not just talking about throwing pointless tea parties where we sneak condoms on the saucers."

Oh dear. Perhaps she had sampled a little too much champagne.

"Really, Perse?" Shoshana said. "And what direct impact are you making?"

Persephone bit her lip, regretting. "Well. I'm very involved in Frida's family."

"So you give extra money to your nanny? Wow."

"I never do that," Kayla said. "First of all, you never know where the money's really going. Some abusive boyfriend for beer, probably."

"And—"

"Tell them about the rhino project," Amanda said, putting down her cup with a clear, percussive snap on the table. The sound was so sharp, Persephone could see Margo jump.

"What?"

"The rhino project," Amanda said. She gave Persephone a sly wink and turned back to the Trailers. "The first day I met Persephone, she told me how much she loved rhinoceroses. Wow, hard to say in plural, isn't it? Rhinos, I mean. She said she wanted to protect them in the field."

Persephone nodded. She'd just been babbling, but she *had* said it. "Well, since then she's been working on her own nonprofit to safeguard the animals. It's quite revolutionary. Actually, I'm helping her manage it." Amanda looked at Persephone and grinned. "I'm her COO."

"I didn't hear about this," Shoshana said, looking hurt.

"What is it?" Jeffrey asked, before taking one last gulp of his spiked coffee. "Your nonprofit. Explain, Phoney."

"Oh, *Jeffrey*," Shoshana scolded him, clearly delighted.

"Well." For once in her life, Persephone was truly flummoxed. She patted the back of her chignon. "The nonprofit is . . ."

"It's her dream job," Amanda was obviously trying to jog her memory. "A protection . . . start-with-one kind of thing."

"Start with one?" Jeffrey pressed.

"Well . . . obviously I can't save *all* of the rhinos out there," Persephone said, finding her groove. "So I've picked *one* rhino. It's my responsibility to make sure *it's* protected."

"From poachers?"

"Yes."

Shoshana crossed her arms over her chest. "Are you using money? Because the State Department prohibits——"

"No. *Personally* protecting it, I mean. By visiting it. And . . . you know. Patrolling the area." Oh Lord. She was so in over her head.

"How? With a gun or something?"

"Well. We might have a gun, in the future. I mean, Adam has one. But it's totally nonviolent." Persephone's head spun as she fabricated. "We're essentially witnesses. It's like . . . we're taking a nonviolent stand."

"I call bullshit," Kayla said. "Persephone, you hate camping. When we went camping at Erindi you upgraded to the lodge."

"The view of the animals was better from the deck up there," sniffed Persephone.

"Seriously, though," Amanda said. "I can attest: this is the real thing." Persephone could see why her friend did so well at business. Her present tone could shut down the most perilously skeptical room. "We're meeting tomorrow to figure out the plan. Supplies, and schedule. That sort of thing."

"And where is your rhino?" Shoshana asked.

"The first one is on Shilongo's game farm," Amanda said before Persephone could answer.

"Mila Shilongo?" Kayla's mouth dropped open. "Come on. You and that woman are oil and water."

"Lemons and milk," Margo said.

"Tequila and Baileys," Jeffrey crowed. The other Trailers exchanged glances. "You hate each other."

"She's really turned a corner," Persephone said quickly. "You know, she donated an entire oryx to the Argentina booth for International Day."

All of this was too much for the Trailers. They had arrived at the meet 'n' greet counting on ironclad alliances. Even small shifts were noted among the State Department community and more than a little resented. When the Wilders had gone to Erindi with the Grants, for instance, and left out the Levins, Shoshana had silently taken Persephone off the host list for Margo's baby shower. And when Shoshana gave up Margo's knitting class because she couldn't make it work with CrossFit, Margo had taken her off the WhatsApp list immediately, pointedly barring her from the other social chat that hummed regularly over that line of communication.

One could call it catty, mused Persephone. Someone like Amanda, who was only dipping in and out of the Foreign Service, probably would. But the perceived betrayals were deeper than that. When you made your living moving from country to country, bringing your family, pets, and all your belongings with you every three years in a bloated balloon, you could basically count on nothing. In-country friends were always temporary, Adam was always reminding her. Likely, a local would want something from her, in the end. No, the State Department employees had their jobs to hold them down, but the Trailers only had each other. And when there was a power shift, real or imagined, they reeled and swarmed, like carp fighting for scarce bits of bread.

The party ended promptly at 11:30. The guests all hugged Amanda and promised to be in touch, but through the window Persephone could see Margo, Kayla, and Jeffrey lingering by their cars in heated discussion. Shoshana, it could only be assumed, had dashed off to Pilates class.

Once they were all gone, Amanda and Persephone picked up plates and brought them to the kitchen.

"What *was* that?" Persephone asked. "I can't start a nonprofit. You need *actual* profit for that."

"Yes, you can," Amanda said. "I was thinking about it, even before today, I think it was when you used the term 'dream job.' All you need is a mission. A noble cause and a passion. You really do love rhinos, don't you?"

"Of course. They're splendid animals. The fact that crooks are shooting them and gouging out their horns to make Viagra, or whatever it is, drives me bonkers."

Amanda leaned on the counter as if she were at a podium and about to give a speech. "And do you think this is a good way of protecting them?"

"Sitting beside them and making certain no one murders them at night? Well, yes."

"And do you know people who would donate? If your deb sisters saw you putting your flag out for this, would they throw cash at it?"

"I wasn't a debutante," Persephone sniffed, donning her cheetah-print rubber gloves. "In Virginia we were considered new Yankee money. But yes. I know loads of people who would give."

"Okay, then," Amanda said, beginning to pace the room at a leisurely pace. "We could . . . commit to protecting one. Go out and physically be with it for a few nights. Like Julia Butterfly and the tree."

"I seem to remember she had to poop in the tree." Persephone turned on the spigot a bit too forcefully, and steaming hot water came shooting out. "Drat."

"This is a smaller scale. But the same idea. Then we ask people to pick other rhinos to protect."

"So they would fly to Africa and babysit rhinos?"

"No. Their *money* would go toward protection," Amanda said. "Carried out by a reputable security organization. We don't want to get involved with hiring guards. But we could piggyback onto the World Wildlife Fund, or something like that. We could hire a local consultant to help with that part. So the fact that you would be sitting out there——"

"Oh no." Persephone jabbed her soapy, gloved finger at Amanda. "Not just me. *You're* coming. You're the one who got me into this."

Amanda paused as if to argue, but then shrugged instead. "I mean . . .

okay. Sure, for one night or two. Anyway, our sitting out there would hopefully motivate people to dig into their wallets."

"All right." Persephone relented, reaching for more dirty plates. "I can see how this would work. But . . . does it have to be the Shilongos? She'll probably train her rhino to gore me."

"Look. I don't know where else to find an accessible, photogenic rhinoceros. Do you?"

"Hmmmph." Her new friend certainly did have an annoying habit of being right. "And what if we actually see a poacher?"

"I can't imagine that we would," Amanda said.

"It might be okay if we did," Persephone allowed. "I know how to shoot, you know. I grew up on a farm. Well, it was really sort of a Southern plantation. My dad used to take me hunting. I was actually pretty good."

"What? More, please."

Persephone shut the water off. "Well . . . last month I went on a hunting safari—very big around here, you know. And all the men were so excited about shooting zebras and such. As if it's hard to shoot a zebra! I mean, the stripes are practically *shouting* at you!"

"Totally," Amanda said, looking quizzical.

"So, out of nowhere this leopard came out and started growling at us. Adam wanted to shoot it, but it was most definitely *not* on our kill list. You can't just shoot things not on the kill list. You'll get into all sorts of trouble. Plus it's inhumane."

"You had me at kill list, doll."

Persephone paused, testing the air for ridicule, then ventured on. "Anyway, before he could say *boo*, I shot her in the little toe. Just a graze. So she got away."

"Hold on." Amanda slapped the counter. "You caught a real live leopard by its *toe*?"

"I'm just saying," Persephone said, delicately removing her gloves in order to enjoy one last croissant, "I happen to be very good with a gun."

8

The truth was, Frida Nepembe did think Miss Persephone was a bit dim. Or if not dim, then . . . troubled. For one thing, the poor woman was worried, all of the time. Every meal was a trial. She fretted about what to eat, what not to eat, how to serve it, and on and on. Who ever heard of almost fainting over a breakfast! Frida had her family over after church every single Sunday. People brought rolls, or a boiled goat's head, or rice, and then put it on the old plank table. If there was more food than usual, they praised Jesus. If there was less, they prayed.

Frida and Miss Persephone were exactly the same age. Miss Perseph-one had said so when she had taken pictures of Frida's ID on her first day of work. "One month apart!" she had said, squeezing Frida's wrist. "Imagine."

Frida could not imagine. She could not picture at all where Miss Persephone had been born. It must have been in a shining mansion, in a bed covered with silk and filled with feathers. Frida was born on her grandfather's farm in Otji. Her mother had been walking back and forth on the veld with her husband and sister, waiting for the pain of labor to cease. Then, without a word, her mother had stopped and looked at the sky, and her father had caught baby Frida in a bucket filled with rice. Frida always smiled when she thought of that story. She'd had good parents. She wished they were still alive.

And then there were Frida's children. Miss Persephone's were still small, because she had them when she was very old. Frida had babies when you were supposed to, so they were all grown. All three studying at the University of Namibia. *They* would not be domestic workers. No. Her youngest, Tonata, was already so full of herself, Frida could barely have her in the house.

As Frida walked down the hill toward Nelson Mandela Avenue, she could see the line for the transport to Katutura swelling already. Each time a taxi stopped, it was mobbed by men in blue work suits and the larger, stronger women who muscled in with their bags of food. Frida didn't mind waiting until the crowd thinned. She would get a ride eventually, and it was very fine here in Klein Windhoek, the air far better than at her house, what with the neighbors burning all sorts of what-what and their latrine that didn't drain.

And so she stood on the curb next to Aletta, an auntie she saw often who worked at a house down the street. As usual, Aletta started pumping her for information about the Americans. What did they eat? How many times a day? Did they have a television in every room? And a telephone? And was it true Americans let you take naps? Frida liked the old woman, but she kept her answers short. She had seen Aletta's bosses on the street. The man was a Boer; he had revved his engine when he drove past, just to scare her. The wife was a fat thing with squinty little eyes. She'd probably wanted information on Miss Persephone, and had asked Aletta to spy for her. Too bad for Aletta. She wasn't going to get anything.

Since Frida had started working for the Wilders, many of her friends in the transport line had either acted strangely toward her or stopped talking to her altogether. She was sorry the other women were so petty, but Frida was a busy woman. She didn't have time for jealousy. Everyone knew what a post in an American house was worth. There was no domestic job as valuable. Afrikaans houses were the worst; those people got involved in your life and criticized your house and children; they might yell or even beat you, but you had to pretend to like them, because the kinder you made them feel, the more they would slip you on the side. Germans were fair and would never touch you or ask anything about how you lived. Yet they were notoriously cheap, and so tiresome with their rules and "standards." Frida's friend Lollie had even worked in a Chinese house—there were more and more of them in Windhoek now, and they were getting richer and richer. Her Chinese boss was very generous, Lollie said. They were only allowed one child by their government, and the girl they had was so precious the mother paid top dollar for her care. But Lollie said she could never understand a word, and she told horrific stories of foul things boiling in pots. No, everyone wanted to work for the Americans, but there weren't many of them, and they didn't stay forever, so the posts were bartered over fiercely, either with cash or meat or what-what-what.

Frida had purchased the job from her cousin Elifas. One of the houses he gardened for had a new family, he'd told her. They needed a nanny, and he would give her the name, for two chickens. Elifas had always been a little in love with Frida. He was also a fool, it turned out. The post was worth five chickens, maybe even ten. Because who had ever seen such a house! The only downside was that it was very big for cleaning, but her new boss was nothing like the German lady who would follow her around with a white glove. Miss Persephone was every bit as nice as people said Americans were, and as foolish. She had heard that Americans were silly to work for, but she hadn't been prepared for the money constantly left around the house—five-dollar coins, fifty- and hundred-dollar bills, even, showering from their pockets and drifting in bowls and baskets. At first Frida had thought she was being tested for thievery, but after a year she knew the Wilder family saw Namibian bills and coins as playthings. Each time she gave the money back to Miss Persephone, the woman blushed or stuttered out of sheer embarrassment and guilt. She was hardly clever enough to test Frida; nor did she have the stomach for it. And she was always giving her things, if Frida so much as looked at her in an odd way.

The husband, Mr. Adam. That was a different story. Frida did not like him. She wished she did, because that would have made things nice for Miss Persephone. But there was something about the way he looked at you, or didn't, after a brief glance to size you up. As if he knew you already, so that was enough. Who knows someone after looking at them for just one moment? She didn't think it was just that he didn't see Blacks, like so many of the whites. It wasn't that he was pretending she wasn't there. His manner was more disturbing than that, more chilling.

On her first day, Miss Persephone had brought Frida to meet Mr. Adam in the back garden, where he was scowling into his laptop. At first Frida thought he was an actor she'd seen in a movie once, about a man who kept shooting people and hanging off buildings. His black hair glistened like a starling's wing, and his wrists, peeking out from his shirtsleeves, were tanned and muscular. He wore sunglasses with mirrors on them—Frida could see her curvy form in the reflection—which he removed without getting up to look her over from tip to toe, as if he were her doctor at Central Hospital. It made Frida feel cold, right down to her feet. Finally he rose and shook her hand, then abruptly sat back down.

Later, she was pleased to find out that his hair was fake. She found the Miss Clairol packet in Miss Persephone's trash, wrapped in newspaper. *Ink*, the color was. It was a secret even Miss Persephone seemed not to know. When you worked in a house, you knew all the secrets. Who was leaking piss. Who was having sex out of the house. Who dyed their hair, who hoarded old love letters, who hid bottles of vodka behind the cleaning products. Well, the Wilders had problems. Not drinking, maybe, but vanity. The man, especially, was vain.

"You've checked her references, of course," he'd said to Miss Persephone. She was standing next to him in a white dress that was very pretty, but that Frida longed to iron. Together they looked like an advertisement for Grove Mall, the ones where the white people laugh and hold kittens.

"Of course," she said to him, winking, and then hooked her arm into Frida's to lead her away. Mr. Adam never looked at Frida after that, really. And when he spoke to her, it was as if she were a ghost.

The transport line was finally thinning out. Frida pushed into a cab with Aletta, because they lived on the same side of the settlement and always walked home together. There were no streetlights in her part of Katutura, and the bad boys, just little boys, most of them, would come out of the shadows and try to beat you and take your purse if you walked alone. They had tried to tug Aletta's bag off her just last week, but Aletta had beaten the little boy with a stick. He had yelped like a lost puppy as he trotted away, blood running down his face. Aletta was a good walking partner. Still, she started in again with her questions as soon as the taxi started speeding toward Katutura, this time with six other bodies packed in.

"So you won't tell me about the lady in white," Aletta said, settling her round body and her bags next to Frida. "Hold this, will you? Soup bones. For once Miss Tessie threw something away." Aletta's bosses were not only nosy, but notoriously cheap. No one in that house would tell you not to call them *Miss*. Although it was so ingrained in Frida to do so after twenty years working in German and Afrikaans houses, she knew she'd never be able to remember not to anyway.

It was confusing, though, with Americans, when you got down to it. Sometimes Miss Persephone could get very grand with her ideas and desires to change things. Of course, Frida wanted more food and more rest and a bigger house that was not made of tin that did not have to be readjusted after every rain. But not everything needed changing.

"You work in two houses now?" asked Josie, another lady who worked near them, on Olof Palme Street. "Two jobs?"

Frida was quick to quash this notion. No one wanted to be seen as greedy.

"Just once a week, for two hours, I go over to Miss Persephone's friend's house. Miss Amanda."

"Nice?"

"Quiet."

"Good pay?"

"Fine."

"And the meneer?"

Frida thought for a moment. Mr. Mark, he was different from Mr.

Adam. He was very tall and very thin. He needed feeding. He was old but had boyish hair, the kind that fell into the eye. He did not dye it; the brown was marked by rivers of gray. Mr. Mark, he saw all of you. And he liked to talk. Sometimes he asked so many questions, Frida had to go in another room to finish her cleaning. He was very curious, for instance, about Oshakati and who she knew there.

"Oh, he is a good man. They are good people. But Miss Amanda has trouble coming."

"Why?"

"The meneer has another woman, I think."

"Why do you say?"

"He is on his phone all of the time, talking to someone. I heard her voice."

The other women in the transport clucked their tongues.

"I am sorry for her," Aletta said. "I will pray. And I am sorry for you. You will lose your extra job."

"God will provide," Frida said. She did not like this gossip and had said too much already. They were coming to the Engen station in Katutura now. She loved coming back to Katutura, with its familiar sounds of friends laughing and rich smells of cooking. She often felt in the white neighborhoods that she could not breathe; the air there seemed stale with years of loveless fear. Now she and Aletta had to hop out and convince another taxi to take them to the north side, a place most transports did not like to go. It was already getting dark, so she and Aletta hurried to get off the path before the young thieves came out.

At home, it was soup with a bit of bacon from Miss Persephone. Frida hadn't felt badly about taking it; the family had so much food, it was forever rotting in the refrigerator. Tonata was home from her classes, so they sat together at the table, listening to Elemotho, Tonata's favorite, and reading the newspaper and magazines. It was time for bed soon, as Frida's day started at 4:00 and ended at 9:00. She knew she should go in and bolt the door, as they'd been broken into one night last month, but she liked to sit in the yard with a glass of beer and listen to the chickens before sleep. Their neighborhood bordered the veld, so that on windy nights she could hear the rustling of the grasses and the shepherd's trees, just like at her father's farm.

Tonight, as she sat, she thought again of Mr. Adam and Mr. Mark, of Miss Persephone and Miss Amanda and their unhappiness and all the things they didn't tell each other.

She refilled her glass one more time. They were all getting there.

God would provide.

9

Hello?

Hi!

Does it work?

Hi!

Hi!

Hi!

What r u doing?

Stuffies.

I'm listening to a CD.

What's that?

It's a circle that plays music. You put it in the mouth of a machine.

Cool.

I found it in my Mom's things. It's fintastic

OK!

U r my only friend with a phone!

Well u gave it to me

Good thing my mom has so many.

How many

She has like ten iphones.

U are pretty rich

Yes, we are because my father is in government

It's not like that in US

No it is your ruler is the richest in the world I think I saw it in the news. He seems to scream lots. So yor country is like Africa now!!!

okay

Did you see Susie's sunhat today? It had little trolls on it. My word.

It was nice I think

Meg. It was not nice it was horridness

Gotta go my mom is coming if she finds this fon she wil kil me.

See u at school I have a good idea to talk to u about byeeeee

Biiiiiiiiiii

10

During Mark's three-hour drive to Swakopmund—first through the brown hills of the lower Erongo, then through blistering veld that graduated eerily into seven-hundred-foot mountains of pure desert sand—he ran over the story he'd made up for Amanda. He was going, he'd told her, to write a report on a vandalized German monument in the main square. This was true, actually . . . though it was only a tiny part of why he was making the trip. As expected, Amanda had been as interested as she usually was when he talked about his work. As in, not at all. He'd given her the name of the hotel and said he'd be back in three days, knowing the name thoroughly off the hook. Still, as he drove closer, he grew more and more tense. He hadn't been to Swakop since—

Where are the girls? Fuck you, man. Listen to me! Where are the girls?

He shook his head, switched on the radio, kept driving.

It was only when he got away from his family's unhappiness (whether actually voiced or beamed silently through their ever-changing moods) that he was able to truly revel in his unbridled love of Namibia. The way he could observe shadows as large as skyscrapers meandering across an entire range of mountains; the fact that he could see for three hundred miles around him with no strip malls or houses marring the landscape. So vivid were the colors—the watery pale sky, the burnt red sand scarred with yellow and green weeds, the white sun, always relentless until mercifully shrouded by angry, blue-green storm clouds—they exhausted his vision. The lonely roads, where the slabs of granite rose out of swirling desert sands, made his chest swell with a sort of longing. Amanda found all this emptiness bleak, but it was the very absence of humanity that Mark loved the best.

After three and a half hours, the veld was completely gone. Just mountains of sand now, left and right. This was where the winds of the coast were born. The heat rose with such force that the cool air from the ocean rushed forth to fill the vacuum. Air and fog shot inland, pushing swirling walls of sand and battling even the heaviest of bakkies on the road. As he came down from the rise toward the beach his car rattled and swerved. He could see a hundred miles ahead of him, where the highway petered out to a thin black ribbon on the horizon.

Finally, as if a miracle, some candy-colored dots of buildings emerged against the mist, followed by the blue glow of the sea. Mark drove directly into town, which was much the same as he remembered, with its strange mix of bunkers and run-down German buildings that looked like melting gingerbread houses. Sand blew in every direction, forming mini-dunes in the street.

It was a crystalline day, the sort that only happens in those few places in the world where pure desert meets beach. The cool air filtered the reflection of the brightest sunlight, creating halos in the mist. As the waves struck the sand, puffs of water and steam rose up in tiny clouds.

Just like the last time, Mark thought. The sky and the air were exactly the same. When he stopped the car to look at the empty beach, he could feel her sitting beside him on the blanket. She had been afraid of swimming, but he had coaxed her to wade in. The water had beaded into iridescent drops on her blue-black legs.

Esther, are you asleep?

Esther?

Fucking stop it, he told himself. Stop it now.

Pulling into the street again, Mark drove past the beachside delis and restaurants and ice-cream shops trying their best to be festive and attractive, despite the sandstorms. He drove to the waterfront, where he remembered the main hotel used to be. The Strand, it was called, a large pink structure Esther's friend said looked like a birthday cake. He remembered a fountain, and the girls' faces when he took them into the lobby, which was musty and as tacky as a 1970s-style Holiday Inn. The carpets were smelly, and the sheets so rough Esther had a rash the next day.

As he pulled around the corner, he took a deep breath, trying to quell his nerves. What if it was torn down? Well, it was, but it wasn't. The place had the same name, but gone was that old pink lady, and in its place a bland glass-and-steel structure that could serve as a conference center in Cincinnati. It was clean, modern, charmless, and scrubbed of her memory. When he went in, he found the prices astronomically higher than they'd been in 1997. He booked a big room anyway, because he was a lot older now, and he had money. It was one of the few nice aspects of aging, Mark thought. You can afford the things you think you want.

It was 2:30 when he arrived. Housekeeping was running late, the deskman said in that dignified, unapologetic manner Namibian service people had that drove Americans insane. Walking back into the glare of the afternoon, he decided to tackle his easiest task first: the embassy report.

Since Mark was embarrassingly badly informed on the situation he was supposed to cover, he took some time to sit on a bench to do some research. Hello, class, he imagined saying as he pulled out his phone. I am Mark Evans, professor of history, shitty PhD candidate. My bibliography today consists entirely of Wikipedia.

He got up and walked to the square to get a look at *Marine Denkmal*, the German monument of recent dispute. It was a hideous thing, comprised of one bad statue of a living soldier standing over the sculpted corpse of a dead one. It had been erected by the colonists in 1908 as a *fuck you* to the Nama and Herero rebels they'd mercilessly defeated, then rounded up and ushered into concentration camps. After independence, the sculpture had moldered in the square unnoticed, which was how most public art in this area of Africa ended up. Finally, around two years prior to this sunny day, some Nama kids had realized how utterly offensive the monument was to pretty much everyone in present-day Namibia, and, as their own overdue *fuck you* gesture, they'd doused the thing with red paint.

Mark took some pictures for the report. He was tempted to go back to the hotel bar and write it up, thereby putting his next awful task off another day. But being in this place—the town where he had last seen her—was too much. There was no way he could wait until tomorrow. He put his camera away and walked toward the edge of town, where the Swakopmund Hospital was marked on the map.

It was just the same building as he remembered, a lonely place listing on the outer edge of town, where the asphalt streets gave way to desert sand. He stood outside, a running stream of anxiety coursing through his body, his knees knocking together like in some sort of old cartoon.

This was where he would find out if she was alive or not. There would be no more not knowing after this. Was it stupid to do this?

Jaime had certainly thought it was. "Remember Schrödinger?" he'd asked when Mark had first hatched the plan to come back to Africa. Jaime was the only one who knew Mark was coming to find Esther, and he made his disapproval known, loudly.

"Not really."

"Philosophy class, man. Curiosity. The cat."

"Yeah?" He'd tried not to sound annoyed. Jaime could be so fucking obvious sometimes. "This was twenty years ago, dude. If I open the box, I kill her?"

"You open the box, you kill everyone," Jaime had said. He thought he was so fucking smart. Well, to hell with Jaime. And to hell with Schrödinger. Schrödinger hadn't been in love with the cat. Schrödinger hadn't spent more than two decades thinking about the taste of the skin on the back of her knees.

When he entered the lobby, he was slapped in the face by sharp smells he remembered instantly: disinfectant, biltong, bleach, shit, rot. This was the smell of a third world public hospital, and the very thing that had scared him off from going to medical school all those years ago. Batting away the shame, he approached the front desk.

A smattering of people waited in wooden chairs, looking dusty and resigned, as if they'd been there since Christmas. The white woman sitting behind the desk refused to look up. Mark shifted from foot to foot a few times, then leaned heavily on the counter.

"Hi," he said.

No response.

"Goeiemiddag," he tried again, the slaying of the pronunciation earning him an upward glance. "Sorry! Hi there. I'm here for some medical records."

The lady stared at him, waiting.

"I was in an accident."

"Yes?" She was Afrikaans, which meant her *yes* sounded like *yis*, and to his ear, the rest of her words rolled lazily around the roof of her mouth. "Tih-dey?"

"No—no, not today. A long time ago."

She pushed back her chair slightly and rocked back and forth. "So. You want your records, then."

"No, not exactly," Mark said, clawing for patience. He hadn't been in Namibia long enough for this. Navigating bureaucracy, or any sort of business here, it took a special state of mind. Most Americans—the State Department ladies he'd met, for example—never got there. Once abroad in Africa, they would get indignant and downright abusive if, say, they didn't get the room with the balcony they'd booked, or they were served perch instead of zebra.

The thing was, he wanted to tell these compatriots but never did, Namibia didn't work that way. If you thought about it, Mark felt, it was a miracle that any life survived this arid graveyard of a place at all. A few mighty tribes had made a go of it—warring all the while for bits of water and shade—for thousands of years. Then the Germans had come, and, using guns, ethnic cleansing, and other classic Deutschland tactics, wrestled those good parts away. After a short while, the colonists deemed the whole venture unworthy and handed the place over to the South Africans, who, after a pitiful showing in a tiny, bloody war, had given the government back to the original Namibians, while keeping all the money and the best land.

If any commerce made it through all this, those businesses were intricate webs indeed. Favors had to be paid to keep children alive, food on the right shelves, land protected from poachers, taxes avoided, water running to your house without diversion. So when you asked the bakery counter worker at SPAR for a Dutch crunch loaf, her look of utter disinterest wasn't because she disliked you personally. Certainly she disliked the idea of you . . . you who had once existed in a fairy-tale world away from this place. But the true bottom of it all was history. She didn't give a shit about helping you because the last two hundred years had proven there was nothing you could possibly do to change her life at all.

"Let me start again, ma'am," he said now. "My friends and I . . ." Jesus, just talking about her out loud made his chest constrict as if squeezed by an invisible fist. "We were in an accident. All of us. And I never found out what happened to them."

Namibians like stories. The others in the waiting area leaned forward a bit. Even his rival behind the desk softened. She wore a green uniform and her pink arms were swollen as big as hams.

"Let me get my supervisor," she said finally. "Sit down."

Mark looked at the people in the chairs again. Two were asleep, their heads tipped against the wall and their mouths open. A few others stared at him without blinking. One lady was crocheting a blanket that reached well below her feet.

"I'll just stand here, if that's okay," he said.

The woman disappeared. It was now three o'clock, dangerously near the end of the Namibian workday. He gripped the counter, wondering, if by some miracle, a polite, helpful, educated person—a librarian of sorts—speaking perfect English might appear, guide him magically to the records he was looking for, and solve his mystery forever. Finally, the ham lady returned.

"My manager says to tell you we would not have any records before 2008."

"You mean you don't have them here?"

"We wouldn't have them anywhere." She looked back down at her appointment book. "He says to tell you it is Namibian hospital policy to destroy all records after ten years."

Mark felt his previous queasiness turn to pure acid.

"But why?" His voice cracked perilously.

The ham lady shrugged. "Yah. Why do people need to know if they were sick more than ten years ago? Your body has either recovered or you are dead. This is a casualty facility. Emergency. We don't have electronic records and we have no room for the long-ago past."

"Only, see, I'm trying to find out information," he explained, trying his best to be patient. "I was in an accident in 1997."

She laughed then, unveiling a surprisingly lovely smile. "Well, you needed to know that in 1997!" A couple of idle patients behind him laughed as well.

"I'm just trying to find out what happened to the people I was with."

The woman shrugged. "If they died, you can find that out. Do you think they died?"

"That's the thing. I'm not sure. I was taken here and then taken away. Out of country."

"Out of country," she repeated a tad wistfully. Her eyes slid toward the clock. "The morgue keeps their records. They don't throw them in the bin. But they close at four. Gurirab Ave. Try there tomorrow," she said, dismissing any possibility of further questions.

Mark walked out into the bright mist, caught between utter relief and the familiar shroud of frustration. Not knowing what else to do, he walked back to the Strand. His room still wasn't ready, so he walked through the reception area to the other side of the hotel that overlooked the Mole, Swakopmund's main swimming beach. Taking a seat at the bar facing the ocean, he ordered a double gin and tonic.

For decades, the Mole had been whites-only; even when Mark had come in '97 Blacks shied away from the beach, as if the memory of apartheid laws still tainted the place. Today, Mark was glad to see, it was clear Namibian citizens of all colors had claimed this beach as their own. A group of kids were executing Olympic-level dives off the floating dock; they fought through the waves to get back to the ladder, climbed up, then dove again. Three boys were flipping in sync with each other, their timing executed with perfect precision. As he watched their youth and grace, he could feel what was left of his own athleticism, once unquestionably epic, seep out of him, as if he were punctured and leaking sand.

"Amazing, isn't it? How good at sport they are?" said the man sitting next to him. He was large, and a little older than Mark. Or, at least, Mark hoped he looked younger than this wrinkled old basketball. Namibia was so hard on the skin, with its relentless sun and parched air sucking every drop of moisture away, Mark often found he was speaking with someone he assumed was fifty or older, only to discover that they were barely straddling thirty. "Born for it, the Blacks are. It's een thar blood."

Een thar blood. Mark sighed. Still, maybe this one would be nice, despite it all. Oh, damn it. This one. He hated how Africa did that to him. How it made everyone speak in terms of they and them. As in, different, and not as good as me.

"Yeah," Mark said. "These kids are some terrific swimmers. That much is clear."

"Usually they can't swim at all," Basketball said. "Scared of the water."

They they they.

"Sure doesn't look like it," Mark said, trying to control the annoyance in his voice.

"Course, *these* are coast boys," Basketball went on. "Coast boys can swim sometimes. But not inland. Read the paper? They're drowning all the time in the rivers. They hate dogs, too. I have two rottweilers. Not 'cause I'm afraid, mind you, 'cause I'm not. And I'm not a racist man, either. I'm just saying, there's good ones, and there's bad ones, too. I'd rather not find out in the middle of the night."

Mark took a drink, trying to figure out how to get away from this bigot. He could walk away, but he wanted to finish his gin and tonic.

"They're not stupid, though," the man said. "You think they're stu-pid, and you under-esh . . . esh . . . -ti-mate . . . now, why can't I say that word?"

"Underestimate."

"Right. Don't do that, or you'll get cheated. Or you'll miss out."

"Okay." Mark took another gulp. The man smelled of cologne, tinged with old liquor. He wondered if his room was ready.

"I'm in with one of them now. A smart one. She's got a racket go-ing, and I'm making good money. Not bad on the eyes, eith—"

"Mr. Ferreira." A young woman, dressed in the same smart uniform as the others behind the front desk, stood next to the man. She put her hand lightly on his arm. "I believe your family usually expects you for dinner about this time. Might we arrange for a taxi home?"

"Might you? You getting all fancy on me?" He turned to Mark, swaying a little. "This's the one I was saying about——"

"I'll just call one now," the girl said, leaning over the bar to pick up the phone.

Mark didn't know what was going on here, exactly, but he knew he wanted none of it.

"It was nice talking to you," he mumbled, then hurried away to the desk, where they finally gave him his key. As he waited for the elevator, he watched the girl try to herd the old man out of the bar. The scene bothered him, and not just because the old man was a dirty bigot. It was that the girl looked exactly the same age as Esther had been on their trip here. So very, very young.

The elevator came, and Mark finally retreated to his room, where he lay on his bed, ordered room service, drank more, and let himself remember.

Everyone who visited called the café a miracle. It was hidden in the back of a busy gas station, where combis crammed full of dark bodies raced in to top off with gas before the long trip south to Karibib or Windhoek. Behind the pumps was a small shop, which sold the usual African goods: biltong, cooking oil, two or three varieties of old hard candy, soap, bullets, milk in unrefrigerated boxes. It smelled the way only those shops could: of rotting meat, gasoline, and the occasional sweet drift of fresh marsh wind. If one stayed long enough for the eyes to adjust, they would see a doorway and a beaded curtain—the sort that was meant to keep out flies but never did. Press through that portal, and one would come into a new land altogether: a true oasis, loud with the chattering of birds, crowded with potted tropical plants and flowers.

In the middle of the place was a huge, magical-looking baobab tree, its branches weighed down by teardropped weaver nests. The ground was covered with meticulously swept fine gravel; the tables were refashioned out of old wooden pallets that had originally been used to ship cattle feed for the herds that roamed Ovamboland unchecked. The cook, JoJo, knew how to make entirely palatable schnitzel out of any sort of game brought in that day. The plates he served were heaped with fried kudu, zebra, or oryx, garnished with steaming potatoes and freshly made purple kraut. It wasn't the sort of food that made sense in a place that simmered in swampy, buggy heat eleven months of the year, but Ovambos, Germans, and Afrikaners alike came from all over to eat it.

JoJo didn't own the café, but he ran it and presumably pocketed most of the profits. The story was he'd traded his daughter to the Boer liquor dealer for a refrigerated keg holder. Otherwise, who could explain how a shebeen like this could have such a machine, along with a thumping generator to keep it going when the rains robbed the town of power? Nor could anyone remember how JoJo's had come to exist in the first place. But it did exist, and it was the jewel of Ondangwa, which was why it was purchased, just a few years before, by the adjacent inn.

This was where Mark first saw her. She had a tray of drinks and was making her way through the tables with efficiency and disdain. She was tall—startlingly graceful. Every moment was so fluid she might have been made of water.

Mark was twenty-two and had been with many beautiful girls by this time. He hadn't ever given much thought to the process. They wanted to be with him, and he'd wanted the same thing, until he didn't. But this. Her. He couldn't stop looking. He couldn't fucking breathe.

He didn't try to talk to her that day, or the next. Instead he came every afternoon at two for lunch. She was brisk and heartbreakingly aloof with him when he ordered. He tried to smile, but she didn't seem to notice, busy as she was with bringing out orders and getting customers new beers. Still, he went back.

She had friends, other girls who worked at the hotel. They liked to hang out in the café when they were off, chatting with each other and teasing her when they could. They noticed him quickly, these girls. Soon they began sitting at his table. They let him buy them drinks and called him meneer.

"What are you doing here, meneer?" one of them asked. "Shouldn't you be in Texas?"

"Texas?"

"Texas is on the show we watch."

"*Dallas?*"

"That one. With the old ladies with the nice hair."

"He's a teacher," another girl said. "Yes?"

"Sort of."

"We like the white teachers. The missionaries are no fun. Thorns in their asses."

"No, this one's an aid worker."

"Aid workers are supposed to buy us beer with aid money."

"Get us more beer, aid money!"

Yet making friends with her friends didn't solve anything. In fact, it seemed to push her away even more. Whereas before her avoidance of him had seemed casual, now it was so noticeable it seemed to be an occupation. She sent JoJo to collect money at the end of the meal and served his beer and food from as far away as possible, so that his plates had to be passed down by three or four sets of hands.

He wondered now, lying in Swakopmund in his middle-aged body, if she really was as he remembered her. Could anyone actually be this exquisitely wrought, liquid amber ghost? Her skin always cool, despite the blistering climate? Her voice sparked a physical reaction—water, running down his back. Her dresses were modest and old-fashioned, but they were thin, so that when the wind blew, he could see the outline of her hips and legs. Once, as she unloaded her tray, her sleeve slipped down from her shoulder and he caught sight of the strap of a snowy white bra against her dark skin and his whole body shuddered, as if his own mother had walked over his grave.

He knew he deserved to be ignored by her, the one woman he couldn't bear to leave alone. How many times had he slept with girls back at school, smart girls, nice girls, and not bothered to call them after? There was a girl from his study group, the one who gave him a blow job in the library; he never let her catch his eye again. There was the Harvard girl the weekend of the Head of the Charles who said she was a virgin; after sex he retreated back to Brown without calling and sent James to console her at parties the rest of the weekend. Everyone acted like an asshole sometimes, which made it okay then. But now, with aching certainty, he saw the truth: he was in purgatory, utterly obsessed with a waitress named Esther, with her huge eyes and her tiny waist that flowed out to round hips like a guitar.

"Can I please just buy you a broodjie?" he asked one day after her shift.

"I'm not hungry." Her voice trickled out, pooling in his ear.

It was her friend Amber who saved him, finally. She was a fine girl, a funny girl, pretty as well, though no loveliness could bloom properly in the other woman's shadow. Amber made it clear she was willing where Esther was not. She liked Bruce Springsteen and told dirty jokes about farm men and their animals. She was even friends with the Afrikaans men, yelling at them in their language and making them laugh. Mark appreciated Amber. She drank beer with him one night after the others had gone home. Esther had gone; only JoJo was left to serve, slamming beers onto the tables as the late-night revelers recoiled to dodge the sloshing. In the middle of a story about how she cured her own malaria with cucumber skin, she put her bare foot on his knee.

"I'm sorry," he said, considering. "It's just——"

"You want Esther."

"But not just in that way." He stopped himself. Then what way? He wanted to sit next to her and play with her fingers at the combi stop. He wanted to press his face into the back of her neck. He wanted to bring her to Highland Park and have her watch him play soccer with his brothers on Thanksgiving morning. It was impossible. He was out of his mind.

"How about the ocean?" Amber said.

"What do you mean?"

"If you take both of us, she'll go," she said, signaling JoJo for another beer.

"She won't," Mark said.

"She will," Amber said. "We've never seen it. The ocean, I mean. It will be good, to go with you. We couldn't go just together. With a white man, no one will touch us."

"What do you mean? What would happen if just the two of you went?"

Amber opened her mouth, then chose to take a sip of beer instead.

"It will be better," she finally said. "If you go."

The proposal to Esther, and, presumably, the acceptance, happened offstage. Mark didn't know what she said or how she did it, but a few days later Amber showed up at his little house behind the Pick n Pay.

"She'll only come if you don't pay for us," Amber said pointedly.

Mark paused, confused. "*Can* you guys pay, Amber? For a combi and food and a place to stay?"

"Are you stupid?"

"So, no?"

"She can't think you are paying, meneer," Amber said. "But I can't think how the weekend will cost less than three thousand."

Mark told her to wait and ran to the bank. At that time, three thousand was less than two hundred dollars. Mark didn't have a ton, but he did have his "dead grandmother money" that could be accessed in times of emergency, which this was. He came back with three thousand Namibian in an envelope. Amber looked inside and nodded, satisfied.

"Meet us at the combi stop tomorrow at seven," she said.

Mark didn't sleep at all. He paced the lone room of his house, choosing which three of his eight shirts to take. He got to the stop half an hour early, trying to remain calm as he sipped coffee from his thermos.

When they weren't there at five till the hour, he knew they weren't coming. He'd been cheated out of three thousand NAD. Well, fuck it, he thought. What did the money mean to him? Fuck all of them.

Then he saw them coming around the corner, holding matching rucksacks, the kind local kids were given by the government for school. Amber smiled and waved. Esther didn't smile, but she nodded, slightly. He held his breath as he watched her come closer. She was slow, deliberate. She wore the same dress he often saw her in, but she had added a thick leather belt around her tiny waist. Was it for him? No, of course not. She came closer and closer until she was standing right next to him—the closest he'd ever been to her.

"Hi!" he said, too loudly. "I was afraid you wouldn't make it."

"We want to see the beach, hey," Amber said. She was cranky and looked tired. "It's *my* trip. Of course we're here." She sat on the edge of the bench, leaving Esther and Mark to sort each other out.

"Thank you for coming with us," Esther said. She sat in the center of the bench, leaving an empty spot beside her.

At twenty-two, Mark had done many things in his life people had thought courageous. At eight he'd jumped into Lake Michigan in late fall to pull his little brother to safety when the kid had toddled off Navy Pier. At Brown, he'd stood up for the one gay member of his crew boat, squelching any sort of snide remark. He'd come to Namibia, knowing nothing about what he was getting into. All of this was nothing compared to taking a seat next to Esther. He felt as if he were an explorer, setting off unarmed to map uncharted lands.

"Can I . . . ?"

She shrugged and nodded. He sat, leaving room between them. She didn't move away.

Many years later, in the same-but-different hotel, Mark got distastefully, wonderfully, and expensively drunk. Sitting in front of his television watching cricket—a game he neither understood nor wanted to—he ordered gin after gin from room service, punctuated by a mediocre burger and chutney-flavored Simba chips. He woke up at nine the next morning, facedown in his boxers, his mouth tasting like the fur of a dead cat. Prickling with hungover shame, he splashed water onto his face and called his wife back.

"Hey," Amanda said, her voice disinterested, flat. "How is it?"

"What's wrong?" His heart skipped a beat. The enormity of his secrets was becoming unbearable.

"Nothing. Just Meg, being aloof. Where does a nine-year-old get off being aloof?"

"I don't know," he said.

"How's your research?"

"Not very good."

"Make some action items," she said, suddenly all business. It was the only time he could get her attention, it seemed. When he was somehow failing her expectations. "Get it done."

"Okay." He felt overwhelmed with relief at her bossiness.

"Meg, I told you to get your lunch box. What are you—"

"I love you," he said. But she'd already ended the call.

He showered and went downstairs to the bakery, which was trying very hard to be hip and French but still served telltale items such as impala carpaccio and tongue. He'd dreamed of her all night, unpleasant dreams in which he could see her and touch her but then she morphed into different sorts of animals. Not African animals, but cats and gerbils. He fucking hated dreams. It was time to go to the morgue.

It was a cool and bright morning. There was no wind or fog, so he decided to walk. In this unusual weather, the post-and-beam and stucco buildings looked neat and well kept, and Mark felt, if he squinted hard enough and used his magical thinking, he really could be in a town in Germany. The fantasy dissipated as soon as he left the tiny tourist district. Within half a block the buildings and houses became bleak and run-down; barefoot children and their angry mothers spilled onto the street.

Located behind the police station, the morgue was no exception to the shabbiness of the neighborhood. A small, squat building, it knew no end of sorrow. Almost no one left this place, Mark thought, with news they wanted to hear.

The office, however, unlike the hospital, was clean and efficient, seemingly run in a different sort of Namibian bureaucratic style. No one was waiting. The middle-aged Black woman was pleasant and quick and helped him right away.

"I'll be right back," she said, her heels clicking away down the hall. As Mark waited, he thought again of Esther's face, those worn dresses.

She had a thick blue leather bracelet, intricately etched, that she said was made by a Himba woman way up north, on the border of Angola. Would she still have it? Would she even remember who he was?

Before he could ruminate further, the woman came back with a file in her hand.

"I'm sorry," she said, sliding the file over to him.

"For what?" he asked dumbly, before, with a sickening thud, he understood. "I can open it?"

"Yes."

"Are there——"

"There are no pictures. Don't worry, sir."

The file contained one piece of paper: a death certificate. Esther Kaaronda had died on February 21, 1997. Cause of death was blunt force from a traffic accident.

"So . . . she died," Mark said. He seemed unable to physically feel anything. "She really did die."

The woman nodded empathetically. "According to this record, yes."

"Could it have been someone else, maybe?"

She put her hand out gently, taking the file back.

"Usually the police require positive identification, sir. I don't think so. I'm sorry."

She was good at saying that. I'm sorry. But Mark could tell she only meant it as much as she could allow herself. It was the same sort of sorry one got at the deli after receiving the wrong type of sandwich.

"It's okay," Mark said. "Good to know, at least."

"I would think so, yes."

"All right, then," he said, lingering. He had come such a long way. Was this really the end? The woman smiled at the awkward pause between them.

"Goodbye," she said, and went back to the file room and shut the door.

Mark returned to the street, blinking in the harsh glare. His entire body was coursing with adrenaline, but at the same time, his limbs seemed paralyzed. She was dead. Dead. He repeated the word in his mind, but nothing changed. Maybe he would be fine with this. Yes. It was okay that she was dead, wasn't it? He had a family already. And maybe her life would have been awful. It had been so long ago, anyway—

A combi rumbled past. The van they'd been in looked just like that, Mark thought. It had flipped and hurtled through the air and she would have been so scared, and then—

A sob escaped his throat. He stopped and bent over, his hands on his knees, and threw up.

A few hours later, after he'd checked out and paid the enormous bill, Mark shuffled through the streets looking for a present for Amanda. He still felt sick, but like any bad news—say, the death of his father—it was beginning to settle in, like a thorn one's skin learns to live with. Still, as he trolled the shop windows, he had to stop and take a few deep breaths.

The coolness of the morning was gone now, replaced by throbbing desert heat. He ducked into a shaded alley and found himself standing in front of a window filled with modern jewelry. One necklace, a thin silver chain with a stunning green stone on a pendant, seemed like something Amanda would wear.

He stepped inside to look at it more closely. The shop smelled of the chemical-laden pine gel adored by all Namibians—a neon goo that cost twenty NAD and was strong enough to clear out clogged drains.

"That's a chic choice," the shopkeeper said as he peered closer. "Tanzanite. Namibia is famous for them. The mine is just two hundred kilometers from here. Karibib side."

"Oh. I . . ." He looked up. "Hey, wait. I know you. You work at the

Strand." He felt enormous relief at recognizing the woman, a relief that he realized, of course, was misplaced. "You were . . . helping that old guy at the bar."

"Oh." The girl looked a bit distressed at the association. "Yes. That was me."

"Double shift?" Mark asked, standing up from the counter self-consciously.

"This is my good job." She rolled her eyes. "I just work at the hotel because my parents want me to. They think the hotel is better."

"What do you think?"

"I think it's boring," she said. "I'm going to quit."

"Well, it's nice that you want to please your parents."

"I want them off my back, you mean."

"Okay," Mark shifted on his feet. "I don't know. My daughter would do anything to piss me off."

She gave a ladylike snort. "I doubt that. How old is she?"

"Nine . . . No, ten."

"Don't know her age, eh? That's a fail."

Mark looked at this girl more closely. She was tall and thin, like a fashion model. Pretty cheekbones, slightly crooked nose. She could tell he was studying her, and, instead of shying away, she put her hand on her hip and posed.

"What's your name?" he asked.

"Anna."

"Nice to meet you," he tried. She shrugged and moved to the window. "This store seems to do well, though. Is it yours?"

"Okay, boomer," Anna said, smirking. "Why would I have to work at a hotel if I owned a fancy jewelry store?"

"Right." Mark blinked rapidly at the retort. "Sure. They sound like good parents. What do I know? So how much is that necklace?"

Anna didn't move, but looked over at him, her lips twisting a bit. "It's six thousand Namibian. I'd give you a discount, but it's not my shop."

"Can you wrap it? Like a present?"

"Sure," Anna said. He wasn't sure, but he thought he could see an almost imperceptible raise of an eyebrow.

"That's cool," Anna said. He wasn't sure, but he thought he could see an almost imperceptible raise of an eyebrow.

"That's cool," Anna said. "It's for my wife."

"Good. Let's do it. It's for my wife."

"Are you fine?" Anna asked. He could feel her curiosity, could see her staring at him out of the corner of his eye. He went to the window, pretending to look at the sky.

"Do you think it will rain today?" he finally managed. His voice shook a little, but other than that he was all right.

"No, boomer," the girl said, giving it up. "It's the desert, hey?" She pulled out the wrapping paper in a sleepy manner.

"I'm not a boomer, actually."

"What? You're not old?"

"Not boomer-old. Those are people born as a result of the return of American soldiers from World War II. I was born in the seventies. That makes me . . ."

Anna gave a loud, pointed yawn.

". . . uh, Gen X, I think."

She shrugged and lifted the necklace out of the case.

"Look, can I ask . . . who was that man at the bar in the hotel?"

She glanced up, then focused on her work again. "Troy Ferreira. He owns Ferreira Properties, which is, like, half of Walvis."

"He seems pretty nasty," Mark said, coming back to where she was and leaning on the counter.

"He's fine," Anna said. "He's investing in my jewelry line."

"No offense, but I don't think that's a very good idea."

Anna stared at him for a moment, considering, then treated him to a slow, dazzling, yet condescending smile. It reminded him of something. Probably because he was often treated like an idiot these days.

"Mr. X. I don't know if you've thought about it, but it's sort of hard to start a jewelry line? You need money, hey? Mr. Ferreira has *money.*"

"Mr. Ferreira is gross," Mark said.

"Whatever. It's not me he's interested in," Anna said, crossing her arms over her chest. "It's money."

"What do you mean?"

"I have a gem connection. Rubies. Amethysts. Not diamonds, but everything else. You can only get them from a guy I know. I can get them for much less than they are worth in the States, or Europe, or even South Africa."

"How? I mean, why does he give you the price?"

"He likes me," she said. "And I buy a lot of gems."

"What kind?"

"I told you," she said impatiently. "Amethyst. Topaz. Smoky quartz. Spessartite."

"Come on," Mark said. "You made that last one up."

"Google it, X-man."

"Okay," Mark paused, drumming his fingers on the glass case. When she frowned at him, he took his hands away and shoved them into his pockets. "Like, how much does he invest? And how much does he get back?"

"He gave me ten thousand NAD," she said. "He got back thirty thousand."

"Really?" Three thousand return for a one thousand U.S. dollar investment, Mark thought. Well. *I have a thousand dollars.*

"Do you have a business plan?" he asked her. What a fraud he was. As if he'd know a business plan if it landed in his beer.

"Sure," Anna said. "People give me money, then I give them back more."

"If you give me proof that I'll make money, I have money to invest," Mark said. His chest swelled with . . . was it elation? Hope? Was he just trying to distract himself from the fact that he'd finally found out that Esther really was dead? He couldn't think about that. Amanda.

How happy his wife would be when she found out he was making them money in Namibia, as well as working on his career.

"I can prove it, boomer," Anna said. "Just try me."

Mark gave Anna his credit card—well, Amanda's, actually—and paid for the necklace. The girl handed him the package. It was an exquisite thing. His very future, one might say. Wrapped in gold paper, tied with a silver bow.

Fall

'N Aap wat 'n boom klim, sal jou dadelik van sy hoër posisie misbruik.

A monkey who climbs a tree will immediately abuse you from his higher position.

—Oshiwambo proverb

11

Hi

Hi who are you with

Uni

Your unicorn???

Yeah. I line all my stuffies up in a row like they are a crowd and I talk to them.

Perhaps you need a pet

Yeah I want a dog but when you take them back to America they have to be cornitined.

My aunt Selma had a dog in Katutura and the neighbors ate it

????????

I found the things I was talking about this weekend at the farm. This will certainly work.

Why would anyone want them?

I do not know but according to google people do very very much

Wow. OK.

And the website is organised

Cool.

So you willC arrange the mailing Meg?

Yeah. Super easy. This is so great Mom will be so happy

I am glad your mom is pretty and kind

Your mom looks like a movie star

Yes she does she has been a model before in fashion shows

!!!!!

your mom is not pretty like that but she has a nice face and that is what we see first when we look at white people

?????

Its true my grandmother says so

What about my face

Girls all have meerkat faces. We don't get our real faces until we bleed

?????

My grandmother again

Where is she?

North. Let's talk behind the trampoline tmrw morning

Hearts and stars!!!!!!!!!!

Unicorn rainbows!!!!!

The thing was, Amanda was just not taking the embassy Leprechaun's Leap seriously. And though Persephone was really coming to adore her new friend, her nonchalance toward embassy events bordered on . . . well . . . *rude*.

Kayla, who was unofficially in charge of all the children's events, had questioned inviting little Meg at all. After all, it was at the ambassador's residence. And Mark Evans was not officially *with* the embassy. Kayla had a point, of course. And there was still an open question, in Persephone's mind, as to what had motivated Mark Evans to come to this country. The possibilities were endless. Just last month, a little Brazilian girl Lucy adored had to leave abruptly when her parents were extradited for fraud. And then there were the hundreds of thousands of (American!) dollars embezzled from the school by the brand-new Afrikaans accountant last year. Though Mark Evans had a nice face, and in Persephone's experience, people with nice faces were generally not fraudulent.

In the end, Persephone had convinced Kayla that it would be cruel to deny little Meg the chance at new friends. It seemed that lately she was absolutely glued to the hip of that Taimi, which simply could not be in the embassy's best interests. No one wanted the Americans mixed up in some sort of corruption scheme. Even though, Persephone supposed, Taimi herself could hardly be involved in her parents' affairs. (Probably not, anyway.)

But when she asked Amanda at pickup what she was wearing to

"the Leap" (the invite called for green or gold), Amanda said she hadn't thought about it. Hadn't thought about it! The event was in *two hours*. And when Persephone—ever calm!—had asked if little Meg wanted to borrow one of Lucy's old leprechaun outfits (she had two from previous years) the answer was: "That's okay, Meg's got a green T-shirt, I think."

At which point Persephone had given up.

What she had been trying to get at, albeit indirectly, was that she had gleaned some information from the other Trailing Spouses about Amanda's husband and the job he was doing. Persephone wasn't the only one onto him. Word was that the ambassador, Ms. Julia Spier, appointee by the White House under the Great Orange Oompa Loompa, was *not* impressed with Mark Evans's work on the Nama situation so far.

It would make the Evanses' heads spin, Persephone thought smugly as she carefully lined her own eyes with greenish-gold eye shadow, how quickly State Department privileges could be rescinded. No more red diplomatic license plates (though, honestly, Persephone had never been sure of the advantages of those), no more diplomatic passports (ditto, as State Department employees were discouraged from using them during recreational travel), and no more diplomatic pouch. (That was huge. Amazon Prime!)

In the name of her new friendship investment (Amanda!), Persephone herself had been trying to help the Evans family in a subtle fashion. The last thing she wanted was Mark getting fired. Amanda would hightail it back to California faster than you could say *biltong*. Therefore, during the last couple of days, she'd been dropping these little hints that Mr. and Mrs. Evans should kiss the ambo's bottom just a teeny bit. As in, maybe little Meg *might* want to consider wearing something other than a "green T-shirt."

But no. Amanda was not taking these indirect hints. Fine. It was what it was. *Her* family (minus Adam, who said he was "interviewing scholarship students in the north" but was obviously on some CIA trip) was now ready to roll at 4:45. The twins, dressed in green jackets and shorts complete with hats and boots—adorable!—and Lucy, glittering in gold, just like the pot at the end of the rainbow. Doni would cry if she saw how sharply her protégé was nailing it.

Without Adam (again! But she supposed she was serving her country), she loaded the girls into the 4Runner. It was just four blocks to the OR (Official Residence), so she didn't bother with seat belts any more than she worried about the one to three glasses of champagne she'd had as dressing drinks. The children adored the lack of seat belt rules in Africa; once Persephone had made the huge Instagram mistake of showing them all frolicking in the back in the corner of a selfie, which had drawn a backhanded "like" from her sister (*Soooo cute but the car seat thing is killing me!!xxx*), as well as a light slap on the wrist from the ambo's assistant and protocol advisor. But four diddling blocks! She could make it.

The street was already clogged with red-plated SUVs. Two security guards stood out front, waving their arms at the self-entitled diplomats in futile attempts to direct their parking. Persephone gave them a wave and a smile (she always treated car guards to tips, though not as outrageous as Amanda's) and parked in her usual spot around the corner, where no one would admonish her for leaving her car on the sidewalk. She glossed her lips one last time and led her little green gnomes (wait, were gnomes different from leprechauns?) through the gate, again smiling at the inside guards who flanked the door wearing AK-47s.

The Big A. was at her usual station, by the door, greeting the guests.

"*Miss Ambassador!*" Persephone said, kissing both cheeks.

Sadly, Persephone and the ambassador were still not on a first-name basis. The ambassador was single, so Persephone obviously had to say *Miss*. Which made her feel like she was in a *Little Miss Important* storybook. She had met the Big A. a few times now, and was still waiting for her to say, *Just call me Julia!* After all, the Big A. called *her* Persephone. It was the Frida problem, only backward.

The Big A. now granted what Persephone hoped was a warm hand-shake.

"Persephone. Don't your little ones look lovely."

The ambassador had no children herself. She was fifty-five, African American, spoke with a European accent no one could place, and had never been seen in anything but Armani suits, even on safaris and during outdoor events in the 120-degree Namibian heat. She wasn't a career State Department employee. In fact, no one knew how she had been appointed to her post, though the question was so bandied about at informal gatherings that the very topic, in Persephone's opinion, had become as tired as an over-sucked lollipop stick. All the embassy employees knew was that the Oompa Loompa had plopped her in there the year before, no questions answered or asked.

People liked the Big A. well enough, as she asked very little of her staff. She was often traveling with her assistant. No one knew where she went, and though there was much conjecture, no one really cared. She never fraternized, and if she did engage in conversation, it was rarely about Africa. What she really loved was food trivia, which meant all of the bum-nuzzlers were studying up on taste bud chemistry and the origin of pink salt.

Yet, for all of that trying, the Big A. seemed to have no real friends or anything resembling a partner. Her companions were two stunning Rhodesian ridgebacks, flown in from their previous post in Switzerland on their own plane. Naturally, it was discussed among the embassy community that *perhaps* a Rhodesian breed was inappropriate given their proximity to former Rhodesia, now Zimbabwe. But the dogs had been acquired three years ago. How was she to know her choice of breed might be an international faux pas? As for kids, the ambassador always stared at them as if she'd forgotten such creatures existed, and that their very appearance in her vicinity was an unpleasant surprise. Which made things quite awkward when one went to a children's party at her residence.

"Thank you for hosting," said Persephone.

"Tradition!" the Big A. said. "Did you know, I didn't even know why we did this instead of the Easter egg hunt? Just found out this year. I never even put together that Easter eggs had any religious significance themselves. But it turns out the eggs have some sort of ancient reference to the Christ figure."

Persephone smiled politely.

"Whereas, St. Patrick's Day is absolutely derived from a religious holiday. Saint Patrick, after all, drove the snakes out of Ireland and then was sainted for it, obviously. But the church never took ownership. This is a completely commercialized version. Important to have something for the children, I've been told. Now, *where* is Adam?"

Persephone, ever the pro, kept her game face. Obviously, the ambassador knew very well that Adam was on a secret mission. But hell's bells if she couldn't play this game.

"Oh, around!" she said loudly. The children were squirming behind her. "Thanks again for giving our little ones something fabulous to do!"

She pushed her leprechauns through the sitting rooms filled with breakable furniture and art, then herded them into the courtyard. The previous ambassador—Obama appointee, bird lover, and universally adored for serving very good wine—had opted to cover over the pool during one of Windhoek's more serious droughts. The result was an enormous Olympic-sized patio that sizzled like the worlds' largest grill-pan. From December to February, any event out there was lethal, but autumn had arrived, and from the steps to the house, Persephone could observe the embassy community as blatantly as if they had been on a stage.

There was Kayla in a green pantsuit. Shoshana wore gold exercise tights tucked into boots with a green jacket. Margo had on a dowdy little green dress and had fashioned some sort of crafty hat of green feathers. It did not look Irish or becoming, yet *did* indicate how she'd spent her free time today.

"*Perse!*" Shoshana crowed. "No white! For once! I like it." Her voice dropped. "So, how are you guys surviving bidding season?"

One of two times of year when one could apply for open jobs, bidding season was a fraught period in the embassy community. It was stressful, and competitive, and the more graceful Trailers knew not to talk about it. Shoshana was not one of them.

"Oh, surviving just fine, thank you."

"Adam put in for . . . what? Morocco? Paris?"

Persephone tried not to look annoyed, though Shoshana knew perfectly well Adam had applied for posts in South Africa, Germany, and Bermuda.

"We're just waiting to see."

"Me, dying over Brussels. Just dying. The I-School is *ah-maz-ing* there. Though the kids already speak French, so . . . maybe we'll go local?"

"*If you get it,*" Persephone couldn't help saying. No one was to hear about their posts until May.

"Yeah, well. I'm feeling pretty confident," Shoshana said.

"Why? Did you hear something?"

Shoshana shrugged, suddenly maddeningly vague. Persephone spotted Mark and Amanda near the bird feeder, looking marooned. After all her worry, the pair looked perfectly respectable, she in a short green flowy dress, he in a tie with clovers.

"Well, I should—"

"I mean, I might have a back channel," Shoshana said. "I can put in a word."

Persephone had to physically restrain herself from rolling her eyes. What kind of *back channel* would Shoshana have that Persephone didn't? Shoshana, who had a part-time job in the Facilities office, whose husband was in Public Affairs, for heaven's sake? Especially as everyone knew the Big A. had no friends?

"Did I tell you I've been running with the ambo?" Shoshana cooed.

Wait. *Running?*

"Julia wants to run the Two Oceans . . ."

Julia?

". . . but she has no idea how to train. Something about being able to try whatever food she wants. So I offered to help her," Shoshana said.

"We have an eight-week plan. I mean, it's coming up, so she's lucky she said something. She hadn't even signed up."

Every State Department member exercised. It was practically part of the job. As a way to socialize with someone who had no friends, it was perfect.

"Isn't the marathon booked?" Persephone asked hopefully.

"She just had someone make a call," Shoshana said. "And she got me a place, too, of course. It's good to be friends with the queen!"

Thankfully, Amanda was waving now.

"I'll see you in a bit, dear." Persephone attempted to sail across the patio, but something caught her heel and at the end of her traverse she lurched into Mark. Over her shoulder, she thought she heard Shoshana giggle.

"Hello, there," said Mark, righting her.

"Oh, hi," said Persephone, taking the opportunity to get another good long look at Mark, the mysterious fake scholar. Amanda's husband was tall and gangly, almost giraffe-like. A bit too good-looking to be a convincing historian, really. Too thin for her taste, but she'd always liked larger men. Beefy, even. Like Petrus, the Namibian IT manager from up north who serviced the embassy . . . Persephone had befriended Petrus because every Embassy Wife worth her salt knew that getting to know the IT man was key. Yes. Petrus, now, he was her *real* type. Such a large, strong man, and his voice boomed so. Being around him always made Persephone feel like a tiny, delicate doll . . .

Suddenly Persephone had *quite* a clear picture of climbing on top of Petrus's mountainous form in her very own Garnet Hill—swathed bed.

Hold on. *Petrus?* Where did *that* thought come from? Because Adam, of course, was her ideal! Adam, with his chiseled pecs, his maddening abstinence from alcohol, his imported protein shakes. For some reason, she shuddered.

"Cold?" Mark asked.

"Spritzer went down the wrong way."

"Huh."

"Meg having a good time?"

"I think so. She's over there." Persephone looked in the direction where Amanda was pointing and spotted the gaggle of little girls, who were lounging with alarming ease on barstools. Meg was, indeed, wearing a green T-shirt, but her manner was so offhand, Persephone had to admit she looked pretty cool next to the other fur-lined, trying-too-hard kids.

"I'll get us some more wine," Persephone said as she sailed to the bar, pretending to peruse the Big A.'s art choices (the administration had switched the paintings out as soon as she took up residence) while eavesdropping on the children. Which was hard to pull off, because Miss Ambassador favored very dull western landscapes.

"You should come to my house for a playdate," Ali, Kayla's daughter, was saying. "The nannies barely check on us at all and we have the awesomest pool because my dad's, like, in charge of who gets the biggest house."

"Yeah, but my house has a tennis court," Alec, Shoshana's son, said.

"We totally did not have that in Turkey."

"You have a pool, right, Meg?" Ali said.

"Yes," Meg said.

"That's pretty sweet, that you have a pool," Lucy said.

Persephone felt the warmth of pride. Her girl was being nice!

"Though it's sort of weird, because your dad isn't really with the State Department. Right? I mean, he's just, like, temporary."

Oh dear. That was not as nice.

"We get to go somewhere new every three years," Ali said. "Every house is better than the last."

Persephone frowned. What the State Department trainings did not tell you about moving your family abroad, she mused, was that while you thought you were doing your children a great favor by exposing them to different cultures, they would also inevitably be steeped in an international *Mean Girls*-like reality show.

"*I'm* moving to France," Alec said. "Everyone wants to be posted there."

"Nah-uh. I heard you have to live in, like, an *apartment*."

"What?"

"My best friend Abbie's in Thailand. I wanna move there."

"I'd just like to go home," Meg said, soliciting hostile, awkward silence. Persephone turned away. Maybe little Taimi wasn't such a bad match for her after all. Meg, like her mother, seemed determined *not* to be an embassy child. But then, if you had no State Department ambitions, why would you?

Briefly, her mind went back to a time when she was beholden to no protocol. Back when she could act like she wanted to at a party without having to make anyone think well of anyone else. When she could just wear fishnets, if she wanted to, and swim in the punch bowl. Just imagining it brought on a rush of freedom. It would be nice to be Amanda, she thought. Aside from that shifty husband.

Persephone grabbed three glasses of white from the kindly-looking bartender (who, she knew, counted every glass each guest was having and then reported who was drinking what to the Big A. after the party) and carried them back to her friends.

"Treasure hunt should begin any minute now!" she said. She took a sip and puckered. Clearly, this Big A. was not as generous with the wine budget as the previous lead diplomat. There was a flutter of activity—a telltale sign that the Big A. was leaving her post by the front and moving back to the patio. If one wanted a word tonight, now was the time to hover. Because after the welcoming remarks and the hunt, it would be time to clear out. No ambassador liked guests who hung on to the party after the call time.

Persephone watched coolly as Shoshana sailed over to the ambo's side. The Big A. was holding court with a few people; it didn't look as if she was any closer to Shoshana than to anyone else in the circle. But . . . training plan!

Persephone sighed. It was nothing short of brilliant. What busy athletic woman *wouldn't* want a training plan and a personal coach to cheer you along? Shoshana would be guaranteed to have the ambo's ear for hours and hours. Persephone knew she shouldn't be worried; after all, her husband was doing double duty with the most exclusive organization in the government. Still, Shoshana was working out with the Big A., and here Persephone was, still relegated to *Miss*.

"What are you staring at?" Amanda asked.

"Excuse me?"

"It kinda looks like you're shooting the ambassador a death stare."

"Oh! No, I was just . . . thinking about how I need to work out more."

"Weird," Amanda said, grabbing two mini-droëwors from a passed tray. "Here."

"Thank you," Persephone said, stuffing the greasy meat into her mouth. "Well, this ambassador . . . socially, we're very restricted, you see. But it would be so wonderful if Adam and I could get to know her better. For us, I mean. I know it's backwards . . ."

"No, I get it," Amanda said.

"Once Tim Cook visited Amanda's company and the nerds were swarming all over him," Mark said. "I was there. And he thanked Amanda for the gathering and it was like Cook had slimed all over her, *Ghostbusters*-style. Everyone was so pissed and jealous. Remember?"

"Business socializing is worse than high school," Amanda said. "Just be straight. Ask her to lunch."

"No! I can't. It's . . . it's not *done*."

Amanda finished her wine and handed Mark her glass.

"I'll be right back."

Persephone watched as her friend marched across the patio to the tight, fraught group of people by the door. She couldn't hear what they were saying, but Amanda tapped the ambo's arm and started talking. Oh Lord Almighty.

"What is she *doing*?" Persephone wailed. All the other Trailers were openly staring. Shoshana looked positively murderous.

The Big A. listened, head tilted. Then she nodded and smiled, and said something back. The two shook hands and Amanda came back.

"More wine, please," Amanda said. Mark dispatched himself.

"What on earth did you say?" Persephone asked, even as Kayla glided by them slowly, in the manner of a shark.

"I told her about our rhino project. How you and I need to know the ins and outs of how diplomats and American nonprofits work together. She suggested lunch."

"She did?"

"Yes. So, you and I are lunching with her sometime in the next couple weeks. Sound good?"

Persephone beamed. Perhaps Amanda would make a bona fide Embassy Wife after all.

On the drive home, Persephone quizzed Lucy on little Meg. The twins were completely useless; Kayla had been predictably lazy about hiding the candy and, after placing about fifteen pieces in the bushes, dumped the rest of the Costco jumbo sack of chocolate doubloons into the garden shed. So the twins and some other kids, royally pissed at finding no candy, broke into the shed and shoved about thirty pieces into their mouths each. Now her two youngest were so cracked out on sugar, she'd had to relegate them to the way back with the emergency dehydration kit.

"But what is Meg like at *school?*" Persephone said. "Bullied? A bully? Which one?"

"No one is mean to her. She plays with Taimi," Lucy said. Her daughter, who was used to her mother gathering intel from her, was by this point a fairly reliable spy. "They sit on the trampoline and play Servants."

"What's that?"

"That game where kids pretend they have servants." Lucy said this in a tone that indicated Persephone knew perfectly well what the Servants game was.

"Is Meg a servant?"

"No. Though it's really Taimi's game. She used to play Ministers, where she was president and the other kids were her government. Now she plays Servants, where she and Meg are fancy ladies and all the other kids are supposed to do things for them."

"Huh."

"Seems like she's having an okay time," Lucy said. "And of course, they have their company."

"What company?"

"Hey, is that Daddy?"

"What?" Persephone looked out at the street. "Where?"

"I just saw Daddy getting into a car. With a lady. But he's gone now."

Drat. This was getting serious. She was proud Adam was tapped for spy duty, but honestly, he should have let her in on the plan for tonight. This lying was getting tiresome.

"Daddy's in Katima," Persephone said, pulling into her driveway. "Remember? Interviewing scholarship people for the Mandela fellowship. We'll call him now-now."

She waved at the night guard and closed the gate, then handed Lucy the phone. As she prodded her mad children up the steps, she heard Adam's voice spill into the kitchen. Booming, reassuring, cocky.

Good man.

She poured herself the second glass of wine she'd skipped at the hunt to keep her count down and sat, kicking off her shoes. What had Lucy been saying about Meg and Taimi? She was exhausted suddenly. She caught a glimpse of herself in the dining hall mirror and went to take a quick bath and moisturize. Dermatological upkeep is important, she imagined telling Amanda. Despite everything, the newbie was still her protégé.

13

One of the many surprising things about Namibia, Amanda thought on her morning run a couple of weeks after the Leap, was how reminiscent the place was of South Carolina during the 1980s. The acknowledged segregation, the reliance on an actual paper newspaper to get local news, the importance of a man's being home for lunch. And then there was Windhoek's Radiowave radio station—the sort that spewed inappropriate jokes and top forty hits 24-7. Amanda made a point of streaming the station as she jogged around the wide, hot streets of Eros, just to stay in tune with what was happening in the city.

She adjusted her headphones, which kept slipping out of her ears because of the sweat. *Sheryl . . . Yes, babe? . . . I'm dumping you. I've found someone thinner, hotter, and better! And who will pay me big bucks . . . Nooooooo . . .* CALL HOLLAND INSURANCE THE HOTTEST INSURANCE BROKER IN TOWN . . . *I'm having the worst time with my maid. All of my stemware is cracked! And then there are my missing earrings. Who can I trust? . . .* CALL MARTHA MAIDS, 'CAUSE IF THEY STEAL, WE CATCH 'EM . . . *George, I was just dreaming of the first time we met . . . Really, Renata? Because I was dreaming of that new hunting rifle down at Agra, complete with a complementary round of ammo at just two-triple-nine . . .* VISIT AGRA FOR ALL OF YOUR SHOOTING NEEDS. AND MORE!!

In other news, a Russian billionaire was buying an illegal amount of hunting land after paying off SWAPO. A toddler had drowned in a latrine in Omaruru. And a springbok had gotten stuck in someone's garden in Kleine Kuppe. The police thought about tranquilizing it, but, not having the correct equipment, just shot it instead. No one could decide who the meat belonged to, so they had a braai in the garden that afternoon for everyone involved.

Running was hard here, as the sun screamed down all day beginning at seven, and the air was so dry it slurped every bead of moisture out of Amanda's lungs. But she had noticed that the other Trailing Spouses went one of two ways in this town: they either became alcoholics, or they got very fit. After choosing health for the day (perhaps tomorrow she'd opt for booze), she jumped into the pool with her clothes on, changed, and headed over to the school.

When the bell rang—as if released from a swollen pressure chamber—children in sun hats shot out of the classrooms, spraying across the dirt play yard. Idly, Amanda watched the parking lot show. There were Persephone's girls, pushing each other to get on the trampoline. There were Kayla's girls, strutting in the shade in mock-designer clothing Kayla had her seamstress copy from magazines. And, finally, there was Meg.

Amanda nearly cried when she saw the blissful smile on her daughter's face, as she walked arm in arm with Taimi Shilongo. Their heads drew together as if they were conspiring, then Meg, spotting her car, sprinted over—narrowly missing being run over by a Malawian diplomat in a BMW tank.

"Hi, Mom." Meg gave her a look she couldn't read. "Everything okay?"

"Of course, pumpkin."

"Not sad about anything?"

"No more than usual."

Meg frowned.

"Kidding, honey! I'm totally fine."

"So you're over the orphanage thing?"

She smiled at her daughter. "Thanks for remembering that, honey. It was a while ago. But yes, I was terribly disappointed, honey, you're right. Nothing would make me happier than helping out those kids. Other than you, of course."

"Maybe there's another way to help them?" Meg's eyebrows were drawn together, and as she waited for an answer, she sucked her lip.

"Don't do that, honey. You'll get chapped lips. Anyway, it is what it is, I suppose."

"Okay." Meg looked back at the playground. "Um, can Taimi come over for a playdate?"

"Sure," Amanda said. "Tell her to hop in."

This solicited an onslaught of squealing, as all clouds of previous seriousness drifted away. "Good afternoon, Mrs. Evans," Taimi said a moment later, climbing into the backseat. "Thank you for this excellent visiting opportunity."

"No problem. Here, girls. Snacks." Meg took the bag wordlessly, ripped it open, and stuffed a handful of pretzels into her mouth.

"May I ask what these are?" Taimi asked.

"Oh. Yogurt-covered pretzels."

"Aha." Taimi looked them over thoughtfully. "And may I have some water?"

"Sure, here's my water bottle. It's iced, so——"

"Oh no. I *never* share bottles. My father says it is dirty. I will need my own water, please."

Meg stared at her new friend.

"Well, I . . ." Just then Amanda saw Persephone across the parking lot. "Hang on, girls. I'll just get one from the tuckshop. Lock the door, okay? Don't open it."

"No," Taimi said. "We will not. And you will leave the air-con on. Of course."

"Uh . . . sure." Amanda slammed the door, feeling vaguely apprehensive. Though if a predator did happen to approach the children in broad daylight in the parking lot of Windhoek's fanciest school, Taimi could probably handle it.

"Amanda!" Persephone cried. She was wearing a white jumpsuit and her red hair was ironed out silky straight, though she seemed to have missed one spot on the left side of her head that stuck out like a little pipe cleaner. Persephone truly was always almost perfect; it was the *al-most* part that made her so damned lovable.

"Ugh. I am so over Adam being away. Not that he does anything, but without him there's *no* discipline. I mean, this morning I caught the twins comparing each other's poop in the toilet." She rolled her eyes. "With a ruler, no less."

Amanda shifted to position her face away from the sun. "Future scientists at work."

"Anyway, I still can't get over what you did at the Leap. I know it seems silly, but Trailers usually don't invite ambassadors or their wives to things. There's a strict unspoken protocol. I swear, it's like from 1955. I love that you just stepped out!"

"Actually, that reminds me. We need to get our eyes on this rhino ASAP. Before we meet with her. Like, next week."

"All right." Persephone looked over her shoulder. "Is that Taimi Shilongo in your car?"

"It is. Playdate."

"Ah! *Well*." Persephone was visibly trying to smooth the peeved look off her face. "Obviously I'm the only one who thinks Mila's crazy. *And after my husband.*"

"Persephone. Be a big girl."

"*Amanda.* I am an *Embassy Wife*, representing the United States of America. I would never knowingly hang on to a grudge."

"Never."

"It's just that she's so——"

"Rhinos, Persephone. Do it for the rhinos. 'Cause I think she's got a real live one that will make this nonprofit a reality. That'll impress Miss Ambassador, don't you think?"

Persephone squeezed Amanda's arm and floated away in an aura of satisfaction.

The fact was, Amanda was almost as thrilled about Meg's finding a new friend as she'd been about her own burgeoning friendship with Mila Shilongo.

She loved Persephone, of course. And when she and Mila began spending time together (you couldn't use the term "hanging out" with someone like Mila) she even felt a little bad about it. Persephone disliked her so, and she'd gone to so much trouble to try to make Amanda like it here, however impossible. And they had a bond, as Caucasian middle-class Southern women born into the seventies; they shared a complex lexicon of Laura Ashley, white guilt, Dave Matthews, ma'am, hot rollers, Boone's Farm beverages, and the kind of teenage sex that happens in a car during a church picnic.

But her friendship with Mila . . . really, it was a foreign-girl crush. Mila's beauty, for one thing, was almost debilitating. Amanda never got tired of looking at her face, how it changed in the light as she moved it from one direction to the other. She imagined this was the way artists felt when they found a muse. She had never been physically attracted to women, and she wondered if this mild obsession was what it felt like.

It was not a casual friendship. Their meetings were arranged well ahead of time. The appointments were always lunch. Amanda usually hated going out to lunch; it reminded her of hot afternoons in Charleston with pink, frilly cousins. Yet Mila never granted her an audience anywhere else. If the women ran into each other elsewhere—say, at school pickup or at a social function—Mila acted cool and formal, as if she were Amanda's boss.

Still, their lunches. Amanda loved them. During the first few minutes she was always too dazzled to be comfortable, but then Mila would make a joke, and she would grow more at ease. Mila was catty and funny and wise. She always arrived dressed beautifully in white pants and an exquisite blouse, or a tailored dress. After showing up for their first two meetings in shorts—a move which elicited obvious disapproval—Amanda made an effort to dress up, too, sometimes buying a last-minute outfit from Poetry just to pass inspection.

It was really something, to walk into a place next to someone as beautiful as Mila. She would open the door, and life would just stop. Amanda loved to see the variety of expressions on people's faces: dismay, envy, lust, surprise, joy. Mila seemed utterly impervious to it. Amanda wondered if she even noticed.

"You must get any table you want, looking like that," she whispered once as the servers scrambled in the Stellenbosch courtyard. But Mila gave her a look so cold, Amanda felt it shoot right down to the bone.

"No," Mila said. "Of course I don't."

Her friend had rules about where she would eat and sit: always a table in the back of the Stellenbosch, or at Sardinia Blue Olive in the manager's section. Sometimes she insisted they move tables two to three times. After a few lunches, Amanda figured out that Mila would only sit where she was certain to be served by a white person. And then, as if to personally rectify all the past wrongs of apartheid right there in the restaurant, she would set out to torture the server.

"Where is the food?" Mila asked once, five minutes after ordering. "Is it being born?"

"No one had to kill the cow to make this steak," she snapped another time to the manager. "It's so tough, it must have died naturally. Of thirst."

During their conversations, Amanda would try to glean information about her new friend's childhood, and the snippets she did get were fascinating. Mila didn't have a father. She had no education. Her name used to be Esther; she'd changed it so her family up north wouldn't track her down later. (They did anyway.) She met Josephat while working a desk at a political conference. And she was the most glamorous person Amanda had ever known.

"Where did you get that outfit?" Amanda asked breathlessly each time Mila arrived.

"Oh, someone made it for me," Mila would always say with a wave of her hand. If Amanda pressed, Mila said she would send her the name of the tailor, but of course she never did.

Sometimes Mila would talk about her husband. Amanda had never met Josephat, as he never did school pickup himself. But one day he happened to walk into the courtyard of Stellenbosch as they were finishing up their oxtail and Greek salads. He was a formidable figure, tall and built like an American football player. Amanda must dress him, Amanda mused, as she looked at his tailored suit and gleaming shoes. The effect of the beautiful clothes on his husky frame was splendid.

In a completely unexpected moment of vulnerability, Mila grabbed her husband's hand. "Join us, Josephat."

Man, Amanda thought. The way she looks at him. I wish I still looked at Mark like that.

"Sorry, darling, I've got Reginald over there," he said, patting her shoulder. "I'll see you back at the house. Nice to meet you, Amanda."

Mila, obviously hurt, avoided Amanda's eyes.

"He seems great," Amanda said, trying to smooth over the awkward silence. "Hey, would you guys ever like to get together for a playdate? Like, we hang out as couples while the kids play?"

Mila was horrified. "Watch the children . . . *play?*" she said incredulously. "Amanda. I cannot think of anything more dull. We do not *organize* things around our children. That's awful."

And yet. Mila seemed interested in her problems. She would sit across from Amanda, her cappuccino or champagne sitting untouched on the table as she listened calmly, hands folded, to Amanda's neurotic drivel:

"I know sex is important to a marriage, but let's just say my interest was drying up already. In Namibia, I've become Sossusvlei. Should I make myself go there?"

Or:

"My God, Mila, I'm dying of boredom just listening to myself. How do you do it? I need a fucking job."

When Amanda was done, Mila would take a sip, sit back, and say something like:

"A jackal would eat its foot over being chained."

"Right," Amanda would say. "Right. But wait. What does that mean?"

"Your daughter is ready to grow. Give her room."

Mila told Amanda calmly that she had to have sex at least once a week if she wanted to be married. That sometimes it is a job to have no job. That we were all getting there, to the same place at different times, and she needed to enjoy the time she had with her husband and child. She said the word *enjoy* with delicious languidness, as if the very vowels were ripe peaches to be savored.

"You're an oracle," Amanda said, after a second glass of wine.

Mila smiled. "I am glad to have a new friend." And then, to the closest white waiter around, "You, there. This coffee is *far* from hot, my friend."

In fact, the more she got to know Mila, the more interested Amanda was in Meg and Taimi's friendship. At first she'd just been thankful that Meg *had* a friend, period. But today she was shamelessly eavesdropping as the girls sprawled on the trampoline, pointing at fake servants.

"Pick up that garbage!" Taimi shouted at someone invisible.

"And bring me my gown!" Meg echoed, a bit less stridently.

At first Amanda had thought something was wrong because they were yelling, but when she took Meg aside, her daughter just rolled her eyes at the interruption and spoke to her in a tone she used only to express the utmost disdain.

"Mom. We're playing Rich Lady," she said. "Of *course* we have servants."

Amanda decided to shelve the lecture on class and society for another time. She looked at the clock. Three o'clock. Time in Namibia did not exactly fly by. The truth was, she needed more to do. Guarding a rhino was nothing short of ridiculous, but—in the absence of anything else—maybe it wasn't. What was so great about making phone apps, anyway? Why had she thought herself so important a year ago? Money? Why were rhinos any different?

She slid her laptop over the counter in front of her and did a quick google.

In 2016, 1,054 rhinos were poached in South Africa. More than three per day.

Rhino horn has been fetching prices as high as US$50,000 per kg.

Professional poachers have prior access to information about the farm they intend to target. They use tranquilizer guns, helicopters, and high caliber weapons.

Many poachers have had military training.

"Military training?" Amanda said out loud. Jesus. What was she getting herself into?

The double beep that notified her of a car coming into the gate rousted her from her online session. It was Mark, back from a research trip. She closed the laptop and ambled out into the driveway. Mark rolled down the window. Amanda was struck by her husband's tan, which brought out the warmth in his eyes. It was good for him to go away, she thought. Otherwise her daily annoyance with her new life got in the way of realizing just how appealing he was.

"That bad in there?" he asked.

"What do you mean?"

"It's just you've never met me in the driveway before."

"Oh. Well, I . . . missed you."

Mark looked surprised, and Amanda felt a rush of guilt. She knew she wasn't affectionate enough. Sometimes she was so cold, she bordered on frigid. What would Mila do? she wondered, then leaned through the window and kissed him.

"Taimi's over for a playdate, though. So, yeah, maybe I did need a little air."

"Well. Cheer up. I stopped at that weird shop on Nelson Mandela and got us a fancy bottle of Shiraz." Mark held up the bottle with one hand and opened the car door with the other. Only, as soon as he stepped out, he tripped. Amanda heard the shattering of glass and saw her husband on the ground, purple wine seeping out from under him.

"Shit," he said. "See what happens when I try and do something nice? How do I manage to fuck everything up?"

"It's okay," Amanda said automatically. Though she couldn't help thinking it was a fair question: Why *did* Mark fuck everything up? And how could she possibly save their marriage when she was so damned annoyed by him all the time?

"We have plenty of wine," she said feebly.

"Yeah, but this was from Drakensberg. I picked it out after hearing this guy drone on and on about varietals—"

"Where's Drakensberg? Germany?"

"I thought we could drink it and then . . . I don't know . . ."

"Run naked through sprinklers?"

Mark smiled at her in a surprisingly tender manner. Were his eyes misting over? Oh God, and she'd been such a bitch lately. She was immersed suddenly in an entire new onslaught of guilt.

"That was fun," he said softly. It had been the night of their wedding at a plantation outside of Charleston, after the last of the guests had staggered home. Having already overused the honeymoon suite and all of its tubs, sinks, and surfaces, they'd been sitting out on the balcony wrapped in sheets when the sprinklers suddenly shot on. The smell of the water hitting the grass, the percussive *shushing*, had awoken something in them both.

"Let's go," Mark had said.

Let's go. Mark used to always say that, and she had blindly followed. But he never seemed to anymore. Because where would they go? Back in time?

"Thanks for reminding me of that," Mark said. "I've had a really shitty day."

"I'm sorry. I'll make you a martini or something," she said, but neither of them moved. "We could still do the drunken sex part, you know."

"Now?"

Amanda bit her lip. Once a week! Mila had commanded. Okay, then.

She grabbed Mark's bag and went to the kitchen. Forgoing the drama of martinis, she poured two vodkas over ice, with a little extra for good luck. Then she unlocked the device drawer and took the iPad into Meg's room.

"One *Littlest Pet Shop*," she said. "That's it."

Taimi smiled. "Thank you for letting us enjoy video entertainment, Mrs. Evans. May I have some juice?"

"Meg, go get Taimi some juice. Mommy and Daddy are doing some work. We'll be out in a little bit."

She went into the bedroom and locked the door to find Mark already naked and waiting under the sheet. He had been doing that lately, and it made her want to jump out of the window. Was it the clinical nature of it? Or the presumption? Amanda took a long draw from her drink.

"Always wear shorts, okay?" Mark said, running his hand up her thigh. "Like, every day. Even when you go back to work."

"I guess if Zuckerberg can wear a hoodie, I can wear running shorts." Through the wall, they could hear the prattle of a preteen cartoon. *Oh my God, I am so going to take Fluffy down before the Big Finale . . .*

"That doesn't sound like PBS Kids." Mark always forbade all media, except in emergencies, which this sort of was. And if he did allow Meg to watch, then it was supposed to be quality public television programming or something archaic and charming like, say, *National Velvet.*

"Yeah, I let them watch trash," she said. "They're eating candy and drinking rum. What are you going to do about it, Officer?"

"Come here, beautiful." As he pulled her onto the bed, she cringed a little. "I love you, you know," he whispered.

Oh God. She should just drop it. Mila would drop it. She couldn't, though.

"Why are you naked already?" she blurted. "Don't you think that takes the . . . throw-down out of it?"

He looked at her blankly. "I don't know. I was hot. The bed looked nice. What?"

"But what about foreplay?"

"You never want foreplay."

"Yes, I do."

"No, you don't. You always just want to get to the sex part."

"Only at night. When I'm tired."

"I can put my clothes back on, if you want."

"No, that's okay. We only have one *Littlest Pet Shop*," Amanda pulled off her shirt and shorts and got in next to him.

Once they fell into their motions, she had to admit they had pretty good sex. She still loved Mark's rower's body; it was softer now, but she could still excavate the former version with her hands. He knew she liked it with him on top, moving up and down slowly so that she could press the headboard with her hands and rock herself back and forth until she came. They didn't always do it that way. She thought of herself as a generous lover—though her patience had waned with age—so she would still (occasionally) bend over a couch or flip Mark over so that she was on top, causing her breasts to bounce in the way that he liked. Yet those couplings always felt like a show to her. Actually, they were a show, she thought now. She never came when they had sex that way, but she'd pretend she did, so as not to disappoint him.

Is that normal? she wondered now, before she actually did come. Do all women pretend sometimes? Do all marriages require acting? Or does it mean our relationship is dead?

She knew who would have the best answer. Mila. She would ask her the next time they had lunch.

They ate outside, under Mark's favorite tree. Taimi had informed them that her father's assistant wouldn't be fetching her until eight, so the little girl joined them to make an unfamiliarly even table. Amanda liked this, having four at dinner. She had always wanted a second child, and Mark had always wanted another, but no baby had ever materialized, so that seemed to be that.

They'd already downed plenty of vodka, but she went ahead and made the martinis anyway. They had tagliatelle with pesto and a Caprese salad she'd made earlier. For the moment, she was doing the very best she could to pretend Namibia didn't exist.

"Thank you for this lovely food," Taimi said as she sat down. "And let us thank God as well."

"Good idea," said Mark.

"And Jesus."

"Now you're going a little far." Mark spooned the tagliatelle onto the girls' plates.

"It is *green*," Taimi said, looking at it curiously. "Is there no meat?"

"Not tonight," Amanda said. "This is Italian."

"We're going skiing in Italy next year," the little girl stated.

"Wow. So what does your mother like to cook?" Mark asked.

"My mother does not cook."

"Your dad?" Meg asked.

"The maid." Taimi swirled the pasta onto her spoon and pushed it into her mouth. "Strange color. Hmmm. Yet this is very delicious. Yes, I *do* say so." Taimi nodded with curt approval.

Mark looked over at Amanda with slightly raised eyebrows. "So, looks like you girls worked everything out, eh?"

"Dad," Meg hissed. "We don't want to *talk* about it."

"Sit up straight," Mark said. Meg's face grew red with frustration. "And pull your chair in."

"Mr. Evans, we did indeed get through our differences. I am no longer angry that your daughter struck me in the face."

Meg giggled. "Nice one."

"Don't talk with your mouth full."

"And how was the crime scene?" Amanda asked, trying to remember the German thing he had to investigate.

"What?" Mark's tone was so sharp, all three of them snapped to attention.

"The statue or whatever."

"Oh." Mark scowled and looked at his plate. "It's not that bad. Just vandalized by some rightfully pissed-off Nama kids."

"The minister of health is from the Nama tribe," Taimi said, her mouth full of pesto. "He has a very nice villa. I like their swimming pool. It is on the roof."

"Ah," Mark said. "Taimi, I forgot that we are dining with a minister's daughter."

"Indeed. My father is the minister of transportation. In charge of all of the roads."

"Very nice. I'd love to talk to him." Mark looked at Amanda. "I wonder if he could do anything about the damned Boer drivers."

"Dollar," Meg said. She leaned in toward Taimi. "They have to give me a dollar every time they swear."

"Swearing is untoward and common," Taimi said.

"I agree, Taimi," Amanda said. She turned back to Mark. "So what were you doing, exactly?"

"Talking to people. Research. About the damned Nama holocaust."

"Dollar," Meg said.

Taimi sat up straighter. "What holocaust? That sounds untoward also. I will ask my father to address this."

"What does *untoward* mean?" Meg asked.

"Bad," Amanda said.

"That's okay, Taimi," Mark said, looking a little nervous. "We should let your father focus on transport."

"He *is* very powerful," Taimi said sagely.

"Must be a good feeling."

"And he has a mistress."

"I thought we were done talking about mistresses," Amanda said quickly, knowing that it was impossible that any man married to Mila would ever have one.

"I want to be a mistress," Meg said. "Like Mistress Bonfamille in *The Aristocats*. She has a huge house in Paris and the cats all have their own beds."

"Her name is Madame," Taimi said. "I just saw that movie."

"I want to be a madame, then."

"*The Aristocats* is quality entertainment," Mark said. "I would watch that with you. What do you say?"

"We're going to play," Meg answered flatly. "May we be excused?"

"Not until you clean your plate and eat a tomato," Mark said.

"Dad," Meg said. "I have a guest."

"Tomato."

"I have eaten all of my tomatoes," Taimi said. "Though I think this practice is somewhat cruel. What if her tummy is full?"

"What—"

Amanda reached over, plucked the tomato off Meg's plate, and popped it in her mouth. "Go," she said.

Mark shook his head as the girls pattered away and shut the door to Meg's room.

"Mandi. Why do you *do* that? You undermine me every time."

"No, I don't."

"You do. Now you're the nice one. And I'm the asshole. Again. She doesn't even like me these days. I can't even get her to watch a damned movie with me."

"Her friend's over." She began to pine for slightly more vodka. "Just let her be."

"Excuse me," Taimi said. Amanda and Mark turned to see the girl standing there, looking at them with wide eyes. "May we please have some juice?"

"No juice," Mark said. "Too much sugar too late at night."

"Christ." Amanda sighed. "Just let her have the fucking juice."

"Oh my," Taimi said. "I believe you owe Meg one dollar, per your swearing game. That makes three. If that is U.S. currency, that would be about three hundred and sixty Namibian. My father taught me to convert."

"We mean Namibian dollars, Taimi. Here." Mark dug into his pocket and handed the little girl the coins. "Put it in the jar. When's your mom coming to pick you up?"

"I believe she'll send the driver. Eight o'clock."

"Okay, well, go get your juice. And tell Meg we're watching *The Aristocats*."

"That will be very enjoyable," Taimi said. She looked at Amanda expectantly. "Glasses, please?"

Amanda poured them two crystal glasses of juice—stemware Mark never let Meg use. As they watched Taimi disappear down the hall, Mark got up and cleared his plate.

"I just can't help feeling that you hate it here," he said. "That you hate *me* for bringing you here."

"I don't hate you. And I don't hate it here, actually. It's . . ." Amanda glanced down at the pool, where a pair of frogs seemed to be fornicating. She got up and leaned against a pillar. "Okay. I do hate it here. But mostly I just feel stuck, you know? I miss my job. I miss American things. Going to the store and buying miso."

"Miso?" He threw his plate into the sink with a clatter and came back out onto the veranda.

"Shut up. I'm here. *We're* here. For you. So just . . . please tell me you're making great strides on your book. Please."

"I am!"

"Can I read it?"

"Look," Mark said, his cheeks flushing. "Look. Life is not terrible, okay? You get to live like this"—Mark gestured to the house—"and live in a fascinating place."

Amanda groaned. "Do you notice that's what everyone calls Namibia? 'Fascinating'? It's like calling the weird sister 'interesting.'"

"Well, I happen to think it's gorgeous. I'm just saying, I've never heard you be a whiner before, Mandi."

"Because you took everything away from me!" Amanda burst out. The vodka had firmly taken hold of them both. "I never wanted to be this person, this . . . *carpooling* woman who sits around waiting for her kid to get done with lessons! I went to business school, for Christ's sake. And it's not like we're so flush, either. We should be putting money away for Meg's college, and I'm just *sitting* here."

Amanda hadn't been looking at Mark as she had delivered her alcohol-induced soliloquy; she'd been peering at the garden, trying to come up with the words that would make him understand they needed to go home. So when she heard the sound of the metal chair toppling over, she could only think he'd tripped again. But as she turned to look at him in the darkness, the chair was still skittering across the terrace from being kicked, and her husband, her mild-mannered, adorable husband, had both fists clenched and was looking at her like he might want to kill her.

"You've got to be fucking *kidding* me," he said quietly, his voice quavering. "You see the way people live here? How people die here easily as flies? And you're complaining about fucking *miso*."

Amanda took a step back. Was she really afraid of her husband? "I'm allowed to say how I feel."

"Not when it makes you sound like an insensitive bigot!"

"*What?*"

Mark spun away sharply, running his hands through his hair. He was taking the time he needed to calm down again. She knew this because she'd lived with him for so long she'd memorized his every gesture. Which was why something was very off here, this unexpected outburst. She could feel it.

"Is something wrong?" she asked quietly. "Is the book not happening? Because if we need money——"

"Look, the money thing will work out," Mark said.

"What? How?"

"Maybe I'll get a raise. Or more fellowship money. Look, I've got this, Mandi. Just, please have some faith in me."

Amanda looked at her husband. The wide shoulders, still intact, but losing shape; the coffee-colored eyes, slightly bloodshot. She wanted to believe him, she really did. But the thing was, she'd never had blind faith in anything. First one mother had abandoned her, and then another had died. Had her father had his way, she'd be a spinster right now, serving him Hamburger Helper. No, she was used to making things happen herself. It was something she'd mentioned to Mila once, during one of their wine-soaked conversations.

"The woman has to be in charge," Amanda had said. "Or the woman figure, in a same-sex partnership."

"Amanda," Mila said, wineglass poised. "What are you talking about? Woman figure?"

"I mean in a gay marriage . . ."

Mila waved her hand. "Don't talk about that. You don't know about that. I'm not . . . what do you call it . . . correct. *Politically*. You're saying in a marriage, the woman must be in charge."

"Right. But she needs to make the man—ugh, I sound so fifties housewife."

Mila shook her head, not understanding. "She needs to make the man what?"

"The wife needs to make the man *think* he is in charge. Like, make him think all the ideas were really his. When they're really yours."

"Of course," Mila said, finally satisfied. "Every woman in Africa knows that."

"Every woman?" Amanda asked, in that pseudo-academic way Mark did. "Aren't you generalizing just a little, Mila?"

"No," Mila said. "I am not generalizing, Amanda. Every woman in Africa knows that. The man must think the ideas are his. It is our job to fool them."

Amanda looked at Mark now. Every woman in Africa, Mila had said.

"Okay, Mark," she said. "I have faith in you. Take it away."

"Thank you," he said, then vanished into the dark garden, far beyond the trees.

14

Josephat himself had advised Mila to befriend the Americans. Yet when asked if she could invite her new acquaintances, along with their families, to his prized property in the Erongo, the answer was a flat no.

"It's too dangerous, Mila," he said now, looking at his phone. The Shilongos were on a family outing to CamelThorn, Windhoek's most popular plant nursery. Because only shrubs grew in the barren ground surrounding Windhoek, plant nurseries almost always housed other businesses—cafés, boutiques, spas, and, in this case, a huge playground with real grass.

"But why?" she asked, willing him to look up. As usual, the plant nursery was packed. Windhoek residents would pay any fee to be somewhere near anything green. The first time they'd brought Taimi here when she was two, the grass looked so succulent to her she'd gotten down on her knees to lick the ground.

"We don't want diplomats in our private home," he murmured, continuing to scroll.

"Why not? There's nothing untoward happening at Osha. We bought it with our own money. What could happen?"

Josephat breathed a sigh of annoyance and looked up at last. "It's too grand, Mila. People know we have a lot, but not *how* much."

"That's the point," she said, taking his hand. "It's grand. *We* are grand, Jo. See? Namibia is not nowhere. It's a place where two people can grow up with nothing and become *us*."

"I don't like it." He gently took his hand back and folded his arms, watching as Taimi and her little friend Meg jumped up and down on a bouncy castle, then abandoned it because of the burning surface of the plastic. "How did this even come about?"

"Well, they have this rhino protection program, and I thought, how perfect." Mila could feel her mood spiraling downward. She had worn a new blouse, handmade out of Ovambo pink fabric. The old Ovambo dresses of home were just tents with holes for the arms and head, but this shirt was a copy of one she had by an American designer, Marc what-what-what. The sophisticated cut combined with the simple nature of the material was meant to be a statement on the present government's progress. Josephat loved clothes; he relished her outfits when they were correct, admonished her when they weren't. And here, she had designed this wearable treatise on Namibian politics for *him*. The order had to be altered twice; the whole thing was six months in the making. And he hadn't so much as noticed it—though every other man in this wretched place had.

"I invited them that day you snubbed me at lunch," she said now.

"I didn't snub you," he replied, shrugging. "I had a meeting."

"I'm your wife. Sometimes you could choose me over business."

"Mila," Josephat said soothingly, finally putting his arm around her shoulders. He glanced around, making sure people noticed. They did, of course. People noticed every move the Shilongos made. "The meetings I take, they're for us. Our family. You know that. I just don't think this rhino business would help us."

"Maybe I want to help a rhino," Mila said. She realized her mood was dangerous, but she didn't care. "I don't mind making you look good to cover up whatever you're doing. But I do have a conscience, Josephat. I happen to believe in anti-poaching measures."

He took his arm back, moving away from her. "Whatever I'm doing? Mila. Please. You of all people know exactly what I'm doing. Also, I've never known you to be much of an animal lover. I wish I'd known before I had the boys shoot that oryx for you."

"*You* told me to make friends with the American."

Her husband smiled at a pair of mothers who were throwing

admiring glances his way. "No one is really your friend unless they are related to you," he said.

"Well, I *like* her," Mila said. "Amanda Evans. So I invited her. And while we're on the topic, Adam Wilder's wife is coming, too."

"What?" Josephat took hold of her arm a little too tightly and led her to a bench that had opened up in the shade. "That one I *know* you detest."

"I tolerate her. The way I tolerate a lot of things." She followed his lead and sat down. She hated bickering with Josephat. He was the one thing she loved in the world, other than her children. It threw her very center off-kilter.

"All right. I suppose this all can happen, as long as Adam Wilder doesn't come. He's all right as far as embassy work . . . the arrangement makes us look good. But something is off about him, Mila. He absolutely cannot see Osha."

"Fine," Mila relented. "I'll make sure he doesn't come."

"Look at how elegant Taimi is," Josephat said, changing the subject. "Much prettier than that white girl. Though I don't like what my daughter is wearing. She is too old for short pants."

"All the girls wear them, Josephat," Mila said, sitting up straighter so as to be in his view. "Do you like what I am wearing?"

"Rhinos," Josephat mused, pulling out his phone again. "All of the foreigners are so worried about rhinos. How about kudu? Poached by the hundreds. Or wildebeests? Are they out of fashion? What about the kids dying of hunger in the south? Are they not adorable because they don't have big fat horns?"

"That's not what the American ladies are focused on." Mila sighed. "They want to save rhinos. They adopt one, or some what-what-what. They plan to camp near it and make certain no one pesters it."

A waitress came out, bringing them two rooibos teas and a huge piece of Afrikaans cake. Josephat pointed at the table, indicating that she should set the tray there. He never bothered with speaking to servants.

In fact, the purchase of Osha had been a necessity. Three years before, the Shilongos found themselves with entirely too much cash.

Josephat had always been careful about kickback payments from companies to whom he awarded building contracts; the installments were never too big and never came all at once. They were always diverted through one colleague or another's business—for a fee, of course. Then a new Chinese company he'd started working with dumped millions into his Swakop account. He'd transferred the money to Mila in a day, but still it made him nervous.

And then his lawyer, Reginald, who had just taken a job as one of the president's many legal counselors, had told him about Osha. Previously known as Steinveld, the forty thousand hectares had been a grand German farm established during the sixties, when the South African government issued low-interest loans to landowners to make land purchases attractive. Except these particular Germans, it turned out, were children of hardcore Nazi émigrés. They hadn't been willing to pay even the three percent interest, they told the bank, because they found the very concept of interest "Jewish." In the end, the Namibian government had simply seized the property, and Josephat plunked down his offending cash to buy it.

Osha was the Shilongos' crown jewel. None of the other ministers had a farm this far south. And it was grand. A castle-like farmhouse built with thick walls in a sensible German style that even at midday barred the searing heat. There had been no pool, as such pleasantries on remote farms were purely a South African invention. Well, Mila quickly had one built. There was plenty of housing for caretakers' quarters, along with the land, already stocked with exotic game. Not to mention a barn full of Nazi paraphernalia, highly illegal in modern Namibia, which Mila was still figuring out what to do with.

"Can't you just uninvite them?" Josephat said now. "I'm sorry, but I must bring this up again. The Americans don't have the best reputation right now. Something about the president urinating on a bed."

"I can't. It is too late. Anyway, look at these two, they are like sisters. Just look at them."

The Shilongos looked over at Meg and Taimi, who, having played themselves into exhaustion, were now lying together, feeding each other melted ice cream under the playground's biggest tree.

In fact, Mila had grown truly fond of Amanda Evans. Perhaps it was the American woman's honesty, or the fact that she had done most of the question-asking. Or maybe it was that Amanda sought out advice and help in a way that her proud sisters never would. Or maybe it was the simple yet unsolvable nature of Amanda's issue. Her husband was clearly failing her.

The sun had gotten unbearable, even in the deep shade. It had reached the time of day when the only thing to do was to retreat inside to your air-con, if you could afford it, or to whatever part of your home had the thickest walls and the most powerful fan or swamp cooler. Even Josephat, her ever-crisp husband, was wilting. He dabbed his brow with a starched handkerchief, one of many he stashed in various pockets and, just to be safe, in Mila's purses, where they were wrapped in Ziploc bags to keep their laundered scent fresh.

"What shall we do with them?" Mila said, a bit hopelessly. All she wanted was for Josephat to come home with her. Sit in the living room, watch the big TV, hips touching. Holding hands, maybe. She so wanted, once more, to feel loved. "Shall we go home for lunch?"

Please, she thought.

"I have a meeting, darling."

"Really?" Mila kept her voice down and a smile on her face. "You're going to Reginald's? Today?" She watched him run his finger around the top of his teacup. When they'd gotten together all those years ago, she'd known he was impervious to her beauty. It was one of the things that had attracted her to him. She'd been working the desk at a SWAPO conference—a temporary job, which was all she could get back then—and he had been impressed with how she'd handled the long line of needy delegates. He'd been so businesslike when he asked her to lunch, she'd thought it was a job interview. But no, he'd wanted to know more about her, he said. Though, in the end, she thought, it was a job interview. He'd been on a search for the perfect government wife.

Mila often thought about how lucky she was, to have been found by Josephat. She'd been so adrift then, after the loss of her sister, that anything could have happened. Instead, she'd struck a bargain with this up-and-coming SWAPO star. She knew he didn't love her passionately—not the way other men had. But he was a human promise. She would never have to go back to menial labor, she would always have enough to eat and a clean bed.

In fact, as time went on it was clear that Mila would be wealthy beyond anything she could have imagined. But he was becoming so secretive. It made her lonely. And in terms of business, well, it had been a long time since she knew what he was into. Mila had been Josephat's accomplice in concealing several large bribes in the past, but now he was involved in far bigger schemes, deals she had no idea about.

Mila's phone rang. Josephat fished it out of her bag, at the same time fetching himself another handkerchief.

"It's Anna," he said. Their oldest daughter. He answered the phone. "Hello, sweets."

Mila watched him carefully. Anna had come with the marriage; Josephat had adopted her legally after the ceremony. This, Mila was painfully aware, could have gone either way. They hadn't much money then, but as a father, he had spoiled the little girl with love. She looked nothing like Josephat, but anyone who might have questioned her paternity would quickly dismiss such thoughts upon seeing the way Josephat doted on the baby. He even changed her nappies, though certainly not in front of other Ovambo men.

Once Anna was in their lives, Josephat had insisted on conceiving another child, one of his own. For some reason, it took years to produce a child. But sure enough, ten years later, Taimi had arrived, and Josephat finally had what he wanted: a real family.

Mila leaned in to listen to what her husband was saying to her older daughter, who lived in Walvis Bay. He was shaking his head.

"I already sent this month's allowance," he said. "Anna. You must learn responsibility."

Mila frowned. Anna hadn't had the advantages Taimi had of a private school education and a privileged childhood. They had still been struggling when Anna was a little girl, with no money for nannies, and often Anna was toted along on trips to Congress meetings and conferences. After graduating from Windhoek High, Anna showed no interest in university—even U Nam. She wanted to get practical experience in the tourism agency, she told them. Besides, neither Mila nor Josephat had gone to college, and look how things had turned out. After years of Anna living in their house and arguing with them, Josephat found a job for her at the Strand in Swakop and set her up with an allowance.

"Give me the phone," Mila said. Josephat relented and handed it over. "Anna?"

"I called to talk to Dad, not you."

"Why are you out of money already?"

"Mom, I told you both, I'm starting a jewelry line."

"Jewelry is a hobby. Hotels at least are a career."

"A career? In your case the hotel was just a place to meet the man who would save you."

"Don't you—"

"Mila," Josephat hissed. Taimi and Meg were both looking at her, ears pricked. "Keep your voice down."

"Anna," she said slowly, "you must make do until April first. Do your work and stay out of the clubs." Mila hung up the phone, shaking her head. "Cheeky."

"I don't like her not having money," Josephat said.

"Don't even think about sending any, Josephat."

Josephat sat back on the bench, relenting. "All right." He stood up, smoothing his Italian skinny jeans. "I'll take you home, and then I really must go."

Six thousand dollars NAD. That was the tuition for one year at the new university in Windhoek. Everyone was talking about it, the big new college outside of Pioneerspark built by the government as soon as independence took hold. A grand new Namibian institution, established expressly to fill the black hole in schooling left by apartheid. The buildings were big and shiny and filled with foreign teachers, and if you graduated you could get a real job, whether you were a man or a woman. Namibia was opening up, new companies were coming in from Europe and China and America, diamond miners and mineral companies and tourist businesses of all sorts. The government even paid most of the fees for tuition and housing, but it was up to the students' families to find six thousand. And between them, at the Oshakati Country Hotel, Esther and Saara made just four hundred and twenty per week.

It was clear to Esther, now that they had been living together in the same tiny, hot room for two years, that her sister Saara was more than clever. She read every book in the "library" of castoffs left by travelers, both in English and Afrikaans, then read them again. She helped up in the front office with the accounting, building mind-bending spreadsheets that magically calculated how to save money on supplies and groceries for the café, how to charge more for little services like towels and breakfast to up the bottom line. On top of it all, Saara sang like a bird, often taking on night shifts in the café performing with JoJo, who played guitar. On those evenings, she called herself Amber, so that Mrs. Van Wyk, who hadn't darkened the door of any eating establishment since apartheid ended, would never hear about it.

Saara was crafty as a businesswoman as well. For one thing, she made herself indispensable, learning the accounting books backward and forward, better than anyone else. When, inevitably, she was put in charge of procurement, Esther's sister was able to buy soap and potatoes in bulk, sell a bit on the side for extra money, and still come in with a huge savings for the business.

If Mrs. V.W. suspected foul play, she didn't admit it. "I don't mind trusting the Blacks," she often said. "No Black is smart enough to fool me."

Everyone liked Saara. Her presence was happy and light, her jokes smart and cutting. "God gave you the face of a goddess and me the brain of a cat," she said one night as she played cards with Esther on the floor. "If only we were melded into one."

"You're just as pretty as I am," Esther said.

"The fact that you are saying that only proves what I'm saying about your brain."

"If you went to school," Esther said, carefully switching the subject, "would you study accounting? Or literature?"

"I'd study it all, you giraffe," Saara said, laughing, and Esther knew her little sister simply had to go.

But four-twenty a week, with an extra two hundred Saara sometimes brought in. And four hundred out again for food and washing, as the hotel didn't feed them and charged them to launder their clothes. They had to do something. They had to make a plan.

And she had to do it soon. Girls like Saara, clever girls with nothing who worked at hotels, who lived too close to the riches of others, who were constantly made to touch the clean white sheets slept in by wealthy tourists, who daily witnessed the way the privileged were able to look nonchalantly at a loaded buffet table of food and walk away with one piece of bacon, those girls were not able to be patient long. Esther was smart enough, but she would be happy to work quietly at the hotel until something nice happened, perhaps a marriage to a good man or a slightly better job at a business down the street. Already Mrs. V.W. had promoted her to the front desk because of her looks; more things would probably happen soon. But Saara didn't want to wait. She was constantly using her big mind to scheme, to plan.

"If I get Mrs. V.W. fired, maybe I'll be in charge, hey," she said one morning, braiding her hair intricately and peering out the tiny window at the parking lot. "I can make it look like she stole some money by fooling with the checks and the banks."

"You can't get anyone fired," Esther scolded. "Please. This is our job. This is where we live. Don't mess with the hotel."

It was about this time, just when Saara was beginning to move on from drinking beer to Four Roses, just when she was beginning to show up to the accounting office, with its lazy, beating fan and pictures of Jesus pinned to the wall, so sloppy and reeking of booze Mrs. V.W. put them both on probation, that the American came to Oshakati.

That's what everyone called him. The American, otherwise known as the young, tall man with the brown hair and the fancy trainers who spent his days at the clinic. The American, it seemed, thought he blended, what with his volunteer job where he sat with sick patients, and his meager little shack. But everyone knew who he was. An American! Here! In Oshakati! the aunties crowed at the shebeens and grocery corners. Who is tall and looks like he is from television! Who wears glasses that make him look like an owl! Who in real life probably lives in a house with a piano and marble floors and has Popsicles every day!

The maids at the Oshakati Country Hotel, including Saara, knew everything about him. He had his own bungalow near the Pick n Pay. He didn't have a gate or a dog, but he padlocked his door when he left the house. He went to the post office every day, sending letters and packages. He ran on the tar road in the morning, usually with a trail of boys following him. He didn't live like an Afrikaner. He was friendly. He tried to invite people in for tea. He said he wanted to learn more about their country.

"Our country!" the aunties said, laughing. Well, no one came to tea. Everyone knew this was a trick. How many times had Ovambos seen these volunteers who came for a year, befriended you, and pretended to be like you? They insisted they understood. They said they were your friends. They let you cook for them and gave you oranges and their running shoes and drank with your father and bedded your sisters or even sometimes your brothers. They would promise plane tickets, jobs in America, all sorts of things they could never actually give you. Then they would go back to their air-conditioning and mountains of food and never write you back.

Still, word was this American was polite. Mrs. Solumbe, the laundress, invited him over after church, and he brought her a month's worth of groceries. He drank, but not too much. He was helping at the hospital, and he had sat with the Angolan boy while he was dying after being run over by a tractor.

No one was surprised when he began coming to the café every day to stare at Esther. She already had a group of admirers kept at bay by JoJo. It was a fine line; JoJo wanted them to come to the café to ogle his waitress, but if she took up with any of them, it would be bad for business.

"Don't worry," Esther said. "I'm not interested." Her beauty had become a hindrance. She wanted a nice man, not someone who hung about drinking all day. She wasn't stupid enough to be a foreigner's slut. Nothing good ever happened to those girls. Sometimes they had mixed babies no one would accept; other times they went back to their villages, scoffed at and shamed. As the café was the hub of town; she'd had a front-row seat to more than one example of ruin.

Saara, though, was not as careful. She noticed the American the first day he came to the café, and positioned her body his way, singing just for him. When she saw that he only had eyes for Esther, she drank her way into the night and took it out on her sister.

"Of course he only wants *you*," she spat. Her skimpy dress was covered in stains. "They always want the pretty stupid one."

Esther was growing tired of Saara's rants. It was four in the morning, and she had to work at the desk at six. Though Oshakati Country Hotel was in town, it butted against the grasslands. She could hear the mosquitoes and the hornbills outside, preparing their morning warm-ups. "I'm not stupid enough to think his attention can do anything for me."

"What about us?" Saara cried. "Do you know how easy it would be for him to give you two thousand NAD? That's probably what he pays for one of those trainers he wears."

"*You* go after him, then," Esther mumbled.

Saara shook her head and put her shoes back on.

"Where are you going?" Esther asked.

"I'm getting more Four Roses from JoJo."

"Please," Esther begged. "You have to be at the office at eight.

Mrs. V.W. says the books aren't up-to-date. She was going on about you yesterday."

"She can't fire me, Esther. She doesn't know how to do anything by herself."

"She ran the place before we got here, Saara," she said, suddenly very tired. But her sister had already left.

Later that morning, Esther was at the desk at six. She was exhausted, but her uniform was pressed and her hair was clean. She concentrated on checking out the guests who were moving on that morning, her eyes burning as she looked at the numbers. The desk was busy, and the hours went mercifully quickly. Then, a little before lunch, she heard Mrs. V.W. screaming in the back.

"You get out of here, you thief! And take your slutty sister with you! You kaffirs, you can't help but steal, hey? Get the hell out!"

"I didn't steal anything!" Saara yelled back.

"Oh? The till's been short for days, so I marked the bills. You know where they turned up? JoJo's *wallet*. Says you paid him for liquor. Little bitch."

Esther felt the floor drop away as she watched Saara stagger out, still wearing her clothes from the night before.

"I didn't!" Saara protested, more feebly this time.

"What happened?" Esther whispered, shooting a placating smile at the guests.

"Your sister's a thief, is what happened." Mrs. V.W. swelled through the door, her mottled cheeks aflame. "You're both out. Go pack. Now."

Saara looked at Esther, tossed her head, and strutted out the front door. The only thing left for Esther to do was leave the front desk and follow. She could feel the eyes of the waiting guests on her back. Outside the gate, the birds and animals of Ovamboland were approaching their dawn crescendo. As the sisters circled behind the building to the staff dorm, fear gripped her chest, and she felt as if she might faint.

"Saara," Esther whispered. "What have you done? We have nowhere to go."

"I'll fix it," Saara said through clenched teeth as she climbed the back stairs.

"How? We have nothing. Not even our house in Onesi. Don't you know what happens to people like us?"

"I said I'd *fix* it."

But Esther had opened the door to their little room and collapsed on the mattress. Flies batted the light bulb above. She could hear the tin sounds of JoJo's cooking pots below, and the tickling fingers of hunger crept into her belly.

So this is despair, she thought as a heat worse than fever enveloped her.

Saara went down the hall to the washroom and showered, then came back and dressed. "I'll be back," she said, but Esther had turned over to face the wall. The door closed, and Saara went out. Esther stayed in bed for a long time, mostly because she had nowhere else to go. She knew JoJo would come up soon to force her out upon Mrs. V.W.'s orders. But hours passed, and nothing happened. She finally fell into a light sleep, only to startle awake when she heard footsteps outside.

"It's me," Saara said, tiptoeing in and shutting the door behind her.

"I fixed it. I told you I'd fix it." She opened her purse, and a shower of money fell out.

Esther sat up slowly. "How much is that?"

"Three thousand."

"What? Saara, if you stole that——"

"I didn't steal it." She sat on the bed next to Esther and took her hand. It had been a long time since the sisters had been this close, and Esther couldn't help feeling a tiny bit hopeful. "Look, sister. I have good news."

"How?" Esther asked, sitting up.

"The American wants to take you to the beach."

"What?" Esther moved away. "*What?*"

"He gave me the money so you'd come to the beach."

"I'm not . . . You can't pay me for that!" She gave Saara a sharp push.

"I'm not a prostitute, Saara!"

"It's not like that." Saara's face was resolute. "I'm going, too. He just wants to go on a trip."

"He's paying for our company?"

"Look," Saara said. "I said it's not like that. Esther, we're out of choices. We've got to get out of here. The American can get us to Windhoek. He gave me three thousand, and he has more. He didn't ask you to do anything. He just asked you to come."

"No," Esther said. "No. I don't like this. All he does is stare at me."

Saara's lips twisted. "He didn't ask for sex with you. Not specifically." She grabbed Esther's hands. "And he's not bad, is he? He's not old. He's not fat. You should see some of these Boers I had to—"

"I don't *want* that," Esther cried. "Oh, Saara. This was a good job." Esther put her face into her hands.

"All right." Saara stood above her, her hands on her hips. "Esther, if we don't do this, I can work for Duncan. He can give us a place to sleep tonight."

Esther's head shot up as she looked at her sister in horror. Duncan was the town pimp. His girls were forever being found beaten and dead on the outskirts of town. Sometimes they weren't found for weeks, and their bodies would be picked clean by jackals, their bones bleached by the sun.

"Duncan."

"I've already sent him a message."

"No," Esther said. She stood up and found her knapsack under the bed. "No, Saara. Go get the American. Tell him I'll go."

Back in Windhoek a lifetime later, it was now time to leave the plant nursery and go home for a family day in an estate more luxurious than that former version of herself would have dared to imagine. Except she was going alone with her daughter, because her husband, it seemed, didn't want her anymore.

"I should take a lover," Mila said suddenly.

Josephat glanced around at the other tables nearby, making sure no one had heard her. "Mila, what has gotten into you?"

Patrons were gathering their bags and blankets and drifting toward their trucks. It was Saturday, nearing one o'clock, signaling the deadest stretch of the afternoon. Already the café staff was shutting down the slushy machine and hovering near the front door with a bouquet of keys; Mila could almost hear the simultaneous crash of the iron gates slamming across the entrances to the shops throughout the city.

"Mila," Josephat said now, bringing her attention back. "Don't think I don't understand how you're feeling, my dear."

"Oh?" she said, foolishly hopeful at his kind tone.

"Yes," he said soothingly. "You're over forty. Soon men will not want you at all. I can see why that would make you angry."

Mila was so surprised it took her a moment to speak. "You think this is about my *age*?"

"Of course. But, Mila, you must get yourself together. This close friendship with an American woman? The oryx prank? The fits? I have to think you are going through your change. You're not thinking correctly." He draped his arm around her, patting her shoulder. "Go on a trip, why don't you? Take Anna to Paris."

I should fling his arm away, she thought. But it feels so very nice there, him touching me.

Oh, it was maddening. When had she become so pathetic?

"That would be the very worst thing for Anna," she finally managed. "Reward her for being spoiled?"

"Then take Taimi. Or better yet, go to the north. Visit your village and see how far you've come. And watch yourself. Just remember what happened to . . ." He stopped himself, obviously thinking better of it.

She did pull away this time, so that she could face him. "To whom, Josephat? Saara?"

"Yes," he said, finally. "You could have been Saara."

She could kill him. She *would* kill him.

"Mother?" Taimi said. "Are you quite well? You're shaking."

"I'm fine," she said, looking away from Josephat. "Mummy and Daddy are just having a disagreement. But it's over now, girls. Let's go." She let Josephat walk ahead with the girls. Dropping behind to take her phone out of her purse, she sent off a quick text to Adam Wilder, inviting him to see Osha.

God help her. She would show these men something about control.

15

Mark sat in a café in Omaruru, his back facing the street. Not that he would ever see anyone he knew in Omaruru. But then, this was Namibia, the second least populated country in the world. (People always said that, he mused. What was the very first least populated? Mongolia? Siberia?) The point was, *someone* might see him. One of those embassy people who were always chasing him for historical reports, or some college buddy, now rich as Midas, here on a luxury safari. Then Mark would have to explain just what the hell he was doing in rural Namibia, without his family, meeting up with an extremely sexy twenty-year-old with a jewelry habit.

Today was the third trip Mark had taken to meet Anna. Just as a year ago he never would have guessed he'd be hanging out alone on the veld, and he definitely never dreamed he'd be taking multiple gem-purchasing trips with a woman who wasn't his wife. But something—funny? interesting? no, strange—had happened since he'd gotten those morgue records a month before. He'd stopped giving a shit. And it was just easier not to tell his wife. But he also didn't feel that nervous. If someone as beautiful and alive as Esther could be extinguished so easily . . . well, the worst would happen eventually anyway, wouldn't it?

As fate would have it, things were actually working out. Once he'd made the oddest decision of his life and given Anna a thousand American dollars, she brought him back three thousand. He gave her back the three; she brought him nine. Now he was giving her five. It was going so well, Mark was actually beginning to hope that this easy little avenue out of the dreariness of his current profession might actually be successful.

Before returning to Namibia, he'd really tried to ignore how much he hated academia. It was a difficult thing, to admit you'd wasted twenty years of your life. But the moment he boarded that 787 to Johannesburg for the first leg of the trip, he'd felt the great weight that had been sitting on his chest for years just lift and disappear. The millstone had been there so long, he hadn't even known he was miserable. The job he had was fine; he liked teaching the kids, because he felt like one himself. Well, he didn't care about the Holocaust in France anymore. It was sad, true, and he found the stories compelling. He'd even sobbed upon reading the letters he'd come across in a French archive, handwritten notes from doomed children to their dead mothers.

But another scholar had already covered those. And yet another historian had written about the conspiracies in the 4th arrondissement, and the secret tunnels used to transport food to refugees, and the farms where Resistance heroes hid families in root cellars. There was nothing new to say, and, worse, Mark didn't care if he said it. He didn't want to read any more books on the mechanics of persecution, or persecution's long-term effects, or, actually, anything about persecution ever again. He didn't give a fuck about history. He wanted out. So he was hoping, out there as it was, that this crazy gem thing might be the answer.

Mark did run the idea by one person: Jaime. Mark loved Jaime, but he didn't really like him anymore. The red Tesla, the imported beard oil, the endless parade of young women, puffed to perfection by implants, who festooned his Instagram page . . . If Mark met his oldest friend now, he would instantly dismiss him as a douchebag. But one truly wonderful thing about this douchebag was that if you were his buddy, he backed you. Even if you called him up with a notion that would clearly lead to self-annihilation.

"Sounds so fucking Indiana Jones," Jaime had said. "I say go for it. A few thousand bucks? Chump change."

Mark hadn't corrected Jaime by telling him that a few thousand was very much *not* chump change to his family, especially since he'd insisted that Amanda leave her job and follow him here for a small government stipend. But he didn't need to tell his blatantly competitive best friend everything, did he?

Anyhow, Anna seemed to have things under control. She was much more sophisticated than her years should have allowed; her manner was all business. Their routine was to meet at the transport stop. Each time she alighted from her combi, she always looked as if she had been magically beamed from the streets of Manhattan. Heels, tight jeans, some sort of blouse in an African print. She wore her hair tied in a chic turban. She was undeniably pretty, but were anyone to approach her, she cut them to the quick. Unless, of course, you were a gem dealer. Then you had every opportunity for her attention.

Their other trips had been to Karibib and Maltahöhe in order to meet gem dealers and exchange cash. It was easy to convince Amanda he was away on research. And by now Anna and Mark had a rhythm. Mark would pick her up, then take her to lunch at whatever place in town seemed decent, usually a coffee shop at a guesthouse. Anna would inevitably look at the menu with disdain.

"No, I do not want *that*," she'd say, flicking a painted fingernail against the page. "No, I do not want *that*."

In the end she would settle on two to three large plates of food—chicken schnitzel or pasta—and wolf them down like a football player. It had been a while since Mark had been around a girl so young. He appreciated the unguarded way she devoured her food, as well as her assumption that everything in the world should be available to her.

"Look at that car," she said today as a shiny Land Rover drove past. "I'll have one of those someday."

"There's more to life than fancy cars," Mark couldn't help saying.

"Really?" Anna tilted her head. "Like what, Mr. Rich American?"

"I'm not rich."

"You had a thousand dollars in your pocket to just hand over without a problem," Anna said. "You're rich." Clearly he was just the moneyman. Which seemed fine for the moment.

"We need to go to Klein Aub now."

"What?" Mark reached for his battle-worn map. "Why?"

"We're getting some rocks polished ourselves. Claus will do it. We can sell them for more that way."

"Claus?"

"In Klein Aub, Richie. I just told you."

"Okay." He flipped the map open. "Klein Aub is, like, four hundred kilometers away."

"Four hundred kilos. That's close in Nam," she said. "Let's go."

Mark let out a sharp sigh. He wanted to press her further, but she obviously wasn't having it. They got into the car, and after punching the buttons on his radio to look for a decent station, Anna settled for a playlist on her phone. They seemed to be coming into a particularly cruel section of country; the road provided little hope, as it humped ahead, revealing more and more dust. The settlements they did pass were just clusters of crouching houses, children and chickens clawing about in the yards. As Mark drove on, the uneasy feeling in his stomach spread to his chest, then to his groin. It had been hours. He needed to pee.

"I'm making a pit stop," he said, spying some dilapidated buildings on the horizon.

"No," Anna said. "We're here." Mark glanced at her in surprise. He'd thought Klein Aub would be an actual town, but it was little more than a string of tin shacks and a low-slung school dotted with bullet holes. "There," she said, pointing to an ancient corner store. He parked in front, and they got out. His legs felt as if they were filled with plaster, and he did some quick stretches while Anna smirked. "It's not the Olympics, hey."

"I'm old," he apologized. She didn't disagree, and together they surveyed the place. The building looked as if it had once been green before being covered under decades of white dust. A man leaned in the doorway, and behind him Mark could make out the usual sundries—canned vegetables, beer, long-life milk. The only thing in the window that wasn't covered in dust was a lovingly kept royal portrait of Princess Diana in a gilt frame.

"Claus is a royalist?"

"She wore an emerald he cut, once," Anna said, starting up a rickety staircase clinging to the side of the building. "Come on. It's up here."

The stairs groaned and bent under his weight. Anna banged on the door, holding her hand out at Mark to stay back. They could hear shuffling inside, and the door creaked open.

"Goeiemiddag!" Anna crowed.

"Guten nachmittag."

"Ek het my vriend gebring."

A man emerged into the sunlight, shrunken and gray. He peered at Mark and backed inside again.

"Good, yah. Come, come."

Mark shuffled behind Anna, elbowing into the tiny space. Claus's apartment was minuscule and cramped, every surface crammed with rocks and books in German. A tattered German flag hung above the stove. Even in the dim light, Claus looked close to a hundred; Mark could only guess he had come to Namibia during World War II. He hoped Claus wasn't a Nazi. Though his research had slowed down a bit, he'd done enough to know there were plenty of bona fide ex–SS troopers in Namibia, and, even as a lapsed Jew, he didn't particularly care to hang out in the house of a Nazi all day.

The apartment smelled of decades of cooked meat; the air was so thick with it Mark could taste the char on his tongue. He claimed a wooden chair, trying his best to look like Anna's heavy. The ancient man was in no hurry. He puttered around, making tea and extracting an ancient tin of cookies. Following his initial greeting, he didn't speak again. After he had set the tea in front of them, he took the bag into a closet off the kitchen and shut the door.

For the next three hours, Anna and Mark waited, listening to the sawing sound of the polisher in the next room. Every once in a while, Claus would come out of his hole and pour himself some more tea before giving them a distracted wave and returning inside.

"Should we go for a walk or something?" Mark asked, getting up to stretch again. He did some light lunges, pumping up and down.

"This is weird, this thing you are doing," Anna said. "Can you not wait until you go gyming?"

"Gyming?"

"That's what we call it."

"We *are* gemming. Get it?"

Anna rolled her eyes and picked up her phone again.

"I used to be a coach. That's why I stretch all the time."

"I hate sport," Anna said.

"This was rowing," Mark said. "You might like it."

"I would not." She looked up at him. "Anyway, you never leave your rocks. Claus is good, but someone else might come in."

"Really? What would we even do if that happened?"

"Claus has a rifle somewhere."

"Toto," Mark muttered, "I don't think we're in Kansas anymore."

"Are you fine?" Anna looked at him dubiously.

"Sure." They were silent for a few minutes. Other than the grinder, there was only the clicking of Anna's fingernails on her phone.

"Anna, you're twenty, right?"

"Twenty-one."

"And how did you learn to do all of this?"

She tossed her phone in her bag and sat back, crossing her arms, as if resigned to the fact that at the moment there was nothing better to do than talk to Mark. "I had a boyfriend. A gem dealer."

"He got you in?"

"No. He was killed, and I got his contacts."

"He died?" Mark felt an acute prickle on the back of his neck. "From this?"

"No, Coach. Relax. He got a Boer girl pregnant, and they killed him."

"Excuse me?" This explanation wasn't making him feel any better. "Who killed who?"

"The father, we think. He's gone, hey. All his stuff was at his place, but he was gone. Even his phone was there. No one leaves their phone, not in the Location. Your phone might cost more than your house."

"So you don't *know*."

"Oh, he's dead. Or else I would have heard from him when I started using the contacts in his phone."

Mark looked out at the miles and miles of rolling sand. The prickling he'd been experiencing on the back of his neck had morphed into a burning.

"Didn't you tell the police?"

Anna smiled a bit sourly and got up to put the kettle on again.

"The other girl got his baby, and I got his gem contacts. It worked out okay."

Mark swallowed, trying to force whatever was happening to his nervous system down his throat. "Did your parents know about the boyfriend?"

Anna poured the water into the pot. "They don't know what I do." She looked at him sideways. "What about your family? They know you're here?"

"No."

"I thought so." She brought the teapot over and refilled his cup. "Why?"

Mark shook his head. "Never mind."

"A secret!" Anna said, grinning. Her smile was crooked, but she was truly lovely when she showed her teeth. She looked like a child who'd gotten away with something. "Thank God. I was beginning to think you were boring."

"I am boring."

"Not anymore. Now there's something to find out." She sat back down in her chair, looking at him. "Didn't you say you were here before? You were some kind of do-good missionary, right?"

"The Peace Corps."

"Missionaries, Peace Corps. They're all the same. White Americans, sticking out like bad thumbs."

"You mean sore. Sore thumbs."

"Sore and bad, Coachie. Why did you come back? When people leave Namibia, and they go to South Africa or America or what-what-what, they *don't* come *back*. Not if they're clever."

"I . . ." Mark paused. Behind the closed door, Claus cleared his throat violently, spat, and started up the grinder again. "Something happened. Something I had to fix."

Anna narrowed her eyes. "What?" she taunted. "Did you kill someone?"

Mark looked out the window again, biting the sorest hangnail on his thumb until it stung, then filled his mouth with the flat, metallic taste of blood.

The combi stopped, and everyone exploded out, pent up for too long in the too-hot van. Mark got the bags, and the girls swam through the heat down Nujoma Street, straining their necks to see the ocean. Amber and Esther stared at the German houses the color of icing, the restaurants with their wooden benches and polished brass signs. He followed them carrying their small sacks of clothes. He couldn't stop looking at Esther, her polished calves, at the way her hips swayed their pendulum beat.

She still wasn't talking to him; his hope was that she'd be pushed into friendliness by the sight of the sea. But it was all wrong, somehow. In fact, Esther didn't like the water at all.

"The waves are just snakes," she complained. "Look at how they whip and spit."

They sauntered down the boardwalk anyway, looking at the fishermen. The girls linked arms and walked ahead, only talking to each other. Mark was split off by the heavy burden of what he was doing there, why he was with them.

"We need a hotel," Mark said at last. His gut rolled at the very suggestion, but he was tired of carrying their bags. "We'll get two rooms. It can't be that much."

"Sure," Amber said.

"How about there?" He pointed to a huge, ornate pink building squatting next to the ocean.

Amber and Esther exchanged glances. This was independence, yes, but the Germans and Afrikaners didn't think so. There were stories, bad stories of Blacks being thrown out of high windows after checking into formerly all-white hotels.

"Ovambos stay in Walvis," Amber said. "And we can't afford that place."

"Let me just go ask. I bet it's not as much as you think."

"We cannot stay there, meneer," Esther insisted. He felt a blade of desire slice through his skin. The way she said *meneer* out loud. The way her mouth and tongue curled around the words. The way she delicately rubbed the top of her Tab can with a napkin before drinking. The way her ill-fitting dress fluttered around her legs. He couldn't have her; he knew he couldn't. It made him want to gnaw wood.

"I'll just go in and ask," he said. "See what the price is."

"I'll go with you," Amber said, trailing after him. He watched Esther walk to the pier, standing as close as she dared to the edge in order to study the white foamy waves that licked the pilings.

"She likes you," Amber said as they ambled toward the hotel.

"No, she doesn't."

"Don't be stupid, meneer. She does. You'll see."

The lobby was shabby enough, but to his twenty-two-year-old eye it seemed pretty fabulous, with its mahogany walls, peeling paint, and weathered fixtures that could be yanked off by any halfway determined child. Old chandeliers hung from the ceiling, dim with the preponderance of burned-out bulbs. The German reservationist was spectacularly unfriendly, particularly as he eyed Amber, who was making herself comfortable in one of the lobby's cracked leather easy chairs.

"Two rooms will be five hundred U.S. dollars," he said.

"Wait," Mark said. "Hold on. That can't be the locals' rate. I have a Namibian visa."

"There is no manner in which you can take two rooms for one local." He nodded at Amber. "And *she* is not a local."

Mark looked around. He could make a scene about segregation being illegal. Or he could just get on with it.

"Okay. One single room, please, then," he said. "For one local."

"Our bachelor rooms are in the back, overlooking the parking. The local rate is seventy-five U.S. And they are *single*. So your friend must find a different . . . hotel."

It was a lot to him, seventy-five dollars. Yet being broke for a month seemed worth it, particularly when he walked back to the pier where Esther was iridescent—a true Aphrodite—hovering in her own blaze.

Their room overlooked the parking lot, and was decorated grimly with orange carpet and green-and-orange wallpaper. There was a battered dresser with what looked to be actual bullet holes in the side and a tilted bed covered in a spread spotted with waxy-looking stains. Mark went to the store and bought a pack of Tafel, then they walked down away from the hotel and spread out a blanket stolen from the room over the sand.

It was dusk now, the sky caught between blush-pink and a blue Esther said she found sad. Mark begged the girls to swim, but they refused. Esther's cousin, Leva, had gone over the falls at Epupa, they said. Water was not their friend.

They wouldn't drink, either. At least not at first. Esther was steadfast, shaking her head no. She seemed happy to watch Mark dive into the waves, and he spread his arms so that the muscles in his back formed a satisfying V. Amber threw rocks at the water. When Mark came up, dripping, she had him open a beer for her.

"You shouldn't," Esther said.

"You're just boring," Amber taunted.

"I'm not."

"Then have one." Amber put her head on Esther's shoulder. "Just one, omumwamemekadona."

"Fine," Esther said, letting out a defeated sigh. Before she could change her mind, Mark opened one for her. She straightened up at the crisp sound of the cap flying into the air. By dark, Amber had drunk three of the beers. She announced that she was going to find the bathroom.

"I'll go with you," Esther said.

"No," Amber said. She leaned over and whispered something in Esther's ear, then stood up and brushed the sand off her legs. "And don't come looking, You, either, meneer," she said loudly. "I'm going farther down the beach, where the other Ovambos are. I'll see you all later." She waved, then tripped away.

Esther had her hands on her hips. She was frowning. He knew he should tell her that Amber would be okay, but he didn't actually know if she would. He felt incredibly stupid. He should never have brought them here.

"Don't worry. She's like this," she said after a moment, surprising him. She seemed to have decided something; the tone of her voice had completely changed. "Shall we get something to eat?"

To be twenty-two, walking down a foreign sidewalk next to this perfect creature! He could die from happiness. He tried to imprint every detail in his brain, so as not to forget any of it, as surely it was the peak of his life. He wasn't hungry, as he could live forever on the very swish of her skirt. They didn't talk, because when he did, his words dropped heavily, awkward as stones. She seemed happier with silence, and all he wanted was to please her. The Germans had been drinking since the middle of the afternoon, and their slurred voices ricocheted off the walls of the beer halls. At the end of the boulevard, Mark motioned for Esther to follow him into one, where the tables spilled out into the streets. A few Afrikaner tables looked them over and then turned decidedly away.

"I don't want to go here, meneer," Esther said at the door.

"Why?" he asked, a note of impatience coloring his voice.

He hadn't meant to do it; the word had just slipped out. Yet her lack of response was as loud as a yawp of anger. It was natural for him not to notice the white men staring at them. What did he care? He was the same as them, protected from poverty, illness, death. If he was robbed, he would call his bank and get more money. If he contracted malaria, he would go to an expatriate clinic and heal. If a man pulled a knife on Esther, he could rape her, and no one would care. There was no more money just sitting somewhere behind the ATM. Malaria would likely cause her to die. All of these things, Mark knew, meant he would never, ever understand Esther. And also they were why she would never, ever let him near her.

But she surprised him again, by breaking free from him and marching right past the table of men who were audibly jeering. As if on a dare, she smiled at Mark brightly and sat down.

He knew she was using him. For what? Protection? A lark? He didn't care if she used him. He'd be happy if she used him for the rest of his life.

She had another beer, and she started, at last, to talk to him. She asked him about his school, about what he knew. She liked to tease him. "What do you even know about Namibia?" she asked. "Katima is where? South or north?"

"Ah, south."

"No. And Chobe?"

"North."

"Botswana. Wrong country. Do they teach you nothing in your American school?"

"And what do they teach you?"

She smiled dangerously. "Math. English. Geography. How to cook an oxtail. How to skin a zebra."

"Really?"

"No. But I know how."

Mark realized, at that moment, what an utterly shallow person he was. He'd been just like those guys at the Peace Corps headquarters who bragged about their conquests. You're just a tourist until you fuck a local, one of them had said when they were all wasted at HQ. Mark had avoided that particular asshole from then on, but he was no better. His interest in Esther had been simply lust.

Well, not just that. He'd flipped over pretty girls before; what he was now was bewitched. If she told him to jump off the pier and swim in the shark-infested waters to Elba, he would. But once she let him talk to her, he felt himself falling down a deep hole, pausing every so often to marvel at a new, poisonous bloom. Her intelligence was bottomless. Every new corner she revealed was a mystery.

"So how do you skin a zebra, then?"

"Like any animal," she said. "You slit its throat and hang it upside down to drain the blood, then flay the skin, starting with the neck." She put her fingers to her own throat and made the motion of a guillotine.

You don't have to do that, he thought. I'm already dead.

By the time they returned to the hotel, both were a little wobbly from the beer. They filed quietly up the back stairs, opened the door, turned on the light. Amber still wasn't there, a fact that shot him through with both joy and terror.

"Well." Mark yanked open the doors to the ancient, hulking wardrobe. A family of moths flew out. He swatted at them like a bear, extracted a blanket, and spread it on the floor. "I bet this thing has seen some adventures."

Esther didn't answer. Was it his stupid joke that made her close up again? God, he was a fucking nob. She took her things and went into the bathroom. Mark could hear water running, and the avid brushing of teeth. When she came out, he was already on the floor under a blanket, so that she wouldn't think he was a sleaze. He could have been a sleaze, of course. He had been so many times. Well, he would make it up to all of them now by suffering through this night, lying next to the most exquisite woman in the world, the one he could never have.

She shut off the light and climbed into bed. He waited for a while, staring at the ceiling. Every cell of his body was aware of her breathing. He would never be able to sleep, he thought. What was the point of trying? But the pounding heat of the sun and the surges of his heart throughout the day proved him wrong. His eyes closed, and a comforting heaviness began to pull him under.

And then he was awake again. He could hear her turning over, back and forth, could hear her skin brush the awful scratchy sheets. Should he say something? What? His eyes flew open. She was out of bed. It was impossible. Wasn't it? Oh God, she was kneeling next to him.

Mark had received many things he knew he hadn't deserved. This ethereal being next to him now, it was by far the most preposterous. Oh, he knew he would pay. How could he not pay? He sat up slowly, daring to get close enough so he could smell her clean clothes and the cinnamon tinge of her skin.

"Can I . . ." Again, his words felt like bricks. Why was this happening? Was he drugged? She took his hand, felt his fingers, as if she were curious and was learning them. He didn't dare move or even breathe. He could just make out the outline of her exquisite lips in the dark. Should he kiss her? Was that what she wanted? But no, it seemed to be his hand, solely, that interested her.

Fine, he thought. You can have that hand forever, Esther. It's yours.

She took it now, bringing it to her velvety neck, the same one she had pretended to cut open a few hours ago. His breath caught in his throat as she guided his fingers back and forth over the material of her nightgown. When had she put on a nightgown? How had he missed that? It wasn't sexy, just another cotton dress, but looser, and soft, so soft. She pressed his hand against one of her nipples, leaning forward into his hand. When he dared to move his fingers, she stayed very still, and the skin that had been giving a moment ago hardened into a point. It was a perfect breast, a perfect sphere tipped by the nipple, oh Jesus, was he going to get to see—

But no. Something was wrong. She wasn't pulling away, or saying no. But she wasn't moving. She seemed frozen, staring at the floor.

"Esther?"

"You can go ahead, meneer," she said. "I'm ready."

Mark drew back, looking at her.

"Ready for what?"

She didn't take her eyes from the floor. "For what you paid for."

"What I paid for?"

"Isn't that why you gave us the money?"

"Esther." He stood up, pulling her up with him, then guided her to the bed and had her sit down, taking a seat on a chair opposite. "I just gave Amber money because she said you guys couldn't afford to come. I would never . . . pay for sex."

"Oh." Esther blinked twice, then looked out the window. "That was not my understanding."

The streetlamp outside flickered and died. Drunken laughter si-phoned up from the tavern below.

"Look," Mark said. "Look. I like you a lot, Esther. If you must know, I'm completely crazy about you. I mean, I definitely *would* have had sex with you just then. Thank God you said something."

"I'm embarrassed," Esther said, looking at her hands. She ran her perfect finger along the etching of her bracelet.

"No. Don't be. Look, I get it. I mean, I think I get it. You guys must really need money—"

She let out a shuddering sigh. "We're finished."

"Why?"

"We were fired."

"Fired?"

"The day we agreed to come. We don't have anywhere to live, and barely any money."

"Oh fuck. I'm so sorry." He scooted his chair closer, stopping before he got too near. "I'll help you any way I can. But not that way. I mean, I want to, like, date you."

"Date." Esther laughed sourly. "I cannot date, meneer. I have to plan now how to get food to eat."

Again. What a fucking idiot he was. "Look," Mark said. "Look. Let's go to sleep. Tomorrow, we'll have a nice day, and we'll figure this out. There must be other jobs. I know how to put together a résumé."

"A résumé?"

"Let's just go to sleep." He hesitated. "I really, really like you, Esther. I really do."

"That's very nice." She smiled at him, and his heart flipped over, then back again. "Good night, Mark." She leaned forward and kissed him briefly, then got into bed.

Mark lay back down on the floor, carried by a wave of relief. How close he had come to ruining things with her forever. He could hear Esther breathing steadily. He'd given her the gift of sleep, which felt good, but now there was no way he'd do anything but stare at the ceiling all night.

Mark looked at Anna now. Anna, who was the same age but a million years younger than they had been then. Who would never be able to understand.

"I didn't kill anyone," Mark said.

"That's good."

One of Claus's cats came into the room and hopped on the table, turning around twice before settling in to a nap.

"It's just that there was this girl I met here. A long time ago."

Anna raised her eyebrows. "Aha. Love story."

"Yeah." Mark took a sip of tea, now cold. "Aha."

"So?"

"So . . . well. It's been twenty years, and I still think about her."

"Is it?" Anna narrowed her eyes.

"It's like she's right here." He tapped on his head.

"Huh."

"But it's complicated." Why was he telling her all of this? But now that he'd started, he couldn't stop. "See, she's not the one I bought the necklace for."

"That's your wife."

"Right. My wife." As he said the word, it felt unreal, somehow. He was so far away from his wife; hundreds of miles of scorched veld lay between them. "Maybe she shouldn't have been my wife, though."

"You think so?"

"Sometimes." He reached over to scratch the cat's head. The animal sighed in annoyance. "Sometimes I wonder if it was all supposed to be different."

"And what does she think?" Anna asked. "The lady from your past?"

Mark took his hand from the cat, and instead drew a pattern in the dust on the table. "She's dead," he said finally. His mouth had a hard time getting around the word.

Anna frowned. "Sho. That's not the ending I wanted."

"Sorry."

"So am I. I'm tired of the soaps on Netflix." He felt her nonchalance keenly, a blow to the gut. His face must have shown it, because the smile fell from her face. "Just joking, Coach."

"Yeah."

"So when did you find out?"

"Last month."

Anna leaned forward. "And you're sure?"

"Yeah. I went to the morgue in Swakopmund, just to see. I had a feeling, but I didn't know. Then I got the records."

"That's sure, hey," Anna nodded. "The morgue. I'm sorry, but that's sure."

"You won't tell anyone what I said, will you? About me going to the morgue. My wife doesn't know. I mean, looking for that woman was kind of the main reason I brought us back to Namibia."

"The phone would have been easier," Anna said, raising her eyebrows.

"I couldn't bear it. Maybe you wouldn't understand."

"Sure, I understand," Anna said, looking at him steadily. "You think I didn't love my dead ass of a boyfriend who knocked up the Boer?"

She put her elbows on the table, clasped her hands, and rested her chin on the fingers. They were quiet for a long time. The sky ran from white to pink to the purple-blue of a child's bruise. Finally, Claus emerged.

"Your rocks are ready," he said. The old man opened his palm. It was filled with glittering stones.

so, will we see them?

Yeah. I know how to break into the barn.

So so so so kewl.

You won't even believe what people pay for them.

Its weird. And they are right in yr barn? How did u find them

I find everything. Like my Mum's old love notes. And my maid Libertina is 1 millyun years old and she has cigarettes!!!!!

!!!!!!!!!!!!!!!!!!!!!!!!!!!!!!!!!

How is your Mum? Still sad?

She's OK. This will help. Hey did you start book One yet?

Meg, reading is too boring. I live for life.

Harry Potter is not boring.

I'll see the movie.

No no. At least read book 1.

You read to me. You are my servant! Garbage!

Garbage!

Garbage!

Blechgrosssseeyousooooon

Persephone found it curious that in a country with hardly any people, where there was nowhere to go and nothing to do but cook meat on the veld, everyone drove as if they were late to their own wedding. The drive to Osha was supposed to take just three hours from Windhoek, though getting anywhere in this country inevitably took twice as long as Namibians said it did. It was rather a harrowing trip; fancy white trucks loaded with safari gear zoomed past them using the oncoming lane, even on rising hills. But these people weren't going to pressure her to speed up on rutted, potholed roads. No. She was perfectly happy to let a parade of angry pickups pile up behind her. It was what it was.

Amanda, on the other hand, was not so tolerant of the road bullies. "Why don't they take a goddamned chill pill?" she grumbled as the hundredth huge safari vehicle roared past. Twice they'd had to swerve off the road as cars passed from the other direction, hurtling toward them in their own lane.

"Dollar," Meg said from the back. Persephone's children were safely ensconced in Frida's care, but since Taimi, Meg's soul mate, would be at the farm that weekend also, Meg had decided to accompany them. Currently Amanda's daughter was nestled in the back, her nose buried in a Harry Potter book.

The scrubbed-bare land, punctuated by huge red fingers of termite mounds, ribboned past the windows. Every hundred kilometers or so, they'd buzz through a hot empty town, where men sat on crates in the droplets of shade provided by hungry trees, and women stared out from open doors. The tourist industry certainly has its work cut out for it, Persephone said to herself. She decided not to share this with Amanda, who seemed to be warming to the place. Instead, they chatted idly about the rhino project.

"The first thing we need is members," Amanda said. "It's not like we can go out ourselves and protect a rhino every week."

"Why not?" Meg said. "It's fun."

"We have to be home," Persephone said. "To nurture our darling children's minds and feed them nutritious meals."

"Well, I'd camp with you guys every week. It's way better than school. Especially in this thing."

Persephone smiled in agreement. It was wonderful, knowing you had everything you needed, down to a hot shower, right in the back of your vehicle. She knew this was about the animals, but she was particularly excited about the orzo salad she had chilling in the battery-powered icebox, the cold salmon, and the kale pesto pasta. And then there was the biodegradable lavender salt scrub she made from desert sea salt and Dr. Bronner's soap—shipped for the occasion at the government's expense by Amazon Prime.

"We'll need a social media presence," Amanda said. "So we'll have to document this trip and put it all online."

"And what about our name?" Persephone said. "What should we call ourselves?"

"I did some market research on that, actually," Amanda said. "Namibia Rhino Watch is what I think makes sense. The verb *watch* makes members feel active."

"That's boring," Meg said.

"Not *boring*, exactly," Persephone said carefully. "And I do like the watch idea. Though I have to agree with Meg . . . it's maybe a bit . . . flat."

"Well . . ."

"I was thinking we'd call it Tusk. Because, you know, that's what we're protecting, correct?"

"That's cool," Meg said. "Only—wait. Do rhinos have tusks? Or are they horns?"

"I think we can assume they're called either," Persephone said. "Besides, we can't call our organization Horn."

"Yeah, but there's already a Tusk," Amanda said, frowning into her phone. "Here. Look . . . Tusk.org. It's British. William and Harry are into it."

"Oh dear," Persephone said with a sigh. "The royal family *does* have all the good parts of Africa covered, don't they? Can't they just stick to Europe?"

"You can add an exclamation point," Meg said. "That's what China Lisa in my class does. She doesn't like sharing her name with Zimbabwe Lisa, so she calls herself 'Lisa!' She even makes the teacher write it that way."

"That's so clever!" Persephone exclaimed, swerving around a warthog. "I love this idea. Tusk!"

"Tusk!" Amanda said. "It sounds like something you say when you give a toast."

"That's a *good* thing," Persephone nodded. "Tusk! I love it."

The sun was rising; by eight the tar road was already beginning to shimmer with heat. Amanda had packed breakfast sandwiches and a thermos of coffee, so they didn't have to stop. Meg receded once more into the backseat with her breakfast to commune with her iPad. (Since Mark wasn't on the trip, Amanda had declared all devices fair game.)

A small marker indicated a dirt road running north, which, despite its humble looks, was one of Namibia's major thoroughfares. Switching to dirt made the ride much less comfortable; the truck bounced and swayed over potholes and hidden rocks. Still, just fifteen kilometers in, the land was turning from hopeless red to a happier shade of yellow, then green. They could see a long procession of trees marching across the plain, bending eagerly over a thick stripe of sand. It was an empty riverbed, which filled for three weeks during the violent, blink-and-miss-it rainy season, bringing the area a year's worth of water in twenty days.

At 10:08, in a particularly lovely and remote patch of nothingness, the GPS beeped. They pushed open the unmarked gate and roared ahead. The road got worse and worse, weaving through thickets and deep bush. After a while they reached an outcrop of rocks. It didn't seem possible that the road would continue, but yes, this was it, right up on the red, ancient rock.

Finally, they reached the top. Amanda, Meg, and Persephone all held their breath as the pass opened up into an expansive valley rimmed by green mountains. The shivering forest was thick and impermeable. They could see giraffe heads poking up through the trees.

"This looks like Utah," Meg said. "Like, the whole state of Utah. Do Taimi's parents own this whole thing?"

They descended into the valley, and after a few more kilometers, the road widened, surprisingly, into a pleasant country lane. Soon they reached a pretty stone wall with a large wooden gate.

"Good Lord," Persephone said.

She didn't like common exclamations, but she was now truly flummoxed. Standing beyond the gate was a stone castle—a small one, yes, but . . . a castle nonetheless. The drive was lined with leafy elms, and the grass was as thick and luscious as it might have been in England in the summer.

"Are we still even in Africa?" Meg asked.

"Yes," Amanda said. "There's an ostrich."

There were, in fact, two ostriches strutting about the lawn, as well as a few grazing warthogs, and, in a pen at the end of the garden, a fat, sleeping leopard.

The three got out of the truck, looking around in a daze.

"I feel like I'm in Oz," Amanda said.

Just then, an engine roared as a cream-colored safari vehicle whipped around from behind the house, kicking up dust and rocks. Say what you will about African travel, Persephone thought, there is nothing as glamorous as a safari vehicle roaring to a stop. Mila proved this true by swanning on the back, holding only the roll bar. She was resplendent in black jeans and a black T-shirt, her neck wrapped in a gauzy cheetah-print scarf. Persephone couldn't help bristling. Her *own* intended camping outfit was to be set off by a cheetah-print shawl. Now she would have to reengineer.

"Hey, Mila," Amanda called out when the jeep roared to a stop in a cloud of golden dust.

"Welcome," Mila proclaimed. She banged twice on the roof of the cab, and a hulking blond man in his mid-sixties scrambled out. He had a kind, leathery face, with smile lines etched deeply into his skin.

"Hallo!" he said in a booming voice, shaking hands with a crushing grip. "I em the ker-tak-err." German. Persephone loved him immediately, the same way she instantly fell for yellow Labradors and turkey clubs with crisp bacon. He pulled a stool out of the back, and helped Mila elegantly dismount. "We verr looking for your rhino."

"Did you find him?" Meg asked.

"No," Mila said. "Though we did find excrement."

"What?" Meg asked.

"Poop," Amanda said.

"Awesome!"

"Hector," Mila said to the driver. "We'll have lunch in twenty minutes."

"Yah!" he called back, smiling.

"It's so nice to see that," Persephone said idly.

"See what?" Mila asked sharply.

"Oh." Persephone blushed. Of course Mila would call her out this way. "I mean, such a symbiotic relationship. Um . . . that a man like that can work for you with no . . . er . . . fuss."

"You mean a white man working for a Black woman?" Mila asked. Amanda looked at the sky, studiously pretending nothing was happening. "He came with the place. His family's been here for generations. He's a better worker than the lazy Damara who live around here."

"Mila!" Amanda said. "Aren't you being racist?"

"Of course," Mila said. "I'm Ovambo. We're as racist as you can get."

Just then Taimi ran out, linking arms with Meg and pulling her into the house-castle-palace.

"Show me the tower!" Persephone heard Meg squeal.

"Come, I'll show you around," Mila said.

Persephone knew she was supposed to like Mila now, but she couldn't help but notice this was an order, not a request. She and Amanda dutifully followed their hostess through the property as she showed them the parlor and drawing room, furnished with antiques from Bavaria, the kitchen with a brick oven the perfect size for cooking children, the whitewashed bedrooms, and the veranda, artfully studded with oryx skulls and overlooking a broad, reed-lined watering hole.

Lunch was served outside on the porch by an ancient-looking German woman named Heidi who staggered out under plate after plate of salami, roast pork, cabbage, and various salads swimming in mayonnaise. All was washed down by steins of ice-cold beer or glasses of cool Riesling, as the guests preferred.

Mila sat at the head of the table, and midway through the soup course a tall man joined them and introduced himself as Josephat. Persephone wasn't often affected by good-looking men—Adam himself was a bit of a knockout, which only added to her problems. But she had to admit it: Josephat was, well, stunning. And when he looked at her with that shock of a white porcelain smile, her head started swimming. Hoping her cheeks weren't turning splotchy, she took another large sip of wine.

"So you ladies are after our rhino," he said.

"Only in a good way," Persephone said, putting down her fork. "Do you think we'll find him?"

"If you do, don't get too close," Josephat said sternly, sending a pleasant shiver down her spine. "He's a mean one."

Persephone frowned. She hadn't considered the possibility that the rhino she was trying to help might not actually *like* her.

"Have you had trouble with poachers before?" Amanda asked.

"Just local people looking for meat."

"How do you know?"

"They leave the trophies behind. The heads. And we found bones at the local settlement."

Persephone was beginning to feel sleepy. She picked through her plate of mayonnaise, thinking of something to say. "Well. This is a fabulous farm. It must be *quite* expensive, though—to run, I mean. It's nice that you have the money."

"Why would you say that?" Josephat asked sharply.

She looked up to find Mila's husband staring at her *most* unkindly.

"Oh, sorry. Just . . . all the people, I was thinking. And the vehicles. I grew up on a farm like this in America, you see. Well, no rhinos, of course!" She flashed her most charming grin, but, disconcertingly, Mila's husband seemed immune. "Most people with big farms seem to run guesthouses. I just—well, I admire you for keeping it all up."

"It's actually not so expensive," Mila said. "And perhaps one day we'll open a lodge."

"Yes," Josephat said. "Certainly a possibility." Persephone couldn't be certain, but it seemed that Josephat was shooting his wife a nasty look. He pushed his chair back.

"Well, ladies. I'm so sorry—but, alas, I have to attend to some business. Good luck, then, with the rhino. And let us know if you need anything."

Persephone had one more glass of wine and then asked Mila if they might lie beside the pool before they left.

"Of course," Mila said. "It's still early."

Persephone tripped down the lawn to a cushioned pool chair. *Farm* was pushing it, wasn't it? This was more of a resort. Within minutes she was lulled into a relaxation so deep she was dreaming. Time poured by. When she woke up, it felt as if there was a warm hand wrapped around her ankle. She rubbed her eyes, looking around. What was happening? Oh right. She was sleeping off a wine headache in the middle of the veld at a former Nazi stronghold, now owned by stupendously wealthy Ovambos. Of course.

But wait. There *was* a hand on her ankle.

"Adam!" she cried. "What are *you* doing here?"

"Mila and I are working on our transportation project, remember?" he said, grinning. "I was in Omaruru with the Big A., because there's some art center we're thinking of helping out. A new way to look good after this whole presidential shithole thing. And anyway, since it's practically around the corner, I dropped by."

Persephone's ears pricked. This did not sound kosher.

"You dropped *by*? We're in the middle of nowhere."

"Mila gave me the farm phone."

"And the GPS location," she said, leaning closer. "Right?"

"Well, yes." He cocked his head as if confused.

Nice try, Persephone thought. "So you used one of those secret tools you have to track us?" She tipped her head down, looking into her husband's eyes. Truly, she felt like a cat with a sparrow in its mouth. "A . . . secret *gadget* of some sort?"

Adam patted her arm a tad condescendingly, as if she were Lucy having one of her fits. "Perse. Darling. What are you talking about?"

Persephone looked around. No one was anywhere near them. And since her own house was most likely bugged, she felt she might as well bring it up now. "I *know*, Adam."

For once, her husband looked appropriately alarmed. He withdrew his hand from her leg. "You know what?"

"I *know* that you're the CIA plant," she whispered.

He blinked, then blinked again. "Excuse me?"

"I figured it out."

"Um, sweetness . . ."

"Don't deny it, okay? Just accept that I'm smart."

"I know you're smart. But why the hell do you think—"

"Come on. You're gone all the time on those mysterious trips. You're always on the phone where I can't hear you. I mean, what else could it be?"

"Well . . ."

"And, frankly, you haven't been doing your *actual* job at the embassy very well. If at all. So . . . if you're *not* the CIA plant, then you're just a lazy State Department diplomat, coasting on your looks. Or you're having some big affair, right out in the open. And I *know* you'd never do *that*."

Adam paused, looking at her. Then he flashed it. The killer smile. No wonder he got away with spying right under everyone's nose. "You are a wonder," Adam said, rubbing her leg. "You know what? My God. I'd like to fuck you right now."

"Ugh. Adam. *Language*."

"So you've figured me out," he said. "You sly little minx. Go ahead, then. Shoot. What do you want to ask me?"

"If this were that movie *True Lies*, and I were Jamie Lee Curtis, I'd hit you right now."

"Never saw it. And you're much cuter than she is."

"So . . ." She leaned back triumphantly. "How long has this been going on?"

Adam looked at his nails, giving his best handsome scowl. He practiced it. Persephone knew, because she saw him do it every morning in the mirror. "About . . . four months?"

"And have you had to use a gun on anyone?"

"Can't tell you. Classified."

"Oh, you devil!" she said, swatting his arm. "Well, is it fun, being in the CIA? It *seems* fun."

"Mostly it's just gathering information. I'm not exactly in Kabul. Now, you're not going to tell your girlfriends, are you?"

"Of course not," she said indignantly. "I would never jeopardize your mission."

"Good," he said. He leaned in a bit.

"So why are you here?" she asked breathlessly. "To investigate the Shilongos?"

"Why would I do that?"

"You don't think it's suspicious they basically own a Safari Hilton on a government salary?"

"Nah, babe. No one as hot as Mila could be corrupt."

"Oh?" Persephone said, annoyed. "Is that a CIA rule?"

"I'm really just here upon invitation. Besides, who says no to a free private game drive?"

Persephone sighed. This part did make sense. Adam was nuts about game drives.

"Can I help? With the intelligence part? Because I think Mr. Shilongo is a bit shady."

"No, darling. You enjoy yourself. Though easy on the sauce, eh, cupcake? Let's abstain for the rest of the day, shall we?"

We shall not, Persephone thought, but flashed him a smile in the name of patriotism.

"Well. The game drive is about to start, I think. Should we go?"

Persephone nodded, taking Adam's offered hand and standing up. She'd slept longer than intended. By the time they entered the parlor of the farmhouse, it was full of people, all khakied up and ready. Spotting Josephat Shilongo in the corner, casting positively livid looks at his wife, Persephone wondered if her instincts might actually be right about him being not exactly completely aboveboard.

"Are you not coming along, then, Josephat?" Persephone asked. She was trying for a purring voice, but it came out all scratchy, as if she had sand in her throat.

"I don't believe there is room now," he said, glaring at Adam. "Because of the surprise guest. Is there, Mila?"

"Don't be silly," Mila replied. She glided over to Adam and put her hand on his arm. "Don't worry, Adam. He's just jealous of you. And I'm just so glad you made it all the way here to see our farm."

They made their way out to the Land Rover. After two years in Namibia and multiple jaunts to neighboring game parks in Zambia, Botswana, and South Africa, Persephone was no stranger to game drives. At first they had been thrilling. The open-air vehicles, the proximity to hippos and lions and giraffes!

Sadly, though, American State Department employees didn't always have good manners, as she did. Like the time in Erindi when Kayla had briskly informed their driver that if she didn't see at least one lion, he wasn't getting a tip. Or the time in Etosha, when Shoshana was so drunk on Erongo wine she fell off the truck when they stopped to look at wildebeests, effectively ending the safari.

As an Embassy Wife, Persephone always concentrated on looking interested at every show of fauna, be it leopard, meerkat, or ant. But she had to admit, it wasn't easy: after a while, well, a giraffe was just a giraffe. The twins didn't even look up from their iPads anymore unless it was to witness a predator making a live kill.

And finally—proud as she was of Adam's investigations!—she had to admit she enjoyed game drives a whole lot more when her husband wasn't along. His eyes were remarkably keen, which was wonderful, except for the fact that he inevitably made the driver stop for every single show of wildlife, even if they had already seen the species on that very drive ten times already. And today, for some reason, he had brought a camera the size of a NASA telescope.

"Stop!" he commanded before they were even beyond the shadow of the house. "Giraffe at eleven o'clock. Little closer, please? A little closer? All right. Look at the color of the spots, Persephone," he instructed. "At least fifty years old, I'd say."

"Giraffes live at most twenty-eight years," Hector said from the driver's seat.

"I don't think so, friend. Okay. Got the shot. Go. Wait—no, stop! Zebra, four o'clock. Back it up, please? Back it up?"

Amanda, who was free to have a G and T, sipped from her silver thermos, shooting Persephone amused looks. "I had no idea Adam was such a wildlife enthusiast," she said.

"Oh yes," Persephone answered. "Isn't it wonderful."

"Yeah, but we're not getting very far," Meg said. It had been an hour now, and the castle was still visible.

"Meg," Amanda warned.

"Excuse me, Miss Evans, but I have to agree," Taimi said. "I do not wish to offend Mr. Wilder. Nevertheless, if your goal is to find the rhinoceros, we may want to go a bit faster. He never stays near our house."

"Hush, Taimi," Mila said. But Persephone could see that she, too, was getting impatient.

"Darling," Persephone said, "I really think we must press on."

"One more shot." Adam stood, clicking at the landscape. "All right. Done."

Mila rapped on the roof of the truck, and Hector took off down a road so narrow, it was little more than a walking path. The girls screamed with excitement as they were thrown to the ceiling with each bounce and rock of the chassis. Finally, after what seemed like hours (but by her silver watch was only forty minutes), Hector came screeching to a stop. He turned off the vehicle; the shutting down of the perversely loud engine was so violent, the very newfound silence ricocheted throughout the trees. In response, the noises of the African afternoon—birds, geckos, snakes, beetles—seemed to swell.

Hector turned to them and put his finger to his cracked lips, then pointed. There, almost completely camouflaged by a crop of gray boulders, was a huge rhino, its massive muscles rippling with the simple act of swaying its block of a head.

"It's a male," Hector whispered. "Shhhh. Very important. *Be totally silent.*"

"Can he see my zebra print?"

"*Shhhhhh.*"

Persephone had seen a rhino before, but never this close up. Its haunches were pure muscle. The horn was terrifying and magnificent, sharp enough to gore any huge predator that came its way. What she wasn't prepared for were its eyes, which were huge, soft, and kind. He reared his head and looked right at her. She could have sworn it. He blinked, slowly, and Persephone felt an odd, long-forgotten twinge.

It's the damnedest thing, she imagined saying to her sister over FaceTime. I fell in love with a rhinoceros, Delia. I had to leave Adam, naturally. It was literally the call of the wild!

Everyone in the jeep sat frozen, even the children. And then, after a few precious seconds, out of the corner of her eye Persephone sensed something horrible happening. It was her husband. He held up his enormous camera, positioned it for the shot . . . and *clicked*.

The reaction was so instantaneous, Persephone later wondered if the rhino hadn't started running before Adam even took the picture. Maybe the animal *hadn't* been looking at her. Because the next thing they knew, the animal was moving as fast as a train. And he was coming, all five thousand pounds of him, straight toward their jeep.

18

Amanda was not a sentimental person. She had never particularly liked any babies but her own, and she was in no way an animal lover. Pets were, in her eyes, a nuisance. Animals had their rights, of course, but she preferred getting close to them in the zoo.

But then, she had never been in the path of a rhinoceros, running toward her at thirty miles an hour. The beast was so large and forceful, its drive moved the branches on the trees near its path. The ground shook. The manufactured wind sounded of sails batting above a churning sea.

The first thing Amanda did was sit on Meg. The second was to turn her entire body toward the incoming animal. Hector threw the jeep into reverse, so that by the time the rhino managed to hit the vehicle with its shoulder, they were already moving at full speed. The car careened for a moment onto two wheels, and, as if the delayed fear had suddenly caught up with them, Meg, Taimi, and Persephone started to scream.

"Hold!" Hector shouted as the truck righted itself, and, jamming the gearshift out of reverse, he slammed his foot down on the accelerator and drove them back the way they'd come.

With the worst of it over now, the group let the dusty wind roar over them in the grateful, horrified silence of people who have just witnessed something awful yet spectacular.

"Well," Persephone said after a few long seconds. "That would be our rhinoceros."

Amanda still couldn't speak.

"Why the hell did he charge like that?" Adam asked.

"Because he's a wild animal," Mila said. Her tone was polite, but Amanda saw her cut her eyes at him. "And he didn't like the sound of your camera. Did you not hear Hector's direction to remain silent?"

"Sorry," Adam said. "I just got . . . excited." He turned to Persephone. "The good thing, babe, is that I got some great shots."

They got back to the castle at six. Eager to get home before dark, Adam promptly kissed Persephone and left. As soon as his car was out of sight, Persephone accepted a large gin and tonic from Hector, who hugged them all.

"Very lucky today!" he boomed before disappearing into the garage.

"Your husband is very attractive, and I certainly am enjoying working with him on the transportation safety campaign," Mila said. "But perhaps he's not the wisest around animals."

"True," Persephone said. "But then, who among us has ever been charged by a five thousand-pound animal before?"

Amanda glanced back and forth between the two women. They were trying, but it was clear enough that they'd never be the best of friends.

"Well, we'd better get going if we're going to set up our camp," she offered.

"You're still going to do this?" Mila asked.

"Of course," Persephone sniffed. "We came all the way out here. We have *work* to do."

"Yes," Mila said. "What's this club called again?"

"It's a nonprofit or-ga-ni-*zay*-tion," Persephone said. "And it's called Tusk. No. Sorry—Tusk!"

"Shall I lead you back to the spot?" Hector asked, reappearing.

"No," Persephone said. "That's okay. Thank you. I have a GPS, and I remember the way. Just give me a minute." She went outside and disappeared into the camper, then reemerged wearing a khaki cargo miniskirt, a white tank top belted with a leather belt, and silver earrings shaped like rhino tusks.

"Nice touch," Amanda said.

"So happy I happened to pack them. But only because of my Insta-gram duties," Persephone said modestly.

"Let me just find Meg to say good night."

She went back inside the cool, dark house, wandering around the maze of rooms. She could hear the low, musical voices of the staff in the kitchen, punctuated by the hysterical laughter of nine-year-olds coming from above. Upon climbing the stone stairs that curled like a shaving of wood, she found Meg in Taimi's cavernous bedchamber. The girls were lying on the floor, listening to African pop and staring at a CD cover.

"So, you'll be all right?" Amanda asked. Both girls startled and sat up.

"Yup!" Meg said so brightly Amanda felt her heart flip with happi-ness. "I've never *slept* in a castle."

"Well, you know where I am if you need me."

"Oh, she cannot reach you out in the bush, Mrs. Evans," Taimi said. "Though if there *is* an emergency, such as a fire or an invasion, she will be quite safe with Hector."

"Invasion?"

Taimi nodded. "Oh yes. There have been many farmers murdered recently. Poor farmers, I mean. Mostly by disgruntled workers. But my father has top security. Also, we are not white. Usually they only kill white farmers." She smiled.

"I'm white!" Meg said.

"That's all right," Taimi said soothingly. "We like you anyway."

"Have fun, Mom. Don't worry, we'll be fine."

Reluctantly, Amanda went back downstairs. Then, after accepting wishes of good luck and a bit more gin from Mila, she followed Per-sephone to the truck and they pulled out, heading back down the road toward the rhino spot.

She was the sort of tired that only seemed to happen in Africa: the get-up-before-dawn, spend-hours-lurching-around-in-a-jeep, put-your-life-in-danger kind of tired. The sun was going down, and already the bush was coming alive with the noises of night animals: the chirpy purrs of mongooses, the lonely yowls of genets, the scratching mating sounds of millions of unidentified waiting insects.

"I'm going to suggest we don't get *right* on top of him this time," Persephone said. "I saw a really good spot right around, let's see . . . 22.2566 degrees south, 15.4068 degrees east." She steered the camper through the trees. Mila's property really was otherwordly; the border mountains stood green-gold and deceptively lush in the evening shadows, while the heat that remained shimmered voluptuously on the red floor of the valley. Silver impalas, stick-thin and quivering, darted back and forth between the trees; above, hornbills, weavers, and starlings flew in frenetic patterns in a fierce fight for their suppers of long-legged insects, newly visible in the cooling sand.

When her friend turned off the camper with a percussive *per-chunk,* Amanda saw that she had indeed found the perfect location: a large, flat rock covered by a thicket of tall, shady trees, about a mile from where Adam had taken his witless picture. The two women ambled out of the vehicle and started unpacking. The sun was now a gentle-looking orange ball sinking sleepily toward the horizon; on the veld, the wind was beginning to pick up. Even Amanda, with her ambivalence toward Namibia, wasn't immune to the cool, dry desert breeze as it brushed her cheeks and arms and made a soft rushing sound through the grass and trees.

The truck had so many gadgets attached to it, it was impossible not to get a little excited. Persephone popped the roof tent and made the beds, while Amanda set up the camping table, chairs, and unpacked the food. Persephone was serious about glamping; the sheets were sundried, ironed cotton ("Frida doesn't mind *too* much"), the comforters goose down, the tablecloth white linen. She insisted on setting the table with silver, china plates, and candles. Hors d'oeuvres included kudu prosciutto, deviled eggs with truffle oil, Manchego cheese, and quince paste.

"Are you going to propose to me or something?" Amanda asked, looking at the table.

"Even Doni Oppenheimer would be proud," Persephone said, beaming.

Amanda snapped photos of everything, posting them onto the brand-new Tusk! Instagram site. After a while the two women settled into their camping chairs with their cocktails. They'd done the best they could with the food, but the table was still covered with half-full plates.

The only sounds were the crickets, the wind, and the clinking of ice. The stars were beginning to pop out of the inky sky, and it was tacitly agreed that the two new friends would now get very drunk.

"Is this what life without Mark will be like?" Amanda asked, looking up.

"Why will there be life after Schmark?"

"There wouldn't be," Amanda said. "There *won't* be."

"Only that's a strange thing to bring up," Persephone said, wagging her finger at Amanda.

"What?"

"Life without Mark." She leaned back, stretching out her legs. "What's going on with that?"

Amanda shrugged, swirling the ice in her drink. The watery gin was slightly red with dust. "Nothing."

"Nope." Persephone shook her head forcefully. "Not nothing."

"Well." Amanda took her time, knowing this was something she had to admit to herself. "He's . . . changed since I first knew him."

"Why?" Persephone withdrew her marshmallow from the fire. It was perfectly toasted, brown but not burned. She spread it delicately on her graham cracker. "What was he like when you first knew him?"

"He was my rowing coach." She frowned as her own marshmallow combusted into flames. "We all worshipped him. He could do no wrong."

"And now he does wrong?"

"I don't know. In the last few years it's like he's gotten lost or something. He was so into his PhD at first, and now I swear I wonder if he's working on it at all."

"Maybe *you've* changed," Persephone said between tidy bites. "Here. I'll toast one for you. Put that down." Amanda tossed her marshmallow gadget to the ground. "I mean, you got that big job in Silicon Valley. Maybe it makes him feel in-at-quite . . . inquiet . . ."

"Inadequate."

"Exactly."

"Mark does say I'm too controlling," Amanda said. "Do you think so? That I'm controlling?"

"All mothers are controlling," Persephone said crossly, spearing the pillowed sugar. "The good ones, anyway. If we weren't, everything would slip into chaos."

"I guess." Needing more gin, Amanda got up—no small task after drinking in a low camping chair for the better part of an hour. She winced as her knees cracked.

"And speaking of chaos!" Persephone said, accepting Amanda's pour, "I was about to *kill* Adam today. Idiot! There's a wild rhino twenty feet away! None of us are breathing! Now is *not* the time to click your camera!"

"Well . . ." She agreed with Persephone, but she would never say so. Nothing good ever came of co-bashing a friend's husband.

"And can I vent, darling?"

"Vent." She took a long swallow. Who invented gin? It was so delicious.

"Do you *know* what he says during sex? The *worst* things. I'm going to *f* you in the *c*. I'm going to put my *c* in your *a*. Oh, baby, let me *f* your *d*."

"Your *d*?"

"Of course, I did find out something today that makes him a bit sexier." She leaned toward Amanda, as if there were anyone other than bugs and rhinos to hear her. "More than a bit. I'm not supposed to say anything, but—"

Suddenly, from far off, there was a sound that didn't fit in.

"Oh my God," Persephone said. "You don't think—"

"The rhino? No. I read they wouldn't charge unless they felt threatened because we approached. Like today. This is . . . hang on." Amanda wrestled herself out of the camping chair again. "No. It's an engine."

"Poachers?"

"I don't . . . Shit. Okay—let's tap into those rifley skills you were bragging about."

Persephone rose and put her hands on her hips to listen. "I would, darling, If I had actually brought a *gun*."

"You packed capers and paprika, and no gun?"

The sound was getting closer now; it was most certainly an engine. It seemed to be stopping now and then, as if hunting for something.

"Let me just turn on the headlights," Amanda said. "You know, to scare them off."

She climbed into the seat and turned on the camper. Immediately the sound of the other car grew steadier and louder. There was no question. The truck was coming straight for them.

"Persephone," she said, trying and failing to sound calm. "Come hide with me behind these rocks."

"Oh, what a bother," Persephone said. "And we were having *such* a good time." She paused. "Do you think they'll kill us? Or just plunder?" She staggered a bit. "I'm very drunk."

"Shhhh. Come on. Pretend you're at . . . pretend you're at your father's farm."

"My father breeds alpacas as a hobby," Persephone said. They climbed between the boulders into the bush, flattening down several yards away from the camp. "And we have a small polo field."

"Just lie down."

"Ants," Persephone said. "Bitey ones."

"Shhhh."

They watched, breathless, as the blaring headlights of a truck approached their camp. The vehicle choked to a stop, and two people hopped out, both holding huge flashlights that beamed left and right.

"They found us," Persephone whispered. "I'll flank left and distract them. You run to their jeep and see if the keys are in the ignition. If they are, drive like hell. Don't worry. I'll get away."

"Who are you, Rambo?" Amanda hissed. "Just stay here." But Persephone had already scuttled into the darkness. Amanda crouched behind the rock, her knees aching. Damn it, Persephone. She couldn't steal a vehicle. What if they had guns?

"Amanda?" a voice called through the darkness. Relief flooded through her, warming her limbs. She jumped up, brushing off the dirt and insects.

"Mila!"

"What are you doing?" Mila exclaimed. "Why are you back there?" Far off, there was a swishing in the bushes. "I believe the rhino is right over there. Hector, investigate?"

"It's not," Amanda said. "It's Persephone, trying to distract you so I can make a run for it."

"What?" Mila shook her head. "What is wrong with you ladies?" She put her hands on her hips, calling out toward the kopje. "Persephone Wilder! Come out from there! Leopards prowl on the rocks at night!"

"I know that," Persephone scoffed, emerging from the trees and brushing her white clothes off with indignance. "What were you doing, ambushing us like that?"

"Hector forgot to give you the radio. Just in case." Mila shook her head.

"You absolutely terrified us," Persephone made a show of stomping to the bar table. "I now have ant bites on my *cheeks*."

"Sorry, sorry," Mila said. "Are you fine?" She looked at the table and the almost-empty bottle of Gordon's. "Oh. You are."

"Join us?" Amanda said.

"I'll just take a ride around the perimeter," Hector said, taking a camping chair out of the back of the truck and setting it down for Mila by the fire. Before she settled into it, he covered it with a blanket. "I'll be back now—now."

The women watched the cloud of dust dissipate as he drove away. Persephone was still silent, drunkenly fuming. She got up to make Mila a gin and tonic.

"Squeeze the lemon in first," Mila commanded. "Over the ice. Then the tonic, *then* the gin. Stir it for ten seconds exactly."

"The woman knows what she wants." She made the drink to Mila's specifications and another, sloppier one for herself.

"What were you ladies discussing, then, before we drove up?" Mila said, accepting the drink with a nod of thanks.

"Sex," Persephone said, tipping her chin into the air; in response, Mila threw her head back, even more haughtily.

These women are going to need chiropractors if they don't become friends soon, Amanda thought.

"Well, then, how did you meet Adam?" Mila asked finally. "You seem very well matched."

"I don't know what *that* means. But . . . college. He asked me to a fraternity formal." She sipped her drink. The day's extreme heat had now torn itself away, replaced by the heavy, cold air high above. It fell upon them quickly, cruel and damp as a wet blanket. Amanda moved as close as she could to the fire without burning herself.

Mila swiveled her head toward Amanda. Her cheekbones reflected the glow of the firelight. "How did you meet your husband, Amanda?" she asked.

Amanda dragged her hand through her own short brown hair, pulling out bits of leaves from her escape into the bush. "He was my coach. In college."

"I see."

"And you and Josephat?"

"I met him where I worked. At the Oshakati Country Hotel. Josephat was a customer of mine."

"Hey," Amanda said. "You know, my husband used to live in Oshakati."

"Is it?" Mila said. "Why?"

"He was a Peace Corps volunteer," Amanda said. "He worked at a health center. Not as a doctor, but as an assistant."

"When was that again?" Persephone asked.

"The late nineties," Amanda said. "In '94 maybe? No—1997."

"Such a long time ago," Persephone said to no one. "I'm younger than everyone else here, I guess! I was still in college."

Mila was looking at her glass as if there was something strange in it. Nearby, two unidentified small creatures made ecstatic shrieks as they mated in a tree.

"But it's a big town, right? I doubt he hung out at the Oshakati Country Hotel with the SWAPO bigwigs," Amanda said.

"Yes, that doesn't sound correct, that he would," Mila said.

"He loves it here, though," Amanda went on. "He talks about those two years all the time. I met him a couple of years after that." She took a long sip and sucked on the ice. "Oh, and you know what else? This is so weird. He says people there didn't even call him Mark back then. They just called him 'meneer.' Colonization is so fucked up." She looked at her empty glass as if there were a surprise at the bottom. "I need to go to bed."

Persephone, whose eyelids were fluttering, agreed. From down the path, they heard the growing roar of Hector's engine.

"Ah. There is my ride." Mila stood up quickly. "I believe you are safe now. No poachers, no rhinos."

"Thanks, Mila. We'll see you in the morning?" Amanda asked.

But Mila Shilongo had already disappeared into the bush.

Winter

Ovengi ve puka nu kave karara.
Many people get lost but do not sleep in the forest.
—Herero proverb

19

There was something happening in the shepherd's tree. Amanda was in the kitchen, checking the Tusk! Instagram page, which was going through a large uptick of activity. She and Persephone had posted daily photos of Mila's rhino, whom they'd affectionately started calling Mr. Sharp, for no particular reason. Adam had taken quite a lot of pictures, after causing all that trouble, so there were enough angles to make it seem as if they were all exciting new shots. Persephone had even gone so far as having one of her UVA sorority sisters—now a style editor at *The Washington Post*—write a tiny profile of Tusk!, complete with shots of Mr. Sharp and Persephone looking uncharacteristically pensive on the game drive.

Yet the *Post* feature didn't appear to be the cause of the uptick. Persephone's profile had brought on a few hundred followers, certainly, but it was the addition of the tag #rhinopoaching that seemed to have pushed them into the thousands. Amanda tried to discern a pattern among the followers in order to target others, but the demographic was all over the place. Tusk! followers were from Europe, Asia, the United States, and a very few from Africa itself. And then there was a large subset who didn't identify their nationality and represented themselves with photos of stuffed animals.

"Perhaps those are the fuzzy people," Persephone had said when they had stared at the page together earlier in the day.

"What?"

"No. Furry. They're called furries. People who like to fornicate in animal costumes."

"For someone with so many etiquette rules, your knowledge of the seamier side of life never ceases to amaze," Amanda said.

From a marketing standpoint, Amanda knew the furry theory couldn't be the case. Something else was causing this interest. And she was right in the middle of funneling the profiles into a complicated graph analysis when she heard what could only be called a bird commotion. Stepping outside, she gingerly approached the tree, in the limbs of which a swarm of birds seemed to be roosting. Was she imagining this Hitchcock moment? No, there were hundreds—maybe *thousands*—of birds in her very tree.

"Hello?" Amanda called out timidly. "Can I help you?"

In the very next moment a text came in, signaled by a cheerful *ding!* And, as if on cue, all of the birds took flight at once, momentarily darkening the sky before scattering in all directions.

It was eleven o'clock, exactly the time of day when she inevitably found she had nothing to do. She'd already run four miles, so there was no need to do any more exercise. During the first few months of their time here, she had filled the vacant hours with various sorts of clerical tasks: itemizing receipts for next year's taxes, trading a bit of stock, reading about the latest Silicon Valley news.

This particular morning, Amanda had also fielded a biweekly email from Ronnie, a developer she worked with back at GiaTech who was convinced he was in love with her. Amanda had twelve years on Ronnie and a college and a graduate degree to boot, and, snobby or not, she felt that gave her the upper hand in judging his supposed feelings. (Ronnie was one of those Silicon Valley wonders who'd stepped into a two-hundred-thousand-dollar salary right out of high school.) He'd worked for her indirectly, though, when he presented himself to her. She couldn't remember him being at any of her meetings; but then, most of her meetings consisted of her acting brisk and bitchy in front of a whiteboard the size of a movie screen, and the (mostly male) developers, designers, product managers, project managers, and other human flotsam quaked at her "hard stops" and "delivery dates."

The week before Amanda left for Namibia, the company threw a goodbye party for her at a club in the Mission called the Church, which was exactly what it sounded like: a once-holy place of worship, it had now been bought by tech millionaires and converted "ironically," to a bar that served overpriced kombucha cocktails. Amanda and Mark had gotten into a huge fight, which resulted in two things: his absence from the party, and her getting more shitfaced than she'd been since Dartmouth. And it was those circumstances, she'd repeatedly tried to explain to Ronnie, that had led to her making out with him in the alley, when she had innocently gone out to share her first cigarette in twelve years.

It was Amanda's opinion that Ronnie's consequent hard crush on her was the result of her presumed power. She tried to explain, in response to his multiple flirty-yet-desperate messages, that she had no power anymore, she was just a housewife, a MILF on her best days, if you squinted. Ronnie wasn't buying it. But Amanda, in her hungover state the morning after the party, had made the colossal mistake of replying when he emailed her at 6:12 a.m. about their "awesome night together." Which meant there was an email chain on her company email server. Which meant, in the #MeToo era when Silicon Valley journalists would kill their firstborn to get their hands on a story about a female-sexual-predator boss, Amanda had to handle Ronnie very, very carefully. So she did. She told no one, and she responded to each of his messages in a friendly, motherly tone. Someday, she prayed, he would find a GiaTech babe his own age, probably while stuck in traffic on the luxury GiaTech shuttle bus.

Having sent her placating missive of the day, Amanda wandered out onto the patio. She was finding the torpor of Africa in general increasingly seductive. Amanda often found her mind going back again and again to the night she and Persephone had spent camping out on Mila's farm. The wild animal and insect sounds drowning out all things human, the delicious warm desert wind on her arms and cheeks. Yes. She'd liked it. And navigating Windhoek, after six months, was becoming less impossible. She knew how to go to the bread lady and ask to have the health loaf, sliced. She knew that *banting* meant Paleo. She knew that *now-now* meant "in a little while." She knew that when the butcher said that the minced lamb was "finished," if you just stood there, smiling expectantly and not moving, he would eventually go put more through the grinder.

So Amanda was learning Namibia. And yet, she couldn't help feeling that she would never truly understand everything. As a foreigner, she was always half in the dark. Like this thing with Mila. She was certain they'd been good friends. Positive. And it couldn't just have been one-sided, could it? For three months, they'd been going for two-hour lunches at least once a week, sometimes twice. But ever since the trip to Osha, Mila had shut Amanda out. She never returned Amanda's calls or emails. Amanda looked for her at school, but Taimi was always picked up now by a government car or an assistant. Mila hadn't gone as far as keeping Taimi and Meg apart (thank God), but when Taimi came over for playdates, again she was ferried in the government car, and when Amanda dropped Meg off, her daughter was ushered in by Libertina, the nanny.

Amanda had gone so far as to ask, via email and even a handwritten note delivered via Meg, what she had done wrong. But there was no answer. Which led her to believe that, no matter how much she thought she was coming to understand Namibia, really she must have remained completely blind, because just by being herself she had managed to alienate one of her very favorite new friends.

The phone dinged a second time, reminding her of the text. It was Mark.

Halfway home. Got you a present. You're perfect in every way and I love you.

Amanda raised her eyebrows and sighed. Where the hell was this coming from? It was exactly the sort of thing she would have consulted Mila about.

Stop texting and driving, she wrote back. Then, a few seconds later: Love you too.

She got up to straighten the house, as Frida wasn't coming for two more days. She knew she should leave Meg's room to Meg herself. Giving her the duty of straightening up and taking care of her own things would surely impart a sense of responsibility; if nothing else, it would help ensure that when she got to college and lived with a roommate she wouldn't be an asshole slob.

But just the thought of enforcing this, along with the chore chart Mark had constructed, exhausted her, so she went ahead and started. She separated the disturbingly perverse Barbies from the sweet stuffies, folded Meg's cute mini-sized underpants, made the bed, and alphabetized the books. The only area of the room Meg managed to keep neat herself was her desk, where framed photos of her friends from California were organized lovingly and propped up in pink frames. As she surveyed all those images of Los Gatos kids skiing and becoming geniuses, something caught her eye: a book decorated with a sparkly unicorn. It was the diary with lock and key Santa had brought upon request that year.

Other, more respectful mothers, Amanda knew, would hesitate. Not Amanda. She sat down in Meg's little desk chair, slid the diary in front of her, and looked carefully around the surface for the key. Her daughter had not yet developed the teenage skill of concealment—something that would surely come, Amanda knew, when it came time to hide pot and condoms—and so the key to the diary, too, was behind the framed photos, in a mesh bag that had contained Meg's first pierced earrings (yet another cheer-up bribe that Amanda had paid for by facing Mark's wrath). She turned the sack over, and, sure enough, the key—a cheap metal thing—clattered out. She put it into the lock and turned, opening the book with a little, satisfying *sprong*.

MEG EVANS, read the inside cover.

AGE 9. Home: CALIFORNIA. (NOT AFRICA!!!!)

Do not read. If you keep reeding, you have lost a very big freindship.

Amanda paused at that, but then decided that she and her daughter were not exactly *friends*. So she turned to the first page.

My name is Meg. My dad made us moov here. I have friends but I am not sure they like me. On the playground they sometimes won't eat with me. Then sometimes they will.

Amanda felt a punch directly to her heart. Those little bitches.

I wish Dad could just do his work in America. I miss America. I miss air Castle and my friends. But Wakaberry is here and that is ok.

I stole a Kit Kat from the Christmans candy jar.

That was it for Day One. Amanda flipped past a few drawings she couldn't decipher and went on to the next entry.

Dad and Mom are always talking about secrits. They had a secrit they won't tell me I think. What if we have to move to a different county now? China Lisa has to move every single year. I felt bad for her but then she put sand in my lunchbox so now I'm glad she is moving to Prog.

Another entry:

Today, Taimi and I got:

1670
280
5772
977

She told me to keep trak bc I am the tresurur. Except that is boring. Next time I will be president.

Another:

Taimi is my best friend here. We did not like each other at first but then we fought and her mom made us talk. Our moms are friends too. Her mom is so pretty and dresses like she is going to a party every day. That is not what my mom does but my mom looks OK most of the tim.

Amanda looked down at her outfit—blue shorts and flowered mom shirt. Fuck.

Another diagram of a man and a woman. The man had an X over his face.

My dad always yells at me at dinner.

The last entry:

Taimi and I don't play Cheetah anymore. We play spy. But since we are spies, we tell everyone we are playing cheetah. We run around the playground like we did before, but we're really listening to what people are saying. They don't know it because they think we are doing something else!!

Taimi is really good at spy. She especially is good at listening to grown ups. We hid in her mom's closet and heard her mom on the phone talking about something. She was telling Mr. Shelxx?? that she was mad because Taimis dad was at his friends house too much.

She makes me hide by myself to listen but I get bored so I just read.

Taimi showed me her sister's bra. We put it on her head. Ha. Taimi is so smart. Our spy store is perfect. But it's a secrit so I better not rite anymore!!!

Our favrite music is Sextopia. Taimi had a silver plate with songs on it we listned to it on something very very old called a Disk Man. She is so pretty. Taimi says she is from the south of africa.

Also, sex is what happens when a man pees into a woman's urethra.

GROOOOOOSSSSSSSSSSS

That was it.

Amanda closed the book, locking it again and replacing it in its hiding place. She stood for a few minutes, staring at the wall. Then she left the room and closed the door firmly, as if doing so could convince her that she had never read any of her daughter's words.

Sextopia?

"To hell with that," Amanda said out loud. "Goddamnit. Now she *has* to talk to me."

Deciding the mom shirt wouldn't do—not for an unexpected visit to Mila's—she pulled out a robin's-egg-blue Armani pantsuit (an ode to Hillary she'd worn a few times in her Silicon Valley days), then pulled her hair into a chignon. She even put on some eyeliner, and was just deciding whether or not it was worth it to wear heels when she heard the gate beep.

Mark. Why on earth did he have to come home so early? She looked at herself in the mirror, trying to decide how much to tell him. But the thing was, they had always been honest with each other, from the beginning. That was how they worked.

He walked in, calling for her.

"In here!" she called back. Mark came into the bedroom, dropping his bag heavily. He came over and pulled her to him so tightly her ribs hurt.

"Hi," she squeaked. He laughed and let her go.

"You look fancy," he said. "Pretty, too. I missed you, Mandi."

"Look, I have to talk to you."

"What?" He looked at her strangely. "Did Jaime call?"

"God, no. Jaime? Blech. No. It's Meg. I think she's in trouble, and it's my fault, because, well, I didn't see the signs."

"What?" he said, alarmed.

"I think she's involved in something strange," Amanda said. "She and Taimi are listening to something called Sextopia."

"Sextopia?"

"She's a singer."

"I don't know," Mark said. "I don't really think you can control what kids listen to, can you?"

Amanda couldn't believe she was hearing this. From Mark. Mark, who freaked out if Meg ate a Skittle.

"She's nine!"

"What did Taimi's mother say when you spoke to her?"

Amanda toed the carpet. "That's another thing I haven't really told you about. See, we don't really speak anymore."

"What?" Mark said. "You love Mila. I was really looking forward to meeting her. Why didn't you tell me?"

"I don't know."

Of course she knew. She was just like Meg. She felt rejected, and she didn't want to talk about it.

"Well, what happened?"

"I don't know. I must have said something," she said reluctantly. "Or maybe it was a cultural thing. I mean, we didn't talk about anything. Persephone can't figure it out, either—though Mila's fine with her now, oddly. Anyway, I'm going over there. Now. Because . . . what the hell, you know?"

She realized her eyes were welling with tears, and brushed them away angrily.

Mark sat on the yellow ruffled bed. "I guess I'm feeling a little behind here, babe," he said. "And how do you even know all of this? About what Lolo's doing?"

Amanda sighed and leaned on the indestructible State Department dresser. "I didn't," she said. "Only, then, today, when I was cleaning her room—"

"She's supposed to clean her own room."

"While I was *doing* that, I found her diary."

"Okay."

"And I read it."

"Wow," Mark said, scratching the back of his neck. "I'm sort of impressed, actually. That's, like, the very worst thing a mom can do, isn't it?"

"I could sell her into prostitution. Or burn her alive to appease the war gods, like in that scene from *Game of Thrones*. That would be worse." Mark scooted back to lean against the wall and folded his arms over his chest. "I really don't think you should be reading her diary."

"Well, I did. And I found out she's into Sextopia. I mean, what could that even *be*?"

"I don't—"

"And then there's some kind of pretend store . . ."

"What?"

"Oh, I don't know." She smoothed the wrinkles in her jacket. "Anyway, I'm headed over to talk to Mila about it, even though she's been freezing me out for two fucking months."

Mark moved to the edge of the bed, putting his elbow on his knees. "This is a lot to process, having just walked in the door."

"Yeah, I know. Sorry." She leaned down and kissed him on his head, then righted herself to look at him again, waiting for the old rush to wash over her. There was a sense of powerlessness that used to run through, sharp as an electric current, when she looked at the different elements that made up his face: bridge of his nose, slightly crooked, that tiny plump place at the top inner corner of his cheek. But now, hard as she tried to conjure that frightening, often inconvenient experience, she found that she couldn't. All she was doing was scratching an itch that wasn't there.

"Will you come?" she asked, finally. "To Mila's? So we can have a united front?"

"Sure," Mark said. How completely unaware he is, Amanda thought, of how close I am to blowing up our life. As if responding to her thought, he got up and hugged her reassuringly. "Listen—it'll be okay."

Amanda gave a weak snort into his chest and turned her face the other way, as if to move from the lie.

Amanda drove, while Mark flipped the radio from Radiowave to a classical station that played favorites like Beethoven and Brahms punctuated by Afrikaans hymns. Amanda was a slow, careful driver, allowing Mark to look out the window at the high, pastel-colored walls surrounding the hulking houses of Ludwigsdorf, laced on top with broken shards of glass and electric wire.

It was three o'clock, and crowds of workmen dressed in blue suits were already waiting to fight for cabs to the Location. Purple clouds billowed over the southern mountains, signaling their empty promise of storms that wouldn't come. On the few afternoons it did rain, Amanda had noticed, Namibians walked about on it without coats or umbrellas, holding out their hands and saying things like, *Isn't it a beautiful day?* The rest of the time, everyone was just waiting for it to come back.

They wound their way up Joseph Ithana Street, climbing farther yet up a spectacularly steep hill, then pulled in front of a fortress of steel, glass, and white cement walls.

"Man," Mark said. "These Shilongos aren't fooling around, are they?"

Amanda didn't answer, but rolled down the window and pressed the call button. They waited, then heard a muffled crackling.

"Yes?"

"Libertina," Amanda said, before pausing awkwardly. "It's Persephone."

What? Mark mouthed.

Amanda made a motion for him to stay quiet.

"Yes, miss?"

"Nothing serious, but I need to speak to Miss Shilongo, please."

"Just a moment." The speaker crackled off again. A few moments later, she came back. "Miss Shilongo is in a meeting."

"Tell her it's very important. It's about International Day. It's just . . . too much work, and so I wanted to ask her to be chairwoman again."

Libertina disappeared again.

"Mandi, this is weird."

"You said you'd come. Now go with it."

The speaker outside the window crackled.

"She will come out. Yes. Please drive in."

Mark and Amanda exchanged glances. The gate rumbled open, and Amanda navigated up the circuitous drive.

"Won't she recognize your car?" Mark said.

"Too late now," Amanda said. "We're in!" She pulled directly in front of the front door. "Stay here," she said, getting out. "It'll go better if I talk first."

Mark obeyed, slumping down in his seat with the newspaper. The door opened, and Mila stepped into the sunlight. As usual, she was dressed to the nines, in a black sheath dress and heels. The moment she saw Amanda, she froze in her tracks.

"Mila," Amanda said. "I'm sorry, but I had to figure out a way to talk to you. I know you're mad at me, for some reason. And I don't care even about that . . . truly—I'm sorry for whatever I did. This is more *important* than that. I'm concerned about our daughters."

Amanda could have sworn that in that moment her friend's face softened. Was she finally going to talk to her? She could almost hear what Mila would say. A baboon and a baby elephant, they make their own mischief. Or, hard is the baobab that only drinks wine. And Amanda would stare at her, and Mila would give some brilliant insight, and they would laugh and be friends again.

But instead, the very opposite happened. Mila glanced at the car, then back at Amanda, then turned and stepped back into the house, slamming the door.

Amanda stood, stunned, in the doorway. Brushing an angry tear off her cheek, she descended the steps and slowly got into the car.

"She didn't even give me a chance," Amanda said.

"I'm sorry, baby," Mark said. "I couldn't see from here. Did she even look at you?"

"It's just so strange," she said. "What do you think is going on?"

Mark rubbed her shoulder. "I wouldn't worry too much. Look at Meg. Look at *everyone*. You never can really know what's going on in someone's head, can you?"

Amanda bit her lip, looking away from her husband. Did he know what she had been thinking earlier? That they would be better off without each other?

"No," she said. "You really can't."

20

Mila stood on the balcony, watching the Evanses' station wagon retreat down the white gravel drive. So it had happened. She had seen the American. And it had been every bit as bad as she had feared. Her only consolation was that she was fairly sure he hadn't seen *her*. He'd been gazing downward, either at his phone or the car radio, and she had stepped back out of his sight before he had time to look up.

Yet it was unmistakably him. Her Mark, her meneer. He was older now, wizened, even, but he had the same shaggy hair and the same glasses. He even still wore the same sort of plaid, rumpled button-down shirt.

The rest of the world had grown up, but not Amanda Evans's husband. He had seen no consequences. He had found another woman to take care of him, a woman who, because God was a joker, had become Mila's friend. It had been so long, but the old hate rose, white-hot and metallic, as soon as she'd glimpsed him.

Amanda was lucky all Mila had done was slam the door.

Esther's eyes opened slowly, blinking away at the unfamiliar, milky morning light that seemed particular to the sea. She sat up, rubbing her head, which felt full of cotton. Last night's alcohol rang in her mouth. The man on the floor nearby was still sleeping. She sat up in bed, looking at him more closely. His head rested on his arm, which was flung out in front of him. His hair was long for Namibia; it fell in a silky curtain across his forehead. His skin was tanned brown, and his cheeks looked as if they'd been rubbed lightly with strawberry jam. His glasses rested by his wrist.

He didn't look like any other man she'd seen up close for a long time. The Afrikaans men who came into JoJo's were usually purple from drinking and sun, and the English South Africans were often quite handsome, but they were so proud of their looks Esther had always found them repellent. She had avoided looking at Mark as well until now, but he was something different, according to his behavior last night. Or if he wasn't, at least he was asleep, affording her the privilege of close observation.

She leaned over, taking in the details as she would those of an object. The color of his hair was complicated—a very shiny brown, but with other strands, lightened by the sun, shot through, giving the effect of burned gold. His lips were pink like a little boy's and crusted with drool. His lashes were dark but not long, resting on the top of his cheek. His bare shoulder, freed from the sheet, was a round, beautiful thing, sculpted by whatever gyming he was doing in his spare time. His body was tall and strong, with all the same indentations and shadows as the men in the donated book of Greek myths she and Saara would pore over in school. Overall, he was very fine, she decided. And his beauty was more useful than hers, in that it was approachable, and would never cause him trouble.

Esther drew up her knees and gazed out the window. Being paid money for sex, that would have been crushing. Yet she wasn't against having sex for recreational purposes. The politics of giving one's body over in Ovamboland were so complicated, there seemed to be no joy in such things. But she couldn't say she wasn't curious.

When she came out of the shower, Mark was up, dressed, and moving back and forth on the balls of his feet.

"Good morning!" he said a bit too loudly.

"Good morning."

"I was wondering if you'd like to go to the beach today."

Esther did want to go to the beach again, as yesterday had been very nice. But it struck her that this was, actually, what he had paid for. Going to the beach with this American was the job, which meant she would derive no pleasure from it, no matter how hard she tried.

"If you want."

"'If you want'?" Mark frowned. "Still nervous, then, about swimming?"

She could only bring herself to shrug.

"I'll help you. I was actually a lifeguard for a couple of summers."

"I'm not going to swim. I don't have a bathing suit."

"We can buy you one. In the store downstairs."

"Stop buying me things," Esther said crossly. "That was the whole problem in the first place. You paying me."

"We've been over this, Esther," Mark said. "Your friend had me give you money. She said you guys couldn't afford it. Listen, you can pay me back if you want."

Esther couldn't help laughing at his American sense of how money worked. "Do you have any idea how long that would take?"

"Look," Mark said. "I said I'd help you. Can we just have fun today? When was the last time you had fun?"

Esther looked at him, considering. Fun was another thing tourists in JoJo's were always talking about. *Safaris are so fun! . . . That drum circle place near Vic Falls—have you been? So fun!* Esther did not know much about that sort of fun. She was too worried about how to feed herself and not having to resort to selling herself for sex. But here it was. Fun. Shouldn't she try it, for once?

"All right," she said.

Once she had given herself over to it, the commitment to fun, which, she now knew, equated to not caring, she found it very easy. She let Mark take her to the shop downstairs for a bathing suit. He waited shyly outside while she fingered the material of the different garments, and she even considered buying one that came in two pieces, but she knew that would be too much, even for the new, fun Esther. Finally she settled on a black and red one; the shopgirl, who was Ovambo, let her slip it on in the dressing room.

"All set?" Mark asked when she came out.

"I have it on," she said, turning away at the strange, frustrated look on his face. She was used to men desiring her, but she wasn't accustomed to them trying to hide it.

He bought fruit and sodas, and they arranged themselves side by side on the Mole. The sand was searing hot, so she kept her feet on the blanket. They didn't talk much; Mark seemed tired. After a while, he asked if she wanted to go in the water.

"Ovambos don't swim," Esther said. "I told you."

"Just your toes, Esther. Come on." He jumped up and held out his hand. He looked so lovely there, above her, so tall and friendly. She found that she couldn't say no. She took his hand and let him pull her up; together they walked to where the water licked the sand. Heart beating fast, she let him lead her to where the water reached her ankles.

"Now you don't have to be afraid of the water," he said, smiling. "See?"

"Not afraid of the water," she said, fighting back the panic as the sea rose above her knees and thighs. "Yes, all right."

My feet cannot breathe, she thought. My knees, they are drowning.

But something happened as she went out deeper. She was up to her waist when Mark put his hands on both sides of her waist and held her up. Esther had never been held from any danger before; not as a child, not as a baby. As an infant she learned the hard way not to go near a fire, or not to toddle in front of a bakkie. Now someone was protecting her from anything bad that could happen in that moment, and it was as if a lifetime of worrying slipped away. Relief coursed through her so strongly she started to cry, and turned her head away so the meneer couldn't see.

Everything had gone so well the night before, they did the same again: same walk, same restaurant. Though Esther didn't drink tonight, and there was no fuss tonight from the others, perhaps because the staff remembered them from the night before. As they walked back, they were silent; she didn't know if he knew she'd made the decision, but she guessed that he did, as he took her hand as they climbed the back stairs, and didn't flip on the lights when they walked into the room. She closed the door behind her and he came so close she could feel the day's sun radiating off his body.

"Is this okay?" he asked.

"It's okay," she said.

He put his arms around her and pulled her so close, she felt that he could hold up every part of her body were they somehow to fall. They stayed that way for what seemed like a long time before he kissed her slowly and moved her to the bed. After each thing he did, he'd look up at her to see if she liked it. When he was finally inside her, he went deep, moving back and forth at half the speed of a slow heartbeat. He wouldn't speed up, even when she was clutching the cheap metal bed-frame and clutching the limp pillow with her hand.

"I'll never leave you, Esther," he whispered. She could barely hear him for all that was happening in her body. He promised her again and again, as she rode away on a wave of something that was the opposite of water.

After weeks of scheduling conflicts, the Big A. had decided the best location for the rhino lunch would be the Official Residence itself. Persephone tried not to be irritated. Half the fun of having lunch with the ambassador was other people seeing you. It was an unspoken rule that if you saw the Big A. out and about at a meal or in a conversation, you didn't interrupt, as she was likely to be engaging in some sort of foreign policy. Persephone nearly salivated at the thought of Kayla or Shoshana being kept at bay from the window of the linen shop, paralyzed by protocol. But no, the email from the assistant summoned Persephone and Amanda to the OR, at 1:00 on a Tuesday for some "cold salads." Anything to get an audience, but it was disappointing.

"I'm not sure the ambassador even *cares* about rhinos," Persephone had grumbled to Adam one evening as they brushed their teeth side by side.

"She does," he said. "She mentioned your club the other day, actually."

"It's not a club. So were you getting an assignment?" she asked, searching his face for clues.

"Never mind that, honey cunt."

"Adam!" She drew away. "You're disgusting."

"This is the trust tree, sugar! Anyway, she said she was looking forward to it. Now, speaking of assignments, I'm missing dinner again and can't tell you why." He kissed her cheek noisily. "Cover for me with the kids, will you? I'm so glad you know now, sweet ass. It really is helping my work, because I don't have to spend valuable brain effort, you know, dissimulating."

"Good," Persephone mumbled, disappointed with the lack of information he was dropping. "Only, I'd rather be helping in a more . . . meaningful way. Isn't there anything I can do?"

"*Little* meeting?" Persephone repeated. She really was impressed that her husband had turned out to be an agent for the Central Intelligence Agency, but today everything he said made her want to stab him in the eye. "By the way, can you tell me if anyone else is working with you on your missions?"

"Absolutely not."

"Because the girls saw you out the other night with a brunette. Ainsley, perhaps?"

Ainsley was a little slip of a thing whose official title was "Assistant to Procurement," flown in all the way from Chattanooga, Tennessee. Every time Persephone had been at the embassy, she'd observed that Ainsley was: (A) never at her desk; (B) always talking inappropriately intensely to male officials more highly ranked than her—as in, Shoshana's husband, Kayla's husband, or Adam; and (C) allergic to bras and skirts bigger than postage stamps.

"Dear heart, if the girls saw me with Ainsley, it could have been any sort of embassy task, secret or not." He straightened his tie. "Though I'll give you a little dribble and tell you I can neither *confirm* nor *deny* that she is a fellow agent. But, really, that is all you get. Now scram!"

He slapped her, a bit too hard, on the bottom.

"You *know* I hate that."

"Back to the salt mines, sugar," he crowed, pressing his key fob to elicit a loud chirp from his BMW.

After Adam left, Persephone found herself uncharacteristically indecisive about her outfit. She started out in a white pantsuit that any other day would have been perfect, but today made her feel like Elvis. Her white crochet dress was too short. (Ainsley!) Boots over white jeans made her look like a pirate. Finally she settled on a knee-length flared snowy dress with a silver pendant around her neck shaped like—what else?—a rhino.

"Too on the nose?" she asked when Amanda pulled up in front of her house to pick her up.

"You pull it off," Amanda said. Her friend was considerably less dressed up, in one of those "sporty" dresses of nylon that could, in Persephone's opinion, double as bathing suit material. But then, Persephone had never been drawn to California fashion.

The Official Residence was meant to intimidate, and as they parked in the guarded lot, sifted through the layers of security, and rang the gongy bell, Persephone had to admit that she did, indeed, feel quite small. The walls were even taller than any other fortresses on the block, which was nothing compared to the armed guards. An attendant opened the door and ushered them inside.

"Greetings!" the Big A. called out, emerging from the depths of the mansion. Persephone looked around thoughtfully. At parties, the OR looked cheerful and opulent, but in the daylight, empty of guests, the place looked like a rather uninspired hotel event space. Why, the furniture was the same as in all the State Department houses, now that she looked at it, just covered in fabric that was maybe a little more expensive.

"Hello, Miss Ambassador," Persephone said dutifully.

"Thank you for having us, Julia," Amanda said. Persephone felt her eye twitch slightly. *Julia?* Though now that she knew Adam's real role, she could see why the Big A. chose to keep her at a distance. She gave her a small wink to let her know she understood.

"I hope you don't mind chicken salad," she said, nodding blankly back at Persephone. "I adore it." She gestured at the table, which, Persephone was heartened to see, was set properly with diplomatic china and silver. "Do you know its origin?"

"No," Persephone said, trying to sound interested.

"It's from your town, Amanda. You're from Charleston, yes? The first mention of it appeared in a housewife's cookbook in 1840-something. A Miss Sarah Rutledge. Her recipe suggested adding oysters, which even I am not adventurous enough to try. Particularly in the desert! And then another recipe became quite famous up in Rhode Island at a certain butcher's shop in 1863. That might have been one of the few things the North and the South agreed on. Chicken salad!" The Big A. looked at them brightly, waiting for a reaction.

"I knew that, actually," Amanda said, looking at the platter a bit glumly.

"I had my assistant look it up. She has the time, and I just love these little factoids, don't you? Every time she plans a menu, she sends me a briefing with the historical origin of the food. It's especially handy before long dinners with diplomats from other countries I have nothing in common with. Which doesn't mean you, of course! Still, now we *all* know all about chicken salad. It's a win!"

Persephone sat delicately in her chair, waited for Amanda and the ambassador to serve themselves, then put some lettuce and the driest bit of chicken on her own plate. She abhorred chicken salad, whatever its historical backstory. Though the ambassador *did* seem to adore it, as she was already tucking into a pile of it that reached up toward her chin.

"So I looked into this organization of yours," said the Big A. "This rhino society."

"It's a conservation effort, really," Amanda said.

"An action group," Persephone added.

"Whatever it is, it's very impressive. Fifteen thousand Instagram followers, no less! However did you do that?"

"It just grew," Persephone said.

"And, of course, there were some targeted marketing efforts," Amanda added.

"Yes. And then there was the article in the *Post*," the Big A. said.

"Oh! That was *me*," Persephone confessed, delighted. "My girlfriend from school is actually an editor at the Style section."

"That was a mistake, of course."

"What?" Persephone felt her cheeks go scarlet. She did not make mistakes. Ever. "Why?"

"Don't misunderstand me." The Big A. dabbed her lip with a napkin. "It was a fairly positive story."

"Fairly?" She could feel Amanda giving her a warning glance. She didn't care.

"It's just—when we gave you our resources, ladies, we didn't exactly think your organization would garner this kind of attention."

"What resources?" Persephone protested. "You haven't given us any—"

Amanda held up her hand, effectively silencing her. The ambassador looked amused at the discord.

"Well," she said, "you've been using the Internet at your homes, which of course the government pays for. And then there are office supplies, which I happen to know, through PeerWatch, you've been ordering on Amazon through the pouch, another government-subsidized program."

"PeerWatch?" Persephone put her fork down more forcefully than she would have liked, which was unfortunate, because it sprang off the table. PeerWatch was a particularly controversial unofficial State Department program that rewarded officers for delivering evidence of "unpatriotic behavior" shown by colleagues to their superiors. A remnant of the Cold War, PeerWatch kept State Department personnel and their spouses steeped in fear when, for example, they used their diplomatic passports to get good rooms on vacation in Cape Town, or snuck to Chinatown to get one of those beautiful and very illegal zebra purses. PeerWatch, in fact, was the very reason Persephone could not have cocktails—or associate at all, in fact—with Kathy Hanley, a charming friend from Hotchkiss who happened to live in Windhoek after marrying a Russian construction oligarch. Which was a real sacrifice, as Kathy had a private plane. And now this stupid policy was getting in the way of her *cause?*

"Who was it? Kayla?" Persephone growled. "Because *I* happen to know that she—"

She felt a sharp pain as Amanda kicked her shin.

"What can we do to solve this problem?" Amanda said, in a corporate tone with which Persephone was wholly unfamiliar.

"It's not a *problem*," the ambassador said. "Don't get me wrong. It's simply a matter of . . . credit."

"But I—"

Amanda kicked her again. "Tell us more," her friend said.

"The State Department isn't about *individual* ideas. Persephone, you know that. It's not about *one* person shining. It's about our country doing the right thing in Namibia."

"Who was shining?" Persephone cried. "What was too shiny?"

"The article was about you. The pictures, the work. But you are here to support the State Department. It's not against the rules, per se. But since you used our resources, we think you should share the credit."

"Well, that sounds fine," Amanda said.

"*Why* does that sound fine?" Persephone trilled.

Down the hall, a door opened and shut briskly, and footsteps clicked toward them. It was Ellie, the Big A.'s assistant, bartender, and wineglass tracker.

"Miss Ambassador?" she said. "May I speak to you for a moment?"

"Excuse me," the Big A. said. "Duty calls."

Persephone and Amanda waited until the door shut again.

"Look," Amanda said. "You need to cool it. Where is Charming Persephone? The one who dresses her kids like professional leprechauns? Because that's who I need right now."

"I can't help it. I'm so mad." She picked up her glass and took a gulp of water, then put it back down, as her hand was shaking. "I *know* Shoshana and Kayla spied on us. They're so *jealous*."

"It doesn't matter, sweetie. Look at the endgame. Though I honestly had no idea this rhino thing was so important to you."

"I don't know . . . it was just . . ." What was it? Why was she getting so worked up? "Mila's rhino . . . I keep . . . *thinking* about it. How it looked at me, and how we could hear it breathing. This enormous animal. He—Mr. Sharp—*means* something to me. Truly. And now we have all these followers. It's like we're actually *doing* something. I haven't done anything in so long."

Amanda patted her arm. "I understand. But just . . . cool it. Okay?"

"Right," Persephone said. "Hold yo' bek."

"No idea," Amanda said. "Just stop talking."

The door opened again, and the ambassador returned, looking grim.

"Everything all right?" Amanda asked.

"Let's finish this conversation," the Big A. said, pushing her plate away. "At the end of the day, the goal is the same here, isn't it? More protection, more attention. But I believe, if you're going to continue, that you have to include more of the embassy community."

Persephone sucked in her breath. "How so?"

"Obviously, our officers are very, very busy. Yet our spouses are not. And so I need you to include more people. Specifically——"

"Shoshana Levin," Persephone said through gritted teeth, hoping she looked like she was smiling.

"Well," the Big A. said. "Certainly. But I was going to say, specifically, the spouses."

"No problem," Amanda said. "We'll make it happen. Of course, Persephone, as the head of Tusk!, will delegate duties."

Persephone sat back in her chair. Oh. She would be in *charge* of Shoshana. Well, that would be okay. More than fine, in fact.

"Terrific," the ambassador said. "And now I'm afraid I have two bits of bad news. The first is, I have to leave now, before dessert. Though you should have some. It's chocolate mousse with bits of real cocoa. I brought the pods from Brazil myself. Chef wanted to make a milk tart, but I get so tired of it, don't you?"

Persephone sniffed. No, she did *not* get tired of milk tart. Ever.

"The second item, I'm afraid, is much more serious. Apparently, some poachers broke into the Shilongos' farm, and there was an attempt to poach their rhino."

"Oh no," Amanda said, covering her mouth. Persephone couldn't process the words. All she could think of was little poached eggs.

"What do you mean?" she ventured.

"Someone shorted out a small portion of their electric fence on the north side. They cut the wire and went in by foot. Luckily, the caretaker was alerted by the electric disturbance and managed to chase them off."

"So Mr. Sharp is okay?"

"Oh yes. You named the animal. I forgot. Yes. Grazed, but fine."

Persephone felt a lurch in her stomach, firmly disagreeing with her chicken salad. "Do you think it was our fault?" she whispered.

The ambassador looked thoughtful. "You know, I hadn't thought of that. Maybe! That's an interesting lead. I'll get our security team on it right away."

Amanda put her hand reassuringly on her arm. "Persephone, we didn't give any locations. They couldn't have tracked him from us."

"We'll look into it." And with that, the ambassador stood and rang a bell on the sideboard. Ellie brought her bag and coat. "For now, just assure me that you'll widen your circle. And look, you should feel proud of raising awareness! Even if you did almost kill this one rhino. At the end of the day, a gain is a gain. I'll see you ladies."

The front door slammed. Persephone wilted in tears over her mousse.

That night, after lulling Lucy and the twins to sleep by reading them an article from *The Economist* (a directive from Adam to prepare their young brains for the business world) Persephone poured herself a drink and logged on to Instagram to look at her pictures of Mr. Sharp. Tusk! had posted thirty-five photos total. Sixteen were of Mr. Sharp, taken by Mila's caretaker, as well as Adam with his gargantuan lens. Persephone loved looking at the photos of the animal. His liquid eyes were placid and almost understanding, and she could still hear the loud, comforting rhythm of his breathing. She took another sip of whiskey and scrolled down through the profile. Who had commented? Had anyone left strange posts? Certainly there were a few serious rhino voyeurs. Fuzzylove, who said she was from Tokyo and represented herself with an image of a panda, had left short novels about rhinos on just about every post. Mr. Chakalaka, from Johannesburg, posted links to hundreds of rhino fan sites. There were comments under every posted photo (including some about how her own backside looked in white jeans—good Lord, why hadn't she been monitoring this?), but the most popular by far were the photos of Mr. Sharp himself. One follower had even posted a portrait she had drawn of him, adding a party hat as a third horn.

And then she saw it. Numbers. A user with the name bearhunt245 had posted numbers right under the photo Adam had taken. She went to the other photos of Mr. Sharp. Under each of them, bearhunt245 had posted numbers. Different sets of numbers, but numbers all the same.

She drained her glass and went to find her cell phone. Petrus had once given her his phone number after too many Tafels at an embassy event. In case you need any computer help, he'd whispered in that sexy Namibian way he had. Well, perhaps they'd both had too many Tafels. Harmless. Her own mother had told her often that flirting was nothing more than a "Jane Fonda workout for one's charms."

"Hello?" Petrus rumbled now on the other end of the line.

"Petrus."

"Yes?"

"It's Persephone."

There was a confused pause.

"Persephone Wilder."

"Oh *hey*! Hallo!" There it was, that wonderful voice of his. "Good evening. What a surprise. Sorry, I was asleep."

254 / Katie Crouch

"Did I wake up your wife?"

"Not at all, not at all. Did I tell you we put Faiza in the International School? After your chat with my wife, we decided to make the move. It's expensive, but she really seems to be doing well there."

Hmmmm. Persephone didn't even remember chatting with Petrus's wife. Tafels, indeed.

"Are you fine, Persephone? Because, you know I wouldn't know anything about where Adam is at this hour."

"What?" Odd. "No, no. It's a computer thing, Petrus. Instagram, actually. You said you might be able to help with these things?"

"Yes, my dear! Yes, of course."

Oh, she loved that voice! It was like jumping into a warm bath. Naked.

"So—if someone has an Instagram account," she said, "you can find out where they're posting from, right?"

"It's tricky. Lots of firewalls. But yes! Your Petrus can do it."

"Oh, good man. Well, let's meet as soon as possible. Stellenbosch? Noon? Tomorrow?"

"Fine, fine."

"Petrus, sir, you're going to help us save some rhinos."

"Good, good."

"Goodbye!" she said, before automatically adding, "I love you!"

Realizing what she'd just done, she threw the phone into the sofa cushions, hoping he hadn't heard it.

Oh dear oh dear oh dear.

Dear Mrs. Geingob,

This receipt acts as proof of payment for the goods to be received. We are very interested in the other artifacts you may have. Such objects, as I'm certain you know, are incredibly difficult to come by in this day and age. This is a free country, but in the interest of further business, we appreciate you keeping this exchange discreet.

Please send photographs of the other objects when you have a chance.

Yours,

Hans Eichler

P.S. My wife and I notice your last name is the same as the president of your country. Is there, by any chance, any relation?

Mark sat outside the Windhoek International School, feeling more fucking awesome than he had in a long, long time. Mostly it was because he had called Jaime . . . who, as usual, had a great idea of how to go big.

"Let me get this straight," his friend had said. "You were just fronting the cash before. Now *you're* the gem dealer?"

"Not exactly," Mark had said. "Or not yet, anyway. But I'm thinking of getting more involved. She wants to cut out the middleman, see, so we just sell directly to jewelers. We already go all over Namibia finding stones, and then we have them polished. So, really, why do we need anyone else?"

"And this is legal?"

"Yeah. I mean, I think so. It's a lot of driving, mostly. And knowing the right people."

"Give me the numbers," Jaime had said impatiently.

"Okay—take, like, an amethyst. Usually you buy it raw for, like, fifty dollars a carat or so. We'll pay twenty."

"Then what?"

Mark spoke as fast as he could, pausing only to take short breaths. His heart was racing and his palms were cold. "We have it cut and polished. We've got a guy who does it for five percent. The usual is twenty percent, so that's key. Then we sell it for market price. Like, a thousand for a good three-carat, polished stone."

"Buddy. You sure those numbers are right?" Over the phone, Mark could hear Jaime typing. "Okay, so they are. This is *good*."

"Right. I mean, it also matters who you get to polish them. We have this really great guy named Claus. He's a Nazi, but—"

"You should run with this, man."

Mark felt a combustion of excitement. As much as he hated it, Jaime's approval meant everything to him. "You think?"

"Absolutely. *Yes*. Come on. Who do you know in this world who is an African gem dealer? It's singular. Except you need to go bigger."

"Bigger?" Mark echoed doubtfully.

"As in, don't waste all of this time on the little deals. Go for broke, you know? These small deals are going to be a tax nightmare. The bigger deals end up being less work for you, so then you can do more. Get it?"

"I guess. Yeah." The excitement was curdling into anxiety. "I'll think about it."

"I'm proud of you, man," Jaime said. "You've really made this Africa thing work for you. And hey, let me know how this project goes. If it takes off, I'd love to invest."

"You got it." Suddenly he desperately wanted to get off the phone.

"Thank you, man. Seriously. So I—"

"Oh hey, and how's the Fulbright?"

"What?" Could he feign a lost connection?

"The proposal I wrote. Are you doing any research at *all*?"

"Yeah . . . Listen, I gotta go. My kid's just coming out of school."

"All right. Well, keep it up, man. I'm seriously impressed."

When Mark hung up, the elation returned. Rarely, in recent years, had Jaime been impressed by anything he was doing. He threw the phone on the seat and climbed out of the car to surprise his daughter. There she was, whispering conspiringly with that pretty little snob she liked to hang out with. What the hell? Was she a teenager already?

"Meg!" he yelled across the yard.

Out of the corner of his eye, he could see the coiffed international mother heads over at the PTA shack swivel his way.

"Dad? What are *you* doing here?" His daughter's voice practically dripped with disdain.

"Greetings, Mr. Evans."

"Hi, er . . ."

"Taimi, sir." The little girl danced in front of him. "I dined in your home."

"Of course, I remember. Greetings, Taimi."

"Ah! There is my mother's assistant to pick me up. I must go. Meg, enjoy your time with your father. He works very hard. You should be glad he has the time to be with you."

Mark waved as she trotted away. Meg regarded him sulkily from under her hat.

"I thought I'd surprise you and that we could get some ice cream," Mark ventured.

Meg shrugged. "Mom takes me, like, every day."

"Every day, huh?" He put his hands into his pockets, wishing he could let her in on his new profession. Would she be more interested in her father if she knew he was heisting tanzanite? Well, he considered. Probably not. "Want to feed the ducks in Zoo Park?"

"Dad. I'm *nine*."

"Right. Okay." He was really failing here. What had Anna said the other day? *That's a fail.* Then he remembered her mentioning someplace where he could take Meg. "How about the Independence Museum?"

"Sure," she said, surprising him. "That sounds cool."

"Okay," he said with a grin of relief, leading her back to the car. After pulling out of the snarl of the school parking lot, he made his way through Northern Industrial to the mayhem of downtown. The Namibian Memorial Museum had been erected as a monument to an independent Namibia. Funded and constructed by the North Koreans—who, at one time, had a keen interest in Namibia's uranium, as well as the country's potential socialist tendencies—the hulking building squatted over a slight hill one block north of Independence Avenue, casting its shadow over the center of town. The local joke was that it looked like a coffee maker, though in Mark's opinion what the building really resembled was an enormous golden toilet.

He parked on the street, negotiating with an idle man who offered to "watch the car." It had taken a broken car window during their first month in Windhoek for him to learn that if one turned down the car-watching, no matter how politely, one's car would definitely be robbed. He led Meg past the Stalinesque rendering of Sam Nujoma, the country's first president, and rapped on the ticket window, where the attendant reluctantly tore herself away from her phone to sell him two tickets for ten Namibian each.

"This might not look like much," Mark lectured Meg as she looked up at the toilet. "But it's an important symbol to all the people here who fought or died to get out from under South Africa's iron fist."

"Yeah, it's cool," Meg said. "I like the glass elevator."

"Me, too," he said.

They rode up together, looking at the town. Despite the frantic scrabblings in the five-block center, the rest of the streets were gener-ally quiet. The museum was on an upper floor, below a rooftop bar. Afrikaans rock dripped down from above, but the gallery was empty. Meg's dirty sneakers squeaked ahead on the linoleum floor.

"What's this?" Meg asked, pointing to a huge mural of a half-naked woman in chains. It was more graphic than he remembered, with nip-ples fully realized and the rest of the curves painted with positively por-nographic abandon. Shit, he thought.

"Well . . . it's supposed to represent . . . see . . . Okay. Do you know what apartheid is?"

"Kind of." She looked up at him. "Like, Taimi—before—would have gone to a different school than me."

"Yes." Mark felt the warmth of pride at his daughter's perception. "She would have had to live in a different place from you. She wouldn't have been able to do certain jobs—"

"Right, except Taimi's super-rich. So she doesn't *need* a job."

Mark nodded. "Well, that's just it—I'm not sure she would have been rich then. Anyway. You two going to school together, yes, that would have been an impossibility. But Nelson Mandela changed all of that. Now people of color can go to good schools."

Meg wandered ahead, taking in a morbid murder scene in the next room. "Back home, people just pay for better schools."

"Well, sometimes, but—"

"*We* paid."

"We did, that's true . . ."

Meg shrugged. "My school was almost all white at home. Except for Ling."

Mark scratched his neck, wondering how to get her off this subject. "It's complicated. Our class system is . . . well, a little messed up. We're working on it. Sort of. But let's focus here." He gestured at the wall. "See, Africa has a history of much more violence than we've ever dealt with. In this mural, the artist is showing that apartheid is like being chained like a slave."

Meg peered up at him through her shaggy bangs. "But in our country, we *had* slaves, right?"

"Well, not *us*. But a lot of Southerners did, yes. A long time ago."

"Like Grandpa Albert."

"Oh . . . no, not Albert. He's too young. Also, he was a civil rights supporter. I think."

"His grandfather, then?"

"I mean, maybe. We can do research."

Meg nodded, then turned to amble down the hall. "So I'm descended from slave owners. That's what you're saying."

"What do they teach you at that school? Litigation?"

"Huh?"

"You're not descended from slave owners really, because Mom's adopted anyway."

"Yeah, but what about *your* family?"

This outing wasn't going at all the way he'd intended. He pretended to check his phone, leaving Meg to scowl at the end of the mural's progression—happy, strapping Namibians prospering in business suits—before wandering to the window to look out again at the spilled milk of a town that was Windhoek.

"So your work's going okay?" Meg asked, coming to stand next to him.

"Oh sure—my work's going great, actually," he said, suddenly defensive. "Why?"

"'Cause Mom says we can leave once you finish your book."

"Oh." Mark thought guiltily of the eight hundred words he had written. "I'm actually doing a new kind of work," he said. "And if *that* does well, Daddy might not even *have* to write books anymore."

Shit. What was he doing?

"Why are you calling yourself Daddy, like you're not here? That's, like, weird." She had wandered back to a part of the mural where another naked woman was carrying a huge basket of stones on her head. "You don't like writing books?"

"It's okay," he said. "I mean, honestly, I've been thinking that academia may not really be for me."

"And you like this new thing better?"

"I think so."

"That's like Ling," Meg said knowingly. "I thought she was my best friend, but now Taimi is. I mean, I like Ling, too, but Taimi's right here, you know?"

"It's sort of like that, yes."

Meg narrowed her eyes. "But we're still going back to California, right?"

"Oh yes."

"Okay," Meg said. "Can we go home and play Scrabble now?"

"Sure," he said.

But they didn't play Scrabble. Instead they did what they always did, which was retreat to opposite sides of the house. Tonight his daughter was on the landline, conspiring with Taimi, while he sat in the garden and brooded over his laptop. Amanda was out somewhere, so he was free to stare online at the particulars of their joint savings account.

The Evanses had stretched themselves to come to Namibia. Selling the house, it turned out, hadn't been a great idea. Having bought the place only three years before, they'd been nowhere even close to paying off the mortgage. And the taxes had eaten most of what little profit they had made.

He knew he should tell Amanda about his new business. But, of course, then he'd have to explain all those trips he'd taken that hadn't actually been research. Trips that had been taken with another woman, too—innocent or not—and that had involved no writing at all.

So far, the gems had netted him $22,000. Pretty good, but nothing to live on. Jaime was right. He needed to invest more if he was going to make more. And so, taking a deep breath, with the click of a few keys, he liquidated $100,000 of the GiaTech stock in their joint account.

What was it Jaime had said, exactly, about playing and winning? This had to be a win, didn't it?

24

Every school, everywhere in the world, had one: the annual fundraising event. It didn't matter if the money was for scholarships or books or soccer uniforms or a new gym floor; it always amounted to something painful, be it a car wash or dress-up ball or auction dinner, the planning of which transformed ninety percent of the mothers and fathers involved into complete lunatics. (The other ten percent just got drunk.)

Thus far during Meg's school career, Amanda had managed to avoid these functions, claiming "work," and sent Mark instead. (He was always part of the drinking crowd.) But this year she had no other activity that might excuse her beyond posting Instagram photos. So here she was, on the morning before the event, toiling like a carnival worker.

International Day had to have been the most ambitious school event Amanda had witnessed. Back home, PTAs mostly held parties at night that could be corralled into a few hours in the evening. WIS, however, threw a party that stretched on from 10:00 a.m. into the evening. Every grade had to represent a country, and the *fuck-you-I'm-better* aspect of *this* particular fundraiser was varying degrees of booth extravagance. So far, Brazil seemed to be winning, as one of the mothers had arranged for a truck of sand to be dumped on the ground to make a miniature Ipanema, and workers were bringing in actual palm trees. Cuba was selling authentic Cuban cigars, while Japan was hiring a real sushi chef. (Though sushi in the desert, in Amanda's opinion, was a tall if not hazardous order.)

China, set up by the Chinese Embassy, as no one would dare assign China to a grade, was building a real pagoda, but since none of the other countries wanted to be affiliated with China during the poaching crisis, the largest country in the world was marooned at the end of the field, under the goalpost. As for the U.S., it wasn't even represented. Trump's America, it was decided, wasn't appropriate for children.

Half of the families, in a tradition from Mila's reign, had sent their housekeepers and gardeners to work their appointed shifts for them. Persephone had discouraged the practice, but in the end she threw up her hands, deciding that help was help. Although, as Amanda couldn't help noticing, out of the range of their employers' eyes, most of the housekeepers and handymen sent to WIS for the day performed their work with all the enthusiasm of a ninety-year-old cancer patient with access to the morphine drip. Then again, since that was about Amanda's own level of excitement about this project and she *had* a kid at this school, she really couldn't blame them.

Actually, the only person with any drive at all in the setup area, Amanda observed, was Persephone, who was running around like a coked-up sorority girl before Pledge Night.

"Excuse me, sir?" Persephone called to Kayla's gardener, who was sprawled on the ground. "Do you think you can be in charge of erect-ing that canopy?"

The man smiled affably, then rolled over and went back to sleep.

"Amanda!" Persephone said, running up to her in ladylike bunny steps. "Didn't see you here behind all of these crates."

"I may have been hiding."

"Are you waiting for the beverage truck? I hope so! Someone needs to do that."

"I am now."

"Ah, *thank* you," she said, reaching into her shoulder bag and pull-ing out a walkie-talkie. "Kayla, Kayla, *come in, Kayla*."

A crackle of static erupted by way of an answer.

"You there? Listen, we have to rearrange. Brazil cannot be *anywhere* near Ghana, okay? I'm talking the kindergarten booth and year four. Copy?"

Crackle. "Yeah, Brazil's already put down their sand." *Crackle.*

"Then move Ghana, or else there will be a body count, I swear to you. Not kidding. Thank you." She rolled her eyes at Amanda. "The kindergarten teaching assistant slept with the year-four teacher's husband. Now these ladies are threatening to kill each other, and since they're cooking, they'll both have knives. Not to mention alcohol. God save us." She shook her head. "This is hell."

"I really hate it when people say this to me," Amanda said. "But . . . I told you so."

"Yes. I literally asked for this, didn't I? Am I using that word correctly? Literally? As in, the words came out of my mouth. I want to be in charge of International Day, I think I said."

"That's right."

"Well. I sort of thought Mila might be here to just give me a tip or two. I mean, can you believe how AWOL she is?"

"I haven't talked to her," Amanda said.

"Really?" Persephone said, feigning indifference. Amanda hadn't told Persephone about Mila freezing her out, but Amanda could see her friend had noticed and was taking stock of the development. She braced herself for more prodding, but Persephone's radio crackled again.

"Persephone! *The pork is here.*" Amanda couldn't be sure if it was just the radio interference, but Kayla's voice sounded hysterical.

"Right, we've reserved the tuckshop refrigerator——"

"No. Oh my God." *Crackle.* "The supplier misunderstood. They've dropped off warthogs, Perse. *Live* ones."

Amanda and Persephone lifted their eyes to the field entrance far on the other end, where, sure enough, there was a truck full of wriggling warthogs in the back.

"Oh my Lord. Look, I'll see you later," Persephone said to Amanda. "*Do not* leave your post. The only way we'll save this day is with alcohol. Anyway, see you . . ."

Persephone's voice trailed off as she sprinted toward the hogs. Amanda began ambling toward the beverages. Really, what she wanted to do was sneak off and disentangle herself completely from this shit-show. But she supposed she couldn't let down her friend—especially when that friend was obsessed with shows of loyalty, however large or small.

Just then, Amanda's phone vibrated angrily. An international call—Amanda knew she had to answer. She took refuge in a quiet shady spot in an empty tent and picked up.

"Amanda? Hello. It's Rita del Porto."

Rita was the financial advisor Amanda had hired when it became clear she and Mark were unable to handle their money. Amanda, who had grown up with, if not lots of money, enough of it, had never considered hiring a financial planner until two years ago when she began to take home four times as much as Mark.

Los Gatos was an expensive place to live. ("Listen closely. You can hear the invisible vacuums coming for your wallet," Mark used to say as he walked into the grocery store.) Mark detested Los Gatos, but Amanda adored it. It was clean and charming, and the school was stellar (even though they indulged in private), and the place was so utterly different from Charleston. But it was an incredible strain on their finances. One day she went to the ATM to get some cash, and she found the balance at zero. An impossibility, it seemed, as every two weeks GiaTech automatically deposited thousands into the joint account. Yet when she'd looked up the debits online, it was true. The Evans family's Los Gatos lifestyle had them hemorrhaging money. Daily trips to Whole Foods, private riding and swimming for Meg, any clothes anyone in the family felt like buying at any time.

Amanda, thoroughly alarmed, had called her father for advice. For some people, not being able to budget was a mark of shame. Well, Amanda was long over shame—she had given that up when she waited around for Mark Evans for two years in college.

"You have enough money to hire someone to manage it for you,"

Albert had said. "A financial person. Someone to protect you from yourselves and even budget for you. And yet . . ."

"Yes?"

"You and Mark must be on equal footing."

"Huh?"

"Equal access to accounts. No matter who makes the money. That's what a marriage is."

"Of course," Amanda had said. She knew that she and Mark could always tell each other everything. They had never had secrets. Until, that is, Mark had set up a life for them in Africa and not said a word to her about it.

"Rita," she said now, "what's up?"

Rita was Italian and gleefully thrifty, so Amanda was more than a little surprised that Rita was making an international phone call. She was the sort of person who got a physical high from saving money. "Don't you love this chair?" she'd crow. "Yard sale. Three dollars!" "See this dress? My dead aunt's. You can barely make out the oil stain on the chest. A little lemon juice, and—*boom!*—brand-new-to-me St. John's knit!"

She was also, in Amanda's mind, a little too opinionated about Amanda's marriage. "You need to watch out for yourself, girlfriend," Rita had said. "*Your* retirement is in tatters. He has his university pension. What are you going to do if he leaves you for a succulent grad student?"

"Succulent?" Mark had said. "Like a plant?"

"Luscious."

"I don't teach grad students."

"I don't worry about the college kids, Rita," Amanda had said. "They still have pacifiers. Anyway, I have a 401K."

Rita had thrown up her hands in feigned hopelessness. As if Amanda—an educated businesswoman with a salary her father would chortle over—were a hopeless wilting violet who let her husband walk all over her.

Mark and Amanda had bonded over laughing at Rita, in the same way they'd gleefully picked apart their couples counselors. Her cheap furniture. Her (they imagined) angry, spinster-like existence filled with trolling for bargains at various outlets. Never mind that the only two times they'd spotted Rita outside of the office had been in opulent surroundings—once at a play opening at ACT, the other by the pool in Napa. She didn't know *their* relationship. She had no right to pull the *girlfriend-you-need-to-protect-yo'self!* act.

Yet here Amanda was, two years later, listening to Rita tell her the very worst.

"Technically, I shouldn't be talking only to you," Rita said. "But you're both hopelessly unreachable. Mark's email actually bounced *back*. I thought he might be dead."

"He's not dead."

"That's too bad for you. Because he's withdrawn almost all of your savings."

Amanda tried to make sense of the way the leaves on the tree she was looking at were starting to swim.

"Come again?"

"Not your retirement, of course. And not Meg's college account. I've protected those. It's your GiaTech stock. The stuff I advised you to put into the mutual fund so it would be less liquid. But you wanted to see if the stock would rise."

Amanda stiffened. That was their rainy-day fund. They hadn't agreed on what the fund would build yet . . . Mark wanted to buy an inn in Northern California. Amanda was thinking of an old, rambling house in whatever town Meg eventually chose to settle in. Uncertain as it was, this was their future. Their own personal Dream Act.

"Did you know that he had taken the money out? A hundred thousand dollars?"

Amanda didn't reply immediately. It was one thing to lay her financial and marriage foibles in front of Albert. It was another to tell a gloating Rita she'd been right all along.

"Of course I knew," Amanda said. "I can't tell you what we're using it for, as it's top secret . . ." Wait. That sounded like something out of a bad version of *The Americans*. "What I mean is, still in development. Everything is under control. Thank you so much for the call, Rita. And international, too."

"I'll bill you for it," Rita said, and hung up.

Amanda held the phone in midair, still looking at it. The flaps of the tent began to beat wildly in the wind, which was picking up. The hogs grunted noisily. Someone was yelling in Brazil.

All of the GiaTech stock?

She tried to think what he could possibly be doing. Now that she thought about it, he had been looking uncharacteristically happy lately. He was tanner, thinner. He wasn't drinking as much. Maybe he *was* having an affair? But if he was, was he really going to take all of their money with him?

She rummaged in her pocket madly for her keys as she made her way to the parking lot.

"Amanda! You're not leaving me, are you?" Persephone called, sounding desperate.

"I'll be back . . . I gotta . . ." Her voice trailed off as she climbed into the oven-like heat of the car.

It was still somewhat early, but the traffic was already beginning to snarl in the city center. Laying on her horn, pulling out aggressively through the choked intersections. She tried to calm down, but her pulse was doing that thing where it rocketed ahead, no matter how much she tried that fucking Californian tantric breathing. God, she was so stupid. He'd been going on trips every other week, staying over nights. *Of course* something was going on. And, honestly, why wouldn't he look elsewhere for sex? Lately, she'd been as warm and welcoming as a sea vegetable.

Mark had leased a second car since he'd started taking his trips. When she pulled in through the electric gate, she was both relieved and furious to see it was there.

"Mark?" she called across the patio. "Are you here?" Her husband must have heard her come through the gate, because he shot out of the house as soon as she called, looking flustered. Goddammit, she thought. It's totally true.

"Hey," he said, his voice flat. Had she been willingly ignoring his weird behavior?

"What were you doing just then?" she asked.

"I was . . ." He paused. "I was reading your email."

Amanda blinked rabidly. "What? Why?"

"Yeah. I know. It's nuts, because I was so disapproving about you disregarding Meg's privacy. But, Amanda, you've been acting weird lately. Ever since we came here."

She couldn't believe what she was hearing. Was this all just an elaborate plot to make her crazy? *I've been acting weird?*

"Yeah." He didn't come closer, but instead stood a few feet from her, his arms crossed, as if they were about to have an old western showdown. "So I looked through your emails. It took me like five seconds to find out what's been going on."

"What could you possibly be talking about?" Her indignation grew as she realized she wasn't going to immediately be able to stomp on her high ground, which seemed like the only bright side to all of this.

"Ronnie?" Mark said quietly. "The guy who keeps emailing you about your night together?"

Amanda shook her head in disbelief. She fought the urge to burst out laughing. "Oh my God. Ronnie? That's who you think I've been having an affair with?"

"You can't get out of this one, Mandi. The messages are right there."

"Get out of what one?" Her voice was shaking. "Mark, think about it. When have I ever tried to get out of anything?"

"He emails you all the time. You email him back. Yeah, I can see you're trying to cool him off. But I don't blame him. Sounds like it was quite an experience, his night with you."

"No," she said, attempting to sound composed. "You're misinterpreting . . . the material." Oh God. She was awful at fighting.

"No way." Mark shook his head. "No way could I have it wrong. I mean, the guy's not talking about a night of bowling."

"Look," Amanda said. "First of all, I can't believe I'm getting beaten up here. *You're* the one who messed up, not me. I was just coming to——"

"While that's usually true and probably is now, I don't think it's fair of you to change the subject."

"Fine," Amanda said, trying to slow herself down. "It was the night of that goodbye party they threw me. When you were being a total asshole and wouldn't help with any of the packing or the shitty logistics that came with this trip. And then you didn't come to the party."

It was true. After putting his stake in the ground about how it was his turn, which meant uprooting themselves and moving to a new, wild land, Mark had handed all the details of the transition to her. When she'd task him with chores like going to UPS or looking for storage, he'd procrastinate until she did it, or do such an inept job, she couldn't help wondering if he was failing on purpose. The straw that broke that particular camel's back was a shipping quote—he had spent an hour on the phone and gotten prices, but only for the cost of sending his two mountain bikes.

"Well, you were being a total bitch!" Mark retorted. "You wouldn't even let me be happy about the Fulbright for two seconds! So, what, you got pissed and went and screwed some guy?"

The rawness of his anger was so out of character for Mark, it startled her. "We didn't have sex," she said in a low voice. "I was really drunk, and we made out. It was gross. Normally I would have told you, because it was just this funny thing . . . but then we weren't speaking, and by the time we were, I'd forgotten about it."

"No way do I believe you." He shook his head. "You've been barely able to stand touching me since we've come here."

Amanda considered this. "Well, that's just . . . resentment. Textbook."

"Then why do you email him back? Why not just blow him off?"

"Because I was his boss. Do you know how much I could get sued for?" Mark put his hands in his pockets. She could tell that he was doing that thing where he chewed the inside of his cheek. "Anyway," she said. "What right do you have to accuse me of these things? After what you've been doing?"

"What I've been doing?" Mark repeated.

"Yes, Mark. I know everything, okay? So just stop blowing smoke and tell me what the hell is going on."

Mark leaned against the railing and threw up his hands. "Okay, Mandi," he said. "Fine. So you know. I'm glad you know. It's a huge relief, actually."

Amanda's knees felt weak, but no way was she going to sit if he wasn't. In business school, there had been a whole week spent on something called "body tactics," during which she and the other aspiring businesspeople had studied body language. If it was your office, the professor said gravely, sitting while the others stood indicated power. In any other situation, *you* stood until everyone else was down.

She'd also learned from business school that in negotiation, it was important to let the other party talk so that they felt (falsely) that they had some control. So right now her tactic was to remain standing, unfold her arms, lean loosely against the wall, and shut up and listen.

"I met her in Oshakati," Mark said. "Before I knew you."

The weight of this statement—*before I knew you*—bore down on her. It was so completely not what she thought he would say, she could feel its actual heft pressing down on her body.

"We were only together for a day. I mean, physically. I knew her, back, uh . . ." He paused, as if choosing the right words. "Back when I was a volunteer. And then I got into that accident, and I didn't know if she was dead or not. So I knew I had to . . . that we . . ."

When Amanda looked back on this morning later, she saw, in hindsight, that this was the point where she might have steered them all away from the upcoming danger. She might have said, You know what? Never mind! I love you—let's forget it! Let's just go get Meg from school and take a surprise vacation to Cape Town! And everything might have gone along, exactly as it was.

But that's not what she said. Instead, she pointed to a chair for him to sit, and when he did, she pulled another over and sat across from him.

"So," she said. "What happened?"

25

As Mark sat across from his wife, with her tan runner's legs, her sensible haircut, her impeccable sense of right and wrong, he felt an enormous flood of relief. He'd been holding all of it back—this terrible thing that marked him as an awful person—for so long. Finally, he wouldn't have to be alone with it.

Mark and Esther made their way to the Engen station at dawn for the combi back to Oshakati. They were sheepish with Amber, having not seen her for two days. But Amber just laughed and punched them. She smelled of old liquor, and seemed smug.

"She's had a good time," Esther whispered.

It drove him wild, when she whispered. He could feel her breath in his ear, could smell the clean-soap/new-rain scent of her. They were in that new-lover time, brief and precious, when everything the other person did was wizardry. He knew she felt it, too. He caught her smiling at his calves and fingering the worn material of his T-shirt. She liked to kiss the place his cheek left this upper nose. Was it the apple? She couldn't leave it alone. She said it was delicious.

It was dangerous and heady and everyone noticed. The driver, upon seeing him—a white American—had pulled the people out of the front row to give him the prime seating.

"Go to the back!" he said. "We need that seat for the meneer."

"No, no," Mark said, insisting that the boy and his mother stay in the front along with himself and the two girls. Once they were settled, though, he'd pretty much trained his focus forward. He hated to admit it, but the heat and the smell of so many bodies, along with whatever food and the exhaust fumes, made his stomach turn. Anyway, it was just a short ride from Swakop to Karibib, where they would get out and hitch north. Two hours, at most. But this leg of the route was packed. Amber leaned against him, her head on his shoulder. Esther sat on his lap, her hips moving with the bus's rhythm.

And that was the last he remembered. The sweetness of that feeling, the hot combi, Esther swaying. The rest he learned only later, when he woke up in the private hospital in Windhoek. He'd been thrown, the doctor told him gravely, his spine bruised and his knee torn.

"Still, you're one of the lucky ones," the doctor said. "You're *alive* and your brain is in your skull, and not all over the highway."

"But how did I get here?" Mark whispered hoarsely. The room was white, the bed was white. "Where is Esther? Where are the girls?"

"You have to understand, you came here privately," the doctor said. "Privately," Mark repeated.

"You were picked up by some Afrikaans farmers," the doctor said. "They did not think it was wise for you to stay in the road."

"But I was with friends," Mark said. "Two girls. What happened to the girls?"

"No. No one was with you." The doctor shook his head. "The farmers brought you to Swakopmund. They went through your things and found your identification. American. They called the embassy, and those people had you flown here." He paused. "Were the girls American?"

"No! No, they were Namibian."

"I see." The doctor looked at him. "Then they were taken care of, sir. Namibians take care of their own people."

"But where *are* they?"

"I can't know that. I don't know anything about the people on your bus. The farmers brought you first to Swakopmund. You are white, so you went to the private hospital. Maybe your friends are there, too."

"They're not white."

The doctor looked at him. Mark was too drugged to read his expression. He guessed it was disapproving. There was a pressure against the back of his head that wouldn't be ignored. A sensation ripped through his knee as if it were being torn from the socket. He arched his back, groaning.

"Ah! You're in pain. Just a moment." The doctor fiddled with a dial connected to Mark's IV drip, and a warm, thick syrup of bliss and utter lack of care coursed through him. "Is that better?"

"Where are the girls?" Mark mumbled with what remained of his consciousness.

The doctor looked thoughtful. "If they are not white, then they were taken to the Central Hospital. Which is also fine. Namibian doctors are South African doctors. Educated in Cape Town. They should be fine."

"But how do I . . ."

Only it didn't matter anymore as Mark relaxed into an opiate sleep.

The next steps happened very quickly. The colored doctor performed an excellent operation, leaving Mark only a tiny scar and a knee even better than the one he'd had before.

"And now it's filled with titanium and what-what-what!" said the nurse cheerfully. She was lovely, her eyelids painted gold. (Or did Mark just imagine it that way?) But she wasn't nearly as pretty as Esther, whom he loved. Love? Did he love her? He didn't know if he loved Esther. But he certainly wanted her to be here, and alive.

Yet no one would help him. Someone had talked to his mother, who had become hysterical and pleaded her case to his stepfather. Mark's stepfather was the mayor of their little suburban town outside of Chicago, and he knew someone who knew the governor. So the governor called a senator, who in turn called Al Gore's office, and it was decided that

Mark should be discharged from the Peace Corps due to "hardship." Never mind that Mark didn't want to go home. He tried to explain as much to the doughy, sympathetic man from Maryland who was sent from the consular office to take him to the airport.

"But I'm *fine*," Mark said. His head ached. The doctor came in and gave him a pill. The pills helped with everything. He later came to believe they were a magic concoction derived from the desert plants of Namibia, because no doctor in the United States could (or would) give him anything like that ever again.

"I'm sorry. The organization has simply decided you are, well, a liability. This is a government organization, and the government, you must understand, no longer supports you."

Mark pressed his hand to his forehead. He could hardly process the words.

"But what about my stuff?"

"A representative has already been to Oshakati to gather your things. Well, that was me, actually. Usually an assistant would have done it, but I don't have one yet. The embassy here is still pretty new." He drummed his hands on his knees. "Anyway, I paid up your rent and explained the situation to the people you served at your post. Everyone was very understanding." He beamed at Mark. "They all like you very much, actually. You should feel good about your work here."

Mark took a deep breath. Surely this man could help him. He was *American*. "So, the bus I was on—I was on a trip. To Swakopmund. With friends."

The embassy man nodded. Mark felt a surge of hope.

"They were girls."

The man nodded again, encouragingly.

"Can you help me find them?"

"Were they American?"

"No."

The embassy man smiled again. Then he shook his head. "I'm sorry, then. We only have jurisdiction to track down Americans."

"But they were on the combi with me. And I don't know if they died. *Did people die?*"

"I can't tell you that information, Mark."

"It was in *The Namibian*, asshole. I know people died."

"There's no reason to get ugly."

"Look. Mr.—"

"Call me Bill, okay? Bill Mulherin."

"Well, Bill, I was with my girlfriend, okay? She was sitting in my lap. Help me out, here."

Bill Mulherin looked as if this were entirely too much information for him to handle. "Look, when you get back to the States, you can make inquiries. But I'm sorry to say, right now your visa has been revoked. So you're going to have to come to the airport tonight. The doctor has declared you fit to travel."

"What?" Mark cried. As if he'd been eavesdropping, the doctor appeared in the door. "I'm still bleeding!" Mark shouted at him.

"The Namibian and American governments have made it very clear that you must go home," the doctor said. "It's quite safe. And your pain is perfectly managed."

"This is fucking insane," he said to them both, whereupon the doctor handed Mark another pill and a plastic cup of water. Mark knew, from the movies, that he was supposed to bat the pill away, or pretend to swallow it and spit it out, then make a run for it. Jaime probably would have done that. But he liked the pills, so he took it and swallowed.

"Listen," Bill Mulherin said as Mark swam back into those warm, dreamy depths. "You can come back. Or make inquiries from home. People use email, you know. Even in Africa."

Mark would have laughed if he could. He knew Esther and Amber were as likely to use electronic mail as they were to communicate via smoke signal. Yes, he murmured. He would find them later. Right now he was battered and high and twenty-two and penniless, and his much-alarmed family was waiting for him back home, so Mark went with Bill Mulherin and got onto the plane. The flights were a paper chain connected by pills and beer; Windhoek to Johannesburg to Atlanta and then at last to Chicago. His mother and stepfather met him at O'Hare Airport, and as soon as he saw them, he wept like the child he still obviously was.

"But wait," Amanda asked now. "I don't understand. Why didn't you go back . . . back *then*?"

"Because I was twenty-fucking-two," he said. "I had no money of my own. And it wasn't like I stopped worrying about her. I did, all the time. I mean, I couldn't sleep for months."

Amanda looked at Mark for a moment, then got up and went to the kitchen. When she came back, she had the Brita pitcher full of water, and two glasses. She filled both, slid one toward him, and sat down again.

How like her, Mark thought grimly, to think about hydration at this time.

"But then?" she said.

"Then, time went on, and I got really scared," Mark said. "What if I really had left her to die? If I came back, I'd know the truth. And it wasn't something I could have done before now. I mean, I had to be older."

Amanda nodded. It seemed like she understood. After all, she'd had her big secret, too. He'd deceived his wife, but he never actually cheated on her. Not the way she had. God, the thought of it. Her actually in bed with this prick named Ronnie. His stomach clenched dangerously.

"Anyway," he managed, "then I went to Dartmouth for grad school, and then I met you, and then . . . and then . . ."

He made a rolling motion with his hands, then dropped them in his lap. They sat in silence for a while. It was the dead middle of the day now. Nothing was moving. No cars passed on the street.

"Anyway. What I found out a couple of months ago was . . . that she was dead. I mean, she died in the crash. I got the records from the morgue. So maybe it was lucky that I didn't come back. I don't think I would have been equipped to deal with that back then."

"Wait. She *died*?" Amanda said. He could see a shock go through her. "Then why did you . . . I mean. Okay, one thing at a time. First of all, why didn't you just tell me about her?"

"It was a pretty awful thing, really," Mark said. "I didn't think you'd see me in the same way. And I didn't think you'd want to hear about her. She was the one person—"

"The one person you loved before me?" she asked. "Or more than me?"

Mark stopped himself. This was definitely not something he wanted to tell his wife. But like a terrier, her eyes brightened as she went in for her catch.

He shrugged. He wasn't going to go there. When he'd let himself think of Esther that one night in Swakopmund before he'd gone to the morgue, he'd almost lost his mind.

But Amanda pressed on, her voice shrill. "And? What is it? Why can't you talk about her? Even now?" Mark got up out of the chair and moved to the edge of the patio. "Why are you still keeping something from me?"

"You don't want to hear this, Mandi. I was super young. Like you were when you met me." He scratched his neck violently, instantly regretting the words that had escaped his mouth.

"So she was to you what you were to me." Amanda said this slowly, as if turning over the reality in her mind. "The first person you fell for. The person who was supposed to change your life."

"I don't know, Mandi." Mark began pacing back and forth. He felt like he was on a runaway train. "I mean, have things ended up being so wonderful between us? You can barely stand me. You hate the way I parent. I'm a total disappointment to you, and now you're having an affair."

"I'm not having—"

"All right, even if you really did just make out with someone else—which, by the way, I find highly implausible—then ask yourself: Why did I do it? Am I really happy? Or am I just living in this construct because I have a kid?"

"I . . ." Amanda seemed not to be able to get her mouth around the words. "I . . ."

But Mark was trucking on now, full speed ahead. His anger was fueled by decades of sorrow. And it felt good, because Amanda was such a believer in prudence. Well, he thought, this is a fucking imprudent moment.

"So do I think about what life could have been like with her? Yes, Mandi. Of course I do. It would have been a completely different path. I would have taken care of her . . . the way you take care of me, okay? I mean you're so . . . fucking . . . *capable*, Mandi."

"You think I'm capable?" Amanda repeated. "That's what you think?"

"Yes! You can do everything! And what's worse, you always have the answers. You're always right. Maybe it would have been better for me if I could be the capable one. If *I* had to be the one who stepped up."

"Un-fucking-believable," Amanda managed, leaning forward to look at him, with her hands on her knees. "You want a less *capable* woman in your marriage, so you can be more of a man? I've never heard you say anything more pathetic."

"See, Amanda? You're always right."

"No one asked you to be such a weakling, Mark. Our marriage would be a lot better if you'd take some of the load sometimes. If you weren't so . . . *lazy.*"

"Well." Lazy. That's where they were. Mark shook his head and picked up his keys off the table. "I guess now you have Ronnie."

"I don't have Ronnie!" Amanda yelled, pounding the seat cushion. "He's nobody! Why can't you get that through your head?"

"I'll go pick up Meg," Mark said. "I need to get out of here."

Amanda shot up, following him as he walked to the car. Mark had never seen his wife out of control before; it was thrilling and frightening at the same time.

"No!" she shrieked. "You can't leave. Not when I have all of these questions, you asshole. Was she better than me? Was she prettier? Did you like having sex with her more? Was she just a little incapable, fuckable lamb?"

"I'm not talking about this," Mark said, getting into the car. "You're being indecent. It's not who you are." He turned the key in the ignition and pressed the gate button; in response, it shuddered awake and began to open.

"What was her goddamned name?" Mark heard his wife scream as he steered the car down the drive. He hesitated, then put his head out the window.

"Esther," he said, then pulled away.

Mila shifted from side to side in the backseat of the Mercedes, opening and closing her palms. She still couldn't believe she'd let Persephone convince her to come to the school in the middle of this mayhem. Mark and Amanda, they could be anywhere. But she hadn't been able to put Persephone off.

"I can't explain," she'd said patiently over the phone the seventh time the hysterical woman called.

"Try!" Persephone had wailed.

"I have a . . . personal problem at present with the Evans family, and I absolutely cannot see them."

"Mila. Mark Evans doesn't even know where this school is, prob-ably. He *never* does pickup. Never. He certainly won't be here setting up for a PTA function. And Amanda's out buried in the beverage tent. I'll meet you out front of the school. Look, I'll come to your car if you want, as if you were a Mafia boss lady. I just really need you right at this moment!"

"And why do you need me?" Mila said, smiling slightly on her end of the line. Persephone had acted very badly. It wouldn't hurt her to eat crow in a pie.

"Because I was an idiot to think I could do this. I don't even know where to plug in the stereo."

"You lead the cord to the stage in the gym."

"Yes, only the cord shorted. Actual sparks came out!"

"You need the adapter, because the stereo is European and the volt-age was set up in 1986 or what-what-what."

"Exactly! How am I supposed to know that?"

Mila had sighed. "Fine. I'll have the driver take me to the lot. Meet me in the car, under the tree by the middle school."

So here she was, in a government car so conspicuous she might as well have hoisted up a banner that said MILA SHILONGO IS IN. Enter Persephone, sprinting over in her customary whites, her red ponytail bouncing behind her.

"Thankyouthankyouthankyou!" Persephone trilled, jumping into the car. The driver, Joel, glanced at Mila in the rearview mirror and looked quickly away. Mila could feel his tiny smile. Persephone was holding a legal pad and a sparkly pen with a feather on the end of it.

"Okay. Look at this floor plan. I have twelve countries on one side and only six on the other. But everyone on this side is refusing to move. All because of Russia. I said yes to the Russian Embassy, and now look! And they're already drinking vodka and the event isn't until tonight. And the smell of the cabbage, Mila. Shame! And oh my God, we let year two be Namibia, and the teachers have constructed a shebeen. A bar, Mila! At a school event! They've even put a picture of a lady in a bikini on the wall!"

"Tell them to take that down," Mila said sternly.

"What if they say no?"

"They cannot say no," Mila said. "You are their leader."

"Okay, yes. That's true. But I sort of think . . ." Persephone's voice trailed off.

"Think what?"

"That they don't like me telling them what to do because I'm white?"

Her voice was uncharacteristically small.

"Tell them anyway, Persephone," Mila said. "You can't solve the history of Namibia. You need to get this done. What did you do about the live warthogs?"

"I sent them to the butcher. He said he didn't have time—he was booked. Booked! I told him he could keep a whole hog for himself on me, though, so he finally said yes."

"Good. Very good. And China?"

"They're alone under the goalpost."

"All right. You can stage the water balloon toss next to them. Then they won't feel so ostracized. It's a fundraiser for the Christian Club, and God won't *let* them say no."

"Brilliant." Persephone snapped her notebook shut. "As I said, I am very thankful. Although, can I say one tiny thing?"

Mila looked at her, silent.

"It would have been nice if you had told me all of this before. I mean, that's the way I would have done it, I might have left a written . . . guide-book of some kind. That would have been the most *responsible* thing, I think."

Mila peered through the window for a moment, then turned back again. "Persephone, I am going to be frank with you because you need to hear it. I am not trying to be cruel, but you must learn. You, my dear, are a FIGJAM."

"What?"

"Good Lord. Do I have to teach you Americans slang as well? I'm saying you're a *Fuck-I'm-Good-Just-Ask-Me*."

Persephone's cute little mouth formed a perfect doll-like O. "Ex-cuse me?"

"Yes. FIGJAM. Write it down, dear. You think you know ev-erything, because you're rich and American and your skin is the right hue. Your event is a mess because you planned nothing. You're sloppy and entitled and you're the whole reason Namibians dislike Americans."

"Mila!" Persephone cried. "Africans *love* Americans!"

From the front seat, Joel let out a barely discernible chuckle.

"You know what?" Persephone wheezed. "I said thank you for com-ing. But actually, *no* thank you! *You're* the snob. And another thing, too: I *know* your husband's a crook."

"Get out," Mila said, cold as ice.

"Gladly," Persephone sniffed before kicking the door open with her tiny white sandal and exploding back out toward the sweaty, lethargic masses of International Day.

Good Lord, Mila thought. She hadn't wanted to yell at Persephone. She wasn't a fan of hurt feelings in general. But the Gecko, she *needed* it.

"Let's go," Mila said. Joel nodded and pulled out. Just then, there was the sound of crushing metal.

Mila had been in one fender bender since the accident. That incident, which happened while Josephat was driving, at the intersection of Robert Mugabe and Fidel Castro Avenues, had sent her into a shock so violent Josephat had thrown some cash at the policemen and left immediately to drive her to Lady Pohamba Hospital. This jolt was worse than that—the crushing was louder, the cracking of shattering glass seemed next to her ear. She heard a shriek that she realized was her own, and curled up into a ball on the floor of the car.

"Miss Shilongo?" Joel said. He put his hand on her shoulder. "Sorry, sorry. That man ran into me. It's just the back window. Miss Shilongo. No problem, no problem. Miss, are you all right?"

The combi had left late, because one of the mothers was waiting for her little boy to come with a delivery of fruit from his auntie's. The driver tried to throw her off, but she enlisted the sympathy of the other passengers, who rose up against him and insisted that they wait. The woman needed her fruit! The little boy had finally come, triumphantly holding a bag of oranges, and after a brief round of cheers they had started off.

They were meeting a transfer in Karibib, and the driver was making up time by overtaking the slower cars. The combi shook and rattled; they were easily going 120 kilometers an hour. The American was scared and gripped Esther's waist, but any Namibian who had ever been on the roads knew this was the way it went. You got into the car. You handed over your life. Then you hoped to get there.

Esther didn't even see the other car coming at them over the hill. She was turned around, whispering in her new boyfriend's ear.

The rest happened too quickly for her to remember. There was a shriek and the crash of metal. There was a flipping and a turning and the sky was on the floor and the endless plains of sand were stretching out in the wrong direction. Esther braced against the ceiling, hard, and stayed roughly in place, but others around her were flying and hitting the sides and top of the combi with sickening slapping sounds.

Then, just as quickly, everything was very, very quiet. She was not in the American's lap anymore. She was so tired. She went to sleep.

When she woke, there was the sound of dripping. Someone was crying. Feet were everywhere.

There is a certain slowness that occurs after a Namibian traffic accident. Whether it be a fender-bender at an intersection or a fatal collision with a tractor trailer, the aftermath becomes a social event. There is a fundamental lack of urgency, as official help will not come for a long, long time. People stop their cars. They move the dead to one side, the bleeding to the other. They bring food and pray. Someone was braaiing just to give the injured people something to eat. Someone else had turned on the radio.

Esther was stretched on the side of the road, where someone had pulled her, simply to be clear of the traffic. When she opened her eyes an auntie was sitting next to her, holding her hand.

"Oh good," the auntie said. "You are not dead."

"Am I hurt?"

"You are not even bleeding. I think you might be bleeding inside somewhere. Can you breathe?"

Esther sat up slowly. There was a slicing pain in her side. She cried out.

"Yes. The inside is bleeding. Lie still until the ambulance comes. I have some rooibos with honey for you."

"Where is my sister? Where is the other man?"

"What other man?" the woman asked in Oshiwambo. "There are many men here."

Esther sat up again, taking deep breaths to get through the agony. She looked around slowly, taking care not to put herself into shock with what she saw.

There was the little boy with the fruit, so soaked in blood there could be no hope for him. Others were eating his oranges.

There was the father, whose body still lay where he was thrown through the windshield.

And there was Saara, her sister, surrounded by people working and shouting. From where Esther was sitting, she could see that her sister's leg was sheared off below the knee.

"That is my sister," Esther said. "You must help me get over there."

"I do not think—"

"Do it now."

The auntie called for reinforcements, and Esther was lifted and carried over to her bloody sister, whose eyes were wide and crazy as a rabid jackal's. A smartly dressed man was holding her sister's head and feeding her sips of Four Roses. She looked behind him, and thought that he must belong to the white Mercedes with gold hubcaps.

"Saara," Esther said.

Her sister shook her head.

Esther sat back, looking around frantically for the American. This well-dressed man could help her, but a white man might pull even more rank in a situation like this. Yet he wasn't anywhere. She scanned the dead bodies laid out in a line—he wasn't there. He wasn't sitting with the injured or standing with those trying to help.

She looked at the rich man, who seemed to have the most authority at the moment.

"There was a white man on the combi," she said. "Have you seen him?"

"He is with the Boers," he said. His eyes slid in the direction of Karibib. "They had a whole empty truck going right toward the hospital. But they would only take the American."

Esther shivered with hate. "And he went with them? Was he hurt?"

"He seemed all right," the man said. "He was bleeding but walking. They threw him in the back and left."

The ambulance came a few minutes later. Esther waited for hours with Saara for the medical help to sort itself. Someone had torn a strip of cloth from her dress and used it as a tourniquet to tie off her sister's leg. The rich man stayed close.

Esther was certain the American would come back. He went for help, she thought. He went for the doctor. He loved her. He said he did.

He held her up in the water.

But as the minutes and hours trickled away and her sister grew weaker, the truth became clear. The American had saved only himself. He was a white man who had used her and, of course, was never coming back.

Finally, Saara was taken to the hospital in Walvis. They stopped the bleeding, but the doctor said they could do nothing in terms of prosthetics and physical therapy. The rich man was more than that, it turned out. He was Kenneth, a developer from Cape Town. He wanted to fly Saara to a hospital there. He would pay for and oversee her recovery himself.

"You will owe him too much," Esther whispered to her sister at the hospital. She herself had been briefly examined and, despite the pain in her side, was judged mostly unharmed. The man named Kenneth would not look at her. He would not give her a phone number.

Saara didn't answer. She pulled the envelope of Mark's money from her rucksack and handed it over. "I only spent three hundred or so. You can use it. Go to Windhoek. Or find me later, in Cape Town."

They left as soon as they could, taking the white Mercedes southward. Saara waved from the window. Esther watched the car as it disappeared into the desert haze, then sat on the bench in front of the hospital.

It was the middle of the day, the very time when the sun would kill you. She would have to wait until four o'clock. No white car would be giving her a ride home. Esther would catch another combi, alone.

As she sat on the bench without her lover or her sister, she thought about how to survive this. How to learn what to avoid next time. She would learn to bear the long ride to Windhoek without her sister or a friend. She would learn how not to look surprised when she was told, when she called an auntie, that the Peace Corps man never returned to Oshakati. That he was fine, according to the embassy worker who came to gather his things. He just wasn't coming back.

She would change her name from Esther to Mila, so no one from Ovamboland could hear of her again. She would learn to be mercenary, and to look for another sort of man. A Josephat sort, with whom she could make a deal that did not bank on love.

She would learn to box up everything that had happened to her—everything that could ever hurt herself or her family—and to put it far away. She would seal it, this box, with thick hate for an American she met in Oshakati. He was the only person who had ever given her true hope, which was the cruelest of life's tricks.

She had only one regret about never again speaking to the American, and that was that he would never own up to his biggest lie. Not the one about loving her; she no longer cared about that. It was what he said about the water. It won't hurt you, he had said.

Yet Mila was from Ovamboland, a territory riddled with crocodiles and snakes. On principle, Ovambos did not swim. They knew how to coax food out of sandy soil, they knew how to survive years of scorching sun. But the ocean? No. Anyone who said otherwise was telling you a story. It was madness, not to be afraid of the sea.

Amanda stood in the driveway, watching Mark's car pull away. She was a woman who always knew what to do, but right now she really had no idea. She could taste the anger in her mouth; her legs were shaking. No one was there—no gardener, no housekeeper—so she peeled off her clothes and jumped into the pool.

As she swam along the bottom, she could barely make out a deflated pool toy, along with the bodies of a few dead geckos. The water hadn't been cleaned in quite a while, mainly because Amanda didn't know how to do it, and Mark had been doing whatever it was he'd been doing. Oh God. Would she have to divorce him now? What would Meg do? At the thought of telling her, Amanda let out an untimely sob and, choking on the algae, shot out of the water.

Then she remembered. Despite this personal Armageddon that seemed to be happening in their family, Meg had a performance at International Day she'd been going on about for weeks. What time was it again? What time was it now? How many seconds, she thought, did it take to blow up your life? She scrambled out of the water, crouching at her nakedness, and ran into the house to get a towel. And what to wear, she wondered, when everything actually was imploding? She decided on a skirt and a tank top—an ensemble that would make Meg be happy to have a normal, stable mom. She shoved her feet into sandals, pulled a brush through her hair on the way to the car, and got her phone out to pull up the performance time: 2:00 p.m.

"Shit," she said aloud, peeling out of the compound.

It was just before 2:00 now—exactly the time that white working-men in Windhoek ambled back to the office after coming home for lunch. The streets were snarled with huge white trucks. By the time she'd gotten to the other side on Mandume Avenue, traffic was at a standstill.

And Esther. *Esther.* Who the hell was Esther? Amanda gripped the wheel, trying to place when that would have been. Would she have been a freshman in college when this was happening? Would Esther have been older than her? What did she look like? Who had she been?

Mark had had plenty of girlfriends before her. Actually, Amanda knew that he'd had a truly unseemly amount. In the first months of their relationship, the part she thought of as giddy and innocent, they'd played the *how-many-have-you* game, and his number had been down-right frightening. Yet the fact that there were so many was comforting, actually, because after all that time, he'd chosen her. Now it turned out she was second to a dead woman. Knowing that at the beginning would have been fair, but finding it out now seemed—

Wait, Amanda thought, turning off the radio with a snap to listen to a small, faraway voice from a distant corner of her brain.

Esther. You *know* Esther.

The air around her thrummed. She was unable to breathe.

And what's more, Esther knows you.

Driving was suddenly an awful idea, so she pulled over and put the car in park. It was 2:10 now. Everyone would be there.

The school was about a mile away—a short distance for a runner. She locked the car behind her and began to sprint as fast as she could.

The road was busy and dusty, and the shoulder treeless, lined only with thorny shrubs. Whenever Amanda had seen people walking along that way to work, she'd always been tempted to stop and pick them up, as it looked so treacherous. Now she tried to breathe deeply and calmly as she ran over the roasting ground. Her shoes were slipping, so she kicked them off and held one in each hand. The fiery asphalt scorched the soles of her feet as they hit the ground, so she ran faster, taking lighter steps.

The line of cars started half a mile back from the school, as everyone was waiting to get to the International Day festivities. As she huffed past, she could feel the inquisitive eyes of the parents as she ran past their cars.

"Amanda!" Kayla Grant yelled, poking her head tentatively out of the comfort of her air-conditioned car. "Whatcha doin', girl?"

Amanda waved, trying to look normal, as if a regular day usually consisted of finding out her husband had brought them to Namibia to look for another woman he'd loved more than her. As if it were typical to learn that Mark had taken hold of her life savings. As if it was routine to realize, before he did, that her husband's long-lost girlfriend was actually alive.

Don't worry, Kayla! It's all cool!

She burst through the entrance, looking around wildly for her husband or child. "Miss?" the security guard asked, in a rare effort to police the area. "Are you fine?"

Amanda froze as she gazed across the parking lot, where excitement was brewing over what looked like a slight collision. It was Mark's rental car, she saw now. He'd rear-ended a black SUV. It was——

—Mila's SUV.

Amanda could just see him behind the car now, talking to someone. "Mark!" Amanda cried. Yet it was just like one of those dreams she'd had when she wasn't on time to a meeting, or her wedding. Or the nightmares where she'd called and called for her mother, but no matter how loud she was, she couldn't be heard.

Five hundred kilograms of meat, Persephone thought crossly. And wouldn't you know it, all these people wanted were the Canadian pancakes.

It had been quite cold for Windhoek over the previous weeks. Chilly enough to provide Persephone with the false hope that International Day would be as crisp and refreshing as one of those delicious fall festivals back home, the ones where you sipped on cider and could wear a cream fisherman's sweater. (Persephone looked terrific in raw wool.) But no, the cold snap had passed, and here she was with ninety-eight-degree weather again. Persephone had already had to change twice—once because Kayla spilled matcha all over her, and the other time because she'd perspired so much she could have competed in a wet T-shirt contest (the only downside of white). Luckily, Doni had taught her long ago to keep backup outfits in the trunk of her car, just in case. No one ever said looking effortlessly perfect really *was* effortless.

Well, obviously this weather was the hand of God, probably wielded by some curse from Mila. And Mila would be right to do it, too. How could Persephone ever have thought that she could run an event this large in Namibia better than an actual Namibian? Why had she been so nasty to her just now? Why hadn't Adam warned her? (Well, she supposed he *had* warned her. As had Amanda.) What was it about her DNA that made her think that as an American, she knew best? Was it her upbringing? Was there subliminal messaging of general superiority in the Pledge of Allegiance, which she had to recite at Hotchkiss every week?

But she was getting distracted now, and God knows she didn't have the time. A downside of the Uniform was that she could be spotted from miles away, which was not so terrific when everyone had questions for her, from the beverage dealers to the soundman to her ex–tennis partner from Sweden who wanted to know if she'd canvassed the food for shellfish, because little Bjorn had an allergy.

"There are twenty-eight booths and thousands of kilos of food, Anka," she'd said, trying to control herself. "I can't be certain that a sea snail hasn't gotten into the mix."

What else? Argentina was next to Namibia, and they were both selling grilled meat. Brazil's sand was getting all over Turkey's rugs. Separating the adulterous kindergarten teacher from the year four assistant hadn't solved the problem, as the wronged wife had come over and dumped a pot of jollof rice on the perpetrator's head. It was 2:00, and many of the fathers were already drunk—some lying spread-eagled on the grass, blocking the pathways. Was there any way they could pull an emergency measure, Kayla was asking, and raise the price of the liquor?

"I don't think I can change prices," Persephone said. "Mila said if we did that, we'd be Zimbabwean grocery store owners. Whatever that means."

Headmaster Pierre was at her arm.

"It's time for the performances," he said.

"Thank the Lord!" Persephone crowed. "Anything to give me a break."

"If you think this is a break," Pierre said, "you've got another thing coming, I'm afraid."

Persephone squared her shoulders, preparing herself. No matter what Headmaster Pierre said, this was *actually* the moment she'd been waiting for. Last year had been her first International Day, and she'd been stuck at the Canadian booth for eons, doling out poutine and pancakes.

Persephone had been covered in maple syrup: her hair, her hands, even her delicate silver-painted toes. She hadn't even complained. It was for the school, she'd told herself sternly. We international women are in this together! And then, out of the corner of her eye, she'd seen Mila's motorcade arrive. Their fearless leader, it seemed, had been running a mission control center from the backseat of her air-conditioned car.

Then she emerged as refreshed and beautiful as a sphinx in a pink and silver dress, taking her place under the tented state at the microphone, while the other mothers, her underlings, remained in the scorching sun. Persephone remembered standing there in the heat, sweating syrup, as Mila had coolly received accolades from the head of the board, several ambassadors, and other diplomats. Adam had been onstage also, serving the ambassador.

"I would have had you onstage with us," he'd said later. "But you looked so disheveled. Though didn't that Shilongo babe do a great job?"

Well. Now it was *Persephone's* turn. She gave her ponytail a quick toss and followed Headmaster Pierre to the stage. Only, as she ascended, she wasn't experiencing the reverent hush she remembered from last year. In fact, though she was determinedly tapping on the microphone, there was no change in the volume level at all.

"Welcome to . . . Hello? Can you please . . . Hey, *Hey!*"

"Let me try," Headmaster Pierre said, patting her shoulder lightly. He grabbed the mike. *"Angolan coup d'état!"*

Hundreds of heads swiveled in his direction.

"Kidding. *Kidding!"* He grinned at Persephone. "I've always wanted to do that. Folks, it's the hour you've been waiting for. Your adorable children are now going to perform for us, class by class."

The buzz that had ceased instantly began again, and several parents headed to the beverage tent to fortify themselves.

"But first, a few words from our organizer, Mrs. Persephone Wilder." Persephone took a deep breath, beamed at the crowd, and stepped up to the podium again.

"Thank you, Pierre. First, I wanted to thank all of the volunteers who made today such a great success. And all of the housekeepers and gardeners *sent* by the volunteers. You've all done a terrific job. International Day is an old WIS tradition, dating from——"

She was cut off by the sound of the marching band, which someone had signaled to begin early.

"Let the procession *begin*!" shouted Pierre, as Persephone wondered for the fiftieth time that day why nothing was going right.

The students, dressed in various international outfits, began streaming into the gym.

"They look adorable," said Kayla, who was standing next to her. And Persephone had to agree, other than the year twos, who, at six and seven years old, were representing Brazil by wearing spangled bikinis and briefs. Parents were crushing into the gym now, which was steamy hot and smelled of old fried chicken and sweat. The veterans had brought camping chairs and were jockeying for position at the front.

The kindergarten class started the festivities with a lip-synched rendition of "Let's Get It On" by Marvin Gaye. Persephone could see that some of the fresher American parents looked shocked.

The majority of WIS families, though, were weathered diplomats who had been through many International Schools. They knew the drill, which was that I-School teachers everywhere in the world are bound to an ironclad curriculum. Every unit, chapter, and topic was strictly assigned, and every student was stringently tested to see how they were faring against the public school kids back home. As a result, the beaten-down, underpaid international teachers had one place to express themselves: the choreography of student assemblies. Which meant that all over the world, if your children were enrolled in an International School, at some point they were going to get up on a stage and do something completely inappropriate.

The kindergartners finished their sexy dance to thunderous applause. Next were the year ones, who were lining up to hump each other

Britney-style to "Womanizer." A thousandth hand tapped her shoulder to ask a question. Trying her very hardest not to look weary, Persephone turned around.

"Petrus!" she said with relief.

"My daughter's out there," he said proudly, his hands on his hips. Today he was looking massive in a tracksuit and bright yellow trainers. Again, she inadvertently imagined being crushed by all of that wonderful Namibian weight.

Stop it!

"She's the one in the white leather boots."

"Adorable." Persephone pointedly applauded extra-hard for the gyrating children onstage.

"My dear," he said. "I must talk to you. Can we go outside?"

"Sure," she said, blushing. Really? He was going to talk to her about his crush *now*? Still, she needed a breath of fresh air, and since her husband was nowhere in sight, why not?

Petrus led her around the far side of the gym. "I was thinking we could meet for lunch to go over this, but things have been moving too fast."

"They have?" She couldn't help but flutter her eyelashes a bit. She *was* a woman, after all.

"I went over the stuff you gave me. You're right. All of those accounts you gave me are suspicious. I did some mining, and they're all sourced right here in Namibia."

"Oh."

"I think those numbers are some sort of code. As to when and where to meet."

Persephone concentrated on shifting gears. From sex to Tusk! She could do this. "Do you know who in Namibia it could be?" she purred.

"I'm getting there. I just need a few hours, but your husband"—he rolled his eyes—"put me on this other thing."

"Oh. Drat."

"Yes. And this thing they're about to do . . . it's dishonorable and disgusting. But it's not your fault, my dear."

"Wait. What?" She felt her brow wrinkle unbecomingly. "What do you mean?"

"I mean . . . Adam saw that I was looking up the IP addresses of those rhino followers."

"Yes?"

"Well, he was impressed that I could do that at all. So he had me . . . use it for something else."

"Petrus," Persephone said, the alarm rising in her voice. "What are you talking about?"

"Petri Dish, my man!" Adam boomed, tossing his arm around Petrus's shoulder. Persephone winced. Anyone could spot the dislike on Petrus's distinguished face from a mile away. "What are you two talking about here?"

"Nothing, Adam," she said.

"Hello, darling," he said.

"Darling."

"Oh, you," Adam said, disentangling himself from Petrus and encircling Persephone's waist. "You and your rhino club. You are brilliant, you know that?"

Persephone bristled. Actually, she was *quite* aware of her higher-than-average intelligence. Thank you very much.

"Your club ended up opening the door to a huge win. The Big A. will be so fucking happy with us. It's my pièce de résistance. A surprise."

"I'm sorry?"

"Your rhino thing. The IP information. It paved the way for a huge win. You'll see." He pulled her close and dropped to a whisper. "And it's not a CIA matter, so I'll get all the credit."

"I thought the State Department wasn't about personal credit," Persephone said.

"Darling, don't get into a tizzy about this arrest ruining your PTA party. POTUS tweeted something inappropriate last night, and we need a distraction. I didn't totally clear it with the ambo, but for once, I'm taking initiative, yes? If anything, it'll make *your* event the only one people remember."

"But what are you—"

"I'll see you later. Just make sure you do some crowd control, okay? It might get a little nuts. And keep up those hobbies, darling. This one was a home run." He kissed her cheek and disappeared.

"Oh, Petrus," Persephone said. "I sort of hate my husband."

"That's quite a coincidence," Petrus boomed. "Because I *do* hate your husband."

"Well." Life was falling apart, but it *was* nice to have an admirer in this middling phase of life. "This will be disruptive, right on my big day. Which I suppose is fine, in the end. For our country."

"Really?" Petrus said. "I think it is not fine at all. That man is a donkey. I'm sorry I couldn't be more helpful. I'd do almost anything for you. You know that." He looked at her gravely. "I do need my job."

"It's okay, Petrus. Thanks, though."

Luckily, the moment was interrupted by a blast of rap, turned up even louder than the other grades. It was Amanda's daughter's class, 3A.

Where was she, anyway? Persephone wondered.

They were treating the audience to their rendition of "Love the Way You Lie" by Eminem. Above their heads flickered a film of burning forests. Persephone had seen the program, of course, and had been quite stern with the teachers about using the Kids Bop! version sans profanity, but it seemed that corner had mysteriously been cut. *Tie her to the bed and set this house on fire!* Eminem screamed.

Oh dear.

Suddenly the music was switched off. Persephone looked around for the aggressive parent who had gotten there before she had. British, maybe. No one else would have bothered to do anything about it. But then something confusing happened. Namibian policemen were swarming the stage. Persephone saw them talking to Miss Ruby, who pointed, reluctantly, to a corner where two girls were huddled together, clutching hands.

Persephone gasped when, like a falling elephant, the realization of what was happening thundered down upon her.

The cuffs were already out. The police were here to arrest two *children*: Meg Evans and Taimi Shilongo.

The traffic around the school, for some reason, was much busier than usual. Mark recalled something about some event that was happening that day, but in this moment, just as before, he didn't care. He just wanted to get his kid and get out of there. Now that he had pulled into the parking lot, he saw there was definitely a to-do going on. There were tents and the kids were wearing . . . almost nothing.

Jesus, Mark thought. Was that his daughter, crossing the breezeway in a sequined miniskirt?

He craned his head to get a better look, not realizing his foot had eased off the brake. There was a subsequent *bang!* and an awful crunching sound from his car.

Mark covered his face, as his car was withstanding a rainstorm of glass, though his own windshield seemed intact. Taking his hands from his face, he felt the need to swear, though he'd used so much profanity already today, nothing seemed appropriate.

"Myaaaaaaah!" he screamed in frustration. *Mothergoddamnedass-fucker.* He was going to have to pay for the damage to this super-fancy SUV. Why does this day have to be like this? he wondered.

Taking a deep breath, Mark got out of the car to cry mea culpa, only to see that some rich person's chauffeur—*Mothergoddamnedassfucker*—was already surveying the damage.

"I'm so sorry," Mark said. "I didn't see you . . . I mean, I was looking at . . ."

"Talk to my boss," the man said, frowning at the glass. He nodded at the open door. "She's in a state. A bit nervous about accidents, hey."

"Sure," Mark said. He made his way to the open door, though he couldn't quite see inside at first. "Hello. I'm so sorry . . . I—"

She was looking at him, the light on her face. After all that time. She was there, uncurling herself from the inside of the car.

It would have been 1998. Another place, another time. The house Mark settled on for his new wife, Esther, was in Vermont, in the hills outside of Montpelier. He'd decided to go to medical school after all, and UVM had let him in after he'd completed a correspondence course in organic chemistry, the one course he'd failed to take at Brown. But Burlington didn't fit somehow; it was too tie-dye, too Phish. When Mark took Esther to the Ben & Jerry's on Church Street (she adored ice cream), Esther had stared wide-eyed at the stoners and the raving homeless men who lurked on the corners. She hadn't complained directly, but he could read her. So instead he'd steered them east to the middle of the state, where the house prices were cheaper and there was less pressure to conform to nonconformity.

Their new home was marvelously decrepit, with slanted floors and window frames warped enough to keep them from closing. Built in 1841, it was on top of a hill. An old porch that looked out on the Green Mountains clung precariously to the front. The farmland all around had already been sold over the years, so corn was planted on three sides of the house, save one acre, which was cordoned off as a yard with a picket fence. The old couple selling had defected from New York in the late sixties with the other artists and writers who, they said, had either moved back or died. They kept chickens and had filled the place with huge mismatching antiques they wouldn't bother taking with them.

"A mixed couple!" the woman kept saying. "It's so exciting! We don't get that much, I suppose because it's too cold."

Esther and Mark laughed at that. What did the weather have to do with it? Before leaving, the old lady showed Esther where to put the buckets to catch the leaks, and hugged her. Mark took out a small mortgage, and the place was theirs.

Coming home to Esther. When Mark would get off 89 for the back roads of East Montpelier, he'd find himself speeding to the house, running lights and pissing off farmers with the dust. He would jump out of the car, sometimes while it was still running, and rush in to find her. Sometimes she was cooking dinner; other nights she'd forgotten and was busy studying, as she was taking basic classes over at Goddard.

Wherever she was, he'd go to her, wrapping his arms around her waist desperately, burying his head in her neck. He would turn her around and hold her, conforming to her body so that she was completely pressed against him. They'd once had drinks down the road with a cattle farmer, and he'd told them how they calmed the cows down before slaughter: they held them, womb-like, so every curve of their body was supported. That was what Mark did for Esther when he came home. It wasn't a matter of whether she liked it; it seemed to be what she needed. Between them, a sort of humming erupted. Her body would go slack in his arms, relaxing completely. Most of the time they would give up on eating and go upstairs to bed, where Mark would make slow love to his wife, marveling at every inch of her body. After, they would sleep like babies until the next morning, and then . . .

And then.

How many lives can we live? That was the question as he gazed now at Esther, who was not dead, and not much older, but standing in front of him, eyebrows drawn together, mouth pressed into an unfamiliar frown. He blinked a few times and leaned forward, but as he did, she moved back away from him.

"Sorry," Mark said lamely. He couldn't read her expression. He was unable to register anything, other than the treacherous thrumming of his own heart. "Esther?" he finally ventured.

"Mila," Mila said.

"You're Mila," he said.

"Mila," he said, chewing on the words. "Mila."

She nodded.

"You changed your name," Mark said.

"You hit my car," Mila said.

Mark looked at her more closely. She was older, after all; her face was thinner, and there were shadows beneath her eyes. He ran his hand self-consciously over his belly, thinking how he must look to her. She wouldn't be accepting of his age. Unlike Amanda, she wouldn't have been around long enough to be used to it.

"Mark!"

Mark's body jolted awake. It was his wife's voice—Amanda, his real-life wife—ripping across the playground and parking lot.

"Oh," Mila said, her eyes widening. Mark turned his head to where the voice was coming from. It was indeed Amanda, but she didn't look herself—she had a dress on, but she was barefoot and her hair was wild. Her purse was strapped to her body like a military canteen, and she held a shoe in either hand.

"Amanda!" he called. "Are you okay?"

Suddenly a voice boomed over the loudspeaker. Windhoek International School had the old-fashioned kind of PA system, the same sort South Africans used in their prison camps during apartheid. It rendered the words of whoever was speaking as ominous and all-knowing; everyone in the parking lot jerked their head at the noise.

"*Attention. Parents. We have a grave situation.*"

"What, did they run out of biltong?" Smiling at his own stupid joke, Mark looked at Esther to share the moment. But this wasn't Esther—this was Mila. And when she looked back at him blankly, he remembered that this was the sort of thing he did with Amanda. His actual wife.

"*Would the parents of Taimi Shilongo and Meg Evans please come immediately to the gym? This is an emergency . . .*" In the background, the crowd could hear the buzz of off mic discussion. "*Excuse me. No casualties, parents. Remain calm. But . . .*"

Now Persephone's voice trilled over the PA system:

"Amanda! *They're arresting the girls, darling! Get the hell over here and talk to the police! Now!*"

30

The art of what is known as modern diplomacy began in Italy. There, nobles would construct beautiful buildings, eventually known as embassies, where they would discuss the business of their city-states. Embassies ranged in size and grandeur, usually in direct proportion to the power of the country represented at the time. For example, the British Embassies in Cairo and Tokyo are architectural marvels meant to show off the arm of the empire. Even today, the brand-new American Embassy in London cost upward of a billion dollars to build, and resembles a sleek museum, filled with modern art.

The U.S. Embassy in Windhoek was not one of these architectural marvels. Designed to survive an attack from above, the squat structure was largely underground and wedged at the end of a shabby street. Entering required a tiresome screening by sleepy guards . . . one that was more than mildly annoying when one's daughter had been carted into said compound by the police for selling Nazi contraband.

Amanda, of course, couldn't believe this was happening. It must be some cruel, elaborate joke. Yet this was what Barry Levin, head of public affairs, had told Amanda on the ride over. Her daughter, Meg—her *nine-year-old daughter*—had been tracked selling authentic Nazi artifacts to Neo-Nazis in Africa, Germany, and the United States.

"They used Taimi Shilongo's computer to set up a password-protected online store," Barry said, rubbing his hand back and forth over his bald head. "That in itself is troubling, if not illegal. Though there are hate crime issues. And probably it was mostly the Shilongo girl. But then there was the fact that they were using the U.S. diplomatic mail pouch to deliver the packages. That's where we get into trouble."

"She used the pouch?" Amanda asked in disbelief.

"It was actually quite clever," Barry said. "They decorated the envelopes with hearts and flowers to make them look like care packages. If she doesn't go to juvie, she can put it on her application to Wharton."

"Juvie? . . . As in juvenile hall?" Amanda felt tears coming on, but she took a deep breath and squared her shoulders. This was not the time to get hysterical. Manage the project, Evans, she commanded herself sternly. "I'm certain this is a mistake. Mark's Jewish, for God's sake. But let's say, for a moment, it wasn't a mistake. What, exactly, is illegal about these . . . sales?"

"Amanda." Barry looked at her in a manner so decidedly condescending, she couldn't help but feel a strong urge to bring his laptop down over his head. "We're a little pressed for time, so I won't give you an *extended* history lesson. But this was a German colony, turned South African, turned independent. The Germans were very, very mean to the ancestors of the people who make up the present government. And the government's been pretty nice to them. As in, they haven't killed a bunch of them, or even taken their farms, like they did over in Zim. But having Nazi stuff is illegal. Selling it is absolutely illegal. The second part of the equation is that they stole it from the Shilongos, who, like I said, shouldn't have had it in the first place. Though it sounds like it was sitting on the property when they bought it. The final problem is that using the pouch under false pretenses and for commercial use is absolutely illegal. And that's the biggie."

"Well . . . well . . ." Amanda struggled for proper words. "What were they doing with the money?"

Barry rolled his eyes to the sky. "They were EFTing it to Our Hope Children's Hostel."

"Oh." Amanda felt the tears coming again. She got it now. Meg did this for *her*. "Well, that seems okay."

They were in the front hallway now. Barry lowered his voice. "It's not," Barry said. "None of this is okay. Precocious as it is. Can't say I'm not impressed."

"Obviously you'll have her out of here in an hour."

"Well, there's not much I can do."

"What about the embassy?"

"Um . . ."

"Isn't that your guys' job? To protect us in internationally confusing situations?" Her voice was veering into the shrill zone. Desperation, thick and cold, was beginning to creep into her gut and chest. And where the hell was Mark? She'd hurried to the school gym as soon as she heard the announcement, but once they'd been briefed on the situation by the frantic headmaster, they'd run to their respective cars. She pulled out her phone and fired off a text:

Meg arrested for selling Nazi gear

cum to US. Embassy we r being extraordinary

no not that

fucking iPhone

EXTRADITED

"Oh look!" Barry said, brightening. "Counsel is here."

Amanda turned to see Adam's graceful figure cutting a swath through the hallway. "Adam. Thank God. Hi." Persephone's husband flashed his killer grin, causing Amanda to recoil slightly. "What are we going to do? What's your strategy?"

"My strategy?" Adam repeated, cocking his head.

"Yes!" She felt her hands shaking, and balled them into fists. "To get Meg out of this mess."

"Amanda, I'm the *ambassador's* counsel. Not your daughter's." He patted her shoulder.

If one more damned diplomat talks down to me today, I'll get myself arrested, Amanda thought.

"What do you mean?" she asked.

"It's my job to protect our country's interests. Which do not include your daughter using U.S. property to sell stolen Nazi gear."

"You don't have proof of that," Amanda said uncertainly.

"We have emails coming from your computer. We have messages coming from a cell phone in your house. We have pouches tracking to your account. We *do* have proof."

"Wait." Amanda shook her head. "I don't get it. Is the U.S. arresting Meg? Or the Namibians? Because they were Namibian police, but she's here."

"We're holding her as a courtesy to you. We didn't think you'd want her in Namibian prison."

"And Taimi? Her friend?" Amanda looked around for Mila or any sign of the Shilongos' entourage. "Where is she?"

"Oh. She's under house arrest."

"What the hell?" Amanda asked. "Why can't Meg have house arrest?"

"Because Meg is not the minister of transportation's daughter."

Amanda put her hands on her forehead, pushing her hair back in exasperation. "So how the hell do I get her out of here, Adam? This is ridiculous. You can't arrest a nine-year-old for opening an e-store."

"Listen. I'll tell you something I shouldn't."

"Okay," Amanda brightened slightly. "Great."

"It's not actually in the American government's present interest to protect Meg at the moment."

"*What?*"

"I mean, the last administration would have. Of course. But these days we're more interested in culpability. We've got to build some cred after POTUS labeled the whole continent a dung bucket. Meg *did* do something clearly illegal here. So any chance to gain—"

"Don't say another damned word," Amanda hissed. "Let me see my daughter. Now."

"Well, technically, I'm not able to——"

"Now, Adam. Or I'll call *The Washington Post.* Who, after our article on your wife, I have on fucking speed dial."

Adam looked at Barry. Barry shrugged, then turned and led them both down a grim hallway that led to an even grimmer stairway, which in turn opened up into a line of cells in the basement. Barry punched in a code and opened a metal door, leading Amanda to a cell with no windows where Meg was sitting alone at a metal table.

"Seriously?" Amanda said to Adam. "She's *nine*."

For once, Persephone's husband looked contrite.

"Mom!" Meg jumped up and threw herself at Amanda. Her daughter wasn't crying at the moment, but her face was puffy, meaning she had been in this cell weeping alone.

"You all are fucking animals," Amanda muttered.

"I'll be outside," Adam said.

"Sweetheart," Amanda said as the massive door clicked shut, "everything is going to be okay."

"Really?" Meg said, looking up at her mother. "Because everyone here says it's not."

"Meg, you are a very perceptive girl. But today you have to believe that Mommy is going to defy reality."

"Okay."

Amanda sat down. "Can you tell me about this . . . store?"

There was a knock at the door, and Barry stuck his head in.

"I just need to tell you we're listening to everything you say."

"Go. Away."

"Right." Barry closed the door again.

"Tell me."

"It was supposed to be a surprise," Meg said. Now the tears started again. "You kept saying how hard it was to help people here. So Taimi made up this way."

"How much did you send?"

Meg sniffed. "A little over fourteen thousand U.S."

"Holy shit."

"Dollar."

"Drink some water, honey. So, how did you do this?"

"Taimi set up a bank account in Namibia."

"She's not old enough to do that, is she?"

"She used her sister's name and stuff. We just did it over the phone. It was easy. And then the money comes electronically, and we EFT it."

There was another knock at the door, and it opened again.

"Oh my God," Amanda said to Mark. "Where the hell have you been?"

"Dol——"

"Zip it, Meg," Amanda said.

"I was getting the full story from those goons in there," Mark said, rubbing her shoulder. Amanda felt tears rising in the corners of her eyes.

"I know it's been a weird day, but let's just focus on this, okay?"

"Okay," Amanda turned back to Meg. "So, honey, I need you to tell us everything about what was going on here."

Meg screwed up her forehead. "The money idea was mine. Needing it. I heard Mom talking about how she was disappointed about not being able to help the kids at that orphanage. She seemed really sad about it, so I wanted to surprise her."

Amanda looked at Mark, as if to say: *See? She is perfect. At which he shot her a look back that clearly said, Perfect, eh? Then I guess we're sitting in a holding cell because you've been spoiling the hell out of her for nine years.*

"The store idea," Meg went on. "The part about selling the stuff in the barn, that was Taimi's."

"Do you have proof of that?" Mark asked.

"Why? Is Taimi getting into trouble? Because I'm not telling on my friend."

"Let's move on," Mark said, glancing at an apparatus in an upper corner of the room that could only be a camera. "What about transport?"

"Huh?"

"How did you get the stuff to Windhoek?"

"We put them in my suitcase when I visited. When Mom was out on that safari. We only sent stuff that could fit in the suitcase. And then Taimi brought other stuff when she went back on weekends."

"Hmmm. Okay," Mark said, scribbling something down on a notepad. "Who gave you the mailing supplies?"

"We took them from Mr. Shilongo's desk."

"Mmm-hmmm," Mark scribbled some more.

"Can I go to the bathroom?" Meg asked. "They haven't let me pee yet."

"Those assholes!" Mark cried. He shot up and yanked open the door. "Hey, fuckers, I'm calling Amnesty International on you. This kid needs to go to the bathroom. Now!"

It had been years since Amanda had seen Mark this passionate about anything. As Meg was ushered to the toilet, Amanda detected a faraway rumbling inside her—the sleeping giant of her lost lust for her husband.

"So what do you think we should do?" she asked. "And what are you writing there? Did you also secretly go to law school or something?"

"Or something." Mark scowled at his notes. "I've been reading a lot about the illegal export and smuggling trade in Namibia."

"Why?"

"For . . . um . . . my research. Anyway—I think we need a technicality. Some adult that helped. Even vaguely."

"I'll take the blame," Amanda said. "She obviously did it to please me. She said so."

"Yeah, but you didn't physically help. Is there anyone else you can think of?"

"I mean . . ." Amanda paused, looking at Mark. "Maybe Mila knew." Mark didn't look up from his notepad, but she could see his hand freeze.

"All of this went on at *her* house," Amanda went on. "She's my friend, but if our kids were selling Nazi crap and she knew——"

"Amanda," Mark interrupted quietly.

"And I know you won't want to blame her because she's your ex-girlfriend." Her husband stared at her, alarmed. "Yeah. She once told me her old name, which I remembered on the way to the school today. So that whole thing about her being dead was also bullshit, huh?"

"No," Mark said, shaking his head. "I hadn't seen her until today."

"You're such a liar."

"No, really, I—" The door slammed open again. Meg reentered, trailed closely by the ambassador.

"Hi, all," the Big A. said. "Sorry for the delay. I've been on R and R. Was at a fabulous little place called Jack's Camp. No phones, no contact. Just lions. You can't even walk anywhere without an armed guard. I guess one year some Finnish woman left her sweater at the al fresco dinner table, and she went back to get it in the dark and the next day all they found of her was—"

"Excuse me," Amanda said. "Can you please tell me when my daughter can get out of here?"

"Right. Sorry." The ambassador adjusted her stance. "Bad news on that front, I'm afraid. Listen, I didn't approve this. It was that witless wonder boy they've given to me as counsel. Went off and tried to impress me, and he's caused a huge mess. I never, in a million years, would have green-lighted this production."

"Can't you stop it?" Mark asked.

"Well, he's started the ball rolling, and I'm afraid the Namibians are being sticklers. And our current administration doesn't want to be seen as overly lenient toward Americans living abroad."

"She's a kid!" Amanda cried.

"Look. I understand. I've spoken to the Namibian minister of justice. I guess there is something that will help us."

"What?" asked Mark.

"Someone over there wants to take down Josephat Shilongo," she said. "If Meg testifies against Taimi, we'll probably have enough leverage to make this all go away."

"No," Meg said.

"Meg," Amanda said. "This isn't up to you."

"Yes, it is," Meg said. "I did it. I'm the one who knows what went on. Taimi's my friend, and I'm not getting her in trouble."

"Fine girl you've got here," the ambassador said. "But, Molly, think carefully. I don't think you want to go to Namibian prison. They're quite uncomfortable. I don't even know where they put the children."

"I'm Meg," she said. "And I'm not a rat."

"Aristocats?" Mark asked.

"Ratatouille," she answered.

"I'm proud of you, sweetheart," Mark said. "For the record. You never have to eat another broccoli stalk again."

For the first time all afternoon, Meg allowed a few tears to fall.

"Thanks, Daddy."

"This is all very touching," the ambassador said, standing. "But also bad news. And tiring, given that I spent all afternoon at the minister of justice's office. All right. I'm afraid little Meg will be here for the night."

"Here?" Amanda said. "There's no bed."

"We'll arrange a cot."

"Well, I'm staying with her," Amanda said.

"Mrs. Evans," the ambassador said. "I don't think you understand. We are just one step away from a prison cell. Moms don't get to spend the night with their kids in prison. Until the situation changes, Meg sleeps here, alone. Your little girl is in a lot of trouble. And this is Africa."

"This is Africa," Mark repeated. He wrote it down. "What does that mean?"

"Pick up a history book," the ambassador said. "Happy endings are not guaranteed."

31

Persephone didn't stick around for the dismantling of International Day. The supervision, a huge task, was definitely a chore attached to her label of PTA president. But after the arrest, Pierre had given her an out. Amanda was frothing at the mouth to kill Adam, and the faces of the rest of the mothers definitely portrayed a collective opinion that they believed the sacrifice of the children was all her doing. And it wasn't like she could say something like, Actually, I have no idea what my husband does over there at the embassy! Her job was to support him, wasn't it? Which probably meant knowing a little about his day-to-day tasks and if he was planning on arresting her best friend's child.

Oh dear.

"Miss Frida?" she called. A few moments later, Frida appeared, causing Persephone to frown into her wineglass. She was wearing one of Persephone's donated outfits, a sunny yellow knit dress from the days before Persephone had figured out the Uniform. Frida was curvy in all of the places that Persephone was stick-straight. The woman had children in college, yet there was an unlikely upward bounce to her bottom, as if defying gravity itself. Persephone knew she was being ungenerous, but every time she saw Frida in one of her hand-me-down frocks, she felt a wave of envy, and she sort of wanted to ask for it back again.

"Would you like a drink?" she asked Frida now.

"No, thank you."

"You don't like prosecco?"

"I don't drink, miss."

"Oh," Persephone said. "I barely do, either. Well. If you ever feel like you want to . . ." She stopped herself. She had already given away half of her clothes. Was she telling the nanny to drink on the job, as well? She smiled sweetly, indicating that Frida could go.

A few minutes later, the doorbell rang. Persephone refilled her glass, trying to guess who it might be. Perhaps Amanda, coming to say she was sorry for practically physically attacking her after they carted her daughter away. Or Kayla, fishing for gossip. Or Shoshana, with some news to lord over her about the fabulousness of her next post. And yet, Frida returned with none other than Mila Shilongo.

It was a strict policy of Persephone's not to gloat, even when she really, really wanted to. Well, maybe to her sister, sometimes. Yet Mila Shilongo, standing here, obviously in need of something, so shortly after dressing her down! It was almost enough to break her rules.

"Mila," she said. "How can I help you tonight?"

"Hello," Mila said. She was dressed in a beautiful green dress, but something seemed off. Her hair was a bit askew, and one of her nails was chipped. "This is a very fine house."

"Thank you. It's not mine, of course. I mean, the family photos are, and some of the furniture. But mostly—"

"I see you are drinking champagne."

"Prosecco."

"I'll have some, please."

"Sure." That was one thing she liked about Mila: she was direct. Persephone popped up and grabbed another glass. The cheerful nature of the bubbles and the way they fizzed over the side seemed perversely incongruous with the mood of the day. "I'm so sorry about Taimi. Is she all right?"

"She is fine," Mila said. "Her father will sort it out."

"Oh, of course he will."

Mila walked to the window, looking at the olive grove. "Josephat has thrown me out," she said.

"What? But that's impossible."

Mila continued as if Persephone hadn't spoken. A rather annoying habit of hers, Persephone couldn't help but note.

"I have nowhere to go. I was supposed to spend the night in Katutura at my sister's house. She is trying to humble me, so she told me to sleep in the living room. My cousin drinks and watches TV all day and night." She made a face. "I have been walking all day. All day in this heat. I walked through Katutura, dragging my bag. Boys made fun of how I looked. Men asked me if I had a price. Dogs were tearing through the trash. I worked hard to get away from that place, Persephone. I abhor poverty."

Persephone was uncharacteristically unsure of what to say. I abhor poverty, too! didn't seem correct when one was inhabiting a mansion in a developing country. "I'm so sorry. I just can't believe he threw you out. Doesn't Taimi *need* you?"

Mila tapped her finger distractedly against her glass. "Couldn't your husband have picked something else to focus on? These are *children*. There are many adult criminals here to arrest, you know."

"I'm sorry. I wish there were something I could—"

Suddenly it hit her. There was something Persephone could do for Amanda and Mila and their girls. She could talk to the Big A.

They weren't friends, exactly, yet, but they had had lunch together, hadn't they? Besides, her husband was putting his life on the line for their country at *this very moment*. Surely that afforded her an audience.

"Mila," Persephone said, "I know it may seem odd hearing this from me, given our background . . . but please feel free to stay here."

"Here?" Mila asked.

"Yes. It's the least I can do."

She prepared herself for Mila's protests, but none came. Instead, Mila picked up an orange from a bowl on the table, inspecting it for bruises.

"That's very kind of you. I will accept."

"Okay," Persephone said, a teensy bit unnerved by Mila's ability to feel instantly at home. "I have to go out, but . . . make yourself comfortable. The fridge, the shower, everything is yours."

"Thank you, Persephone," Mila said.

Persephone hurried about, grabbing her lipstick and keys. "Now, if there's anything you need—"

But it seemed she didn't have to worry. Mila was already taking her suitcase to the sunnier of the guest suites, speaking Oshiwambo to Frida as if they were the oldest of chums.

Once Persephone was in the car, she made two quick calls: One was to the embassy to see if the ambassador was in. The answer, a curt no. The other was to the ambassador's chef, who had given Persephone her card after their disastrous luncheon.

Was she preparing dinner for the ambassador tonight? Persephone asked.

"Yes," the chef said, sounding a bit hopeless. "I'm making a quiche. Do you know the origin of quiche? I know she's going to ask."

"Tell her farm wives created it to feed troops during the French Revolution. Is she dining alone?"

"Yes."

"Excellent." Persephone hung up, spruced up her makeup, spritzed the wine smell away with the Shalimar she kept in the car for such occasions (Doni Oppenheimer!), and drove out the gate. As she drove the two blocks to the Official Residence, she felt positively radiant with pride that she, Persephone Anne Wilder, would actually be the one to fix all of this. There was something so satisfying about solving people's problems. Usually emergencies she took care of were much more subtle. Getting a sick child to the proper surgeon to have an appendix out, for example. Talking a Trailer out of leaving his family because he couldn't stand doing nothing for one more week. Expatriate blues, awkward dinner party guest lists, groping diplomats from other countries . . . she had dealt with them all. But this was an actual political crisis. Children were imprisoned! And she, Persephone Wilder, had the cards to play.

Before she could ring the bell, it was yanked open by the Big A. herself. Persephone almost yelped in surprise.

"Ellie listens in on Chef's calls," she said. "No stone unturned in this house. Please come in. Have some quiche. Which, by the way, was definitely *not* created during the French Revolution."

The ambassador was wearing a silk robe, pajamas, and bunny slippers. Her Rhodesian ridgebacks, usually hidden away in some elaborate kennel on the other side of the house, swirled around her legs. She didn't even have on an ounce of makeup, which actually made her look much younger. Persephone was constantly cross with the complexions of African women, whose skin only improved with age, while her own freckled and cracked without the constant application of salves and moisturizers.

"I apologize for my casual attire, but you are unannounced, aren't you? I'd have sent you off, but it's better for me to conduct this sort of business in person." The ambassador waved her into the sitting room. She plopped onto a comfortable chair with down cushions, leaving Persephone to teeter on the State Department sofa.

"Well, I really wanted to talk to you about the situation," Persephone said. "Given Adam's relationship with the embassy, isn't there anything we can do?"

"I'm afraid not," the Big A. said. One of the dogs hopped up on the sofa next to Persephone, stretching out luxuriously. So that's the intended function of these ghastly couches, Persephone thought. Large-breed dog furniture.

"It's tough, because usually I'd have Ainsley handle the next steps, but for reasons I hope by now you see as obvious, she's not the perfect fit."

"No," Persephone said. "Ainsley certainly doesn't have the skills to handle international law."

"Well," the Big A. said, "she certainly has an *interest* in law. If you see what I mean. But in this case, I'll have to talk to Barry."

"Barry? To handle diffusing the Amanda Evans case?"

The Big A. shifted a bit uncomfortably.

"No, Persephone," she said. "To fire Ainsley. She can't consort with her higher-ups like that."

"Ainsley?" Persephone asked. "Postage-stamp-skirt Ainsley?" The ambassador's face lit up. "Her skirts *are* like stamps. Too brief!"

"She consorted with *Barry*?" Persephone asked, trying not to sound too delighted. This was classified information indeed.

The Big A. cocked her head. "Persephone, have you talked to Adam since he brought the Evans girl in?"

"Why, no," Persephone said. "He told me he had to go to Swakop. For . . ." Was she supposed to keep pretending? "A mission."

"Again, please?"

"I know I'm supposed to deny this, but I can't anymore, Miss Ambassador. The truth is, I know all about it." Persephone straightened up proudly in her chair. "It's not Adam's fault. I just *guessed*."

"You guessed . . ."

"Why, that Adam is your CIA plant."

The ambassador pressed her fingers together, up and down into little tents. It was exactly what Persephone's boarding school headmistress used to do when she couldn't decide whether or not to suspend a student for sneaking a beer into the dorm or pulling a fire alarm. Oh dear. Was she going to be taken to the veld and shot?

"I know I'm not to talk about it," she said. "I'm sorry. I just—"

"Ellie!" the ambassador called, rising. "Set up the quiche in my office. Follow me, please, Persephone."

Persephone dutifully walked behind the Big A., her feet sinking into the thick white carpet. Of course. She was such a ninny to say that out in the open! The entire residence was probably bugged, if not by the Namibians, then the Russians!

The Big A. stepped into a surprisingly small office. This tiny segment of the house hadn't gotten the attention of the State Department interior decorator, apparently. The walls were paneled with cheap brown overlay. The bookshelves were stuffed, both with government tomes and, to Persephone's delight, pulpy celebrity memoirs by the likes of Rupert Everett and Barbra Streisand. There was also a large framed photo of the Big A. standing on the railing of . . . a dock? . . . a yacht? . . . with the Big T. himself, looking puffy and orange as ever—if a little more windblown.

"Is that real?" Persephone asked. It wasn't an out-of-line question. The American Cultural Center had a life-sized cardboard cutout of the Big T. right by the front desk. Diplomats were known to borrow it and snap photos next to it in picturesque places, in order to keep framed photos with the president in their desk drawers. Such pictures were exceedingly helpful when haggling with local diplomats over PEPFAR conference dates and reserving parking spots. Namibians weren't fond of the Big T., but power was power, and if you had a picture of you next to the president of the United States, you were someone to be contended with.

"That is real," the Big A. said. "That was a restaurant opening in Italy. I used to manage restaurants all over Europe, and he happened to come to this one. We talked about golf. I never thought the exchange would result in an ambassadorship, but then, I never knew he'd be president. One of his people remembered me and figured I'd be somewhat neutral in my views toward him." She paused. "They had to fill a lot of posts."

"This is your first State Department job?"

"Running an embassy in a sleepy country is a lot like running a restaurant, Persephone," she said. "It's all honoring rank and throwing decent events."

"Did you even vote for him?" Persephone asked, then instantly regretted it. If you were smart, you never asked another State Department member's political affiliation. It only caused unnecessary conflict. The Big A. ignored her question, proving she was, indeed, worthy of the ambassadorship. Instead she picked up her knife and fork and took a delicate bite of her quiche.

"People don't know this, but it was the Italians that actually came up with savory eggs in a pastry. Not the French. Fourteenth century." She chewed delicately and put down her napkin. "This is mediocre. I can't stand Namibian bacon."

"I'm sorry," Persephone said. She thought about trying a bite, but her stomach was so queasy from nerves she could only manage a sip of sparkling water. "Now, as I said, I know I'm not supposed to know about Adam's status, but I guessed it. You can't blame him. And I absolutely hope this doesn't affect our next post. We're so looking forward to—"

"Persephone," the Big A. said. "Stop."

"Oh right. We can talk outside, if you're worried about—"

"Adam is not in the CIA."

Persephone found that she was blinking incredibly rapidly. The wall was doing that wavy thing that usually only happened to her after too many cocktails.

"Excuse me?"

"He lied to you. I'm sorry to say this, but there's no way in hell or on earth we'd recruit him for the CIA. He's fine as a diplomat, but quite lazy . . . and not exactly brilliant."

"Oh," Persephone said. She shifted in her seat. Of course she knew all these things. She was his wife.

"Between you and me he blends in just fine as a middling State Department employee. Though I'm very annoyed that he pulled that stunt, telling the Namibian police about this Nazi mailing business without my permission. Do you think I ever would have let that happen? In any other world than the one we're living in right now, we all would be burned at the stake for that. Arresting kids for shipping trinkets abroad! But under this administration . . . well. Let's just say, idiocy is celebrated." She took another bite. "And then there's the other matter. Well. We're sending her home. It's not very #MeToo, but that hasn't hit the State Department yet, and he outranks her. Anyway. You won't have to see her."

"What matter?" Persephone asked. "See who?"

The Big A. took a last bite of quiche and pushed her plate away. "Why am I always the one ripping off the Band-Aid? *Ainsley*, my dear. She and your husband are having an affair."

"What?"

"I am sorry. I never was interested in marriage myself, exactly be-cause of this sort of business. Anyhow. You, my dear, are a jewel. A real figurehead of a State Department family. Which is another reason why we're keeping Adam and *not* Ainsley." She patted Persephone's arm. "It makes sense, doesn't it? We just can't let ourselves lose a top Trailing Spouse like you."

32

Mark had dropped his seething wife off, with promises of returning with Nando's chicken. Then he had done what any reasonable father with a freshly imprisoned nine-year-old would do: drive to Embassy Liquors, buy some bourbon, and then head to his favorite bench at Avis Dam in order to figure out what to do.

Windhoek was showing off her full plumage in terms of sunsets. Purples, fuchsias, yellows, and greens seeped through the sky. The more he drank, the more the colors deepened and turned, until he could only believe that he was being offered a true revelation. He felt his phone buzz in his pocket. It wasn't a number he recognized, but he answered anyway, just in case it was good news.

"Yes?"

"It's Persephone Wilder."

"Oh, hi, Persephone," Mark said. "Sorry to sound disappointed. I thought you might be the consulate with news."

"I have something to tell you," she said, her voice decidedly chilly.

"Yes?"

"It's about Shark Island."

"Where?"

"*Shark Island*," Persephone said, "was the biggest atrocity committed during the German colonization of Namibia. You know. The holocaust. The one you're supposed to be writing about?"

"Oh." Mark was totally confused and a little pissed at her attitude, what with his kid in jail and all. But something told him to hold his tongue.

"I'm just giving you the facts. Because I happen to know you're a total fraud."

"What—"

"You see, the Germans were basically using the Herero and the Nama as slaves. Indentured servitude, shooting them for no reason in the fields. That sort of thing. So they rebelled in 1905. Like *you* would, if some Herr Rumpelstein took Amanda as his concubine. Or whatever." Her voice was shaking with anger. "They killed some Germans, which was very bad. So the Germans did what they did at the time, which was overcompensate. They sent fifteen thousand troops to drive the Herero and the Nama to the desert—all of them, not just the fighters, so that the men, women, and children died of hunger and thirst."

"Okay." She really sounded off her rocker.

"But the worst part, the pièce de résistance, was the concentration camp they constructed. It wasn't *in Walvis*—which was how I *knew* you were a faker. As anyone who cares an iota knows, this infamous travesty took place on Shark Island, off the town of Luderitz. They later included the Nama people, too, as they were trying to exterminate that tribe as well. Documents written at the time by the Boers—no strangers to brutality, Mark—said they were so shocked by the conditions they had to leave. Historians widely agree this was the precursor to the concentration camps of World War II."

She stopped. The line was so silent, Mark wondered if she was still there.

"I'm just letting you know," Persephone finally said, "because on top of being a cheater—"

"Cheater?" Mark said. "I'm not a cheater."

"I've spoken to Amanda, Mark. Don't deny it. Anyway, on top of being a cheater, you're also a huge fake. I'm the only one who knows that part. The only one who's figured out that you've used the suffering of the native Namibians for your own financial gain. I was trying to decide what to do with that information . . . like, should I tell the ambassador? But I don't want dear Amanda to be even further embarrassed, so I'm giving you CliffsNotes for when people start asking you questions."

"Well . . ."

"Well, what?" Mark was almost pleased to hear Persephone Wilder give an honest-to-God snort. "Blech. I mean, just . . . sho."

And then she really did hang up. Mark looked at the phone for a moment, then shrugged and pocketed the thing. So some State Department wife thought that he'd been having sex with Mila Shilongo for months . . . as did his *own* wife. As unbelievable as it was, it seemed trivial, in light of his other problems.

Wait. Of course. The situation wasn't impossible. Despite his wife's tears. Despite Persephone's out-of-the-blue wrath. The ambassador had been perfectly clear about how to get Meg out of this. It was her friend, Taimi.

If Taimi took the blame, all she would get was, at most, a large fine, probably—whereas Meg would spend her youth in a foreign prison. What parent of any child would let that happen to another? Even if Mila was angry at him, he could make the case. He could make *her* the savior in all of this. He remembered Esther as a reasonable person. Wonderfully reasonable. Kind. She couldn't have changed that much. All he had to do was find her.

It was dark now. Mark stumbled down the trail, tripping a couple of times on the rocks. Once he got into the car, he popped a piece of gum to cover up the smell of liquor and drove toward where he vaguely remembered Mila's house being, taking a couple of wrong turns before reaching her long, precipitous driveway.

When he got to the mansion, it seemed even more like a fancy psychiatric ward than before. He was thinking what he was going to say when he rang the bell, but he didn't have to. The gate was open, and the Herero housekeeper, today dressed in a stunning ensemble of green and gold, was struggling down the driveway, her arms full of plastic bags of clothes.

"Good evening," Mark said.

The woman grumbled something he couldn't quite make out.

"Is Mrs. Shilongo home?" Mark asked.

"Miss Mila is gone. And I am leaving." She looked defensively at her bags. "Mr. Shilongo said I could have these."

"When will she be back?"

"She will not be back. Gone, I said." She peered at him. "Can you give me a lift to the taxi stand?"

"Sure," Mark said, reaching over and opening the car door for her. The transfer of the bags and her layers of crinoline was somewhat of a production. Her double-horned Herero hat, which up close looked like a brightly colored matador's hat with cone ends, bumped against the roof. He reached over to help her, but she swatted his hand away.

"Okay, okay. So . . . what do you mean, Miss Mila won't be back? I really need to talk to her."

The housekeeper looked over at him, her mouth clamped shut.

"You can try walking with those bags, if you want."

She gave a snort.

"If you give me the information, I'll take you all the way home. No taxi."

The woman looked at him with a taunting smile on her face.

"You will drive this car to Katutura? You're not scared?"

"Of course not."

"You've been there."

"Well, no. But I was planning on going someday. So let's do it. But first you have to tell me what happened."

The woman looked up at the house. "He has thrown her out because the little girl was arrested with the American girl."

"That seems like an overreaction. It's not like it was Mila's fault."

"He thinks it is. He is quite heartless, sometimes."

"Well. I'm the American girl's dad," Mark said, backing down the drive.

The woman whistled. "Things are bad for you, my friend."

"I just really need to find Mila. If her daughter steps up, she'll just get a little slap on the wrist. If Meg takes the blame, she has no rights."

"We'll see," the woman said, indicating with her hand which way he should drive. "Namibian courts are very strange."

"Where should I try to find her?"

"She maybe at the Hilton. She likes it there." She adjusted her two-horned hat, thinking. "She could be at her sister's restaurant on Independence. Or at her other sister's house, in Katutura. I do not know the address. And she hates her sisters . . . Ah! Or with her other daughter."

Mark stopped at the bottom of the drive a bit too hard, propelling them both toward the dash.

"Her other *daughter*?" Mark asked carefully. "Mila has *another* daughter?"

"Of course. I do not like her. Libertina did not raise her, that's for certain." She looked at him. "Libertina. That is me. Anyhow. The other daughter, she had no rules. She is very naughty. Big temper."

"How old is she?"

"Twenty, I think? Perhaps more?"

"Where does she live?"

"Swakopmund. She wants to be a fashion person or jewelry artist or some what-what."

"Fuck," Mark said. "Oh, fucking hell."

"You sound like a Boer," Libertina said distastefully. "Miss Mila would have had to get there on a bus somehow. She has no car. But you might look for her. Her name is——"

"Anna," Mark said.

"Yes," Libertina said. "That is correct." She pointed her gnarled finger, painted gold at the tip, up a long, dark road. "I live just that way. Five kilometers or so."

"All right." They drove in silence. Mark had reached the Location now. The township was nowhere as large as those in Cape Town or Johannesburg, though the structure, Mark had read, was similar. At the center was an organized network of streets lined with proper houses and flats, most with large fences and gates—though the gates weren't nearly as elaborate or tall as those in the white neighborhoods. Those affluent avenues gave way to narrower lanes of smaller houses, shops, and shebeens, which spilled out to dirt alleys lined with corrugated tin shacks of various sizes and complexity. The longer you lived in a place, it seemed, the more rooms you added; some family complexes spread out haphazardly for several meters, as if made of Jenga blocks.

The Location looked fun. Men and women hung out in the streets talking and laughing; kids played soccer on poorly lit dirt fields despite the time of night. No one in Mark and Amanda's neighborhood, Klein Windhoek, would dare go out at night.

Libertina directed Mark past the more prominent streets to a shantytown. A bus in front of them halted, and men in blue coveralls and women in domestic work outfits streamed out, bearing flashlights, as there were no streetlights on this side of the neighborhood. A girl Meg's age ran in front of the car, bringing him back to his seemingly hopeless predicament.

"Man," Mark said. "Have I messed up my life."

"Ah?" Libertina said, raising her eyebrows. "I am interested. How does a white man like you mess up his life?"

"Well, Libertina," Mark said, rubbing his jaw, which was sore from clenching, "I gave away all of my family's savings to Anna, and she took off with it. Like, a week ago. And I haven't heard back from her yet."

"Hmmm," Libertina said. "Yes. That is something Anna would do. Naughty. And to have no money, that is a problem." She shrugged. "But you are white. There's always more."

"Yeah, but I have to ask for it."

"Also not a problem." Libertina looked at him sideways. "Use your voice."

"Okay, I see where you're coming from. But also, I had an affair long ago with a woman. Now it looks like she had a daughter and I never knew about it."

"Affair." Libertina raised her eyebrows. "She had a husband?"

"Oh. No."

"So you had the sex and then she fell pregnant?"

"I guess. But she never told me."

"That's not your fault," Libertina said, folding her arms over her chest.

"Well, actually . . . I could have tried a *little* harder to be in touch." Libertina shrugged. Herero men were known to be scoundrels. Why would Americans be any different?

"And now it looks like the daughter is someone I actually *know*."

They were approaching Libertina's house now. The older woman sat up straight. She was proud of her house. It was in the shantytown, but was a comparatively luxurious bungalow, with two tiny bedrooms, a living room, and an indoor kitchen where everything was blue, right down to every cup, saucer, and the plastic cutlery. There was a wall around the small plot, laced with barbed wire and shards of cut glass. Inside, her daughter was waiting for her. They would drink beer and watch *South African Idol* on the television, and later her husband would be home. So, although she had to have a dog to scare away the thieves who scaled the wall monthly, and although she now had no job, in actuality she had more than this sad white man. She was glad for that.

"Well. Goodbye," she said. "I hope your problems go away." She took up her bags and, with some effort, got out of the car. As he drove away, Libertina thought about giving him a blessing. But she knew the American would be all right in the end, so she saved it for someone in real trouble.

One of the little girls, perhaps.

33

It was two in the morning when Mark walked in the door. Amanda was still sitting at the table, a half-empty bottle of vodka in front of her next to a glass of melting ice and a few massacred lemons.

"Hey," Mark said. He stumbled a little as he made his way to the table.

"Hey."

"What are you doing?" he asked, sitting across from her.

She placed her elbows on the table and rested her chin on her hands, looking at him through her messy dark bangs. "Well. My theory is if I drink all night, I won't have a hangover. I'm alternating each glass I drink with a glass of water. See the water?" She motioned toward a pitcher next to the vodka. "That's the way Swedish people drink. Did you know that? One water. One drink. That's why they look so good all the time."

"I think that's the Swiss, babe. Also, the Swedes don't always look that good. Remember when we watched *The Bridge*?"

She ignored him, pouring more vodka. "I'm also using lemon to battle antioxidants."

"I'll try it with you," Mark said, getting up to fetch a glass. He threw in some ice and came back.

"What do you think Meg's doing?" Amanda said.

"Sleeping."

"How can she sleep in that cell? She needs a night-light. Do you think they let her have a night-light?"

"Yes," Mark said.

"I called three times, but those ash-holes said I couldn't . . . Can't talk right now correctly, *Assholes*." She giggled suddenly. "Do you know that Meg knows what a dickwad is? Like, the scientific definition?"

"That's disturbing. What is it?"

Amanda took a big sip, crunching down on the ice. "A urethra blockage."

"Huh. And here I thought the official definition was Adam Wilder."

"Exactly." They were quiet for a few minutes, listening to the symphony of insects outside.

"So you're pretty wasted?" Mark said. "Because I'm pretty wasted."

"Yeah."

"And we have all these things we need to talk about."

Amanda tipped her head up to meet her husband's bloodshot eyes.

"You've been having an affair with Mila Shilongo who used to be Esther, yes?"

"No!" Mark said. He wagged her finger at her. "Errrrrp! Incorrect. I really did think she was dead. I saw the records and everything."

"Huh," Amanda said disinterestedly.

"But here's the kicker," Mark said. "We had a kid together. I think."

"Huh," Amanda said again. She downed her vodka and dutifully filled the same glass with water. "Taimi?" she asked.

"No," Mark said, shaking his head vigorously. "See, Taimi is Meg's age. When Taimi was born, I was with you."

"Hmmm." She was so drunk, it felt like someone was telling her a bedtime story about someone else. It was delightful, but she already regretted the hangover. She drank some more water. "So you mean Mila's other daughter? The one that's a pain."

"Right. Anna. She's twenty, so that's exactly the age she would be based on when we were together. See, we didn't have an affair, Amanda. We met when I was in the Peace Corps. And then there was the combi accident—"

"Noooooool!" Amanda threw her head back and howled. "I can't hear about the combi accident even one more time!"

"It's *important*," Mark said, slapping the table.

Amanda picked up a lemon rind and sucked it. "You know what I'm going to do?" she asked, standing. Mark shook his head. "I'm going to have a cigarette."

"What? You can't do that."

Amanda smiled wickedly. Their entire relationship started because he was her athletic coach. Smoking was like fellating another man in his presence.

"Oh yeah. I bought some a few months ago at the Portuguese grocery store. That lady with the blue braids was there. You know her, right? And I was complimenting her on her hair, because some braids really are a work of art, you know? These were, like, lavender and silver. She looked like a fairy princess. Anyway, right behind her head were these cigarettes, and pasted on the package was this absolutely disgusting picture of a mouth filled with cancer. It was unbelievable! The tobacco companies would never let the anti-smoking people do that in the U.S., but it's so smart, right? I mean, black goo is literally oozing out of this woman's mouth. Look."

Amanda went to the desk, fetched the cigarettes, and held up a packet wrapped in an image of a mouth riddled with sores.

"And I was there buying pre-cut vegetables or something, because, that's, like, what I do. I make healthy meals for you and Meg. I keep things going. So I put the minced game and the chopped-up French beans on the counter and said, I'll take those smokes, please. So easy. Do you know I haven't had a cigarette since we've been married? We're so fucking healthy together, Mark. We eat kale and we work out and we have sex once a week like it fucking matters. Like doing all of that will keep the bad things away. But now our kid is in an international prison. Prison! And what now? You have some other kid? And also, you took all of our money. Was that for the kid?"

"No."

"Okay." Amanda fished a lighter out of a drawer and lit a cigarette. The sound was so lovely—a nice *crinkle*. She didn't bother inhaling, because she knew the smoke would feel awful. The action of it was satisfying enough.

"Don't you at least want to go outside with that?" Mark asked.

"Where's our money? One hundred thousand dollars of GiaTech stock. You know we have to pay taxes on the gains?"

"I used it to buy gems."

"What?"

"*Gems*. Namibian gems. I was going to surprise you. I've been getting into the gem business."

"Hmmmm." Amanda pawed the vodka bottle, but she realized that she was at her tipping point—any more alcohol would only make her vomit. "How did you do that?"

"Through Anna, actually."

"Your kid?" she asked, scratching furiously at a bite on her knee.

"Right. But I didn't know she was my daughter. I just met her in Swakop and she started talking to me about it."

"You randomly went into business with a woman who is probably your daughter, but you didn't know that?"

"Right."

"Namibia is a fucking small country," Amanda said. "Maybe this is good. Maybe since she's your daughter, she'll come back with your money."

"That's positive thinking."

Suddenly Amanda was very, very tired. She sat again, sliding down in her chair and looking at her cigarette. "You know what, Mark?"

"What?"

"I don't care about that other daughter."

"Well. You might when you're sober."

She shook her head. "No. Listen. Let's get this straight. You brought us to Africa because you were looking for Mila. You have a *kid* with Mila. You've spent all of our savings on some weird scheme, except you didn't, because your partner, who happens to be your kid, absconded with the money."

Mark hesitated, then nodded. "Yes. It does sound bad when you put it like that."

"The thing is, all of that is really, really, bad, right? I mean, you couldn't make up more reasons not to love you."

Mark leaned over and grabbed her hand. "Amanda, don't say that. I know this is all super messed-up, but what I realized today . . ." He squeezed her fingers, hard. "What I really *knew* when I saw Esther was that I . . . just love you so much. I really do, and all this other crap doesn't—you and I—"

"*I'm. Not. Done.*" Amanda's voice through the room was sharp and percussive as bullets. Mark sat up straighter and put his hands in his lap.

"Okay," he said quietly. "I'm listening."

Amanda took a quick drag, made a face, and exhaled. "I've been thinking about this for a long time. That we were over. Like, since a couple of years ago. I've been thinking that we've been just going through the motions, and that we've been too lazy or scared or something to call it a day."

"Amanda—"

"You've been lost, or something, and I didn't like it. I mean, I guess it was this Mila thing? Or this job thing? Anyway, I thought if *I* could be so together, what the hell is wrong with Mark? I just was sort of living around you, doing my thing. And you let me. Except sometimes you'd put up a fight with how to parent Meg, which was annoying. But I would just parent *around* you."

"Spoil her, you mean."

"Shut up. Just shut up, okay? So now you've gone and really messed up. Like, on paper messed up. *Anyone* would say, Okay, Amanda. This is your chance. Time to go."

Mark didn't say anything, but below him, he felt the floor fall away.

"The thing is, I can't seem to do it. I've been thinking about this all night. I can't leave, because I love you. It's not reasonable and it won't make me happy, but it's not supposed to, I guess. Being together isn't always about happiness, is it? Or having this perfect life all the time?"

"I guess not. Though we were happy, sometimes."

"Sure." Amanda nodded and dropped her cigarette into her almost-empty glass, where it expired with a sizzle. "Sometimes. I know. But the point of being with someone . . . marrying yourself to a person . . . is so you have someone around when things aren't perfect. I think. Like now." She shrugged. "So there it is. You're a beautiful, royal screw-up, and you stole our money and you have another kid. But I still fucking love you."

"Dollar," Mark whispered.

Amanda started crying. "Let's get Meg back. Just bring her back, Mark. I don't want anything else."

She pushed her glass away and buried her head in her arms, then let herself cry as Mark picked her up, carried her to the bedroom, and pulled the covers over her. Amanda cried and cried for her daughter, for her marriage, for her mother whose dying wish, long ago, was nothing more than to make her chicken salad.

I will make Meg a sandwich, she thought dimly.

Finally, she was asleep.

/ 34 /

When Meg woke up the next morning, sunlight flooded the room. The air conditioner hummed with a hushed reverence——none of the spits and groans of the wall units at the Evanses' bungalow. The sheets were crisp and white, and she was in a bed as big and cushy as her own parents'. In fact, the room looked a lot like a hotel room her parents might stay in when they all went to Napa or one of those safari lodges near Etosha.

She rubbed her eyes. She had definitely never been here before, and it was also definitely not the room she had gone to sleep in. And now the door opened, and a lady she didn't know came in. But the lady was pretty and wore a suit. In Meg's experience, grown-ups in suits generally knew what they were doing, so she didn't scream.

"Good morning, Meg," the lady said.

Meg nodded. Never talk to strangers, she could hear her mother saying. Even if they are the first person you see in the morning.

"I'm Ellie. Would you like some quiche?"

Meg shook her head.

"Pancakes?"

That was a bit of a stumper.

"I believe we have real Canadian maple syrup. One of the embassy mothers nabbed it from the Canadian booth at International Day."

"Have I been kidnapped?"

"No." Ellie briskly laid out a clean towel, a toothbrush, and toothpaste on the bed. "The ambassador felt it would not do to have you stay the night in the holding cell. But legally, we can't let you go, either, so letting you sleep at home was not an option. Therefore, the ambassador decided to place you in one of her personal guest rooms, as you are under guard here. We have six suites for visitors, so it wasn't a problem. You were so tired you didn't wake up when we transferred you, which is why you don't remember moving."

"Oh." Meg looked around more carefully. There was no phone, and the windows had bars on them. But this didn't mean anything, because all of the State Department houses had bars on the windows. Taimi was the only kid Meg knew with a clear view. "Can I talk to my mom?"

"Absolutely. We will take you back to the embassy where you can participate in proper visiting hours, which are held from one p.m. to four p.m. Providing the security guards are back from lunch."

"Okay."

"The ambassador would like to have breakfast with you. You have no other clothes, but why don't you shower and brush your teeth, then I'll take you to the dining room in fifteen minutes."

Meg nodded. Ellie left the room, and she grabbed the towel and went into the bathroom, which also looked like something in a hotel. She didn't know why Ellie bothered with the towel, because there were towels everywhere, even little hand ones, folded to look like birds.

Usually her mom still ran the water for her when she bathed, and put bubbles in it. Her dad told her mom she was spoiling her, but Meg's mom said she liked to do it, in that *leave-me-alone-you're-being-a-pain* voice. Meg's mom used that voice a lot with her dad, especially in Africa.

Meg didn't know how the shower knob worked, so she used the tub. There were lots of tiny bottles. She didn't bother reading the labels, opting instead to dump all of the contents in the tub, so that the water was a milky, bubbly soup. It felt nice. She stayed in until her fingers were raisin-y, then got out, toweled off, and dressed in her dirty International Day hip-hop clothes. She skipped her underpants because they had skid marks. Those she just threw away.

"Okay," she said, coming out.

"That was much more than fifteen minutes," Ellie said.

"Sorry. No clock."

Ellie didn't reply, but took off down the hall. Meg guessed this meant she was supposed to follow her, so she trailed behind, peeking into the other bedrooms, which looked just like the one she had come out of.

She wondered what the ambassador would say to her. She still wasn't sorry for selling the German stuff and sending the money to the orphanage. The stuff was ugly, and those weird people Taimi found were willing to pay big bucks for it. And anyway, those kids needed someone. She saw them all the time. They knocked on her window when her mom drove her to school, boys and girls just like her, their bare feet covered in dust, crust in the corners of their eyes. They wore the same clothes she did, leggings and cool T-shirts, only their shirts had holes in them and were covered in dirt. The boys wore girls' clothes, the girls wore boys'. It didn't matter. They didn't beg like the old men and the homeless people in San Francisco, who sat under bridges by the grocery store surrounded by tents and dogs. They didn't shout at you or wave funny signs. These kids just looked at Meg, sometimes with eyes yellow where they should have been white. They did a dance with their hands, a kind of knocking. Meg's mom kept boxed juices and bottles of water for them on the passenger seat. She'd crack the windows and hand the juice out, as if she were afraid the little boys and girls would crawl into the car and hurt her. Which was impossible, because they were no bigger than Meg.

So, even though she was in trouble, she was happy the kids were getting the money. Which was what she told the ambassador, who had already started in on a stack of pancakes.

"Yours will be here in a minute," she said. "I have to go to the embassy, so I couldn't wait."

"Sorry," Meg said. "I like baths."

"As do I," the ambassador said.

The ambassador was pretty. She was not fat, exactly, but round, with lighter skin than Taimi's. Taimi told Meg it wasn't proper to talk about the color of your skin, like, its *actual color*. But Meg didn't understand that, because in Africa it was such a big part of how you looked. Besides, she'd told Taimi, if you stick to actual colors, like, compare the skin color to something else in the world, that couldn't be wrong, could it? Like, her mom's skin was tan, especially in Namibia. Her legs were the same color as baked hamburger buns. Her dad's skin was pale, just a few shades darker than typing paper. When he burned, the color was the same as raspberry jam. Taimi's skin was pine-tree-bark-brown with a little navy-blue-crayon rubbed in. It sparkled awesomely on its own, without glitter. Taimi said she was probably Oshiwambo royalty, and Meg suspected this was how you told if you were royalty or not in Africa—the amount of natural glitter in your skin. The ambassador's skin was the same color and polish as that of her dining room table in Los Gatos. It was smooth and looked clean and like she polished it with Pledge.

"Here we go," the ambassador said when the housekeeper came in with a stack of pancakes. "Did you know that pancakes were invented in ancient times?"

"Yes," Meg said. "We learned that in school. The Romans ate pancakes. But not with syrup."

"That's right. Very good," the ambassador said. She looked at Meg, appraising her. "You're all clean."

"I threw away my underwear."

"Oh. Well, we can arrange for you to get your clothes, surely. Though"—she leaned in—"if I had my way, I'd never wear any, would you?"

Meg considered for a moment, and decided it was an appropriate time not to answer.

"Meg," the ambassador said. "I appreciate your motivations for selling the stolen items. And that you didn't *know* they were stolen. But you'll be in a lot less trouble if you just tell me how Josephat Shilongo's daughter set this thing up."

"No."

"No, she didn't set it up?"

"No, I'm not telling on Taimi."

The ambassador put her knife and fork down. Meg noted that she had eaten almost all of her pancakes. "I appreciate your loyalty. But sometimes in diplomacy we must participate in give-and-take."

"I don't know what that means."

"What about Mrs. Shilongo? Did she help you put the site together?"

"Nope. She didn't know anything about it."

"Mr. Shilongo?"

"No. He has someone else do all of his computers when he sells stuff."

The ambassador straightened up.

"Sells stuff?"

"Yeah." Meg crammed as much pancake into her mouth as she could. So far, she had learned that, when in jail, food came only sporadically.

"What stuff?"

"He sells animals," she said with her mouth full. "To hunters."

"Excuse me?"

"Yeah. He has this computer guy tell the hunters where the animals are and when they can come. It's like a club."

"What kind of animals?"

"Um . . ." Meg had to think. She had only been in the room once when Mr. Shilongo was talking to his friend about it. Actually, she had been in the closet, playing Spy, and when Taimi had run in and found her, Mr. Shilongo had looked pretty mad. But then Taimi had said of course they hadn't heard a word of his business and had done a little ballet dance, and eventually Mr. Shilongo had clapped. Taimi was good at snowing her dad.

"There was a rhino they were selling," Meg said. "Two elephants, also. They use a drone to take pictures. And get the . . . um . . . kward-nits."

"Coordinates?"

"Right! All I remember was that Mr. Shilongo said he person-ally could never go online for safety reasons. Which I thought was weird, because what about a computer isn't safe? Anyway. That's how I know that he didn't help with our website."

"That's very good, Meg." The ambassador wiped her mouth and put down her napkin. "That's very, very good."

"Okay." Meg ate some more pancake.

"Ellie?" the ambassador called. "Come here, please."

"Do you think I can go home today?" Meg asked.

"Oh yes, my dear," the ambassador said. "I believe we have come across your bargaining chip."

Spring

Shi ha monathana omuti nomuti; aantu yoompadhi mbali oha ya tsakanene.
Trees stay rooted, but people, they come together.
—Oshiwambo proverb

35

Frida watched from the kitchen as Miss Persephone hopped from room to room like an angry bird. Her employer clutched a notebook that sparkled. Her bare feet were dirty, and her hair was piled on top of her head in a big, tangled poof. Frida had tried to follow and help her at first, but her efforts seemed only to make the poor woman angry, so instead Frida straightened and cleaned where she could in spots that weren't filled with boxes and Mr. Adam's clothes.

Miss Persephone had gone to see the ambassador four weeks ago. In her mind, Frida labeled this as The Day. On The Day, Miss Persephone had found out about Mr. Adam's other woman. She hadn't directly told Frida about this, of course, but when Mr. Adam had come home later in the afternoon, Miss Persephone had screeched like a wet baboon and started throwing dishes; he was only able to escape when Mila Shilongo had emerged from the guest room and held Miss Persephone down. Since then Mr. Adam had been living in the pool house, sneaking in and out the back gate when Miss Persephone wasn't home. He had asked Frida once to fetch him some groceries from the main house, but when Miss Persephone found out, she had become so angry that everyone—including Mila Shilongo—had run for cover.

It was a surprise, how Miss Persephone acted when she was angry. Her face grew red. Her eyes grew wild. She was still nice in her heart, you could see it, but she was almost mad, the same way Frida's sister Leona had grown mad when she was bitten by the pig farmer's rabid dog. But Leona had been given antibiotics and gotten better, whereas

Miss Persephone grew worse and worse. She was still kind to her girls and Frida, but, whereas she had once taken pride in looking like a fashion doll, in these last weeks she had become unkempt. Her hair was wild and pinned into a ball on her head that grew bigger as the days went by. Wine bottles were opened first thing in the morning, and dishes littered the house. Frida had to do twice as much as usual just to keep the place looking half as nice.

Another thing that happened on The Day was that Frida told Miss Persephone that she was leaving domestic service. Miss Persephone had cried and hugged Frida when she'd told her this. "I don't know what we will do without you, Miss Frida," she'd said. "You are our family."

Frida had patted Miss Persephone's shoulder kindly, but she had not replied. Frida was no liar. She was not sad. She never tricked herself into thinking she was Miss Persephone's family—she was just *around* her family. She was not invited to their dinners, or to their parties, or to their meet-'n'-greet breakfasts and the rest of the what-what-what. Her white employers always acted as if she should cry when the job was over, because *they* usually did. One Boer lady had wept harder than Frida had when her own mother died. They assumed she was attached like a mother to their children. Yet she was never sorry to leave a household, no matter how long she had been there. It was unsettling, because it meant she would have less money. But it was not sad.

Yes, this was to be Frida's last house. Her daughter, Tonata, was about to finish university, and Tonata did not want Frida doing domestic work anymore. She already had a good job at a bank, and she said she would rather give her mother money than have her be a maid. Frida relented, but she thought this was silly. She had been a maid for a long time. There were other things she'd rather have done, but they hadn't happened, had they? Anyway, being a maid lately in the Wilder house was more than fine. It was better than the stories on the TV.

There was a crash in the bedroom. The children were at school, and Frida didn't think Mr. Adam was in the house. If he was, that could be Miss Persephone, killing him.

"Miss Persephone?" Frida called. She crept toward the bedroom. To get around the house now, you had to weave in and out of a maze of boxes of Mr. Adam's things. About three weeks ago, they had started extracting his things with a strict system Miss Persephone had used the other times she moved from country to country, involving candy-colored notes that stuck to the boxes and long lists. Cherry-red for suits. Grape-gum-purple for the books. But as the days had gone by, Miss Persephone cared less and less about the lists and notes, and lately she had been simply throwing objects into the boxes with various degrees of force as she passed.

Miss Persephone now refused to wear white. Instead, she wore colors that fought and struggled with each other before Frida's eyes. Red flowers clashed with purple paisley. Yellow stripes battled brown plaid. The whites she threw out of her room at Frida in billowing trash bags, commanding her to take them home. Frida had obeyed, but mostly she sold the things to her friends and the clothing shops some women ran in the richer parts of Katutura. Frida did not like wearing white, no matter how fine the clothes. She was not a bride, and she had already been baptized. White, in a country of red dust, was disrespectful to the land.

"Miss Frida?" Miss Persephone called now. Frida made her way through the maze to the bedroom. Miss Persephone was wearing a formal dress covered in blue and yellow flowers and was sitting on the floor surrounded by piles of clothes and shoes. She was wearing bright pink lipstick, but no other makeup.

"Are you fine?" Frida asked.

Miss Persephone shook her head like a little girl. "I am totally not fine, Miss Frida. My husband has too many things. How did I not know all of these things in our house were his? I have been just pushing them over there. My side. His side." Frida could see now that Miss Persephone had drawn a thick black line down the middle of the room with some sort of big black pen.

"Perhaps you can let Mr. Adam straighten these things and pack them up himself?"

"Mr. Adam is not allowed in."

"I see." Frida was impressed. Miss Persephone was much smaller than Mr. Adam. In her experience, when love ended, the person who was bigger got the house. "Must he really have all of his things?"

Miss Persephone looked at the mound of clothing and possessions and brightened. "No!"

"Then I can help you," Frida said. "I will call Elifas to come with a bakkie."

"Thank you, Miss Frida."

Frida nodded. She really did want to help. Plus, she and Elifas would be able to sell Mr. Adam's things for good money back at the Location.

"Perhaps you should shower," Frida said. "Now-now. Before your children get home."

"Perhaps," Persephone said disinterestedly. She crawled over to the unmade bed and pushed some more clothes onto the floor. "I think I'll sleep, Miss Frida."

"All right," Frida said. No. Miss Persephone was not doing well. She heard the front door open, and braced herself for Mr. Adam, who might be coming in to pillage the kitchen. But to her relief it was Mila Shilongo, who still had a key. Mila had moved back to her own house, as her husband had been arrested for taking part in an international poaching ring. Everyone assumed that the minister of transportation took bribes for awarding government road construction contracts. What wasn't known to anyone—including Mila—was that one of the Chinese construction executives opened up a spot for Josephat in a lucrative poaching operation. His first test of loyalty had been to offer up his one rhino, the famous one Miss Persephone called Mr. Sharp. However, the hired poachers hadn't counted on Hector.

At first the police had suspected Mila as well, but after they investigated, it became clear that Mr. and Mrs. Shilongo, as of late, barely communicated at all. And the fact that she had invited guests to their farm, Osha, the poaching headquarters, pretty much proved Mila's innocence.

Frida and Mila Shilongo had become great friends during Mila's stay at Miss Persephone's. It turned out they had met before, as Frida's mother was originally from Onesi. Frida knew all about the Beautiful House. Once Mila told her she was really Esther, Frida had deferred to her as if she were a celebrity, which Mila appreciated greatly.

The women enjoyed speaking proper Oshiwambo to each other, so their greeting took a while.

"Hello," Frida said.

"Hello," Mila said.

"Have you spent the morning well?" Frida asked.

"Yes," Mila answered.

"Really?" Frida asked.

"Yes," Mila answered.

"That is fine," Frida said.

"It *is* fine. And have you spent your morning well?" Mila asked.

"Yes," Frida answered.

"Really?" Mila asked.

"Yes," Frida answered.

"That is fine," Mila said.

"And are you still fine?" Frida asked.

"I am more than fine," Mila said. "I have received word today that I am being considered to fill Josephat's role as the minister of transportation."

"Ah!" Frida said. A woman minister. This was good. Wives often replaced their husbands in government roles. Over in Zimbabwe, Mrs. Mugabe was trying to do the same thing now that her husband was forced out. Now, a President Mrs. Mugabe was not a good plan. But Mila Shilongo as a minister, that was excellent.

"Where is Miss Persephone?" Mila asked.

"In her bedroom, sleeping in a party dress. She is doing very badly, Mila."

"I see," Mila said, frowning. "Though I do not know why. It is good to shed a bad husband. Who doesn't want that?"

"I don't know. Every day is worse and worse. I'm trying to help move his things."

"I will talk to her," Mila Shilongo looked at Frida thoughtfully. "And you are leaving, I hear?"

"My daughter does not want me to do domestic work anymore. She has a good job now," Frida was proud, but careful. She did not want to brag. Mila's own daughter, Anna, was the same age as Tonata, and there had been some trouble about her taking Miss Amanda and Mr. Mark's money.

"Can you do office work, Frida?" Mila asked. "Can you use the computer?"

Frida thought about it. She had a smartphone. A computer was just a phone, but bigger.

"Yes."

"I will need an assistant. Someone who I can trust."

"You do," Frida said.

"I have been trying to get gossip about Persephone Wilder for two years now. I told Libertina to ask the domestics in Katutura. They all say you never talk. That you keep secrets."

"I don't keep secrets," Frida said. "It is not my business, to tell about the lives of other people."

"I can pay you one thousand per week."

"Miss Persephone pays me two thousand per week."

The women looked at each other. This was a lie, but God would permit it.

"Persephone pays you eight hundred per week. I know because she is *not* good at keeping secrets. But all right. I will pay fifteen hundred per week."

Frida's mind started working. This was even more than Tonata was making. After some months, she'd be able to add another room onto her house.

"All right," Frida said. "When my time with Miss Persephone is over, I will work for you."

"It's settled," Mila Shilongo said, satisfied. She kicked a box out of the way and marched down the hall to Miss Persephone's room.

Frida looked around the massive kitchen and living room. She stared at the American clothes piled high on the government sofas, at the seven types of cereal boxes crowding the counters, at the cabinets full of chips and candy and washing-machine soap. Miss Persephone had tried very hard to understand Frida, but they were from different tribes. And while everyone said that tribes meant nothing in modern-day Africa—especially Tonata, with her big university opinions!—in Frida's mind, they still meant very much, all over the world. It was important to love everyone, of course. God wanted his people to listen to each other and do their best. But in the end, your people were your people. Or at least that's what Frida thought.

In fact, Mila Shilongo was trying some intertribal communication right now. Sho. It did not sound like she was getting very far.

"Get up!" Frida heard Mila Shilongo say. "Get up, Persephone! I am here to get you going."

She heard Miss Persephone groan.

"No more wine in the morning. No more sleeping. You are not a hobo, klein baba. We are free from our bad husbands, and we are not old, and we are clever. Get up, Persephone. It's time to maak 'n' plan, my dear. Get up. Life is waiting for you."

36

The day before the Evanses' departure, Mila and Amanda met for one last lunch at Stellenbosch.

There was much business to clear up, of course, before this meeting could happen. First, Mila had to explain the matter of Anna—who, the Evanses were relieved to find out, was not Mark's child after all. She was in fact Mila's niece. Saara, her sister, had given birth to her approximately nine months after their weekend in Swakopmund. But, as she was a cripple, she felt she couldn't care for her.

"How sad," Amanda said.

"Yes," Mila said. "She died just a few years later in South Africa. Johannesburg is not a nice place for Black women with no money and a handicap."

"I'm so sorry, Mila."

Mila waved the sentiment away. She was so different from the girl Mark had described, Amanda thought.

"Did you . . . ever get another chance to catch up with Mark? Just to . . . set the record straight?"

"He didn't tell you?" Mila raised her eyebrows.

"You know, I just felt, well . . ." Amanda took a sip of water. "It's not my business."

"We spoke briefly. A few days ago, at school." Mila looked at Amanda steadily. "I could see that he was sorry. That he had paid by worrying about it most of his life."

"So you forgive him?" Amanda asked. "He wasn't totally without responsibility. He should have come earlier to make sure you were okay."

"You know, Amanda, it's strange." Mila looked over Amanda's shoulder at the cars and bakkies crawling down the street. "It's been so long, I was holding on to all of this hate. Then I saw him, and heard his story . . . and I just didn't care anymore."

"He was still a bit of an irresponsible shithead."

"Well, he's your husband, not mine." Mila smiled. "So you have to live with him."

"True."

"So everything ended up well."

"Not for Saara," Amanda said.

"Africa is real life, Amanda," Mila said flatly. "Even more so than other places."

Amanda bit her lip and looked away. For all her time here, for all that had happened, she would never really know Africa. She loved the place with all her heart, but would always just be a tourist.

Mila had insisted on sitting in their usual spot, and today the Afrikaans manager was being even more attentive than usual. He sent over champagne, and though Mila thanked him rather grandly, neither mentioned what the present was obviously for—to celebrate Mila's new position as minister of transportation.

"And will he want a favor later for this?" Amanda looked at the wine dubiously.

"No more favors," Mila said crisply. It was her motto. As soon as she was safely ensconced in her role, she had shaken up the administration by calling for complete transparency in the bidding process for road contracts. There would be no more corruption in the business of building Namibian roads, she'd said in her first press conference. Several columnists in The Namibian were wondering if she'd be the country's first woman president.

For lunch today, Amanda had worn the very same outfit she'd worn to confront Mila in Headmaster Pierre's office. It was her very best, and nothing else had seemed to do. She'd been nervous while getting ready—a factor that seemed unfair, since Mila was the one who'd fooled around with Amanda's husband all those years ago and failed to tell her about it. Still. Mila was fucking intimidating. And this was the first time in a long while that they'd be alone together. But everything was fine as soon as Mila arrived and snapped her fingers for service.

"So shall we send back the wine, then?" Amanda asked. "If it's supposed to be an exchange."

"No," Mila said. "That man's parents and uncles did horrible things to my parents and uncles. The wine is the least he could do."

Amanda sipped her champagne obediently and thought about how you could love a place deeply without understanding it at all. And she had, in fact, come to love Namibia. She loved the aching heat and the merciless sun and the way everyone said *How beautiful!* every time it rained. She'd been a tiny dot on the hugest landscape she'd ever seen, and what that told her was that she had power over absolutely nothing. At first it had scared the shit out of her, but in the end it was freeing. Amanda Evans didn't *have* to hold everything together all the time. Not everyone was going to die on her in the grocery store.

Frida, as Mila's assistant, had been the one to call to set up the lunch, breaking the radio silence at last. Amanda had been so excited, she'd cried as soon as she hung up the phone.

"I know you loved her back then, but I think I love her more," Amanda had said to Mark. Her husband, who was now deep in the business of gem dealing, had chosen not to answer. As of late, Amanda noticed, Mark was getting very wise about when not to talk.

The girls had been allowed to come to lunch, though they'd abandoned the table after downing their Cokes to run up and down the tiled stairs and visit the parrot that lived in the beauty salon upstairs. Now they were pitching coins into the fountain from the second-floor balcony. In the two months since the scandal, they'd been reveling in their celebrity status. Both had been immensely pleased with the attention they'd received, and as much as Amanda had wanted to discourage her daughter's potential future life of crime, she couldn't bring herself to rebuke her *too* harshly. They had, after all, raised a lot of money for orphans, and no one seemed to be asking them to give it back.

"Do you miss Josephat?" Amanda asked after the server brought their salads.

"I do," Mila admitted. Josephat was in a holding cell, awaiting trial. The Namibian justice system was so backed up that one might wait years. The holding cell—jail—was better than prison, so he would be all right for a while. But if there is one thing Africans of all colors agree upon, it is justice for illegally slain animals. In Botswana, poachers are often sentenced to death. Luckily for Josephat and his partners, Namibians were more lenient, though they likely faced many years in prison.

"He's my friend, and I love him. I wish he could have been more honest."

"Yeah, but you wouldn't be where you are," Amanda blurted, then immediately felt sorry.

"I would have found a way," Mila said. "And did things turn out so well for me, striking a bargain on a lie? No. In the end you cannot be who you are not. A cheetah cannot be a leopard."

"Right," Amanda said. "I mean, it sort of could, though. They're similar, if you think about it. Both cats, both predators. The cheetah's a lot faster, but—"

"I just wish he had not gotten so greedy," Mila interrupted.

"I know. I'm sorry."

"So am I," Mila said.

Something above them had caught Mila's eye. Amanda followed her gaze. Taimi and Meg had somehow scaled the building and were sitting on the red-tiled roof, their feet dangling above the courtyard.

"Get down from there, you criminals!" Mila cried. The restaurant erupted into laughter. Everyone, it seemed, knew their daughters had done jail time.

Their food came. Mila delicately cut into her steak, then put her knife down and motioned the manager over.

"I said rare," she snapped. "Not breathing."

"We'll put it back on the grill, Minister Shilongo." He picked up her plate and hurried away.

"And you, my dear?" Mila said, turning her attention back to Amanda. "What will you do upon your return?"

"I'm going to run Mark's new company," she said.

Shortly after the girls were pardoned, Anna had returned with the missing money, and, true to her word, she had tripled it and then some. The reason she gave for not being in touch was that she had traveled to Dubai for the sale, as that was where she could get the best price. Now she was back, and Mark was insisting that they start a legitimate business. He was throwing in the towel on academia. This was much more fun and lucrative, and he'd be able to travel back to his favorite country at least twice a year—no book writing required.

Amanda hadn't thought of getting involved at first. She was happy Mark had found something, at long last, that he liked. His new sense of purpose was extremely sexy, she had to admit, and things had so greatly improved in that area that they actually had to use the lock on the door.

Plus, GiaTech had already said they wanted her back. Age, it turned out, was the new trend in the Valley. Her former boss, the very one who told her she would "age out" in a year, was now sending her nonsensical emails that pushed stock options and were riddled with the term "aging in."

But then Jaime had called offering Mark his skills as the head of Mark's gem business. Which was exactly when Amanda—who had never trusted Jaime—had decided what their new family business needed was a top-notch CEO like herself.

"I hope we can stay friends, Mila," Amanda said now. Her eyes filled with tears again, and she let them.

"We must," Mila said. "The girls are almost sisters. We will meet once a year, for lunch."

"Yes," Amanda said. "A springbok does not stray from its herd."

Mila stared at her, confused. "I don't know what you mean, Amanda.

Springboks often stray from the herd. In fact, young males are often exiled by their elders, so that they don't hone in on the young females."

"Fine."

"But I will see you. A promise is a promise."

"It is," Amanda said. She dabbed her eyes.

"My word, Amanda. You are proof that the saying is correct: In Namibia, you cry when you come, you cry when you leave."

"Who said that?"

"Someone like you," Mila said. "Now please stop weeping. I must send these potatoes back. That waiter is looking far too pleased with himself."

37

When Mila had asked how she could repay Persephone for the long stay in her house, Persephone didn't have to think twice. She wanted one more night of camping next to Mr. Sharp.

"And I don't want anyone knowing I'm coming, Mila," Persephone said. "Because I won't be alone."

"Petrus?"

"Petrus."

The liaison had come about one evening when Mila insisted Persephone go with her to the Night Market, a rather fabulous event filled with Namibian hipsters of all colors, shapes, and sizes. They had run into Petrus there, whom Mila knew from social circles; when Persephone had mentioned her crush, Mila more than approved.

"He is from a very good family," Mila said. "They have two farms up north with over eight hundred cattle." Persephone added his family's cows to his list of attributes, and accepted a third glass of wine when he brought it over. He'd driven them home and kissed her good night in front of Mila.

"He's married," Persephone said with a tiny wisp of guilt.

"I know his wife," Mila said. "She is very busy. She won't mind."

Two weeks later, Persephone was on Petrus's lap, taking in the Erongo dusk. They'd sighted her beloved Mr. Sharp earlier in the day, but kept a proper distance this time. Now they were watching the rain come.

"Do you smell the water?" he asked. She didn't, so he dragged her to the top of a large rock and pointed to a group of thin gray lines so faint they looked like a child's feathery attempt at using a pencil. "There," he said. "Let's make tea and watch it arrive."

The air was still as death at first, but then there was a faint rustling in the grass, followed by delicious, damp, howling wind. There was a smell Persephone could only call expectation. The grass and flowers rose up for the water that wasn't there yet. Finally, the raindrops, light at first, then huge and soft and voluptuous, then sharp and pounding and relentless.

"There's no way to listen to this storm and not think of sex," Persephone said.

"Most Namibian birthdays correspond to rainstorms that happened nine months before." He smiled at her. "So, shall we, my dear?"

It was a onetime weekend. Persephone had never thought of herself as an adulteress; yet Petrus had assured her this was normal in his circles, both for him and his wife.

"That's very French," she'd said. "Are you certain your wife has the same privileges?"

"She has six children," Petrus said. "As long as I have the nanny come while I am gone, she is quite pleased with the arrangement."

It had been a lovely weekend. The first night Petrus had prepared a proper braai, not letting her lift a finger, and then he had taken her inside the tent and they had done all the things she had fantasized about all year. It was even better than she'd imagined. And now here Persephone was, propped up on her elbows, next to an Ovambo man with beautiful manners, looking out at the boulder-strewn landscape so foreign it might as well be the moon.

Life was quite extraordinary, she thought. If you let it get that way.

The next day, Persephone walked around the half-empty house, counting the boxes by the door. She was feeling quite herself again. In three days, she would fly home with the three children. She didn't know what she was going to do next, but she couldn't go on leading this pretend life.

It was scary, of course, this change in career. She would no longer be connected to the State Department, with all of its protections and privileges. Still, she had plenty of ideas of where to go next. For one thing, Doni Oppenheimer had actually called her upon reading about the poaching ring in the *Times*.

"You had something to do with this, didn't you, dear?" Doni had said. "I read about your organization in the *Post*, and then about that very rhino being attacked and saved. And now the whole thing has been cracked open! You must have helped in some way?"

"Well," Persephone had replied carefully, "I'm really not supposed to say."

"Clever girl. And might I say, you're aging quite well. This is not backhanded, dear. I can tell you've stuck to a strict skin regimen. Those photos were fabulous."

"Why, thank you, Doni," Persephone said. "I remember how much you prize youth."

"Oh, not so, my dear, not so. My last girl was an absolute disaster. Twenty-six. Ugh! Which is why I am calling. Now, I'm not looking for an assistant, Persephone. It's time for me to wind down, as they say—"

Persephone believed this as much as she believed Doni's no longer prizing youth.

"So I really need more of a partner, someone worthy of taking on what I've built. And you're so camera-ready, darling . . ."

Persephone wasn't sure she wanted to be Doni *Acte Deux*, but certainly it was an interesting option. Life was opening up. If she really left Adam and went home, she would miss being a representative of her great country, but it was, to be sure, getting harder and harder to smile gracefully at other diplomats while Papa President was throwing tantrums and making lewd comments in misspelled Twitter-speak about every woman he'd ever seen. She'd done it, of course. How many times had she and her siblings pretended everything was just jolly at country club dinners, while her mother threw forks in drunken rages and fell asleep in her aspic? But it was not something a lady could keep up forever.

Later in the week, as she prepared one of her first Frida-less meals for herself and the girls, the bell rang. Persephone was pleasantly surprised; unexpected visits were so rare in Namibia, what with the prison-level security. Being a Southerner, she adored a drop-by, which was why she always kept fresh tasties on hand on the bottom shelf of the refrigerator, arranged on a china tray and wrapped in Saran Wrap. As well as a terrine of Brie and chutney, ready to be microwaved for an instant dip. *Homemade* chutney, mind. It gave the guest such a sense of specialness.

Another idea! Persephone noted triumphantly. She could write a book of State Department entertainment tips! *Brilliant.*

"Miss Frida," she called. "Can you see who it is?"

But then she checked herself. Miss Frida was already gone. Yet the gate was opening, which meant it was Adam, arriving to live like a mole. She wondered if he'd noticed that she'd given the majority of his belongings away.

Persephone and Adam hadn't yet spoken about their future. Obviously she would divorce him. The thought didn't bother her; in fact, his absence was the one positive thing to come out of all of this.

It chilled her, how easily she was bidding the father of her children farewell. She'd realized in the past weeks that she'd never really loved Adam. She'd been fond of him, and she'd appreciated his fine looks and the life he had given her. But her camping weekend with Petrus had been more emotionally satisfying than any of her Four Seasons weekends with Adam.

Still, Persephone hated the thought of not being a family unit. Retreating back to the United States as a divorced, single mother . . . well. It was not merveilleux.

Persephone could hear him coming up the stairs now. Usually he ran them two at a time to show off his excellent lung capacity, but today he was heaving himself up rather slowly. He must be dreading this conversation as much as she was. She arranged herself in the living room, looking desperately for a book to pretend to read. Drat—the only thing available nearby was a copy of *I Hope They Serve Beer in Hell*, which Adam had been reading at some point before she'd ejected him from the building. *Swine!*

"Persephone?" a voice called.

Hell's bells. It wasn't Adam. It was the ambassador.

Persephone shot up, kicking the book under the sofa. "Hello! Miss Ambassador! In here!"

The ambassador emerged, looking very ambassador-like in a well-cut pantsuit, though the color, serge green, was a bit sad, in Persephone's opinion. Now that she was back to wearing colors, she was considering herself a bit of an expert at who looked good in what and which shades to don when. Red was for battle. Blue was for peaceful deference and the absorption of new knowledge. Green was for St. Patrick's Day and she didn't know when else. Despite being a redhead, Persephone wasn't fond of green, especially the hue the ambassador was wearing. Mottled? Bottled? It reminded her of old peas.

"Persephone," the ambassador said. "I think it's time you called me Julia."

Then again, green could be fantastic on some.

"Wonderful," Persephone said. "How are you, Julia? Also, how did you get in? Did Adam give you the key?"

"We have keys to all of the houses," the ambassador said. "We also have listening devices and cameras. Though you probably guessed that." She said this offhandedly, as if it were the most normal thing in the world.

"I did not guess that," Persephone said.

"Oh yes."

"In . . . every room?"

"Not the bedrooms. That would be untoward."

"Laundry closet?"

"Persephone, I'd appreciate it if you would join me in my car for a conversation. Given what I just told you."

"All right." The back of a car in the raging heat with the ambassador—*Julia*—didn't appeal terribly, but she supposed she didn't want whoever was sitting on the other end of the hidden microphones to hear more about Adam's tawdry affairs. "Shall I bring us some tasties? I have homemade cheese straws."

"Yes, yes," the ambassador said. She made her way through the kitchen and paused. "My, this is a ridiculously large house. It's a good thing I hadn't seen it before, or I most certainly would have pulled it. All right. I'll meet you in the car."

Persephone sighed. Whatever this conversation was, she didn't want to deal with it. She took her hors d'oeuvre tray out of the fridge, had a quick sip of Chardonnay for strength, then headed out to the ambassador's SUV, which was idling in her driveway.

To her surprise, the ambassador was in the driver's seat. No chauffeur today. Persephone climbed in and placed the tray on the center console.

"So, Julia," Persephone said. The name tripped on her tongue. "How can I help you?"

"Well, Persephone, I'm here to tell you that I know you're thinking of leaving."

"I do have my tickets." Persephone arranged the tasties fastidiously on the tray, placing the cheese knife on the ambassador's side.

"Well. The State Department doesn't want you to leave just yet."

"You don't?" Persephone said. "It doesn't?"

"No. We consider you a terrifically valuable asset. That's why we decided to let Adam keep his job instead of Ainsley, remember?"

"That's very kind. I suppose he is a decent lawyer."

"He's a terrible lawyer, Persephone." Julia gave her an appraising look. "I didn't say he was a valuable asset. I said you were."

"Oh!" Persephone sat up straighter. "Well. Thank you. I'm glad that you've noticed that I've toed the line all these years. I do see it as my special duty to excel at supporting the State Department."

"No, Persephone. I wouldn't say that."

"What? But—"

"You're good, but you're not perfect. You drink a bit too much at government events, and you're extremely expensive. Also, you're a terrific gossip. And now you're sleeping with one of the staff."

Persephone glanced at her reflection in the side mirror. "Petrus is just a onetime thing," she said.

"Good," the ambassador said. "Because we need you to remain married to Adam."

"Need me?" Persephone couldn't help bristling, which was unfortunate, because such emotions always made her nose flare. "You can't control *whom* I marry. I'm not a . . . a bride for *hire*." Did that make sense? No? Well, none of this did.

"Persephone. Listen carefully." The ambassador picked up a cheese straw and considered it as if she were a scientist looking at a specimen.

"Oh." Persephone wrinkled her nose. "No, thank you. I'm not really interested in anything the State Department has to offer."

"I'm here to offer you a job."

"Don't be so sure," the ambassador said. "We're willing to pay quite a lot."

"I'm aware of the State Department pay scale."

"Here's the thing." The ambassador put her hand on Persephone's arm lightly. "You have an excellent education. How many languages do you speak?"

"Oh, let's see!" Persephone *did* love a brag now and then. "German, French, Arabic, Afrikaans, Romanian, Oshiwambo, and *some* Nama."

"Yes. And your riflery skills. Everyone heard about how you stopped that leopard a few months ago. You even managed not to kill it, yes?"

"Oh no," Persephone said. "I knew exactly what I was doing. She's at AfriCat, recovering nicely."

"Exactly." The ambassador gave Persephone's arm a squeeze and took her hand back. "Which is why, Persephone, we want you to be our local operative in the CIA."

"Me?"

"You."

"I . . ." It was a rare moment, but it was true. Persephone Wilder absolutely had no idea what to say.

"They've been watching you for some time. The agency is certain you will be excellent. And they're even more certain that no one would ever guess that you would be capable of anything like this."

"Well . . ." Persephone blinked. "I don't want to shoot a real person, I don't think."

"Oh, we never shoot anyone in Namibia, usually. We gather intelligence. Or, you'll gather intelligence. We've noticed you're very good at that. Oh, and the salary is this." The ambassador wrote down a figure on a piece of paper and slid it over.

My, Persephone thought. A girl could live well on that.

"Obviously I need to think about it."

"Obviously. I'll leave you to it. It's only for a couple of years. We don't want you to be stuck with Adam forever."

"Well—"

"All right. As soon as you give the green light, I'll have Ellie messenger over a lockbox of materials. We've arranged for a fireproof safe to be installed in a secret compartment in your pantry. You'll receive a signal and the code when your official mission begins."

"That's not *really* how it all works, is it?" Persephone asked, breathless. "Missions and compartments and signals and *codes*?"

The ambassador allowed herself a smile. "That's just the beginning, future Agent Wilder. Now, time to get out. I'll take these cheese straws, if I may."

"You may," Persephone said, still stunned. "Good . . . goodbye!"

She slid out into the heat and climbed the stairs up to the terrace as the ambassador's car slipped through the gate. The sky was blinding midday white. Elifas was clipping a hedge.

My Lord, she thought. The CIA? Could she do it? Turn her entire life around like that in an instant?

For maybe the first time, Persephone felt a strange twinge she realized must be self-doubt. She had been an Embassy Wife for so long. Her organizational and calculation abilities were dizzying, but for years they had been put to use only to support her spouse. She had been . . . trailing.

And if she was perfectly honest, it was *nice* to trail. Nothing was ever your fault, really. You could lead without really leading. She had been proud of mastering the household, being in charge of her darlings, making up her little suite of rules and regulations for being a spouse in a foreign land. And this? This was terrifying. Could she really step up and become a government mastermind while being a mother? Could she continue her role and start a new one as a secret freedom fighter? A warrior of espionage? A *spy*?

Catching a glimpse of herself in the reflection of the patio door, Persephone paused to meet her own eye.

Of course she could.

But first she had to serve dinner, find a new nanny, bathe the children, oversee their homework, and take care of the laundry. She had to read to everyone, put them to bed, not have a drink, get a good night's rest, get up, make breakfast, pack lunches, dress everyone, and get them off to school. Once that was done, she had to build a new wardrobe of whites. She had to practice her marksmanship. She had to watch for the signal, and learn the code, and find the secret compartment, and . . . begin her mission.

And, of course, she had to thoroughly brief Adam.

If he was going to be a halfway decent Embassy Husband, he had a lot of work to do.

During recent years, my family and I had the privilege of living in Windhoek, Namibia. We found Namibia to be a stunning country. The sheer expanse of the landscape renewed my hope for our planet, while the Namibians we met, as diverse as they are, were funny, fascinating, and welcoming.

As an expatriate in a nation where few Americans reside, I was also lucky enough to befriend several U.S. State Department employees and their families. These were delightful, smart, and brave men and women who had dedicated their lives to representing and defending our nation. I admired them greatly. Admiration, however, does not make for good comedy, which is why I took many satirical liberties in the name of a story. I hope the dear friends I made in Namibia will forgive me. Making stuff up is the whole job.

Except the part about our American president at the time bungling the name of the magnificent country of Namibia and calling the entire continent of Africa a shithole. That totally happened. It was nuts.

Acknowledgments

I'd like to thank the great Namibian journalist Denver Kisting for his help with this novel, as well as my writing group at the American Cultural Center in Windhoek. Thanks to my expatriate sisters Janet Roscoe, Emily Schlink, and Lisa Transfeldt Atkins. Thank you to my agent, Rob McQuilkin; my editor, Emily Bell; and Grady Hendrix, my dear friend and reader. Finally, thanks to Peter for bringing me to Namibia, and to Phoebe and Roscoe for making our lives there—and everywhere—so very much fun.